AMANECIDA

Artorian's Archives Book Fifteen

DENNIS VANDERKERKEN
DAKOTA KROUT

MOUNTAINDALE
PRESS

ACKNOWLEDGMENTS

From Dennis:

There are many people who have made this book possible. First is Dakota himself, for without whom this entire series would never have come about. In addition to letting me write in his universe, he has taken it upon himself to be the most glorious senior editor and keep straight all the madness for which I am responsible, with resulting hilarity therein.

An eternal thank you to my late grandfather, after whom a significant chunk of Artorian's personality is indebted. He was a man of mighty strides, and is missed dearly.

A special thank you to my parents, for being ever supportive in my odd endeavors, Mountaindale Press for being a fantastic publisher, and all the fans of Artorian's Archives, Divine Dungeon, and Completionist Chronicles who are responsible for the popularity allowing this to come to pass. May your affinity channels be strong and plentiful!

Last of all, thank you. Thank you for picking this up and giving it a read. Amanecida is the continuation of a multi-book series, and I dearly hope you will enjoy them as the story keeps progressing. Artorian's Archives may start before Divine Dungeon, but don't worry! It's going all the way past the end of Completionist Chronicles! So if you liked this, keep an eye out for more things from Mountaindale Press!

Please consider giving us five stars on Amazon, Audible, and anywhere else you'd like to spread the word!

PROLOGUE

Eternium checked the delve details before Artorian and company were thrown into the deep end. "Your realm is Vanaheim, and your zone is the terrible, indescribable thing known as the Darkest Dungeon in quadrant K-nine, designed by Wisp Howard Phillips, L. So you better prepare everything you have before you go spelunking, Artorian. I'd suggest a torch, or a Gnome named Bosco."

The portly dungeon grinned wide, excited by what was going to come next. "Good luck, bud. You're in for an elite deep dive, into the darkest depths of the Arcoplex!"

Artorian the Young-torian pressed his hands to his hips, not sure how he wanted to take that insinuation. Digesting the task, he broke Tim's statement into bite-sized pieces. "Emby and Lucia? Definitely elites. Meg, Oak, and Hans? They're gonna get me killed. They might as well be called Team Liability, and don't get me started on the *sass*. The amount of talking they're going to do alone could fill a book, and I'm not going to have the willpower *not* to personally throw them off a mountain after the pun-slinging and singing starts."

He reached over to rub Zephyr's polished architecture,

being clear on why he hadn't included her. "Not you, Zephy. You're a gem and we love that you're here. I would steal you from Team Dangerlicious if I could, but I'm sure the pirates need their ship."

The High Elven yacht's sails flapped amicably in response, prompting him to smile. "If you could hold the fort down here, so we have an escape route when we get Tisha and haul the whole of Abyss back up here? I'd like that."

Red, green, and blue lighting glowed in sequence along her inner hull to showcase delight. She was most definitely staying until she was forced to accompany her team. Artorian truly treasured reliable people, in boat form or otherwise. "Tim, I have neither a Bosco, nor a torch. That does not mean that, between Ember and Decorum, this place is going to be anything other than a charred kiln by the time we're done here. Speaking of, how is Decorum? Do I need to do this setup in utter haste, or do I have a minute?"

Tim pressed his fingers together, tensing and flexing them against one another before breaking out into a giggle as he snuck a look. "Let me show you!"

A large screen appeared, showing Artorian and company what all the other onlookers from Caltopia must have had access to this entire time. The angle of view in the central portion of the screen was positioned behind his brother's right shoulder. Four other, smaller screens portrayed other angles that faced Decorum from farther away.

Artorian whistled, both impressed and enthused as Decorum, in full Liger mode, tore up and through this dungeon. The visuals of what the dungeon's innards looked like were blurry as the focus remained on his brother, but celestial feces, could Decorum steal a show! Aggro-pulling ignored enemies behind himself to form a monster train, the Liger Prime waltzed around opponents deemed irrelevant at thunderclap speeds. All while simultaneously dicing through opponents that did notice him and reducing them to tethers of sliced cabbage.

Extra style points were earned in his wake. As, rather than

make illumination in this dark place, only the passing swings of claws betrayed his location. The screens did nothing to provide sound, but buffeting winds that preceded Decorum worked to both unsettle and discombobulate his unsuspecting opponents. Before those foes either joined the piles of frayed ribbons as they were struck by claw glints, or joined the monster train tailing him.

As Decorum worked his way through an area resembling an underground cove, each thunderous clap of Liger claw to gem-encrusted clam resulted in two things: a shower of scattered riches that went entirely ignored, and a sound that traveled all the way back up to the entrance gate. A gate that allowed plenty of sound to pass, as one of the doors had not survived the passing of Decorum.

Artorian could eventually tie a specific assault to a specific sound, but they were delayed and ever farther away. Nowhere near enough for echolocation to build him anything useful.

The main screen shifted to showcase what Decorum was seeing, which turned out to be a delectable treat to the senses. Artorian recognized this sight method! This was the type of vision that latched to the ebbs and flows of air, showing the breathing pull and push. The rushes and gusts. Where air did not move, there was a wall. Where the smoke billowed, there was a creature.

This colorless landscape spoke its own language. A language that made the sudden appearance of color all the more appealing. Where did that most interesting multi-colored strand of scent go off to? Artorian knew the answer in his nose. That was the direction of Tisha! How had Decorum gotten past the rotten smell problem? The screens didn't give him that.

Rather than comment, he enjoyed watching Decorum tear through foes like a whale ate krill. Electric and made of haste, the Liger lurched through one twisted passageway after another, always following the curving flows of the multicolored strand. One foe had not seen or heard him coming, resulting in what- ever Wisp was controlling the angle of view to pan the sight out, moving the viewpoint to be in front of the Shambler. A slug-like creature that looked half-molten, covered in plates of chitin.

The slug showed no signs of panic until the glowing eyes of the great predator behind it reared up high. Decorum's glowing claws extended on both sides of the Shambler as he snuck up on this potential threat, causing enough of a change in the environment to make the slug flinch. The Shambler wasn't bothered by wind or thunder, but wasn't given the opportunity to learn that it should be as it was guillotined like stalked prey.

Decorum moved on before the severed slug head hit the floor, the rest of the Shambler's body crushed underfoot by a sea of pursuers.

Artorian noted that, while hard to see, many of the opponents had odd forms. Yet, not a single Penguin or Arachnoid was among them. Decorum was cracking through a buffet of Clams, Crabs, some Undead, undulating oddities, a shrubbery filled with coals for eyes, and several swine that stood as men. Their bacon potluck ended poorly.

Artorian would not be surprised to run into chickens and gander at this rate. Whatever route Decorum was taking was unlikely to be a route he was going to be able to follow, so anything that his brother was running into, he was not going to have to deal with.

That made him pump his fist and cheer. "Get 'em, Gomez! Thanks for buying me time! I'll get through this as fast as I can and come find you!"

Things were starting to look up, until the ominous music began, and every player in Eternia received a global prompt.

Dun-dun-dunnnn!

————

World Event: The City Must Survive.

Fuyu No Arashi, the Eternal Thundercloud, has declared Casus Belli upon the Realm of Midgard due to unacceptable weather patterns. Fuyu No Arashi demands the permanent reinstatement of The Pale, and related conditions. Until these conditions are met, Fuyu No Arashi will assault Midgard with increasing waves of ice, frost, sleet, and snow. Either until its health runs out, due to the inhabitants having weathered the storm, or by capitulation of the current most prominent city on Midgard, upon which the storm will be centered: New Haven.

Survive: Unlock 'Brave New World.'

Perish: The Pale becomes permanent on Midgard once more.

Note: Unlike the conditions of The Pale, which could dip to a constant temperature of minus fifty degrees Celsius, Fuyu No Arashi can force temperatures to dip down in waves, until a final temperature of minus one-hundred and fifty Celsius is in effect. This last temperature drop is also her last hurrah, and surviving that wave signals success.

———

All eyes ever so slowly turned to Tim.

The dungeon whistled innocently, his thumbs rolling across one another nervously as he pursed his lips, and closed down the last of his screens after discreetly packing up. "Told you. I am needed elsewhere."

Artorian squeezed the bridge of his nose. "Was the mention of Henry and Marie's Ardania, and the Decorum show, meant to distract us? Perhaps for long enough that you were hoping to slip away before that notification occurred?"

Tim looked away, appearing awfully small for such a portly man. "…Maybe."

Artorian did not let up from squeezing the bridge of his nose. "Go. Have someone else come do my version three setup process. I can't be in more than one place at a time, and I am counting my lucky stars that New Haven has Lenore. Lenore will pull them through until we can dramatically show up in the final act, if we have to show up at all."

Tim spoke in a hurry and fled, throwing distractions in his wake as Artorian received several notifications to check. "I suppose I'd best get to that. I've finished importing your New Game Plus goodies. Have fun!"

The dungeon threw open his **Order** portal, hustling through with a quick turn on the heel before it snapped closed behind him. The ominous music left with him.

"My New Game Plus... What? I didn't even tell you what my three choices—" Artorian's head shot up from his hand at hearing the Kings and Castles portal *click* out of existence as if Tim had placed a piece down. "Wait, did he actually flee?"

Ember couldn't help but laugh. "Do you have any idea how much trouble he's going to be in with Yuki if he doesn't attend that event? She's the one who devised Fuyu No Arashi when he was asking for unconventional roaming boss monsters and events."

Now Artorian wasn't sure what to think, or how to feel. He couldn't support both sides. Could he? Was that allowed? "Yuki, put together an...? *Ah*. Right. Her **Law** is **Kenopsia**. The eerie, forlorn atmosphere of a place that's usually bustling with people but is now abandoned and quiet. A living storm that turns anything in its path into empty husks and frozen land-scape would qualify. She's doing **Law**-stuff with the game as a medium, isn't she? That's smart. I like that. Doesn't change that I feel bad for Lenore and want to go help when I can, but I like that."

His expression turned complicated. "Emby, I *can* go help, right?"

Momentarily serious, Ember nodded with strength. "You can. Until you choose to either fully step into the role of Administrator, or Divine, you are at liberty to playtest and don't have to remain impartial, neutral, or stay on the sidelines. Regardless if that is to try out goodies, character balance, field test, or throw everything you're given into the trash to start over. Never track your growth by the power you have. Track your growth by the journey you have lived."

Ember crossed her arms, driving the point home. "We are not committed to being field, area, or world bosses. That also means we do not get access to the associated shops or bonuses, but that is not important. That lack of intent is likely also why you have not gotten pressed prompt-wise for Deity stuff, because I have not been getting pressed for mine."

Tapping a finger to her lips, she finished up addressing her boy's concern. "As we are not truly starting from scratch, we will not be considered proper players. We are here to spend time together, in whatever form that may take. If in that process one of us gets a case of fury because something unsavory is going on that we refuse to accept? Neither of us have to grit our teeth and sit on the sidelines. Are you struggling with expectations, sugar?"

Artorian scratched his head. He hoped that whoever was going to show up to help would be here fast. "I was honestly expecting an... Actually, no. I have no idea what to expect from this game right now. Seeing Decorum tear through this dungeon and being a major distraction has started me off on the right foot, and did me well. I can focus less on needing to be some kind of hero, and more on getting this setup done right before diving into the deep end. To support him being the big celestial hero and get Tisha back in his arms. **Love** will prevail!"

Ember was so proud of her boy. "I am very happy with your decision to not jump directly into the fray."

Artorian shrugged with a half-smile. "There is a rush and a pleasure to throw oneself off the cliff and toward the fire. Then again, if I don't know what the rules are, I don't know how to break or circumvent them. If I don't know what my tools do, then I won't conjure up ideas on how to use them. If I don't read the game descriptions of the gimmicks and goodies being thrown at me, then I will make poor assumptions based on what I think they do, rather than what they actually do. My way is not glamorous until I am a font of tips and tricks, and after seeing Decorum steal the spotlight? I am itching for some glamor."

Ember posed fancifully, as if a most glorious statue placed in the center of the limelight. "If a show is desired, then a show we shall have."

Artorian plotted deviously, rubbing his hands together. "I'll just ask Yuki how she's doing next time. I'm curious as to what her toolkit is, and how she has applied it. Knowing that might give me some insight of how the truly serious have approached this beta run. Thank you, dear. You're a beacon of warmth and reason."

CHAPTER ONE

"Only to you, honeybee." Ember grinned wide as she grabbed hold of a lounger, noisily dragging the fancy mahogany thing across the deck. Once she had the furniture settled behind her boy, she tugged him into the pillows with her, enacting the evil plan to attain more cuddles. "Yuki is responsible for testing Cascade Pylons. She likes casting spells where snowballs start launching themselves at her opponents, causing minor status effects. Her favorite spell is called 'Artillery Snowball.' Slow moving, easy to dodge, deals negligible-to-low AoE damage."

She momentarily could not recall if he knew what that was short for. "That's Area of Effect, sugar. Each impact creates physical snow on contact, which seems harmless by itself."

Artorian sat, pressed himself into the pillows, and held her hand before pushing away his prompt. The screen could wait. "Sounds decently harmless so far. A little snowball fight never hurt anyone too terribly much. What does this have to do with Cascade Pylons?"

Ember raised a hand, but the expected prompt did not come up. "That's a terrible time for that not to work. I'll explain without the pretty diagrams then. Yuki's first trait as a roaming boss is called 'Silent Avalanche.' Every time a snowball from one of her spells hits, she casts a free plus-one snowball on the next cast, so long as she's still upholding or channeling the spell that caused the hit in the first place."

Ember placed her second hand atop his before he could once again say that this didn't seem too bad. "I'm going to make you aware that nowhere in that trait does it say the snowball needs to hit a designated target. It just needs to hit. That includes the ground."

Artorian released an 'oh' noise, and let the lady finish. "Her second trait is called 'Silent Death.' Remember that I said her snowballs cause status effects? A tiny trickle of Frostbite, Frostburn, Bleed, and Poison. Barely noticeable. It'll pop up on the status screen with such a short duration that players would dismiss it out of hand if they noticed an early hit."

Ember's boy squeezed her hand, seeing where this was going. "*Cascade* Pylons."

She wriggled in her seat, making a high-pitched happy noise. "You're getting it! This is so much fun when people catch on. Each hit, the snowballs do one more damage, and one more tick's worth of status effect duration over time, if the status effect gets through a player's protections. Since that's calculated per hit? Resisting those effects can become difficult, and Yuki's durations *stack* instead of refresh."

A fire lit in Ember's voice. "So, add about a second to the duration of the status effects, per successful hit of a snowball. Now for the kicker. Because the projectiles are very slow, and easy to dodge? They have no *range* limitation. She can go unseen with her Comet's Coma, skate on ice or snow to another location, and never stop casting in the process. So unless you're looking right at her, you're going to lose track of her, and more and more Artillery Snowballs are going to be sent your way. Each cast being a little more dangerous than the last."

Ember drew a curved line in the air. "Yuki is very good at

spellshaping. She can direct fire. She can arc the shot. Now add the fun factor that the base cooldown between casts is one snowball every three seconds, and she can autocast it. Or channel. So far that means the same thing; I expect that to change."

Artorian frowned, needing to do some mental math. "The first few snowballs... I... doubt I'd even notice them. Some joke about non-player characters pranking players? No, I doubt Yuki would engage first unless the players were high on their hubris. I'm seeing the danger curve, but not what's so frightening if, regardless of the amount, I can sidestep the snowballs."

Ember grinned wide. Enjoying that he too, regardless of his usual cleverness, had fallen into the trap. "I'll give you a hint. When I asked Yuki how people would defeat her, she said, 'What are they going to do? Bleed on me?' I laughed."

Seeing as Artorian was still struggling, she added some more elements, and laced fingers with her boy. Noting that he, unlike the rest of them, was in Faith Foundry pajamas. Not exactly good for a deep dive. "Okay, Yuki likes places that are cold, snowy, and abandoned. She has beautiful mobility in any snow region, and can seemingly vanish without using any kind of invisibility. Because Comet's Coma obscures your advanced senses, not your basic ones. Nothing is preventing her from aiming any amount of snowballs at the ground, giving her instant physical cover. This also adds to her snowball count."

She paused a moment hoping that was enough, then began adding more in the hopes that he would have a reaction soon. "I'll say that again, if—"

Artorian suddenly squinted. His free hand shot up, pointer finger first. "I was tricked! My math is off! She doesn't gain a single snowball every time she casts. She gains a single snowball every time one hits. So it's not a 'fire one, then fire two, then fire three' situation. It's one, to two, to four, to eight, to sixteen, and then it quickly gets dangerous. The damage doesn't seem like it's a lot, but Yuki is the type of person where if you bother her once? She will chase you across the entire realm until you are dead, purely to teach you the painful lesson that you should not have done that. She is also the kind of person that would leave your body behind as an ice-entombed sculpture warning."

Ember used the back of Artorian's hand to make substitute clapping sounds. "Very good! There are fates worse than death, and Yuki is well-versed in most of them. The main damage from snowballs is secondary. The other effects will freeze you in place, make you feel like you're on fire while sapping potential motion, poison you, and make you bleed. All while she's burying and entombing you in an ever-growing snowy avalanche that can crush you with real, physical weight. While dealing *area of effect* damage."

That fire in her voice happily intensified. "She *never* had to hit an enemy directly to apply her DoTs. That's damage over time, sugar, and her area of effect is *biiig*, as another tradeoff for how sluggish the projectiles are. Taking any of them point blank is equally terrible, because until her snowballs hit something, they have the incorporeal trait. Her own snowballs pass through each other just fine, until they hit something else. Get hit point blank, and all of them will become physical and make an instant snow-grave right on top of you. She's also immune to her own spell's effects, because why not, right?"

Artorian's face became a mask of horror and sympathetic pain, feeling the yeowch for whoever encountered her with the intent to cause problems. His mouth hung open, lower lip pulled back. "*Eeesh*, and this lady made Fuyu No Arashi? I'm suddenly not so confident in New Haven's chances anymore. That is one doozy of a tutorial to begin the game with. I overheard Shaka and Tim chattering about making the beginning difficult to set the tone of tension so people wouldn't do what I did, and go in with maximum *wheee*."

He reflected on the information. "This is harsh, though..."

Ember nodded patiently and slowly, her fire fading. "Works, doesn't it? The build does get more intense, as that's just one part of her offensive kit. She has the actual SnowGrave spell at her disposal as well, for when lessons need to be more instant. Her utility kit carries a lot of Silence and Deafen abilities, not merely personal stealth. Silence is great against Mages, and shutting down spells or effects that otherwise won't stop on their own, but Deafening breaks up team cohesion. Also causes panic. Lots of panic."

Artorian cringed, his cheeks tightening. "I would rather slide in a suggestion to have any new players be put through trials instead, rather than suffer a hard dead-drop into the kind of difficulty that should be reserved for people who are after power. I think Cal might have talked about that? Some people simply aren't going to be fit for that kind of gameplay. I mean, I know we're essentially trying to make more Mages—artificially or otherwise—to send out into the real world that's going to be filled with actual problems."

He motioned at the sky, referring to Eternia for a moment. "All the problems and challenges in here will be manufactured to give people the experiences they need to accomplish those leaps. There's still going to be people that are only going to want to farm, or need support from the transition. Some will not even be capable of interacting with this world at all. Abyss, if whoever we find once the door opens is part of a society that can't even grasp the concept of what's going on here? The door being there won't matter."

Ember tilted her head, opening a prompt to note that idea with her offhand. "That's not a bad viewpoint. You think there will be more people who *can't* rise to power through this game, than there will be people who do?"

Artorian looked at her to wonder if that had actually been a question. "Of course? I look at this the same way as people looked at cultivators in the Old World. We're a rare breed, very uncommon, just very influential with the push and shove we can exert. Compared to population numbers, on the other hand, we as cultivators were statistically negligible. The majority of people are going to just be people. The few and rare that are going to thrive and shoot up through the realms? Those people are going to need our attention. Everyone else just wants a good world to live in."

He needed to rub his forehead, bothered at a detail. "A world I'm not going to have the time to invest in. I can see it already. The door opens, and I'm going to need to build society outside, or help whoever ends up being in charge. Administrate."

Artorian puzzled, the architect in the old grandfather on display. "I feel it in my nose. Cal is going to dump both the entire future and current incoming player base into Midgard. I may need to help Henry and Marie before I go. If Fuyu No Arashi gets beaten back, then there's a lot of war in their future. I expect new groups vying for that kind of country-sized control, and few who would be happy with those Monarchs. There's going to be cultivators starting sects, Beasts starting clans, and nobles doing what nobles always do."

He grumbled out loud. "I foresee Ardania having a good few centuries of consolidating ahead of them for a messy variety of reasons. They'll have to contend with today's influx of new players that may not necessarily want to play, as there will certainly be people who only do so in order to gain enough merit and points for an exodus body. Those people will be troublesome, and likely make trouble to fill their time."

He inhaled deep, wrenching his mind away from that topic. "Enough of that. Honey? Thank you for holding my hand. What's next on the docket?"

Ember leaned over to proudly kiss his cheek, getting a happy flush and small smile out of him. "Character sheet making. I want to get right to it. There are several matters that have drastically changed, and we can get started before the assigned help shows up. I also picked up some things along the way, though that was before I heard through the grapevine you wanted to get even less help?"

"If it comes up, then it comes up." He leaned over to peck her right back on the other cheek. "Can I say it yet?"

Ember squinted at him, seriously considering his request to

grace her ears with the words she wanted to hear. "No. Ears want, heart not ready. Good boy for asking me first... I should encourage that behavior and reward you. What do you want, sugar?"

Artorian hadn't expected such a lovely concession! "Train me how to fight? I'm going to make a very melee-heavy build and..."

He trailed off when Ember's face went flat. "And... that's not what you meant at all."

She cocked her head, her lips pursing and unpursing before she licked them and tried to dig her gaze into his brain. "How are you the Ascended of **Love**, picking up these clues for everyone else like they are pieces of honey pie with your name on them, and yet remain so entirely clueless when it comes to your own?"

He smiled all cute.

She held his head, pulled it close, and kissed the top of his blond and brown hair. "Doofus. *My* doofus. I'll surprise you later. Pull up your prompts."

She then snapped her attention to Team Three-Stooges as Hans, Meg, and Oak were all trying to sneak off the ship. A poor attempt, as the *wham* of a door opening signaled that they had been caught.

Lucia filled the doorway with Hans Jr. napping in her arm, a hefty frown on her face. She surveyed the three deer caught in bright lights, and deemed that it would be more fruitful if they were off doing something. She conveyed this wordlessly to Ember with a look.

Ember opted to be loud, rather than budge from her spot. "Bards! Go scout the entrance and report back! We're not ready to sortie, and if you want to go cause trouble anyway, cause trouble in a useful way. I don't care if you come back to Zephyr screaming. Get a move on, use those peepers of yours, and come back with a report. Hans! If you back-talk me, I will drag you through *another* entire desert with nothing but a single leaf for your dignity."

Hans snapped to attention, saluted, and ran off as fast as his pirate feet could take him. Meg and Oak fumbled before falling in behind the Bard-sassin who had the fear of the cosmic fireball put into him long ago. He yelped as he ran, repeating a crucial part of the lesson out loud. "Don't mock the pillow!"

CHAPTER TWO

Artorian opened his prompts, the screens rapidly multiplying until he was surrounded in a globe of them. The amount of soft-light they were emitting changed the theme of the Vana-heim Depths, bathing the reddish area of hot-cheese magma flows in sheens of blue, killing the entire vibe of their implied threat as the cheese that pulsed between stalactites could no longer undulate menacingly.

The string cheese even paused while illuminated, too shy to be revealed as it retreated away from the light.

Artorian had no time for those small details. He needed to know what trick Tim had pulled on him. "Imports… Imports… Which screen is New Game Plus imports?"

The screen in question sparkled when called, spinning in place to make itself noticeable. Artorian's blue eyes snapped to the movement before he smiled and chuckled approvingly. "Screens can be called? I do like that. Come here, you!"

Undocking from its position in the information sphere, the screen descended like an over-enthused magic carpet. Sliding into Artorian's field of view, the flowy carpet became an ordinary prompt once more once.

Artorian reclaimed his fingers, folding them together before his dearest could abscond with his digits, expecting to need mobility to handle the prompt.

Ember squinted at him for doing so, but said nothing as she silently tallied this great grievance. She had, after all, plotted to steal, at minimum, one of his hands away. Her expression changed when Artorian suddenly made a wholly confused face at the prompt. When his brows furrowed, she read the silent 'what the abyss' painted on his face as his mouth opened and forgot to speak. "Sugar?"

Artorian raised a hand, palm up. "I think Tim cherry-picked ideas from the random idea-spillage I was having and went, 'This'll do 'im!' Because while Freedom of Mind makes a lot of sense, as I really don't want to go anywhere with it after the alpha run? Look at this."

Ember pulled the screen closer with a beckon of her hand, the prompt obediently turning and enlarging so she didn't need to squint or lean.

––––––

Congratulations!
New Game Plus importing complete.

––––––

Skill gained!
Freedom of Mind.
Freedom of Mind provides full immunity to possession, mind altering states you do not allow, and grants a powerful boost to any speech-related activity. This does not provide a numerical change, and will instead put you on equal footing with any who use oration of a superior skill level. Regardless of your respective skill level.

––––––

Skill gained!

Hypermobility.

Your movement is unimpaired by your environment. With Hypermobility, any surface can be a valid source of footing. Your skill in Hypermobility determines how consistently you can traverse differing, questionable floor-types, such as water, wayward leaves, clouds, or air. Your skill in Hypermobility determines whether you destroy or damage your floor-type during traversal, balanced with your mass, density, and applied pressures.

———

Trait gained!

Loved by Mana.

Loved by Mana prevents the benefactor from being injured by anything that uses Mana. Any spell, ability, skill, effect, or otherwise applicable cause that uses this energy type will instead be subverted when used against the benefactor. Subversion may result in healing, energy restoration, or other positive effects.

Loved by Mana is considered an 'intelligent' trait, and can choose of its own accord to allow beneficial effects to take hold on the benefactor.

———

Ember had to read those over a second time.

Then a third. "Freedom of Mind looks normal. Hypermobility looks like it was cobbled together out of Freedom of Movement, but in a way that causes no energy consumption problems. I have the feeling Tim made your prior trick a skill that puts the emphasis on how well you traverse the terrain by feeling, rather than the game cheating by providing you immortal platforms to run on. Platforms you didn't need to pay for with energy, if I recall?"

Her finger pressed onto the third entry as her boy hung his head. "The first two are fine, that's balance, but then there's *this*. Loved by Mana. Blanket immunity to a whole energy-*resource* type? What is that lug thinking? I know you used to have Mana

Loved and One with Mana, but one is part of the normal Mage-advancement tree, while the other one was a mess."

She stopped when Artorian beamed, his expression filling with elation. "*Oh, no*, what did you think of? It can't be good with a smirk like that plastered on you."

Artorian wrung his hands together, a scheming look in his squinted peepers. "Not being affected by Mana, while I'm planning a duelist-type character? Using a physical melee kit and build. Focused on training with you and being in the front of the fray? This smells like a good time. I can't prevent my enemies from casting spells on me, but I can surprise them by running right through their casts, getting in their faces, and enthusiastically saying hello."

He inhaled deep, then instantly coughed and gagged as his eyes watered, having forgotten that they were surrounded by the most terrible of odors that Lucia's shields could only do so much against.

Ember patted his back, but with half the normal effort. "You deserved that."

He whined, rubbing his eyes and nose with his sleeve. "Did not!"

Checking on solving that problem right away, he groaned when an important part of his toolkit came up blank. "I miss my Cleaning Aura. Three out of three import slots used, but there's a lot of goodies I'm not sure I can play without anymore. I can likely wiggle around my attributes just fine when we get to that, given that the numbers don't correlate to the meanings one might expect them to have."

Ember had to agree there. "Not for us, no. I think it's less noticeable for you than it was for me? Going from a double-S-ranker to a mortal, subsidized by some numbers, doesn't remotely do the previous equivalent any justice. Having five-thousand intelligence doesn't make me feel any smarter than the average cultivating mortal. I feel stuck at the zenith of C-rank, as far as capacities and capabilities are concerned. The rest is all modified by the numbers, and how much I'm willing to take risks. Running at Mach speeds is doable, but most of the time I don't even remember that I can do it. Whereas when I was an Incarnate, moving between planes and spaces happened almost by accident if I wasn't careful about it. There's a vast difference in scope at play."

Artorian crossed his arms with concern. "Are we supposed to feel smarter with more Intelligence, attribute-wise?"

Ember waffled her hand, settling back into the pillows. "Yes and no? You don't really notice intelligence, so much as you notice the results. When you come to a decision easily and quickly, you usually don't notice that you did. Even when that process happens faster. The numbers do matter, but the more mental and esoteric attributes don't give you convenient markers for what that attribute means at certain thresholds. That's why we used direct markers, like Mana amount, regeneration rates, and such. That's tangible."

She pawed at his arm, making tugging motions so he could do the rest of the prompts while in a half-cuddle. "For people who begin this game *as* mortals? That's a whole different swirl of soup. We come from the land of Mages and Incarnates, we have had capacity far beyond anything this game can replicate, and so we feel limited. Or that the gains aren't really gains. For a newcomer, that increase in attributes will feel like a substantial difference, because they've never experienced that new height before."

Ember flexed, showing off the muscle in her arm. "Physical attribute changes, like from Strength? These can alter players look, depending on how they perceive they would look. We look the same, even if our numbers are insane, because that meaning of Strength doesn't translate the same way with you and I. We *could* get all buff and beefy, the numbers allow it. Yet we look like the children we are. Perception of the self is serious business."

When he relented and pillow-flopped with her, she smiled bright and ran her claws through his messy hair. "The mental attributes are much the same. Wisdom will help you act in ways as if you have a deeper, personally-experienced understanding of something. Intelligence will always increase your raw data processing and problem solving. Charisma helps organize the word order in which you talk, and helps to pick the words you say. That is all still merely the system's 'help,' pushing your own mind in that direction so you begin to do it naturally. If you already had better words in mind to say, the Charisma attribute won't do any pushing."

Artorian was the one to take her hand, feeding her fingers with his by lacing them, an act that instantly improved her mood as she kept speaking. "If you had better existing pathways for problem solving, Intelligence will take a backseat. If you already had the experience, Wisdom will get out of your way. The system takes aggregated knowledge of all the ways people have interacted, organizes and ranks them, and then helps push you to the next threshold based on your attributes. Or holds you back if they're too low, compared to what you naturally have. That's the trick. That's the system's way of making you want to make the line go up. Make numbers bigger."

Artorian pulled up his attributes, noting that the Cultivator title was already in place. He currently had all-even scores across the board. He motioned at them, wondering if she had anything more before he began to fiddle.

Ember nudged her nose at his numbers. "The importance of them all being even has to do with Mage comforts, and the hidden features being built in that I'm pretty sure you've found by now."

Artorian tried to think of an example. "You mean that we do actually have access to dilation, but that we take health and energy burnout damage when we tap into it? Thus, attributes being equal means we don't suffer a deficiency when we're operating in other frames of time? I'd like it a lot more if I had back that alpha run ability that made me not suffer the burnout, but as is… That feature is too double-edged. I would keep it in my pocket as a backup, and once I start needing to use it, I will begin to rely on it."

He shook his head. "I don't want that."

Ember thought to argue, but decided against it. Her boy did not have to play with features he did not want. That answer was good enough, and if that was the one thing he'd discovered, she was going to remain hush about the rest. The adventure was no fun if the players were told everything they could and could not do. The big reveal moments when someone figured a mystery out for the first time were always delicious and juicy.

She squeezed his hand instead, happy to be in the pillows as she buried her face in for a moment. "*Mhm*, but keep testing. Keeping attributes even is important for turning non-Mages into Mages with game features, and important for using tricks like dilation at all. There's a whole system to punish deviation, but nothing particularly effective for adhering. The hidden features are meant as a patch, though I'm worried they're going to be too difficult to find."

Ember salved her own wounded concerns by moving to a more pleasant topic. "I expect we're both going to have a new title that provides us immunity from those deviation effects, so we can both play around with our attribute placement. I don't know if moving mine around will matter a whole bunch, but it will for you. Oh, don't drop any attributes below one-fifty, that *will* mess with you. I'd actually recommend two-hundred, in case you're ever hit with an attribute-reducing effect."

That tidbit earned her a worried look, so she added to her statement. "One-fifty is the game's internal Mage-number, even if people aren't actually Mages. That correlation doesn't translate directly. Not until Cal and Tim can make artificial ones out of normal people. The number does determine if you get the push-back effects that actually limit you. The detail matters for anyone playing that is either a Mage, or at one point was one. For me, my minimum attribute has to be seven-fifty, but you'll never see me with anything lower than a thousand in any value. Seven-fifty is the minimum internal Incarnate number. Any lower than that and I'll get impairments, regardless of the system not punishing me for having uneven attributes to begin with. For mortals, impairments hit any attribute below a ten."

Artorian nodded, satisfied. "Well, I was thinking of actually indulging in being a child, since I had the opportunity. No reason not to enjoy being a rambunctious youngster when given the chance. Not when I already know that version three of this build is going to be temporary. I'm thinking… dumping out the Wisdom and Intelligence. If they actually controlled my thinking, I would be *very* opposed to doing that, but since they're just… numbers? Why not."

She nodded, distracting him as she attacked the back of his head with her claws. Receiving a momentary happy sound for her efforts as he momentarily slumped, Ember felt victorious!

Purring in delight, she didn't distract him for too long. Alright, maybe a little too long, but celestials above, this made her happy. She was having a good time indulging in all these little touches of soft love, without comment or reprimand. "What about Luck? You love Luck. Or are you going to try something different since there's no penalties? You've got your flat and growth bonuses as well, still."

When released from the head rubs, far too soon in his opinion, Artorian grumbled to think as the pleasant and tingly fog lifted. "Let's start the great work."

CHAPTER THREE

Artorian adjusted his attributes screen, the prompt showing total statistics. Showcasing values of seven-twenties across the board, and no more, Artorian raised an eyebrow. That wasn't right. Those should be higher. Time to fiddle.

Ember put her head down for a moment to let Artorian focus, staying in the pillows while activity on Zephyr shuffled and lived around them. The vibrations of the deck told her plenty.

Lucia had zero problems entertaining Hans Jr., the shield-bubble covered baby riding on her back as she walked from Zephy's port to stern in large ovals that decreased the amount of sound erupting from the small child. The activity appeared more soothing to Lucia than it did Hans Jr., but it wasn't like anyone was going to stop her as the child got increasingly drowsy.

Before that, Hans Jr. had been playing super monkey ball deluxe, as the ball, impervious to damage while bumping into all the things within the main cabin. There had been much screeching.

Ding!

Artorian and Ember both looked up, not sure what new notification had just come in since nothing had changed. Artorian and Ember looked about, then sat up some more in confusion, before scanning the existing orb of screens they were in. Why was there a ding if nothing was different?

Lucia yelled from the aft of the ship. "Hey gang? Back here! Some kind of tiny turtle with a castle on his back showed up. A Tactical Tortoise?"

Artorian drew the only parallel he could, yelling to the aft of the ship. "Incursus?"

Lucia yelled back, impressed. "You just made the tiny turtle smile!"

Ember threw her nested pillows off, wriggle-working her way out of the lounger without a second to spare. Forgetting her strength in the process, she sent one of the pillows into the ceiling with such extreme might that the pillow fluff-sploded on impact, dealing a single point of damage to whatever poor thing it hit. "I wanna see the turtle!"

Artorian looked up, saluting the lost pillow before putting his fist to his mouth to make funeral trumpet noises. The loss of a good pillow was always a tragedy.

Pwa-pwa-pwaaaa.

The struck ceiling-entity suffered an existential crisis on realizing that it had taken damage. Had the most esoteric and frightening of living horrors just been challenged to a pillow fight? What? First, its delightful undulation had been taken by accursed illumination. Next, it had been whacked by a mundane pillow—so hard that it had taken actual health damage. How had it taken health damage? It was immune to physical harm! It was cheese! You can't hurt *cheese*.

Cheese hurts *you*!

Utterly curious about how this was possible, Team Sleep gained the personal attention of a Vanaheim Cheese Elemental, native to the gate zone of the Darkest Dungeon. The final surprise for those who entered, delved, and returned. There was little as devastating as being cheesed right before reaching your end goal, having falsely believed yourself safe.

Having let your guard down.

Utterly curious and hungry for information, the Elemental scanned for unconventional weaknesses. The results were surprising, and made the Elemental desire a tiny mustache to curl and preen.

Puns?

Team Sleep was weak to… *puns*?

Given that the Cheese Elemental, undecided on its own shape, wiggled at the thought of having been accosted by a pillow? There seemed some odd, but fair recompense in the strangeness of it all. If that was their weakness, then it would create cheesy puns. At an opportune moment? It would strike! Once victorious, the Elemental would undulate in the darkness once more. Another deep dive, cut short. *Mwahahaha.*

There was a definite need for a tiny mustache.

For now, it would ruminate and bide its time, stalking Team Sleep. What were they up to? According to some intrusive cheesing about, Team Sleep had four members. The two on the mid-deck had moved to the aft, pinpointing three of the four team members. They surrounded a small green creature that had been placed on a table.

Where was member number four?

A quick pulse through the cheese-network, and the Elemental found the fourth member wreaking pure havoc deeper in the Darkest Dungeon. That one kept yelling some strange things, but between the curated, piercing strikes of its chosen weapon, and the sudden claw-mauling it would deliver when shifting into the larger catty form? There was an upset in the status quo. This dungeon was supposed to terrorize players, not the other way around! The Elemental would inform the Darkest One that it was time to release the spores and hallucinogens.

The Darkest Dungeon, in the depths of Vanaheim, was meant as an experience in two categories. Horror, and psychological pressure. The mood and the lighting at the entrance were finely curated. All to give the actual dungeon a grim, gritty, dour, and depressing feel.

Combining strange and unique challenges, complete with several gimmicks that on occasion made standing to fight the poorest possible choice, this dungeon aimed to be devious. Events and enemies were rarely straightforward, and progressing forced players to carefully choose how they balanced their inventory. Torches were worth their weight in gold, and players could only carry so much.

If they survived the encounters, then greed would be their downfall on the way back out. Every tester party had faced inevitable defeat as the Shifters and Shamblers slunk from their hiding places. Or even better! Summoned into place from a wayward hand reaching for treasure that was no treasure at all.

The Cheese Elemental savored the scenario, but savored the lucky party that could return all the way back to the gate most of all. Making one's way to the gate was normally considered a feat, but new information looked to upturn that assumption.

This team had used a shortcut in the shape of a flying ship. How unacceptable. It would inform the others to add sticky cheese netting, preventing that avenue of exploitation in the future.

They were the baddies here!

Slinking away as a mass of heated, cheesy goo, the Cheese Elemental began to plot. First, it would need to choose a name. Then, a form. As the Elemental decided that it would be a he, the name came easy. A moniker was modeled after what had broken the Elemental from its stupor, causing newfound aware-ness to snap to the forefront. Taking a point of damage had jump-started the Nemesis Pylons, which were now rumbling to life, turning the previously system-bound entity into a being with a personalized character sheet.

He would be named... Pillow Breaker. Shatterer of all that is fluff.

A prompt came up for Pillow Breaker upon deciding that

for himself, one he reached out to with a sticky tendril. Unlike the awful blue of Team Sleep's screens, this one was a most comfortable off-yellow. Given the opportunity to accept a class, Pillow Breaker villainously rubbed two tentacles together, then accepted without pause.

Truly, either Vanaheim or the Voice of the World was looking out for him! Accepted most grate-fully, he gained a most pun-worthy base class:

Pillow Breaker, the *Pun-isher*.

This development went unnoticed by Team Sleep, who had repositioned around a visiting Incursus.

To his own dismay, the tiny turtle with an adorable, minis-cule castle built on his back stole much of the attention. Specifi-cally because the girls wanted to hold him, and no work was getting done while they played pass the baton. This lasted until Incursus had managed to vocalize that between being held by Lucia, and held by Ember? The dungeon would rather keep his feet on the ground.

This caused much pouting, but ended with Incursus getting his footing, who then immediately sorted Artorian's problem with his base stats. Eschewing the rolls altogether, thirty points had been slapped into each statistic.

Artorian now had the full seven-hundred and fifty count in each attribute, his missing numbers accounted for thanks to Incursus. He was allowed to shift them about, and the napkin math was keeping his mind very busy. "If I take them all down to two hundred? That means eight attributes would be refunding me five-hundred and fifty points each. For a total of four-thousand, and four hundred points to divvy up."

He kept wanting to theorize number placements, but also kept coming back to the same bothersome, intrusive thought. Did he want to adopt the Glass Cannon trait that reduced his health to one? Did he really? That would vastly change the math on where to put his points. He knew it was a terrible idea, but there was something that pulled him to that binary danger. "Maybe for version four?"

Lucia pulled him from his pacing rut with a soft paw on the head, having gotten cozy in her large basher form so she could keep the napping, ball-shielded Hans Jr. tucked under her chin. He'd lapsed from energetic and bombastic to dead asleep in about two seconds. "What are you mumbling about, kit?"

Artorian showed her the screens he was mulling over, revealing more of his internal monologue. "There was something oddly satisfying about the dangerous difficulty of having only one hit point. I disliked it at the time because it was keeping me from what I wanted to do, but I am *pulled* to it."

A troubling hand motion led into pointing at his health value. "There was a tension in that danger that I find myself unable to *not* think of. Is it dumb? Yes. Can I stop thinking about it? No. I'm wondering about the possibility while I have a person around specifically versed in shields. Both for a good party dynamic, and to not lone wolf it like I have a tendency to do."

Moving his hand, he tapped his temple. "My mind is currently on the satisfactory gameplay sensation that I think the dungeons are wanting me to experience. While I'm in this dungeon specifically to get Tisha out, now that I have all these options? I am drawn to what kind of gameplay I could experience afterward. The intended experience, or something closer to it."

Lucia shot a sharp look at Ember. "You're not the only one who does that lone wolf thing. It's more common than you think."

Ember growled back, but the noise wasn't mal-intended. She was stuck on Artorian's hit point question. Her arms crossed as she stood at militant ease, Iridium eyes flicking from screen to screen for more tactical data. "I would suggest against. Pick up some shield lore from the master of the craft in the party first. *Then.* Otherwise, if something bad happens and you get separated, you basically lose your borrowed life at the first poor roll of the dice."

She made an X with her arms, telling him not to proceed.

"I understand what you meant now, with your version four mumble. Keep it in the pocket, sugar. Maybe make some skills first that let you dodge attacks, or negate area effects. One of Yuki's snowballs would do you in."

Emby had never led him astray, and that advice did help with the tumultuous, intrusive thought that wouldn't behave and go sit in the corner. How dare. So rude. "Thank you, dear. I'll hold off on Glass Cannon for now, see how the excess health affects me. Maybe the Vanaheim damage numbers are equivalent to the Moose we encountered? That would be bad. More health would certainly be better, but without personal sustain and dedicated healing, I'm always going to feel off. The alpha run got a lot right, and much hasn't been replicated."

He leaned into Lucia's Glitterflit paw and added weight to the motion. "I'm sorry, Momma Bun. You protect me really well, but I'm still thinking I'd be able to do it all myself, and that factor not being true is taking something out of me. I'm not less capable, but I can't 'do the thing,' and that bothers me. I am thankful for your Hearthfire shields, in all their funny forms."

Her large paw rubbed his head. "You be good, kit. Finish your screens. Come ask Momma when you've got time and all your other work is done. There's no rush on that, and I can certainly teach you a thing or two. You've barely seen one percent of my true power! My teacher was a real Shaggy Hare. Great sense of humor. Loved eating hay. Skittish to all Abyss."

Lucia retrieved her paw, lowering her chin back down on Hans Jr. to keep the little baby boy warm. "I'll be around, kit. Make your character. Hans owes me Timothy Hay for babysitting work. A whole bale. I'll be busy daydreaming about that while you and your lady do numbers."

Artorian snuck a glance at Ember's reaction before commenting, trying to play it off like he wasn't looking while pulling the attribute screen back to him. She had a blush on her cheeks, but was also not trying to let it show. *Adorable.*

He'd let it slide for now, tapping the prompt. "Incursus? I think you're who I need for help here. I believe I could do this myself, but I'm intending to include more people in my flow. Care for a paddle?"

The tiny turtle was pleased as punch to get into the river, Incursus's speech slow and strained. "Happy. To."

Artorian nodded, finishing the second half of his request now that Incursus had been given some agency in the matter. "After all the statistics are bumped down to two-hundred? Drop eight-hundred points into Strength, Dexterity, and Constitution to start, please."

The calculations happened, but just as the dungeon core's lumbering and sluggish speech took time to cook to medium rare, the results were not as fast as the hare. Not being in his own dungeon, Incursus's prompts were made of clonks.

They clicked and ticked, many gears rolling and moving in an invisible background as the top of the prompt filtered in anew. The text updated line by line rather than all in one go. The lack of seamless change... honestly? Artorian liked it.

Especially the clickety-clacks!

That might get difficult in combat? He should address that. "Thank you, Incursus. By the way? I don't need combat logs. When it comes time to calculate big numbers, I want you to do what's easiest for you, but don't feel a need to give me the results unless I ask for it. I don't want to see numbers pop out of enemies, or some big, difficult calculation spread, or any of the numerical bonus hints that remove the immersion."

The turtle nodded in a languished motion, but Artorian understood, then read over the update.

———

Characteristics:
  Strength: 1,000
  Dexterity: 1,000
  Constitution: 1,000
  Intelligence: 200
  Wisdom: 200

Charisma: 200
Perception: 200
Luck: 200
Karmic Luck: 0

———

Characteristics Remaining:
    2,000.

———

Artorian reached for his beard, fumbling a grip when it wasn't there. Right, too young still. One day, old boy, one day. "Well, there's no reason not to go in hard, if I'm going to attempt this min-maxing. The idea is for a statistics spread that would make a Dwarf proud, so another six hundred in each physical attribute, and then the last two hundred in… Luck, please."

The turtle smiled, Incursus once again making his prompt update with those oddly satisfying clickety-clacks. Numbers rolled in, updating line by line as the dungeon went through the steps and got it all done.

———

Characteristics:
    Strength: 1,600
    Dexterity: 1,600
    Constitution: 1,600
    Intelligence: 200
    Wisdom: 200
    Charisma: 200
    Perception: 200
    Luck: 400
    Karmic Luck: 0

———

Artorian pet the turtle head for his work. "Well done, Incursus. What's next?"

A tiny pre-made prompt arrived for his troubles.

———

To Do List:
  Name.
  Race.
  Class.
  Specialization.
  Profession.
  Flat and Growth Bonuses.
  Traits.
  Titles.
  Equipment.
  Flash Runes.

CHAPTER FOUR

Artorian had a better grasp of the process this time. The first, hand-held walkthrough with Zelia had done him a lot of good. That allowed him to go much faster this time! "Thank you, Incursus. Any commentary or feedback on my choices?"

Incursus moved one of his tiny turtle feet to step on the table with purpose, a prompt appearing. Rather than needing to speak directly, the prompt rolled his spoken words into place much faster, with more bonus clickety-clacks.

Given the opportunity, players will optimize the fun out of a game.
Given the opportunity, curators should encourage fun over optimization.

Well, that gave him much to chew on.

Artorian held his chin, reading the missive again. "So I won't be getting feedback from you, but you're going to try to make the game as fun for me as you can? I can't say I disapprove, Incursus. Fun is a good focus. I like fun."

He then addressed the team leader, her gaze steeled on information prompts. "Emby? Any name preference? I recall you shouting something about avoiding our actual names when we were in Demeter's Dream the first time. I didn't get to follow up on that, but I figured it was important."

Ember nodded seriously, the movement fast. "Everyone else can use their actual names as much as they like. I want the extra layer of security on the off-chance, the *off-chance*, that Cal ever plays with that Truename nonsense. Don't do it."

Ding!

One of Apiculteur's Serenity Bees popped into existence near them, buzzing right over while holding a comparatively massive folded-up papyrus sheet. It was a small note by people-sized standards, but for the single Bee, the item was much too big. The task seemed impossible, but Bees didn't care what anyone else might think was impossible. The Serenity Bee buzzed at them while doing its utmost to butt-waggle a particular flight pattern.

Ember, without missing a beat, replied with buzzing sounds and dexterous head bobbing before accepting the letter. She was fluent in Bee.

The tiny Serenity Bee then saluted, waggled its butt some more, and vanished in a flash of heat while sailing away into the black.

She handed the letter to Artorian. "Here you go, sunshine. Mail for you. An older letter, apparently. Long overdue? He said they're getting the mail up and running, but there's a backlog. Some busy Bee named Lu Ri kicked the project off. Captain Reynolds says that the new mail-hives are abuzz with activity, and he'll be back when the bees-knees kick off in full force."

Artorian took the missive, reading the title while keeping the papyrus folded up. "Last words of Chance the Fateseer."

The silence that followed as he held the letter made Ember curl her arm around her boy. "Sugar?"

This was difficult for Artorian, as he experienced the memory containing the flash of consumption that wiped his friend from the alpha run. After Chance had pushed him out of the way of that very attack. "I'm alright. I'll be alright. I was not expecting that prankster to come up again. Now here I am, holding a missive with his bony handwriting."

Already feeling the emotion swell, he unfolded the letter. "'Dear Sunny. The problem with being a Fateseer is one can see the punchline of a joke before they know the joke. I'm tucking this letter away in the bottom of a pile where it will be forgotten for a while, but I refuse to let this jest pass me by. I finally know the first half, and can share this actor's wisdom. Never perform for cows. You'll get mooed off the stage.'"

Artorian sputtered, needing to look away before composing himself to read further. "'Now I've got the last laugh, *Sunshine*. Ha-ha! The next part was blurry to me, but I could make out that you needed help picking a name. Well, there you go! Use it well, Sunny, and thanks. You're the best friend I ever had. Don't mourn me, or I will make another letter with a pun about seeing my fate coming. A eulogy for my old bones is plenty.'"

He silently read the missive again, before responding to his long-lost friend with a melancholy nod. "The last laugh indeed, Chance. The last laugh indeed. Emby? I need a small funeral pyre. Chance never did get a proper burial. Not so much as an incense stick for my old friend."

Ember held out her fingers, the tips and nails glowing a searing hot orange. He placed the piece of papyrus between them, watching the letter instantly catch flame. The fire swiftly tore through the missive as Artorian gave the Fateseer a short eulogy. "The thing about luck is that luck loves the bold. Luck loves the daring. Luck loves the fair. It loves to play tit-for-tat and turn the other cheek, and as luck would have it, I too have developed a fondness for fairness. Rest peacefully, old friend."

He inhaled slowly, frowning as he turned his chin to Incursus. The name was fated to be. "Sunshine, please."

Clickety clacks rolled within his Character Sheet's entries.

Ding!

Character name set: Sunshine.

Another breath, and Artorian squeezed his wrists behind his back, plagued with memories that he needed to remain quiet for. Processing them so he could think about the game. Though answers for the game appeared to flow as water while his mind was occupied with the remembrance of Chance.

He spoke easily as he kept his eyes on Incursus's handy to-do list. "Profession? Janitor. I want that Cleaning Aura back. This time with a broom that I don't have to surrender. Race? If I'm not already defaulting to Nascent Being, set me as what I am. I believe I've had my fill of the Dragon and High Human, and wish it no further. I must move past those old states of my being. I have no answers for you per class or specialization."

Artorian stopped speaking when he heard the mechanical clacks, giving Incursus time to work.

Ding!

Profession set: Janitor.

Artorian squinted at the text, realizing he made a huge mistake. "Janitor was my class last time, wasn't it? Not my profession?"

Incursus gave him the slow turtle nod, but Artorian couldn't fault the dungeon for doing exactly as he'd asked. "Right. Thank you, Incursus. Any chance I can still have a Cleaning Aura?"

Incursus gave him the slow turtle nod again. Appreciative of what Incursus was dredging out of the waters for him, Artorian sat and provided some well-deserved head-pats, rubbing his thumb over the tiny turtle's head. "Can you show me a list of my overall goodies? I heard much has changed."

Happy clickety-clacks occurred right away.

Ding!

————

Traits:

    Loved by Mana.
    Experimental Attributes.
    Experimental Energy Metric.
    Free from Gaston.

————

Titles:

    Administrator.
    Overdeity.
    Cultivator.
    Roaming World Boss Duo.

————

Race:

    Nascent Being.
    Truesight.
    Profound Sight.

————

Skills:

    Freedom of Mind.
    Hypermobility.

———

Flash Runes:
  Voltekker.
  Cleaning Presence.

———

Gear:
  Silverwood Bracelet.
  Armored Core: Voltekka.
  Pillow.
  Broom of Shaka, the Boom Shaka Laka.
  Tribal C'towl Cloak: Archimedes.
  Zelia's Senate Brooch.
  Faith Foundry Pajamas.

———

Languages:
  Old World.
  Wood Elf.
  Demoniac - Scree-scree.
  Red Panda.
  Aquatic.
  Baa.
  Braille.

———

Artorian instantly searched for other screens while learning this information, his hands up and out to reach for whatever floating screen might be the one. "Wait, what? I need more words on some of these. Experimentals? Cleaning Presence is a Flash Rune? Give! I must know!"

He snap-pointed at his traits screen when he found it in the circular mass.

"You! To me!"

The relevant prompt staggered out of formation, but didn't scooch fast enough. Amending that indecisiveness, the traits screen was grabbed by its neighbors to be spun, turned, and hurled like a wet towel right at Artorian's face!

Sunshine was knocked to the ground when the flexible prompt clapped around his head, the screen holding on for a short moment. Remembering it needed to be a prompt as the recipient hit the deck legs up, the traits screen let go and returned to being a boring rectangle. Hovering ever so innocently in place.

Prone on the floor, Artorian made a concession as he heard Ember devolve into sputtered laughter. "I'm going to pretend that did not happen."

CHAPTER FIVE

Reaching for the wet towel pretending to be an innocent game screen, Artorian encountered an upset error message when he attempted to access his trait information. An irritated little *uack* played, like a moody Darkwing Duck's quack.

He tapped the screen again, but the same duck-based error sound repeated. A warning prompt blocked and overlapped his traits screen. "What are we playing here? Duck-Duck-Goose? What's next? Spitting Llamas in my skills sheet? Goats chewing on my equipment prompt because it kind of looks like grass? Boo the Bat pulling Sugar Gliders out of an overcoat and reverse-pickpocketing them into my inventory? Or will there suddenly be Lilly, the Mer-neko version of a C'towl, biting into the tail end of my titles?"

He tilted his head, still not having figured out any of the prompt colors, except that black was important. He had no black screens, nor multi-colored ones, nor any with shiny, fancy borders. That was fine, he supposed, but he was going to figure it out!

Tapping the error directly, he read what some duck was

quacking about. "Attributes unfinished, user cannot proceed. Please select allotted advancement patterns."

Artorian motioned at his attributes page to 'come here.' When it flew over to be within easy arm's reach, he tapped Dexterity, then the flat bonus entry when it popped up as an option.

Uack!

"Oh, come on!" Artorian tapped the same options again after the errors cleared, wanting that option selected and over with.

Uack!

"Why are you quacking at me!?" He furiously tapped the same set-up miniature prompts again, trying one last time before he was going to chuck the screen.

Uack!

Artorian got up in a flash, took the edge of the screen, and chucked it at the ceiling. His attributes prompt spun and flew like a ninja star, embedding itself into a stalactite. The prompt, realizing this is not where it was supposed to be, quivered itself free. The screen flew right back to him, happily reassuming its prior within-arm's-reach position. A little closer, in relative terms, as the user had their hands pressed to their face.

Poof!

Uack?

The more questioning duck call earned a defeated groan in response.

The glasses-wearing, white-feathered duck which had appeared unannounced cleared its throat, trying again, but in the Old World language this time. Maybe that would have more success. Alfred Jodocus Kwak—Quackbang, to his friends—adjusted his red scarf and straightened the clipboard under his wing. "I said, sir, that the flat bonus option has been rendered unavailable, on account of…"

Alfred adjusted his glasses, reading from the clipboard with a flat tone. "I quote, 'These values stack? What do you mean these values stack? Why are these numbers so big to begin with? You're telling me they stack each time a threshold is reached? That is ludicrous! That is a bigger bonus than our base formulas, and by far too much. Remove those from the pool and leave only the growth-type options. We're going to have to use these for something else, like class-based achievements, or some other form of earned reward type, especially if we're going to keep the numbers the same and allow them to stack. Off with its head! Now show me this Molotov Cockatiel. I am baffled that we have not *once* managed to recreate a Phoenix. Shaka! Shaka, put that down, that is a not a——'"

Alfred moved the clipboard back under his wing. "So ends the statement. I am informed that as compensation, you are allotted three attributes to assign the growth pattern to, rather than two. So ends my task. Quackbang, out."

Uack!

Poof!

Artorian had moved his hands to observe the small duck speak. He hadn't believed there was a small duck there, but he did see and hear it. When Quackbang poofed out with the duck-call and a cloud of feathers, he half-looked at his attribute screen. Artorian touched the Dexterity entry, and swiped down over Constitution and Luck with a *nyeh*. "There. Done. Growth types, the lot of 'em."

Incursus worked, finally able to show Artorian his current base statistics, getting this out of the way before he had to worry about calculating some of the experimental traits. The clickety clacks would flow.

Ding!

———

Base Values:
   Hit Points: 15,950.
   Mana Pool: 2,000.
   Mana Regen: 50 / second.
   Stamina Pool: 15,950.

Stamina Regen: 800 / second.

———

Characteristics: Improvement Choice.
  Strength: None.
  Dexterity: Pattern B: Growth.
  Constitution: Pattern B: Growth.
  Intelligence: None.
  Wisdom: None.
  Charisma: None.
  Perception: None.
  Luck: Pattern B: Growth.

———

Characteristics: Threshold 1,600, Total Bonus:
  Dexterity: Multiplier of 25, replaced by multiplier of 57.
  Constitution: Multiplier of 10, replaced by multiplier of 42.

———

Characteristics: Threshold 400, Total Bonus:
  Luck: Fun Item Find chance, plus 8%.

———

Adjusted Values:
  Hit Points: 66,830.
  Stamina Regen: 1,824 / second.
  Luck: Fun Item Find chance, plus 8%.

———

Current Values:
  Hit Points: 66,830.

Mana Pool: 2,000.
Mana Regen: 50 / second.
Stamina Pool: 15,950.
Stamina Regen: 1,824 / second.

———

Incursus stretched his wittle turtle legs. Success! Now for the hard part. A few clickity-clacks to make the prompt, and send!

Ding!

Artorian received the short message, distracted while utterly baffled at the tiny mana pool and mana regeneration values. Fifty? What did the game mean, *fifty?* Was that number supposed to be that small? Is that what normal players would contend with at two-hundred points in Wisdom? Fifty? That was *normal?* His baseline was Abyssed!

He glanced at Incursus's missive, though the contents were anything but easy to chew on. In addition to a short recap of his traits, which he had wanted, an activation prompt lingered. He was uncertain about pushing the button. Loved by Mana he'd seen earlier, so he scrolled down from that entry to the problematic ones.

———

Trait: Experimental Attributes.

This user may, after initial finalization, move all of their attributes around at leisure, a single time. After this feature has been used, it will lock.

This feature has been locked.

———

Trait: Experimental Energy Metric.

This user may, after having acquired an energy metric other than Stamina, combine that energy metric with their Stamina metric, merging might and magic into a single calculation. A user may only do this once per character, and that character will become unable to use another energy metric from that point. Changing to another class will not alter this merged metric, and may lock a user out of that class's toolkit entirely.

This feature can be activated.

Activate?

———

Trait: Free from Gaston.

This user is free from several system repercussions. In addition to the level requirement of professions being removed, this user will not suffer from system penalties relating to unbalanced statistics. Particularly, their attributes.

Note: This angers Gaston, and Gaston will hunt you.

———

Ding!

Artorian rubbed his temples when he could swear the next part of the entry was sung straight into his head. The addendum to the prompt barged in unannounced. Like a rude brute commencing a bar song without invitation.

———

Requisite addition:

No one stomps like Gaston,
No one romps like Gaston,
No one holds thick and girthy big deer like Gaston.
It might sometimes be said he's exasperating.
But what do you want? That's Gaston!

———

He didn't know who Gaston was yet, but for that ditty alone, he was going to give that creature one beast of a bad time, written in Comic Sans. "Well, that's the traits, then. I have no idea what Experimental Energy Metric is going to do. I faintly remember mentioning it during my high-velocity ideas pitch to Tim, but not well."

He stared at the activation prompt, wondering if he should push the button. Artorian turned to see if Ember was done laughing her butt off yet, but found that not to be the case. His lady suffered at his continued misfortune as she wheezed out the word 'duck' while beet red in the face and slapping Zephyr's deck.

Lucia kept half an ear up, but no more; she wasn't going to be good to ask, either. Zephyr could be a voice, but Zephyr was only going to make him opt for the more adventurous option.

Artorian almost asked Incursus, but based on the prior response, the dungeon had to remain neutral. He stuffed his hands into his pockets, and felt Zelia's brooch. Now there was a solution! He pulled the communicator free, pressed it for comfort regardless of that act not doing anything, and spoke. "Zelia? Do you have a moment for advice?"

The connection was seamless and instant. His brooch picked up the bar-clamor, hang-drum music, and hooting laughter in the background. "Of course, my Dreamer. If it perchance has to do with your choice of pushing the button? Push the button. Many are watching you, and there are loud chants in Tun's Tavern that... One moment, let me turn so the Dwarven Chant can reach your ears."

Some shuffling occurred on the other end of Artorian's communication device, followed by loud, excited cheering and harmonized Dwarven chants of, "Push. The. Button! Push. The. Button!"

Out of pure, sheer, raw curiosity, Artorian reached his hand toward the prompt. Hearing the mad chorus and Dwarven song devolve into raw hollering and mug-slamming.

Pulling his hand away, a sad rebuttal of 'awwws' and 'noooos' instantly followed, the vigor of the Dwarven voices over the connection dying down.

He then, just because he could, moved his hand back toward the prompt, causing an explosion in jeering and Dwarven yelling that each tried to overpower the other as they yelled at him and picked up their war chant once more. "Push. The. Button! Push. The. Button!"

Zelia turned, muting the clamor in Tun's Tavern, located somewhere outside of Nidavellir. "Like I said, my Dreamer. If that happened to be why you called? I hope that helped. Otherwise, what can I do for you, Administrator?"

Artorian placed his hand on the prompt, glancing at it a moment to provide the intent that he wanted it to stay put and act as a support. The screen easily did so as he leaned on it. Though the act caused even more noise to fill Zelia's background. "How many people tend to watch me? I'm not exactly being interesting."

Zelia needed a moment to find that answer, but relayed it simply enough. "Many."

Artorian rolled his tongue around in his mouth as he thought of that. "*Mmm…* and they're all like this?"

He could feel Zelia hide her face with her sleeve as she grinned on the other end, before she took a large gulp of Dwarven brew. "For the most part, my Dreamer."

That gave him a brilliant idea. "Is there any way to get some kind of a lead on what the masses are hungry for? I do like putting on a bit of a show, and if this is making people happy, that does make me happy in turn. I like involvement."

Zelia loudly slammed down her mug. "I'll see what I can do, Administrator. Anything else?"

Artorian shook his head, an act that he was certain Zelia could see. Especially if they had whole prompts functioning as screens currently centered on him. "No, thank you, Zelia. Let me know the will and hunger of the people. I've got a button to push."

Zelia laughed from the other side of the connection before the brooch went silent. Artorian nodded, affixed the object to the left side of his pajama collar, and then snapped into a pose.

Keeping his stance wide and arms high, he yelled to the sky. "Do you wanna see me push the button?"

He heard no reply, but he imagined the sudden question to all the onlookers might have spurred some kind of excited murmuring. He got louder, and did it again, turning his hands palms-up as he walked around the prompt like a gladiator presenting. "I said, *do you wanna see me push the button?*"

Grinning wide as he most certainly had people's attention now. He hovered a hand over the prompt, yelling out his challenge. "Are you not entertained?"

Not waiting for a reply that wasn't going to come, Artorian slapped the button, activating the Experimental Energy Metric. "Let us be entertained!"

CHAPTER SIX

"Insolent wretches! I once more find you in my realm and domain!" Breaking free from a sudden cloud of dark buzzing mosquitoes, the great, the one, the only, the El Mosco spread his many flamberge appendages and multiple, sharp buzz-kill wings as he revealed himself. Having reformed only to find that the team of sleepy miscreants still plagued Vanaheim.

The fools! They had trapped themselves underground, right next to a dungeon entrance. He had them now. El Mosco arrived far more prepared against the dreaded 'beams' that destroyed and haunted him. Now those attacks were a worry no more!

The many giant blades that made up his limbs all gleamed before becoming drowned in the dull, darkened red of old blood. As fog set in around the area boss, he spread his appendages wide in dramatic performance before draping his wings all over himself to uphold an air of mystery. One had to hold to the dramatic order of things!

Opening his act with a guffaw, El Mosco was knocked out of his hovering position in the sky by a perfectly placed pillow as Artorian yelled at him. "Shut! I am trying to put on a show here! You stole my thunder!"

Insulted beyond words, El Mosco trembled with fuming rage as he retook his proper sky-placed hovering position, his compound eyes going bloodshot. Moreso still, that a laughing little girl picked herself up from the deck of that accursed airship only to wipe her eyes with the back of her hand and utter the daring words: "Do your thing, sugar. I got this. Finish your sheet so you can come play while I play with this wet sheet."

The self-proclaimed Vampire Lord of Vanaheim, who could likely have thought over his words before throwing them out in the open, made a terrible mistake as he flourished his flamberges wide in offensive display. "Insolent wretches! I am no mere bedding cover. I am El Mosco. I shall wipe the laughter from you all! You will fear me, weak little girl!"

Activity on the ship stopped dead.

Artorian's shoulders bunched, a discomforted noise peeling out of him as his hands pulled away from his screens. "*Mnnn...* you shouldn't'a said that."

The smile bled out of Ember's face.

Heat rose from her being, distorting her surroundings. The air around Ember twisted, forming desert mirages and the scenery of endless sands. Diamond striations criss crossed over her bronzed skin as she took her first steps towards a brand-new warfront. Her form filled like a container with roiling, pyroclastic solar swirls as the Diamond Body ability spread.

She walked off the deck as Zephyr hurriedly deployed a boarding ramp. The searing footprints Ember left behind were hot enough for Zephyr to feel the burn, marring previously pristine luxury-liner hardwood.

The burning steps proceeded down the ramp as Ember's eyes remained locked onto the noisy, buzzing fly that mandated a harsh swatting. Zephyr retracted her ramp with an instant tug once Ember was off, hissing noises leaving her pipes as if she'd just tried to take a cooking pot off the fire while having forgotten her mittens.

El Mosco, unimpressed by a little lustrous fire and mere display of heat-illusions, reared up in another exceedingly unnecessary flourish to roll into another speech. He got as far as inhaling before Astarte, Goddess of War, had him by the throat. She introduced herself to the fray by violently ripping his proboscis off at the root, El Mosco's passionate speech coming into being as a career-ending scream.

This hello made it very clear that it was not she who had to contend with the area boss. The area boss, far from his assigned domain, had to contend with her. There would be brutality, blood, murder, and an increase in width of the mad, toothy smile developing on Astarte's wide-eyed face. Her eyes became orbs of orange and carmine flame that hungered. Astarte's previously red hair was now a tapestry of fire that put the dull reds of El Mosco's sword-arms to shame.

Getting up to El Mosco had been trivial. Ember had left a tiny pool of molten ground behind where she had stood, cooking and burning the cheese underneath the stone. Launching herself directly at her opponent without a single word being spoken, Astarte's straight-line leap was basic. Clean. Direct. Her laconic ways were alive and well when it was time to put the fear into an ingrate, sparing him no dialogue.

Just as she would not spare El Mosco from devastation.

Astarte gripped the mosquito man hard enough by the left compound eye to crack a few dozen lenses as her fingers wetly plunged in. Her claw claimed a bloody grip as her short, stiletto-shaped nails dug the first nail into El Mosco's coffin. Her boots unsheathed claws of foxfire, hooking into the burning footholds that they carved into the mosquito's chest. The foxfire anchors dug deep, as if the area boss was a cliffside to be scaled. Fire damage rapidly piled on from sheer contact as she turned up her Coronal Aura, Astarte's presence alone out-damaging both her claw-grip and boot-cleats.

El Mosco's screams were drowned out by fire.

Unlike her Sunshine, who preferred his combat clean and kind, Astarte preferred hers to be spartan. Brutal and effective. Dirty and quick. Not at all concerned about optics or the mess made and gore left behind. Finishing her introduction, she stabbed Mosco's proboscis through his right compound eye before he could act, resulting in a bloody, high-pressure smear that erupted from his face. To everyone watching, this development had been lightning fast. To Astarte, this all occurred in slow motion.

Treating the end of the proboscis as a handhold and lever rather than some kind of weapon when the blood spurt had barely begun from her perspective, Astarte opened her mouth to finally speak. The inside of her maw revealed a roiling supernova. Her tongue and lips turned a searing, solar orange. "Shining. Burning. Finger."

El Mosco had enough time to grasp and understand the primal sensation of fear as a sun went off inside of his skull, vaporizing his antennae and wings from the sheer secondary forces at play before he could get his flamberges to do so much as twitch. To El Mosco's credit, his flamberges were all that remained when the rest of his body, head, and limbs all went up like a magma-cuddled firework.

The proboscis in Astarte's hand became molten slag along with the rest of her opponent, before multicolored particles exploded around her as the local area boss learned that it should perhaps not have picked up a grudge against a roaming world boss.

El Mosco wanted dramatic flair, but Astarte did not play.

If you wanted the smoke, you would catch those hands.

She would fade you faster than the curtains could fall.

The flamberges fell and sunk into the stone as gravity took them; Astarte's feet hit the ground not long after. Her body barely registered the impact, transitioning from the fall directly into an active walk back to the ship. The insignificant drop distance was not worthy of her notice, her attention on dropping her Aura since that short-ranged tool dealt horrendous, indiscriminate damage.

The fire and flame faded from Astarte's body as the diamond glint receded, her healthy bronze appearance retaking its original place. Ember traded a body of luster and fire for supple and smooth skin. She hopped back onto Zephyr, who tensed before it was clear that no additional scorch marks would mar her deck. Ember walked the few paces to take Artorian by his gaping mouth, slowly lifting his fallen jaw until it closed before she pecked him on the forehead.

Ember was all soft smiles and sweet words the moment she was back, the war she had begun already ended and done with. "How'd your experimental energy metric come out, sugar?"

Artorian had entirely forgotten that had been the focus before she stole the show. Granted, a very welcomed theft, but he hadn't been able to focus on anything except her viciously taking an area boss apart that... really... should be a lot more formidable than they kept making him seem. A Vanaheim area boss was nothing to scoff at.

Normally.

He turned his head to glance at his screens, noting the previous value of the mana regeneration metric. He still couldn't get over how that number was a mere fifty, at two-hundred points of relevant attributes. How was anyone supposed to get spellwork done with those values? Get cozy on Midgard? No. They'd barely even start with that value, if any. He was going to pay keen attention to newcomers who were effective with the small numbers. Yes, he needed a severe refresher on how proper mortals did things, and managed to get through challenges with the means they were provided. Version four of his character, that he would hopefully begin in the proper release version of Eternia, was going to need to play pretend in the land of the people.

He had too far removed himself.

Ascendancy had muddled the averages.

Ascendancy continued to muddle the numbers.

Artorian felt that he had improperly grasped the problems that normal people, being mortals, would struggle with. Any cultivator could outright ignore issues that were debilitating problems to the person who he used to be before he dabbled with Essence and corruption. Ingenuity and cleverness, alongside the beard-stroking scrutiny inherent in Kings and Castles, were all pathways and roads to find ways around such problems. They had thus become the bread and butter of his pattern. The honey syrup on his toast and crackers.

This would be no different in the game world of Eternia, where numbers ruled the realms.

In the wise words of the Casual Farmer: 'A mortal could brute force nothing. They had to think on their feet and come up with creative ways around an issue.'

Artorian nodded sagely to these words, deeply enshrined in the Skyspear Academy's teachings as they were. The lesson was important, and the words appeared at an important juncture. One should not forget where they started, regardless of the turbulence when rowing one's boat through difficult waters, moving ever on down the stream of life.

He took his screen before plummeting too deep into his thoughts, and turned it toward his dearest. He matched her enthusiasm and smile, showing her the named result of his merged energy metrics. "Determination."

Artorian could not hear the mad cheering from Tun's Tavern, and hoped Zelia would have a fix to be more connected to his over-enthusiastic audience soon. He was, on the other hand, decently certain they were entertained. Particularly after Ember's bloody, short-lived brawl. It made him wonder if he was going to be able to enjoy the game knowing such a powerhouse would always have his back. Right now? That only brought him comfort.

He could always ask to solo!

Lucia would likely bap him with a shield, and Ember would fuss at him about technique. Actually… That didn't sound so bad. That didn't sound so bad at all.

Ember ran her nails through his hair, pleased with the result. "Good. I like that. Now finish up with Incursus. I got all fired up and limber, and now I need to work out some heat. I should also use a custom energy metric. Help test the system."

A confirmation chime played as Ember had hoped, before she shoved her nose over her shoulder to point. "I'm going to poke my nose into the first floor of the Darkest Dungeon, see if there is anything fun I can make sit in place until you get there. I was expecting mobs to spawn where we are, especially with the gate broken down, but no. There's nada. Mosco is anomalous, and not what I was keeping an ear out for. If nothing has accosted us by now, nothing will. We're either missing an activation trigger, or there's nothing here to trigger. It's never that second one, so brooch me if something comes up."

Artorian beamed at her. "Of course, dear. Lay on the heat."

She rolled her arm, itching for another fight like the combat-junkie personality she tried not to let out too much. "I want to start teaching you Ancient Elven fighting styles again! I'm going to have so much fun watching my boy beat the snot out of everything. Can you tell me what lessons one and two were?"

"Lesson one: Never stop moving. Lesson two: Never stop attacking." She'd read his mind! Or she just knew him that well and could read his every thought from the constant, minute changes on his face. Also good! "What I remember of your Pantheon style is that it completely throws out the idea of defense in trade for pure devastation."

Artorian recited a mantra containing a list of 'don'ts rather than dos.' "There is no block. There is a counter. There is no dodge. There is a reaction. Do not stop moving. Do not stop attacking. Do not give your enemy time to breathe. Do not give them time to plan. Do not give them space to move. Do not let them succeed in their attacks. Do not let their commanders speak. Do not let any live. Do not hold back. Do not stop."

She was so proud, pressing a big, noisy kiss to the top of his head. "Very good! I should reward you for retaining that. A heads up on the two lessons after that seems proper? My boy likes his information. Lesson three: Location, location, location. Lesson four: All war is deception."

Artorian adored both the smooch, and the information. "Thank you, dear. Have fun breaking the dungeon. I look forward to fighting lessons that aren't in a desert. Are you going to be alright? I know you lost all your weapons and such."

Ember's eyes lit up, her large Elven ears perking. "Oh! I forgot to show you!"

She rose from her leaning position, standing straight and extended an arm with her hand wide open. "I got new skills and abilities that I automatically received when they were done being made. Including Weapon Modes, Weapon Ignition, and Weapon Adaptation. I should teach you those now that they're actually useful! One of them is called 'Calling.'"

She smirked at the half-pun, the word play being just enough of a not-pun to not cause Artorian injury. Ember then slid into the feeling that was Astarte, the game character requiring a soft change in mindset. Altering her view to the harsher and spartan, Ancient Elf deadly days of her Blade of War life. It was fun roleplay, and good to process bad memories with.

Violence, and **War**, annoying Heavenlies as they were, had been correct that this unpleasant method of processing her experiences would yield positive results. Despite this, Ember had managed to remain happy and pleasant around her boy. The aggressive urges, anger, and fight leaked out only when he wasn't around, or when she was challenged.

She did *enjoy* being challenged. Too much.

Enough reminiscing.

She invoked her ability, utilizing her call. "Surtur!"

Burning into reality, the twenty-foot sword-spear flashed into her hand as her fingers closed around the shaft. Ember nodded, grinning at the ease of functionality. Surtur was too large like this, though. "The twenty-foot sword-spear is good against Titans. Big creatures require big weaponry if I'm going to stab deep enough to strike something vital. For the tight corridors of an underground dungeon? This will not do."

Time for another of her new tricks. "Sizing."

The twenty-foot sword-spear compressed, diminishing in size while retaining its shape as Surtur, the Dalamadur turned living weapon, became a six-foot sword-spear. Her hand cleanly fit below the head of the weapon now, which Artorian noted to sport adorable little cloth tassels with... "Is that my solar sigil? You keep adorable little tassels embroidered with my sun? I love that!"

Ember made the victorious face of a cheeky brat earning her keep. "*Mwahaha*! Sure is, Sunshine! Did you think I was going to sit idly on my laurels while everyone else was making them? I have made embroidered tassels, painted plumes, engraved purity seals, sewn patches, and molded medals."

She upturned a hand, momentarily opening a prompt serving as an image file that revealed a large shrine filled with sun-sigil flags. "I am using your Cathedral of the Luminous Prism as an additional storage site. Your fans may be using your Shrines, Faith Foundry care room, and tucked away corners for all their knick-knacks, but I needed much more space."

Her voice filled with delight, happy to show off all the flags and tassels she'd made with the cutest little blush painting her cheeks. "I have them on all my weapons. All of them! And I have many armories of glorious armaments. One of them being Marie's halberd! All mine now. She can have it back if she succeeds in attaining her fifth specialization in the game."

Artorian felt a word stand out in that statement. "If?"

Ember grinned wide, her eyes predatory as she sported an evil smile. "*If*."

CHAPTER SEVEN

Artorian's curiosity spiked when a different part of Ember's game information filtered in. "Wait. Fifth? I thought specializations went up to four and then stopped."

His dearest held her own cheeks with both hands, her nails trailing down as she thought about throwing Marie through a mountain. "It's experimental. The idea might have to be pushed to sixth, but for now it's fifth. The prompt isn't complete, but I can still show you what I've got so far, and tell you my preliminary ideas. When someone thinks about transcending to fifth from fourth while I'm available? They get this beautiful pop up."

Ding!

Two gorgeously elaborate, carmine-, snow-, and aurum-colored prompts appeared. Their mahogany border was thick, and lacquered in golden paint.

———

You desire the greatest heights.
To transcend your limits.

A goal to climb for.

You are hereby granted access to attempt your breach into a fifth specialization.

————

Breach: Draw your weapon, and Challenge the Golden Sun.
Task: Survive for 10 minutes.
Reward: Fifth Specialization.

————

Artorian saw the delight in her expression. How she savored the gift in her hands. Yet he could not grasp what was so major about it. "I'm missing a detail. Why would Marie have a hard time succeeding in this challenge? Surviving for ten minutes doesn't sound so hard."

Ember's grin spread wider, her teeth looking awfully sharp all of a sudden. For all her predatory hunger, she spoke in whispers at the beginning. "That's the best part. *I* am the Golden Sun. I will show no mercy. I will bar no holds. I will appear as Amaterasu, in my lovely Shiranui Shrine Goddess attire. I shall float above the surface of the Eternia Sun, which will be the entirety of our battlefield. Our fight will take place there for all the realms to see, for anyone who knows how to look. All they need is to have received the prompt themselves in order to spectate, but that's still a high bar."

Her voice resumed full normality as she talked logistics. "Constant damage will assail the challenger from the terrain, that they must learn how to contend with. As, aside from the sun being the only place where one's feet can stand, the battle takes place in empty space and open vacuum. Even if they enter the sun, those conditions will not change, and I will certainly chase them."

Artorian's comfort threw itself out of the window. "That's

horrible! You're not even doing anything yet and the very location of the fight is going to guarantee you'll kill people off."

She nodded fast and quick, utterly excited. "*Mhm*! I rain abilities down on them from above in the meanwhile! Hovering all cute in my pretty outfit. The first Solar Flare I toss out should send people back to their respective recovery area. Whether that's a Seed Core or otherwise. The whole point is that the player who wants to make the breach would need to prepare incredibly well. Both to survive in the most impossible environment, while also being capable of fending *me* off, for ten whole minutes."

Her hands happily clapped together, Ember far too chipper about this seemingly impossible task. "Anyone who manages it will probably be able to traverse actual space, out in the real. Originally, the idea was for a training regimen that would allow S-rankers to individually space-travel. The idea has gone through some turns and twists over the eons? Any who succeed would be able to handle the conditions, and if they kept *me* from murdering them dead for ten whole minutes? A rogue asteroid or otherworldly encounter isn't going to be something insurmountable. There's even a bonus stage!"

Artorian almost didn't want to ask, but his curiosity needed the information. "What, pray-tell, with a blessing for my own sanity on top like a cherry on frozen milk, is the bonus stage?"

Ember squealed, her clapping even faster and more intense as she threw up the window.

Ding!

Congratulations!
   You are one of the few to have breached into a fifth specialization.
   Your journey is complete!
   Or is it?
   Bonus stage unlocked: Breach into your sixth specialization.

Artorian made grabby hands for the screen that followed.

Breach: Draw your weapon, and Challenge the Golden Sun.
  Task: Defeat Amaterasu, the Golden Sun, within 10 minutes.
  Reward: Sixth Specialization.

Ember sighed wistfully. "I can't wait. I really can't. Anyone who challenges this breach is going to think I'm a distance-type Mage or spellslinger, when I'm an up-close and personal, in-your-face fighter. I just happen to have some fun cluster grenades and variations on the good ol' fireball in my pocket. Give or take a coronal mass ejection."

Artorian released a keening peep. "I have so many concerns."

She leaned to the side, dreaming out loud. "The first time someone manages to inflict an actual hit point of damage on me? The sun we're fighting on inverts, and becomes a black hole contained by a glassy sphere. Not only can it break, but if they break it? That's death by environment right away. I won't be affected as it's *my* black hole, but I do expect the clever to try to break the floor and trick me through the crack. Sometimes you just walk off a hill and fall into a wet stream, y'know?"

Artorian shot her a sharp look, but didn't mind the reference from the ancient years. Where he had been tricked by sproutlings into walking off said hill and into said stream.

Ember couldn't help that she liked talking more around him. It was a rare pleasure for her, and made her love being around her boy all the more. "As a flavor difference, instead of dealing constant fire damage, the sun turned black hole will now deal constant cold damage, and I get to shed my Shrine

Goddess attire to don my seamless, full-Iridium Dawn Armor. I get access to every weapon in my armory, and I get to *unleash*."

Her excitement returned in full force. "The environment and long-distance barrage won't be a problem to my opponent by then, and I will have seen them attempt the breach so often that I will know their toolkit and skillset. One I will gladly learn to put those people, who think they have attained the highest heights, back down on the bottom-most peg."

Artorian tactically kept his mouth shut while Incursus bobbed his tiny turtle head with utter enthusiasm. As far as Incursus was concerned, killing people in a dungeon was a socially praiseworthy practice, and great for the dungeon in question to boot!

Artorian, on the other hand, leaned heavily on the information that this was all experimental speculation. Tim had surely told Ember this via an over the shoulder comment as something that might end up being a future plan, and Ember had taken the flame and run wild with the idea.

Ember's fingers interlaced, her eyes entranced as her enthusiasm only grew, oblivious to Artorian's growing discomfort. "To get Amaterasu back, they have to get me down to twenty percent health. Until then? They face Astarte, Goddess of War! There was an alternative suggestion where my stages should instead be between Ember, Dawn, Corona, and Ammy? That might have merit, and I'm willing to hear those Wisps out if that's a better idea. None of this is set in stone. Either way, I want my foes to see my burning smile as I run them through, their last health points bleeding away. To lean in close, and whisper, 'Come see me again.'"

She readied up, flexing and stretching. "*Mmmmm*! What a wonderful day that will be! I completely understand Solo and Melania's dynamic. If my heart was not already taken, that combative method would have been a lovely way to find someone. Words will not help them win the bout, but I do enjoy hearing my opponents chatter away while I break them."

"*Mhm*!" Artorian's lips pursed tight, a nervous nod and

squeaky sound escaping him before his mind threw ideas at the wall to try to get her off this topic. "Aren't you a roaming world boss as well, instead of a super special encounter?"

His lady shook her fist at the sky. "I know! There's contingencies! Most of the roaming world bosses that aren't dedicated world bosses can double as a candidate for the fifth specialization thing, but I want it to be *meeeee*! Everyone else won't go as hard on the players as I will. The choice system isn't finalized yet, but I did hear Halcyon is who you're more likely to encounter if you take the underwater version."

Ember pressed her hands to her hips, pouting. "If I'm encountered on the world map? It's as a raid boss. Likely as Dawn, capable of facing entire armies alone and winning."

Her grin spread once more, the lust for a good fight rising. "For a master of Pantheon Style, I don't think a four or five-person team is going to be enough to actually overwhelm me? Give me twenty. Thirty. Fifty people! I taught you how to assault an army of Demons, inside a fortified position, and win. Abyss, give me five-hundred! I would relish such a stomp."

Artorian sagely, and silently, nodded to agree, as that was a correct statement.

Ember had a great thought as she spotted the broken-down front gate. She leaned over to kiss his cheek before adoringly skipping right off of Zephyr. "Imma go play! Baiii!"

Artorian felt pale. He didn't look pale, but he did feel it as he reached for his brooch with a lilt to his head, pressing down. "Zelia? How many people overheard her just now?"

The connection, clear and smooth, transferred Zelia's voice through. "The number of applications to become players being rescinded has suddenly spiked. The number of applications to be an NPC have suddenly spiked as well. So, one or two, my Dreamer. One or two."

Artorian squeezed the bridge of his nose and nodded with closed eyes. "Thank you, Zelia. I take it that my energy metric has gone entirely forgotten by the crowd?"

He could feel her smile all amused through the connection.

"Entirely, my Dreamer. Please finish your title work, and proceed apace. There may be nothing left in the dungeon if you dally. Decorum is making an incredible headway, though not cleaning up behind himself. The musical scouts you sent ahead managed to instantly tumble and fumble into a hidden passage."

Zelia paused as the sounds of screens being checked were audible through the connection. "In the time it has taken for this conversation to occur... Astarte has already gruesomely ripped the first-floor boss in half. A sight many people cannot look away from. I'm afraid your viewership has tumbled along with the bards', my Dreamer. I suspect you will have some peace and quiet as you finish your character."

He heard a Dwarven mug slam onto a table, with several Dwarves in the background groaning before one of them noisily fell off a stool while claiming to be perfectly fine. Then shouting about this drinking competition being unfair. The clamoring arose like rote commentary, before the connection closed with a feeling of Zelia being awfully smug.

Artorian ran a hand through his hair, looking over at Lucia to spot that she had fallen asleep, protectively cuddling a passed-out Hans Jr. under her chin. He instead directed his attention to the starry-eyed dungeon, who could only dream about having the kind of end-boss that Ember was. Dawny's reputation amongst the player base may be nothing short of terrifying, but among the dungeons, there was a growing sense of reverence. "Incursus? If that's all for the prior material? My titles, please."

CHAPTER EIGHT

Artorian's ears were soothed by the rolling welcome of clickety-clacks. He noticed the turtle make an unpleasant expression as their starry-eyed expression broke, reaching to pet Incursus's head with his thumb. He chose not to follow up since Incursus appeared to be happier when focusing on his tasks.

Ding!

Title: Administrator

Cal assigned. Cannot combine. Can be toggled on and off. Grants deep system access. Bugfix access. Player character modification. World modification. Inspect Quality: All.

Title: Overdeity

Eternium assigned. Cannot combine. Can be toggled on and off. Grants deity system access. Deity features. Divine Energy Point access. Divine Energy Shop access.

———

Title: Cultivator

Cal assigned. Cannot combine. Gain ATB based on personal cultivation rank. F-rank: 1. E-rank: 2. D-rank: 6. C-rank: 24. B-rank: 120. A-rank: 720. S-rank: 5,040.

———

Title: Roaming World Boss Duo.

You have been designated as a Roaming World Boss.

You cannot claim an area as your dungeon or base of operations.

On defeat by another player, you will drop loot based on the World Boss loot table.

You share this title with its bonded counterpart.

In order for your Personal Pylon Hold to be deleted, both individuals with this title have to suffer defeat within 48 Eternia hours. Otherwise, your Personal Pylon Hold will remain intact, and you will respawn with your character as it was before death.

Note: This title will update when the Personal Pylon Hold problem is resolved. We do not know how your new bank was affected with the wiping procedure.

———

Artorian held his cheek as he sat and leaned into his hand. "Looks like the Task Manager continues to pain my behind. Surprising, but not too surprising. This reads like a solid workaround. Both Emby and I have to be game-dead, at the same time? That's unlikely. Well done with the titles, oh great Tactical Tortoise."

He petted Incursus some more, the tiny turtle mighty pleased at the praise. "Race next, please."

The clickety clacks churned, and Artorian had his prompts soon enough.

Ding!

———

Notice!
No Bonescripting detected.
Bonescripting entry blocked.

———

Artorian slapped his hand onto that prompt to pause it. "*Whow! Ho!* Slow down there. I know Mortis was unbricking my mortar, but the whole thing's gone? Does that mean Flight and my platforms...? Oh... Oh, *that's* why I got Hypermobility."

He removed his hand from the prompt, placing it back on Incursus. "Well... It's not the final Eternia version. Maybe I can pick Wisp Flight up again somewhere. Apologies for the pause in the happy mechanical noises, please continue."

Incursus nodded under Artorian's hand, and resumed the blessed clickety-clacks.

Ding!

———

Race: Nascent Being.
As a Nascent Being, your base empirical senses consist of sight, hearing, taste, smell, touch, electrosense, and echolocation.
A Nascent Being is never lost, and always has a vague idea of where to go, regardless of what they are currently looking for.
As a Nascent Being, you are always considered Well Fed and Well Hydrated.
You are immune to the effects of depth crushing, thin atmosphere, vacuum, harmful gasses, inhaled venoms or poisons, and cloud- or vapor-based attacks.
You can breathe in any environment.
Note: The environment does require breathable material.

———

Racial Feature: Truesight.

A sensory advancement to see all as it actually is. Ignoring all forms of obfuscation, invisibility, guise, and illusion. This extends to creatures, objects, and effects. The true form of a creature will be betrayed by the shape of their shadow.

———

Racial Feature: Profound Sight - Complete.

A sensory advancement that denies a greater power. Complete Profound Sight allows the use of Truesight on Heavenlies. While there exists a greatest power that Complete Profound Sight cannot pierce, no other mighty shall escape your awareness.

———

Artorian felt like he could work with that. "Shame about the Bonescripting, but I can do without. I never grasped how to use it very well anyway. Was there more? I've forgotten the list already."

Incursus, helpful as always, provided him with a refresher on what was left via an updated list. Using a mere single click! He was improving! Building out more of his mechanical calculator was pulling much of the weight, but he was happy about the progress regardless.

The head rubs were equally as wonderful, his tiny turtle tail doing a waggle.

Clack!

Artorian perked up at the difference in sound before he checked the prompt. A clack? Not a ding? Better than a quack, he supposed. He'd take a clack.

———

To Do List:
Class.

Specialization.
Equipment.
Flash Runes.
Aura.

―――――

"Auras? *Ooooh*, for the Cleaning Aura from Janitor? I like that. I was wondering what it was doing in Flash Runes. Maybe it's because I asked for it as a profession?" Artorian got up, pacing as the prompts followed him. He'd forgotten that a class was likely needed to get started, but still he had no idea. "It's not like I can slap a concept for the class in, right? I mean, all the classes are going to have something to do with violence, but it's not like that's a viable word for a class."

Incursus thought that supremely amusing.

Clack!

―――――

You have been offered the base class: Violence.
  Accept?

―――――

Artorian had to stop and stare at the prompt. "You are making a joke? Surely this is a gag."

Incursus gave him the most adorable tiny turtle smile.

Artorian looked at it again, shared the dungeon's smile, and pressed accept. "*Eh*, why not! Violent Sunshine. That's going to be a fun thematic."

Clack!

―――――

You have gained the base class: Violence.

71

———

Nothing happened after he'd accepted the class save for the confirmation prompt. He received no explainer prompt, nor attribute gain metric, nor bonus skills. Nothing showed up along with it. Par for the course, though he was already missing the longer string of noises. "Say, Incursus? I know the shorter noises likely mean progress, but I really did like that mechanical click-ety-clacking. Could I have it back? It was lovely music."

Incursus didn't know how to get his machine back to making those noises. Not unless he ripped off the entire new latter-end and remade the whole thing. A chill of loneliness caught him, his happiness taking a sharp nosedive. He could do it… but his progress would—

A hand on his head stopped the turtle's thoughts.

Incursus looked up to a strange sight. Gone was the boy. The face of a wizened grandfather occupied his place as a starry, constellation-surrounded, sweet old man pet his head. The old voice was both soothing and gentle, filled with sunshine. "You don't have to, my boy."

Incursus learned what it meant to keep a stiff upper lip, exercising fortitude and restraint to prevent a sudden expression of emotion. Being given attention and being wanted was one thing. Being provided consideration and care? That was another.

Only his Wisp had been so gentle with him, and only Zelia had looked on his slower, less capable methods with pride. As if they saw something that other dungeons simply did not. Incursus wasn't the best dungeon Core. He was slow, and needed help. He couldn't build or process or create anything very fast, but he could do so well. Incursus excelled in the slow, meticulous, complicated task of crafting calculation engines. He was sensitive to loud noises, vibrations, and sudden bright lights. But he never felt panic. He was able to make strong, effective decisions, especially during a crisis.

His sprightly eyes closed as the pets on his head continued, the dungeon lost in the affection for just a selfish little bit longer. Just a bit longer. He'd get right back to work, he swore, like a good dungeon.

"You don't have to, my boy." The grandfather's words repeated, gentler, softer, more tender still. As if the ancient being could read his thoughts, or see that some dungeons had feelings, and that he had too many. "You don't have to."

Incursus lost the thread of what the grandfather was replying to, but it no longer felt like he meant the prompts, or the noise, or his excessive need to want to be helpful so he could show that he had value. That he was good and useful and could play with everyone else.

Incursus did good! He just couldn't keep up. He made good Grecian architecture, he made good prompts, he made good clickety-clacks to help calculate complicated things. He just couldn't—

He couldn't—

A stiff upper lip did nobody any good when their eyes were leaking, no matter how tight they kept their mouth. A hand laid on his head, and a paw joined it. Then another paw joined, placed on his shell. Then another, and another. Until Incursus was far from alone, surrounded by effigies of pink affection, all bundled close around him.

One yawned wide, a mouth filled with fangs revealing itself. That same muzzle then licked its nose, and licked Incursus right over his tiny turtle face as a mass of wet Mana. The muzzle then bumped noses with him, and the large wolf followed up by bumping their head to his. When the animal pulled away, they pushed their nose to the sky and howled. Starting a call each that each of the other creatures around him picked up, regardless of their shape.

The first wolf stopped to bump Incursus again, motioning with his nose to the sky as the tiny turtle had not made a sound. Motioning to join. Yet Incursus was no wolf. Incursus was a tiny turtle with a castle on his back. A slow dungeon, for whom thinking was hard, who kept falling into introspection, and—

The pink wolf of **Love** Mana licked over his face and stole those thoughts away, panting and more aggressively pointing at the sky.

"Go on." The grandfatherly voice, who could only be heard and no longer seen, spoke with the prior gentleness. Soft pink warmth bubbled inside of Incursus's Dungeon Core. Incursus no longer felt like his perspective was present on Zephyr's deck when he heard the words. He was elsewhere. He was sitting on a rock, in a small pond, in a grassy field, under a deep night's sky filled with bright constellations. Surrounded by glowing pink creatures of all kinds.

Some seemed familiar.

The wolves all flashed him happy grins, then nosed hard at the sky.

Incursus felt out of place, but calmed when the sensation of the soft hand on his head felt present. The grandfather wasn't in this place, but the feeling of the hand on his head was the same, the action ongoing elsewhere. Incursus drew breath, and as the wolves howled to the sky, he managed to release a high-pitched whine.

It wasn't much, and it was small, but it was more than enough to create the sympathy connection. Pink Essence reached down as a soft string from the sky, within reach for Incursus to take. He didn't know if he should, until he noticed that the others around him also had such a string. How nice it must be for them, to all be connected in that way.

A pleasant, chosen family.

He wondered how to reach the string, thinking it out of reach even though the string was close. To which the string replied by lowering more and lying next to his foot. Uncertain, but wanting, he slid over to touch it. An act more than sufficient as far as the rogue Mana was concerned, delighted to accept Incursus into the fold.

Another dungeon connected to the family.

Glowing, soft pink energy broiled from within as his form was overtaken by the light. Incursus became an outline of a turtle, enshrined and detailed by the soft pink. Instantly, he felt other dungeons cheer, other dungeons he had no connection to moments prior. He felt Beasts call out and howl in welcome at the new addition and presence. His presence.

The calls were scattered. In other Soul Spaces. In other realms and places. Yet Incursus felt them all as if they were laying right next to him, under this most pleasant, starry vista. What a wonderful painting someone had made, to cover the sky so.

Feelings hit him from all sides as he released that opinion out into the open. Other dungeons who had needed help, like him, agreed. Other dungeons, who were also slow, loved that they had gained one more friend. The thoughts of both dungeon and Beast assailed him with welcome, and suddenly, Incursus didn't feel nearly so alone.

On Zephyr, Artorian continued to gently pet the silent turtle, who appeared to have gone elsewhere for a while. That was fine. Incursus was doing hard work, and helping him very much. He was proud of the little dungeon, and grasped why Zelia had picked Incursus to introduce to him.

His weakness.

To include those who knew no inclusion with a seat at the longhouse. To make certain that they knew that they had earned their bowl of stew, and that they were welcome at the table. He had spent many a day orating Choppy's achievements to Lunella, Wu, and the family. There would be at least one statue! That great soul would never go forgotten, not while Artorian lived to tell the tale.

Incursus wasn't the fastest, or the brightest, but he had a good spark in his Dungeon Core. The spark of someone wanting to do their all for the betterment of another. Artorian found that terribly praiseworthy, and gave Incursus all the time he needed. When the slow, ticking, clickety-clacks continued like the shy keys of a typewriter, a smile graced his face before the prompt came up. Incursus had found his courage.

———

Approval request:
   Violet Calculation Engine, Evergarden.
   Accept?

———

Artorian gently pushed the confirmation prompt, his voice that of a child, but no less loving. "Of course, my boy. You didn't even need to ask. Thank you for the lovely music."

Incursus had some of his spirit back, as the prompt that followed read like a continuation of the prior joke. Artorian, for one, definitely laughed when the clickety-clacks culminated. Was this how the dungeon felt about him? Or had he unknowingly done a number on Incursus? He wasn't certain of that. What he was certain about, was that he was pushing accept on this prompt.

———

You have been offered the Specialization: UltraViolence.
   Accept?

CHAPTER NINE

Artorian checked his to-do list again, glad Incursus seemed to be doing better. The wayward head-pets continued, helping to soothe the dungeon.

———

To Do List:
    Equipment.
    Flash Runes.
    Aura.

———

"Stuff and things are up; what am I working with so far?" Artorian tapped on the entry to manage his gear. The clickety-clacks sang pleasant notes, and his prompt appeared while slowly filling itself in with information from the top down.

———

Item: Linked Silverwood Bracelet.

Function one: Storage Device. This item stores objects in a linked warehouse. The size and weight of the items stored are limited by the player's ability to lift and manipulate them. No storing mountains and dropping them from orbit!

You may store a maximum of fifty items, twenty-five of which are allotted to you. The linked bracelet stores the other twenty-five items. You may retrieve items from the linked storage space, but you may not place them in the linked storage section.

Function two: Proxy connection to Character Pylons. This item will break in the event of character death, removing the player from Eternia before causal effects are tabulated.

"I sneaky-sneak helpful items to Ember?" Artorian blinked at the entry, the implications dawning. He could already feel what items Ember had stored in her half of the storage space, the sensation of their details crisp and clear. No headache whatsoever was a vast improvement compared to the last time he'd attempted an inventory check.

His curiosity got the better of him, attention drawn to Ember's stored equipment. Surtur was no surprise, the Halcyon Nights were great to see, the Damocles was back in her pocket, and... "The Abyss is a Hemotoxic Proboscis Tracer? Did she kill El Mosco *again*?"

He moved on, not dwelling on that idea, as the next one that was filtering into his prompt made him frown. Voltekka? Voltekka was no item. There better be a good explanation here.

Living Item: Armored Core: Voltekka.

Voltekka serves as an experimental item called an Armored Core. An Armored Core is a seamless, complete suit of skin plate armor, meant to be stored in special items called 'Morphers.' These Cores allow a player to skip the donning and doffing time that armor normally requires, by instantly coating the player with the armor contained in the Core. As Armored Core Equipment cannot be donned and doffed normally due to its seamless nature, this is a requirement.

Skin plate is a new armor type one step above full plate, retaining and improving the defensive capacity of full plate, while vastly augmenting the available Dexterity of the user without compromising the joints.

Armored Core: Voltekka contains a green, white, and silver suit in the form of energy that solidifies into a physical mixture of Mithril, Iridium, and Silverwood. This Armored Core has a slim silhouette and is Dexterity-focused, sporting a wide-shouldered design to house Voltekker-enhancing components.

This suit is representative of a warrior that does not lead from the back, but stands at the front. A living beacon. A flag. A symbol.

Special: The sigil of a roaring sun is marked onto this Armored Core's back, and will project itself as an oversized halo behind the user. When active, it will shine bright for all to see. In the event a cape, cloak, or similar cover is worn, the imagery will appear over the outermost layer available instead.

Special: Armored Cores function on a built-in energy supply that must be recovered by rest over time. Taking damage will deplete this meter. Activating the Armored Core's signature move, Voltekker, will deplete the entire supply. This synergy combination will also increase the damage dealt by Voltekker by a full category.

Note for Artorian: A category means 'times ten.'

Effects:

Voltekka provides an offense-based Armored Core centered around Dexterity and primal aggression. Voltekka is allowed to provide one offensive trait, and one defensive trait.

Voltekka's defensive trait, 'Never Down, Never Out,' provides immunity to receiving Critical Hits, and Critical Hit effects.

Voltekka's offensive trait, 'First Blood,' provides an automatic Critical Hit on the first successful damage dealt in combat.

Armored Cores provide a flat 20% damage mitigation effect, regardless of source, with priority calculation. Meaning that against any damage taken, damage mitigation will happen first, before other sources of damage *reduction are calculated. Damage mitigation prevents damage from all sources at its stated value, except true damage.*

Skin plate applies the special effect of Conditional Condition Immunity, unless an attack overcomes their damage reduction value. Skin plate has a damage reduction value of 800. Any attack that fails to do more than 800 points of damage will not be registered as having taken place, aside from incurred physics being simulated. With Conditional Condition Immunity, this means that any attack that would incur effects like Bleed, Toxic, Hemorrhage, Frost, Slow, or similar status affecting conditions cannot trigger.

Damage reduction applies only against direct physical damage. Including crushing, bashing, piercing, and slashing.

―――――

"I can tell this was made with the prior Critical Hits specialty in mind. Good effort, Tekka. Good effort. There was no way you could have known that the system would fall on its face." A bonus prompt arrived with the Armored Core prompt, which Artorian half-glanced at, as it was written by a Gnome in a hurry. Who else would tell him to get hurt on purpose. Spotters, maybe? On second thought, this list was certainly from the Spotters.

―――――

Experimental Armor Value Table.

Note: We don't know how to balance armor yet, get hit a bunch for us!

Unarmored: Example: Normal Clothing - 0 points of damage reduction.

Minimal Armor: Example: Padded Robes - 50 points of damage reduction.

Light Armor: Example: Leather Armor - 100 points of damage reduction.

Medium Armor: Example: Scale Mail - 200 points of damage reduction.

Heavy Armor: Example: Full Plate - 400 points of damage reduction.

Seamless Armor: Example: Battle Tyrant - 800 points of damage reduction.

Super-Heavy Armor: Example: Orbital Armor - 1,600 points of damage reduction.

———

Experimental Armor Prerequisites Table.

Note: We don't know how to balance this either. Find a glowing, soapstone 'Try Jumping' sign floor-scrabbled at the edge of some cliff, and check the validity.

Unarmored: None.

Minimal Armor: Physical Attributes: 5.

Light Armor: Physical Attributes: 10.

Medium Armor: Physical Attributes: 15. Mental Attributes: 5.

Heavy Armor: Physical Attributes: 20. Mental Attributes: 10.

Seamless Armor: Physical Attributes: 50. Mental Attributes: 30.

Super-Heavy Armor: Physical Attributes: 150. Mental Attributes: 100.

———

Note: An additional category exists below Super-Heavy Armor, tentatively named a War-Frame. However, each time we have attempted to add word choice to the ledger, an error noise has occurred, and one of the Heavenlies has fussed at us. Calling us Dave, and informing us that we could not do that.

The Heavenly of **Copyright***, Hal, calls everyone Dave for some reason. We have chosen not to take this odd joke personally, as Hal prefers to muck almost exclusively with High Elves. Best guess is that this jest has something to do with his favored dungeon Core appearance? Hal is adamant about portraying himself as a stygian black core with a cardinal red center.*

———

Note: The mental requirements for armor signify the difference between wearing protection, and using the armor well. Not meeting the mental threshold of an armor type precludes a player from benefiting from any of that armor type's special bonuses. Such as pivoting, damage transfer, glancing blows, damage nullification chance, and 'I said No.'

———

That was nice, Artorian supposed. His detail-loving sniffer was stuck on other details. "Wish it would tell me if the materials did anything. Or what these special bonuses mean. Incursus, I don't suppose you could dig that up? I dislike obscurity, if my racial traits didn't give that away."

The tiny turtle puffed out its chest. Incursus would provide! Even if he had to provide the entries in separate prompts. A minor inconvenience! He would stack them atop one another, with the button to clear them away all in the same place, so Sunshine could rapid-tap the same spot easily when he was done.

Clickety-clacks preceded a **Ding**!

———

Note: Beta-Trial Material Effects.

———

Iridium.

Bonus: Crysis Adaptation - Iridium adapts to the incoming physical damage type, allowing the armor to retain its full armor value against every mundane type.

Weakness: Crysis Crash - Iridium cannot adapt to absorb two damage types in the same moment. If struck simultaneously with multiple melee damage types, Iridium will only protect against one of them.

———

Silverwood.

Bonus: Energetic Ablation - Silverwood excels at energy transfer. Any energy-based damage affecting the player is reduced by the armor's damage reduction value, as if it were mundane physical damage.

Weakness: Hey! Listen! - Attracts Wisps who will want to talk to you at inopportune moments.

Mithril.

Bonus: The OG - Mithril is extremely durable and light, providing weightlessness, and immunity to durability damage. An armor that incorporates, or is made of, Mithril, has no weight.

Weakness: Ragdoll - Mithril removes all stagger protections, and doubles the player's susceptibility to the physics of attacks.

With that in the bag, Incursus followed up with additional goodies, having unearthed what the armor bonuses were with the help of his overly helpful new family. They were all so excited to be of assistance that Incursus was made entirely of glee. He was also happy that Artorian was making very approving noises at the placement of the confirmation buttons to clear out the log. User ease mattered!

Note: Special Armor Bonus explainer.

Pivoting: Skill-based. Position yourself so that you take less damage from a blow, causing the attack to graze you. Grazing attacks deal only 20% of their total damage.

Note: Incoming damage is tabulated before armor values and associated protections are applied. The calculation of a graze occurs before mitigation and reduction.

Damage Transfer: Skill-based. Angling your armor during impact so that a successful attack slides off and hits a nearby enemy instead, causing both the player and new target to take a grazing hit instead of a full hit.

Glancing Blow: Luck-based. When struck with less than full force, a strike that is uncertain, or made from poor footing, the attack has a chance to fall off to the side. This glancing blow will be tabulated as a graze, even on a direct hit.

Damage Nullification Chance: Luck-based. When struck, there is a truly minor chance that an unmodified melee attack will do no damage, and cause no application of physics. Special effects associated with modified melee attacks will not be stopped. This chance improves per the higher weight class of armor being worn.

I said No: Willpower-based. On the successful trigger of damage nulli-fication, a player is able to press themselves into the resistance, adding a minor chance that in addition to the full negation of the physical damage, any other damage associated with the attack is nullified as well. This chance improves with higher Willpower, but has a ten-minute cooldown once triggered.

———

"Definitely Spotters. Incursus, if there's more pertaining to armor? Enough for now, please." Artorian closed his eyes and rubbed them, moving onto the next item. This one he'd used before, and he was rather fond of the cloak. He wondered if there were any changes. Bonus that, unlike the prior two items, this one had its original formatting! Mostly.

———

Item: Tribal C'towl Cloak.
   Name: Archimedes.
   Material: Darkwind Storm C'towl.
   Rarity: Unique.
   Ability: Shunpo - At will, lightning-themed, short-range teleport.
   Maximum range: 50 Meters.
   Costs: 5% of a mana bar per use.

Cooldown: None.

Toggle: The effects listed below can be toggled on or off at the user's preference.

Effect: 1 meter radius area damage-effect on arrival, equal to mana cost.

Effect: Afflict any damaged valid targets with: Stun - Minor - 1 second.

Note: While Stun trigger is guaranteed, the effect is easy to resist.

———

Artorian rubbed his grubby hands together as the equipment information paused. Incursus was making him something. "*Ooooh*, now that I'm a more front-line build, this is going to come in handy! Can I chain-stun an enemy by hopping back and forth around them? I have to try that for sure!"

Ding!

———

Message from Incursus: It is requested of Archimedes whether he is willing to accept Determination as a metric instead of the stated mana value. Verdict... positive!

The word use of 'mana' has been updated to 'energy.'

Note: 5% of 15,950 maximum energy translates to 797.5 damage.

Shunpo damage will be rounded down to 797.

———

Eager for more, Artorian read the next entry as it clickety-clack rolled in.

———

Item: Pillow.

Material: Basher fluff, Basher cloth.

Rarity: Common.

—————

Item: Faith Foundry Pajamas.
    Material: Basher fluff, Basher cloth.
    Rarity: Common.

—————

A chuckle followed. A normal pillow, and normal pajamas. At least he was going to fight and take after-combat naps in comfort. Based on the slowly populating text that filtered in line by line, the broom was next! This at least should be special!

—————

Item: Broom of Shaka.
    Name: The Boom Shaka Laka.
    Material: Mahogany.
    Rarity: Uncommon.
    Ability: Sweep.

—————

Artorian had to admit, he'd expected something more... special. Was he spoiled? He was spoiled. Voltekka had spoiled him. No, he wasn't going to blame this on anyone specific. Everyone had been trying to spoil him. Though, perhaps, stealing one of El Mosco's flamberge legs as a starter weapon wouldn't go amiss? Unless he could use the broom to clean up his enemies? That would be very thematic. He also did have a pillow as his Soul Item, but that goodie was unavailable.

Did that really matter? He had a beating stick and a smacker. That was enough, in case a good ol' cast of Fist didn't do the job. Sweep didn't have any kind of dropdown when tapped, so he'd have to test that ability later. Thinking of it, he should keep pretending to be a Mage and spellcaster. He'd done well setting up that clever ruse during the bout against the Steamlord, and Dawny appeared to have had the same idea.

"All war is deception!" Oh, that *was* lesson four, wasn't it. Look at him being a good student. His enemies would know to fear the pillow. Hans could lead the song. "I wonder how that would work with my current class and specialization."

Letting his thoughts roam, he read the last item as the prompt filled in, decently sure he knew the description of Zelia's Brooch. This one was certainly special in some way. The old brooch's description had stated the connection was supposed to be limited to Senate members in close vicinity, but unless his close vicinity was the entire Soul Space, someone had snuck features into the brooch not listed in the old entry.

Sneaky spider moves!

———

Item: Zelia's Personal Communication Brooch.
  Name: Entangled Web.
  Material: Iridium.
  Rarity: Artifact.
  Effect: Seat of the Senate - Speak with any Senate members who also wear this insignia. The correct position of the brooch is on or in the left segment of the collar.

———

"*Ha*! Knew it!" No range limitation being mentioned at all made Artorian grin. He loved being clever. "Almost done! Incursus? Flash Runes and Auras, please!"

CHAPTER TEN

Artorian studied the Flash Runes entry as it clickety-clacked onto his screen with satisfying detail. Information filtered into the blank prompt he was holding. Lots and lots of information. Given the sheer size of the blank space in the prompt, this was going to be one of those big ones.

Flash Runes Primer:

Flash Runes, much like the casts of spells, are expressions of patterns that are evoked out into the world. Unlike casts, which form internally and source patterns from within the body before engaging their effect. The version known as flashing forms externally, via Aura. These patterns are evoked at the quality level of a Rune, for a brief moment, which is sufficient for a Flash Rune's intended effect to trigger.

The downside of Flash Runes is that anyone who sees the expression of the pattern for the brief moment it is visible will know what the intended effect is. Even if they do not understand, comprehend, or are able to replicate the pattern.

The upside of Flash Runes is threefold. They are instant, so long as you have mastered the pattern being evoked. They are incredibly efficient, and therefore cheap in cost. They are considered fully potent Runes, and therefore equally potent in output.

Note: While this technique format is still in its infancy, it is theorized that all that prevents a person from casting a Flash Spell, rather than a Flash Rune, is the correct and proper mastery of the pattern in question.

While Inscriptions, Runes, and Spells all have ranks and levels that differentiate between the efficiency output of two identically named effects, not all effects are created equal. The means that create these effects vastly increase in complexity and skill requirement as the bar is raised.

While the game system allots the use of spells to its entities, player or otherwise, that is done due to the efficiency of their cost, and the ease of which they are entered into Pylons that duplicate their effects.

The Curators are very aware that, in Old World measurements, a certain mental capacity is required to grasp and utilize certain quality levels of output without there being some backlash of otherwise unpleasant cost.

Mages cannot use spells without headache-inducing side-effects. Zenith C-Rank cultivators cannot use Runes that aren't utilized through an item, without the chance of blowing themselves up. For the same reason that C-rankers get horribly ill when they attempt to use Essence sight on a Mage, players receive instant nausea and a nasty headache from being unable to comprehend what they are seeing.

This effect, unfortunately, translated into game terms on all levels. Be exposed to a pattern that your brain cannot handle, and your brain will go boom.

The game system attempts to circumvent this by using spells as a standardized function that rely on Pylons to do the heavy lifting. All the effects, none of the strain. No exposing people directly to the pattern, if it can be helped.

Of note, Spell Pylons and Flash Pylons currently do not play friendly. Ordinary synthetic Pylons hold the power that charges and fuels them on their surface, while filled with script. This allows for intensely complex Pylon work, but always has to account for limited available power. Run too much power over this Pylon, and it will go up like a firework.

These new Pylons hold and transfer power internally, allowing for much greater charges and scope of effect, while expressing their script exter-

nally. This limits what the Pylons are able to do severely, but the Pylon will do that one particular thing exceptionally well. If you have Flash Runes, you currently cannot have spells. Even if it is theoretically possible to have both skills in the game, and in the real.

We know this, because our original Pylons could hold power both internally and externally, but our original Pylons were also people. So that's out.

––––––

A reminder of the Old World terminology, part one:

Inscription - A permanent pattern made of Essence that creates an effect on the universe. An inscription is composed of a set pattern, with set Essence, designed in a set, specific, and particular way to accomplish a set, specific effect.

Rune - A permanent pattern made of Essence that creates an effect on the universe. Also called a completed Inscription. This type of pattern is more efficient in the ratio of energy required to achieve a certain set output than an inscription.

Gnome detail: A pattern is considered a Rune, rather than an Inscription, when its combined efficiency and output metrics reach or breach a factor of pi. Whether that value comes entirely from efficiency or output does not matter. That detail merely makes for a different flavor of Rune, and does not change that the pattern in question is of Rune-type quality.

Spell - A 'spell' is a completed Rune that has the correct ratios and affinities included in the pattern! No guesswork with what Mana or Essence you need to convert, or how much. Pre-molded, pre-shaped, pre-tuned!

Gnome detail: Delightfully consistent as before, a pattern is considered a spell, rather than a Rune, when its combined efficiency and output metrics reach or breach a factor of pi. Again, whether that value comes entirely from efficiency or output does not matter. That detail merely makes for a different flavor of spell, and does not change that the pattern in question is of spell-type quality.

––––––

General note: There has been an argument that the function of a Flash is the same as the function of an Enchantment. It is our verdict that a Flash and an Enchantment are the same, in the sense that liquid and vapor are the same. Kin in source, but separate in form.

Flashing specifically requires completed patterns, as a poorly expressed pattern through Aura is highly lethal. While a Flash does temporarily create a pattern, the effect released cannot be sustained, and will be enacted even faster than when done via incantation. Specifically, an incantation without the requisite verbal component. It is not required to call out the name of your Flash Rune in order to activate it. It is, however, very cool. Because that warns the system and flushes the related Pylon with preparatory coolant. The system appreciates warnings.

———

Artorian had to pause a moment. "Is that word underlined? Have I ever seen one underlined in a prompt before? No? No, I don't think so. The system appreciates warnings. I'll keep that in mind."

He got back to studying.

———

Please do not confuse this function with Flash Runes that are applied to Pylons. Pylons using Auric patterns is a whole topic by itself, and the two do not correlate well. Those Pylons are not actually using Flash as a feature; rather, they provide the feature to use Flash. Unless you want a massive headache, do not delve into how this is done.

***Pylon** became a **Law** for a reason.*

———

To contrast:

Enchantments do not require completed patterns, as you're merely throwing out Essence using whatever piece of the technique or formula available to you. A botched Enchantment will yield annoying or unpleasant results, but it is unlikely to be lethal to the user.

The main difference is twofold. One, Enchantments easily apply to items, while Flashing is exceedingly item-unfriendly. Two, Enchantments are suited for internal, or body cultivators. While Flashing is suited to external, or Aura cultivators.

In comparison: The terms Inscription, Rune, and Spell, can double as measurements pertaining to the quality of the pattern. While Enchantments, Incantations, Invocations, and Flashing, are all different methods of expressing your intended effect. One method is not inherently better than the other, but each does have their niche. A Spell is objectively better than a Rune, and a Rune is objectively better than an Inscription.

Note: This does not account for Arrays, Formations, Script, and Sigils. Which are interactions between multiple Inscriptions, Runes, and Spells being used at the same time. Or in tandem, or in sequence.

*Wisp note: This measurement system does not account for your foray into the manifestation of Tower-quality patterns, such as when you pull out the **Sun** Law and make a very real micro sun. There are levels to that, and we're not remotely ready to incorporate any of them. Please don't do that in Eternia. Pylons will explode.*

Spotter detail: Can confirm. They did explode.

———

Artorian took a moment to rub his eyes, then continued reading. He felt like he was back at a college somewhere. All this delicious, dense, juicy mechanical knowledge. Yummy. If he ever had to orate this to a class, this is where he'd remember to drink water, and touch grass.

———

A reminder of the Old World terminology, part two:

Enchantments - A temporary Essence pattern that produces a short-term effect. An effect of pure energy that lasts only as long as the energy invested holds out, or the pattern degrades past a point where it can keep cohesion. Essentially, the pattern of an effect can be placed in or on an item, without the need for physical modification on the item. A conditional activation can be added or triggered to make the effect occur by itself, otherwise, enchantments are always active. An enchantment will constantly drain itself regardless of the effect being enacted or not.

Incantation - An incantation is created from words and gestures. It releases all of the power of an enchantment in a single burst, rather than as a slow, sustained effect.

Invocation - A release of Essence focused via identity rather than pattern or Essence ratios. Effectively an incantation performed from the other end of the formula. An invocation requires maddening amounts of Essence in order to self-form the missing pattern in a way that suits the idea fueled into the effect.

———

Artorian shrugged, and cracked on to read part three. This was nothing he didn't already know. Refreshers were nice, but this was upper-level collegiate content, and by this point he would expect brains to hurt.

———

A reminder of the Old World terminology, part three:

Array - An Array is an older, artistic method of connecting multiple Inscriptions without directly overlapping them. As if arranging multiple smaller pictures to create a single cohesive whole, such as a mosaic. You need a certain number of Runes or Inscriptions that work together to trigger an effect, and they have to be placed a set distance away from one another, in addition to being linked by 'sympathetic connections.' Example: Armor doesn't function properly if you're not wearing all the pieces, even if it does resize to keep the sigils aligned while it tries to refit.

Script - A Script, or scripting, is a more linguistic method of connecting multiple Runes together. Rune-script being its most common form. Script is called such because, from a distance, the Runes look like words in sentences, with individual Runes acting as letters. The method in which the script is arranged alters which Runes are activated and when. Script allows Rune activations to loop back into the beginning of the script, allowing the effect to run so long as it is powered.

Formations - A Formation is most commonly known as a spell formation, or spell-form. Formations are geometric methods of connecting multiple spells together, rooted in mathematics. The correct connections within Formations are based on exacting, calculable variables, resulting in geometric shapes. The geometric lines that form the visual component do not act as a limiter when it comes to spell placement and trigger order. Each spell placed within a Formation can trigger another linked spell, regardless of those two spells not being connected by lines. Choosing geometric designs that connect spells which affect other spells directly does appear to improve the Formation's stability.

Warning: Recursion designs like to blow themselves up. Amalgamating designs will destructively consume existing designs, and replace the newly vacated space with itself. Proliferating designs will eat more energy than the caster has, and thus eat the caster. Always set a completion variable. Ley-Lines, the combination format of these three designs, are currently blacklisted. Consult the Spotters before being clever.

Sigil - A name for a symbol or set of symbols that aids in the function or activation of other effects. This can also reference a set of Runes, Spells, or Inscriptions via a grouping, but confers no additional meaning to them.

———

Artorian rubbed his chin, wanting for a long beard to pontificate with. He wondered why the information did not mention that it seemed perfectly feasible to apply Formations to Inscriptions, or Script to Spells. Also missing was Cal's commentary on spells. An opportunity for puns, missed?

Cal was not making these entries.

How had Cal described spells in the records again? Because one was 'spelling out' the Rune in their body and pushing out what you 'spell,' he was calling it a spell now? Yes, that seemed right. "This explanation is wordy! Are we about done? *Oh*, looks like we're finally getting into what Voltekker does. About time!"

Flash Rune: Voltekker.

*Voltekker is the offensive format of the pattern that comprises the unique creature known as Voltekka, a Teslasaur Beast with an uncommon Tower connection to **Aeris**. The Law of **Copper**.*

Voltekker creates a long, conical blast, in the form of a twisting copper and hunter-green wild roar of annihilation. This blast deals damage, and cannot be negated or countered. Voltekker ignores protections, defenses, and resistances of all kinds. Including physical barriers, which it damages and destroys regardless.

Voltekker deals area of effect damage equal to a ten to one ratio. Where one unit of invested energy deals ten damage of… we're going to call it annihilation damage for now. We haven't figured out what Voltekker doesn't work against yet, but it's also excruciatingly difficult to test.

System note: This Flash Rune is ridiculous.

Please don't use this if you can avoid it. Energy investment also determines the area of effect's range, and we cannot have you carve out another chunk of Vanaheim. Consider this a Mage-level attack in a world of mortals. We are, as of yet, unable to balance this any better, but we can't take this away from you without making a whole lot of people a whole lot of mad.

This Flash Rune is so efficient and so damaging that we are having a convention at the Geneva Point to figure out what to do about it.

Try not to 'accidentally a war'?

Artorian did not mind the commentary being interspersed with game mechanics. That was becoming par for the course when receiving new, previously undescribed toys. He preferred it this way. Eventually some Wisp would come by, look at it, have a heart-attack, and trim it all down to size. Until the Gnomes eventually got their hands on it again after lamenting loudly about what the Wisps had done to the poor thing. Just like

Supreme Weapon Mastery. That would help with balancing, at least. Back and forth was good for fine detailing.

He read the last words again. "Try not to 'accidentally a war'?"

Artorian tapped his chin. "How bad could a one-energy investment into Voltekker actually be? One energy is a measly ten damage. One energy shouldn't make the range terribly big?"

Incursus wasn't giving him any help or answers. Possibly, the dungeon didn't even know. Looking over his shoulder, Lucia was still making happy bunny-nap noises. He could ask Zelia again, but at this rate he might as well keep open communications if he was going to do that. "I could just test it?"

A moment of silence occurred before a prompt appeared that didn't originate from Incursus.

Uack.

———

Message from Vanaheim: Please do not.

———

Artorian stared at that message longer than he should have. He glanced at his class, then back at the missive. "Is this where I choose violence?"

Uack.

———

Message from Vanaheim: Please do not make me send the duck.

———

Artorian beamed, his smile all teeth. Now it was a challenge! "Cowabunga?"

CHAPTER ELEVEN

Uack.

———

Message from Vanaheim: You do not understand what you are toying with. If you persist, I will forcibly reward you with an ability that you will not like.

———

This was childish, and he knew it, but when was he going to have the opportunity to be this much of a child again? Perhaps he should finish the last character sheet entry first, and then decide just how petty he was going to be about this. Brother Moon, now officially Vanaheim, *had* given him some heartache. "*Hmm*. Incursus? Auras, please."

By the power of the clickety-clacks, Incursus delivered. *Ding*!

———

Aura: Cleaning Presence.
  Rank: Novice.
  Special Qualities: Aura, Clean.
  Shape: Orb.
  Description: A field emitting a constant cleaning effect, centered on the user.
  Output: One meter in diameter of cleaning effect per percentage of maximum Energy bar invested.
  Note: You may only have one Aura type effect active at any given time.

————

Artorian thought that satisfactory, wondering how much he was going to invest as another mechanical noise followed. An Incursus update rolled in.
  Ding!

————

Profession: Janitor.
  "Bless the cleaner and his broom. Bless the coming and going of him. May his passing cleanse the world. May he keep the world for his people." - Shai-Hulud, First of the Allsand.
  Effect: All Cleaning-related powers have their cost negated.

————

Profession: Janitor.
  "In his way, there was only the cloy. In his wake, there was only clean-liness." - Shai-Hulud, First of the Allsand.
  Effect: All powers that Clean also Cleanse.

————

Expecting an explanation to accompany the terms, Artorian felt satisfied when the mechanical noises proved his assumption to be true.

Ding!

Explanation of terms: Wisp version.

Cleanse - Cleanse removes status effects that negatively impact the entity, such as Burn, Freeze, Poison, Disease, or similar toxins. Including alcohol, and other detrimental substances. Cleanse can remove status effects that positively impact the entity, if desired.

Clean - Clean removes deleterious and cosmetic effects relating to anything 'dirty.' Including undesirable dust, dirt, particles, liquids, vapors, spores, pollen, and the entire category of anything labeled with the 'filth' tag.

Note: Any entity that has recently been under the effect of both Clean and Cleanse receives the 'Washed' buff for one hour.

The positive 'Washed' status effect provides resistance against being affected by disease. For the duration of the buff, the affected entity will not form odors, providing resistance against detection by scent, while being more pleasant to be around in general.

"Excellent!" Free, constant, pleasantly feeling washed and clean? "Well, that is right up my alley! I think that wraps us up? Or do we have any incoming changes?"

Incursus was glad he asked.

Ding!

Update:

Flash Rune: Voltekker.

Rank: Novice.

Voltekker creates a long conical blast, in the form of a twisting copper and hunter-green beam. This blast deals 10 area of effect annihilation damage per every 1 energy invested at the moment of inception. Voltekker cannot be negated, countered, canceled, or be affected by any effect fueled by blue mana. Annihilation damage ignores protections, defenses, and resistances of all kinds. Including physical barriers, landscape, and structures.

If it is in range, it is hit.

Note: The annihilation damage type deals half damage to shields. Shields must still be broken or brought down fully before the entity can be damaged by the annihilation damage type.

———

Skill gained!

Skill: Voltekker.

Rank: Master.

This skill reflects a user's proficiency with a given Flash Rune. A user must have a full, working knowledge of the Rune or pattern in question in order to successfully bring it forth through the Auric format without repercussion.

———

System note: This skill has been made to separate real knowledge from game effects. Which is why your Voltekker Flash Rune is set to Novice. We are considering moving this skill to a new subsection called proficiency, but so far this lacks the votes.

Unfortunately for us, the Heavenly of **Copper** *has already provided improved versions of the Flash Rune in question. Each with minor tweaks on how to more effectively, or efficiently, translate the pattern being expressed. It is to our great misery that I must thus inform you that your Voltekker can improve.*

Commentary: Fully manifest Flash Runes have been labeled as War Crimes by the Gnomes of Geneva. Should you ever dump the full one-hundred percent of your energy metric into a Flash Rune again, you will immediately be put in time-out. We will squint at you severely if you pull and play the ninety-nine percent card. Yes, also the ninety-eight percent card, you brat!

Note: When even the Gnomes think you have gone too far, and the Wisps agree, we will be convening at the Geneva Point. While the qualifier to measure the rarity of a skill or ability grows the more you can creatively do with it, some imported game entries, much like Magehood in general, are considered unfit for translation and must be subject to subversion.

Emphasis: Sub-version. Not con-version. Conversion would mean we can still work with the tool as is, but it needs tweaks to fit. Subversion means we cannot import the tool, and need to overhaul how such a thing is represented in the game world.

Note: Any game entry gained in Eternia that is not at the rank of Master will not be retained when outside of the game. While the system will still attempt to import skills, abilities, and relevant tools in your kit based on personal experiences, these Pylons are currently non-functional. To fill in your game format character, some functions are being operated manually, but please do not use your trick to force the system to pay attention to you. A few thousand Wisps have developed carpal tunnel from the amount of dice they had to roll to calculate your Luminous Gatling damage.

Wisps don't even have wrists!

Now take these skills that you have earned and have some Abyssal mercy on us. Say nothing. Vanaheim has been sending us Penguin after Penguin to plead for the retainment of realm cohesion. We have had to send him a Duck specialized in problem solving as an emotional support animal. Brother Moon wants you off his rock and out of his bowels, or to, at minimum, and I quote: 'Not burst forth from the chest.'

As far as Brother Moon is concerned, you are the Eldritch Horror. You have been tagged as Nightmare Fuel, so Brother Moon can keep track of you at all times while you remain on Vanaheim. We know that Brother Moon is an unconventional creature, but they are putting in the effort. Please keep it in mind?

Skill gained!
Skill: Effect Shaping.
Rank: Novice.
This skill allows a user to take the system-set shape of a tool and alter

the assigned expression. At the Novice rank, the shape of an expressed effect may be altered offensively into a beam, or defensively into a wall. A user is allowed to diminish, but not increase, the volume of a given area that an effect would take place in.

Each rank of this skill adds an additional allotted shape; such as a line, cone, sphere, cylinder, or wave.

———

Skill gained!

Skill: Effect Cosmetics.

Rank: Beginner.

This skill allows a user to take the system-set cosmetics of a tool and alter the assigned expression. You may alter the color of an expressed effect freely; such as to white and blue, or black and red, depending on the visual theme or style that the user is attempting to go for. This skill cannot make a tool transparent. Invisible effects are considered too potent and have been specifically added to their relevant classes. You are limited to opaque and translucent alterations.

Each rank of this skill adds an additional color scheme.

Novice color scheme: Trans Am. Celestine blue glow, snow white particles.

Beginner color scheme: Villain. Onyx black, carmine red.

———

Artorian's voice became a taunting whisper, counting his second sighting of underlined words. This slate required clearing, and whoever made this system prompt dare to both call him a brat, and tell him to say nothing, in the same message? Mercy could wait on the doormat. T'was time for violence.

"Voltekker."

The hurried prompt from Brother Moon got as far as the *uack* before Vanaheim held its collective Abyss in anticipation of a series of truly unfortunate events, and lots of yellow snow. When no pattern manifested, and no attack was forthcoming,

Vanaheim looked upon Artorian. Who somehow knew the exact place and position in space to gaze in order to glare right back at Brother Moon's intrusive glance. "We are even, now. Yes?"

Vanaheim cautiously reached for the prompt it had sent out, attempting to pull the screen into obscurity and negate the effect. Forcing the screen back into physicality, Artorian snapped it up and caught the disappearing missive between his fingers. "*Tu-tut!* I wanna see this! What was your retaliatory Kings and Castles move, cheezums?"

―――――

Ability gained!
    Ability: Taunt.
    Rank: Novice.
    Cost: Free.
    Activation: Automatic.
    Range: 33L.

―――――

Artorian scratched his head. "Well, I think after Auras, I'm done with setup? Bonus skills notwithstanding. This prompt mostly confuses me. There's no description. What does 'Taunt' do? What is an L, and how much is thirty-three of it?"

Lucia's head snapped upright, the sleep being blinked from her eyes as her ears had picked up some concerning passive information. "Did someone just say their ability had a range of L? Get rid of it!"

Artorian frowned, dismissing the screen. That, unfortunately, didn't get rid of the ability that had rudely added itself to his character sheet. He was decently certain he'd said something about not wanting abilities? At least it wasn't a spell. "Lil too late, Momma Bun. What does L mean?"

Lucia pawed at her own face as the jarring movement let

Hans Jr.'s ball roll free, waking Hans Jr. with a sudden spike of energy as the boy went from zero to hero and decided that he had to run into every single surface on Zephyr's deck. The child was in a shield orb, he'd be fine.

Lucia sat on her haunches. "L stands for league, and it's always attached to trapped chests in dungeons that temporarily latch some effect on you. The L ones happen in an annoyingly vast area, making you unable to escape the effect until the duration runs out. What trap did you activate?"

Pursing his lips, Artorian looked down, wondering about his life choices. He turned his character sheet so Lucia could see it without her needing to use her healer skills to pull it up on her own. "About that. Do you remember how long a 'league' was? I'm rusty."

Lucia took her time to shift into her human shape, still rubbing her eyes as her ears flopped out of her head. "About three miles, or five kilometers, with generous rounding. So y— *Thirty-three*? That's either a hundred miles, or a hundred and sixty-five kilometers of Taunting! Generous rounding or not, you better hope that's calculated in diameter. The duration should be short, at least… It's… It's… not on here. Where is the duration? Please tell me you did not just pick up an ability that goes off on its own, for free, and anger-annoys every possible enemy in a thirty-three-league range? I am shielding you, right now."

Artorian *mmmm'd* painfully at the ability as he glowed different colors, Lucia stacking the shields on him. "I'm going to call it 'The Oof.' Because *oof*."

Ding!

———

Ability updated!
Ability: The Oof.
Rank: Novice.
Cost: Free.

Activation: Automatic, once per minute.
Range: 33L.
Effect: Taunts all enemies within the listed range, calculated as a radius. Taunt makes all enemies aware of the Taunter's position, and they will favor attacking the Taunter over other targets, unless the other targets are too opportune to be ignored.

———

Artorian sought solutions with rapidity. "I need Yuki. She can Silence and stuff like that. Maybe she can Seal this ability, if we cannot otherwise get rid of it. New plan! Get Tisha! Get out! Go to Yuki!"

Lucia instead had a truly simple, and truly genius idea. "Can't you call for her with the brooch and make her come to you instead?"

Artorian instantly squeezed the brooch. "Yuki? Are you on this thing?"

Zelia answered him, both curious and intrigued when the connection resolved out of the static. "No, my Dreamer. Yuki does not have a brooch of mine in her possession. We have been apart since she went off with Team Icy Hot. Do you…? Oh. I see. A brooch will be delivered to Yuki, my Dreamer, along with a missive that you are on your way to her with a truly annoying problem. Good luck. You have incoming hostiles."

Zelia considered ending the conversation there, but slipped him a pertinent detail. "Also, my Dreamer, and this is somewhat important? Hans Jr. has rolled off the boat in that protective monkey ball, and is on a direct and speedy descent path to the broken-down hole where a dungeon gate used to be. If you chase now, you will already just barely not make it."

The connection clicked closed as Zelia relayed important instructions.

"Run, my Dreamer. Run."

CHAPTER TWELVE

Uack.

"Not now, Moon-moon!" Artorian bolted, leaping from the yacht's deck and gunning it to the broken gate as Hans Jr. rolled to imminent doom. "Bun! Get the baby. Zephy! Change of plans. This place is going to be crawling with enemies. Escape!"

The cavern shuddered and screeched as tremors built from below, accentuating the sudden necessity of speed. Ominous darkness in the form of tendrils poured invasively from the open gate, eating away at the blue illumination of all the information screens. A rooster crowed, but that sound went ignored along with the duck call.

Uack!

"Moon-moon, unless your next prompt is taking this Oof away, I do not have the time!" Artorian's feet put pressure cracks in the ground as he pressed forward, tripping as the ground gave way like fine gravel. He missed his platforms already as the ruined footing hampered his acceleration. Spitting out dungeon rocks, he pushed back up and resumed the zoom. "Mo' body, mo' problems! I completely forgot that unbalanced attributes meant that my kinesthetic sense was going to take a nosedive. This was easy when going slow, but if I keep using too much of this new strength, I'm only going to put myself in the dirt."

He needed more speed, and as was becoming the norm, he needed that speed in a hurry. What did he have in this new arsenal that would work? If he could unlock the Running skill, he would likely have it already. No Trans Am or similar attribute booster was to be found in his pockets. Not even one handful of sand. What was he doing out and about on an adventure without pocket sand, or a towel?

"Archimedes!" The solution struck his brain like lightning, as his next step of Hypermobility combined with Shunpo. The sudden spark of electricity stole an extra fifty meters of space between him and the bright monkey ball of Hans Jr. Success!

Artorian tripped again before he could chain the Flash Steps together, as the orb crossed the Darkest Dungeon's threshold. A threshold from which a feathery mélange of opponents were beginning to pour like floodwaters, all of them ignoring Hans Jr. They must have seen him as an egg, or saw their taunting rube messily roll over his own face, as, penalty or not, he had more bodily oomph than his head could keep up with. Pushing himself back up regardless, he oriented himself toward the door and pushed off, breaking just enough of the ground to move him, but not groove him.

"I've got the baby!" Lucia, in full golden Glitterflit form, sped past him and left a trail of light in her passing wake. "Zeph's in trouble!"

With Lucia cleanly beating him in speed and control, Artorian changed the gears on his plans, drifting into a powerslide after he'd freshly built his speed back up. "On it!"

Even if he successfully began chaining these Flash Steps from Shunpo together, Zelia had been right. He wasn't going to catch the shield ball, and her mention currently felt like a warning, rather than a prompting for him to prove the world wrong.

Sunshine turned on his heel on having dug a deep enough divot in the ground to come to a halt, then hurled himself the other way with an instant use of another Flash Step. He was going to liberally lean on the effect of his cloak, which was exactly the kind of reliance he was worried about with time-frame dilation. Better Archimedes than burnout! "Prompt controller! What's the point of testing this minmaxing push if I'm going to be accosted by the normal penalties anyway? I thought the Gaston thing prevented this?"

The telltale chime of confirmation played in agreement. The dissonance between the capabilities of his body, and his mental capacity to keep up with them so he didn't punch himself in the face, vanished. Artorian was most appreciative as his interactions with the world suddenly felt normal, even if the numbers did not reflect that. "Thank!"

If Lucia said she had the baby, then she had the baby, and Artorian would place his trust and faith in Momma Bun. Hans Jr. was too much like his father! His hand snapped to his brooch, pressing in to contact Ember. "Honeybee? Shenanigans! I am constantly taunting anything and everything in a thirty-three league radius, and cannot turn it off. My character is done. Hans Jr. is proving to be his father and has gotten separated with Lucia chasing."

Rolling a perception check, Artorian figured out what his next problems were. "I just learned that Zephyr's escape route is cut off by cheesy netting, and I am being chased by… chickens? Am I seeing chickens?"

Noot!

Artorian was surprised when the Penguin call played instead of the quack or ding. Was this Vanaheim suddenly trying to help? He hurriedly snatched the still-forming prompt out of the air. Zephyr quickly descended from what had looked to be a snappy increase in altitude, having torn herself free. Her masts and sails were entirely coated in unpleasant and clingy string cheese. He spared the second and read the prompt while on the run.

———

Message from Vanaheim: I tried to take it away! Accepting the prompt accepted the ability. Now I can't do anything. I had that ability set to go as a contingency. I thought you'd leave me be. Please let us still be even?

———

Artorian pushed the doubt button, even if it did not exist on the prompt. "That can wait. I need information on these uncooked nuggets. Inspect!"

Ding!

———

You have encountered: Mother Clucker.
    World: Eternia.
    Realm: Vanaheim.
    Region: Darkest Dungeon.
    Terrain: Dungeon.
    Circumstance: The Oof.
    Local Event: None.
    Unique Properties: None.
    Racial Template: Vampiric.
    Species: Chicken.

———

Detected Trait: The Cluckening.
    Detected Skill: Rooster Martial Arts.
    Detected Skill: Hyrule Hatred.
    Detected Skill: Kill That One Specifically.

———

Protection: Resistance to Cold.
    Vulnerability: Weakness to Fire and Melee.

––––––

Attack 1: Peck.
   Attack 2: Wing Buffet.

––––––

Ember's voice pushed through his brooch as his eyes ran down the list. "Is that where they all went? I was wondering where the Army of Grand Cluck was off to all of a sudden. Use your class, sugar! Or maybe don't. Forewarning? For each chicken you kill, another will appear. I am three floors down and got lost. I can burn through the spores, but the hallucinogens are messing me up. Momma Bun, are you on the connection? I need either a Cleanse, or Veracity. I'm going to lose my I.F.F."

Artorian was too focused on getting back to Zephyr, who was having difficulties landing. "Your what?"

Lucia saved him with knowledge as the brooch spat forth information. "Identification Friend or Foe! It's an identification system designed for command and control. She said she's about to not be able to distinguish friend from foe."

"Out-Abyssal-standing." Artorian was not amused to learn that tidbit. Ember was very much not on the list of opponents he wanted to fight for realsies. He punted a chicken by accident during his next Shunpo, accelerating the mother clucker past three thousand eight-hundred miles per hour. This turned the chicken into instant rotisserie at supersonic speeds as an innocuous skill added itself to his class entry.

Not noticing that he had gained a skill called Glorious Overkill, Artorian got to Zephyr as she was transforming from a full yacht into a person. Her hold opened at the bottom of her hull before she did, spilling free a whole host of squatting Spotters who had been napping.

The Spotters all fell into a heap, rudely calling out litanies of insults. This was before the troupe of bald men all crawled over each other to run away and flee from a surging sea of vampiric chickens. The flood of feathers clucked at them with a hunger for blood, and a sudden need to establish a pecking order. They would be fine. What was the worst that could come from dumping an entire SCP foundation in a dungeon populated with the most unknown of horrors?

It'd be *fiiiiine*.

Nobody would remember that elongating one's words tends to make them a lie.

When Zephyr fell to the ground the last few feet, she reminded Artorian that Elves were graceful cats. Unlike what Artorian expected, she shot into the crowd of oncoming chickens, beelining toward the flood rather than away from it. All in high heels, a restrictive, colorful dress, and perfect hair a-flowing. What was her character trait? 'Always Fabulous'?

Manifesting an energy bow of neon, Zephyr proceeded to lay down cover fire.

"Zephy, you did not need to go that hard on the style!" Having no idea how to clean up hordes of smaller enemies just yet, Artorian did the sensical thing for a Janitor. He got out his broom and commenced sweeping. "Sweepidy swoops, chickens go back to their coops!"

Flourishing his cleaning implement like a spear, he scrubbed the floor with windmill strikes. When within ten feet of Zephyr, he turned on a heel again so he could join her advance into the flock.

"Yes I did! Win or lose, you have to do it in style!" The maddened, adventure-loving Elf did not share his initial viewpoint at all. Calling out an ability, her bow unfurled like an umbrella. The energetic lattice spread and widened, allowing her to shoot multiple neon arrows when she fired off the original. "Neon Sails."

Since Zephyr appeared dead-set on being an adventurous little monster and diving nose-first into the thick of it, Artorian abandoned clever tactics and worked with what he had. No retreat. Only advance! "On second thought, time for hard style! Zephy? Music! Do you have a line attack? I need a path to the door! I'm cranking up my Cleaning Aura to full, but that will only do so much."

"Sir, yes, sir!" She was plenty on board with that directive as amplification circles formed on the lattice of her bow.

"Repulsor." Her next multi-shot sank deep into the thick wave of red-eyed chickens before activating the intended ability. Chickens went flying with a sonic bang. Repulsor dispersed the flock with the gentility of a cannonball taking out bowling pins.

As bonus aesthetics, the impact added a satisfactory thud. Like the drop of a beat that would make Astrea proud as repeated thumping pulsed forth from Zephyr's bow. Artorian had forgotten that High Elves were party animals! He was worried about her wellbeing, but regardless of the situation that they appeared to be in? Zephyr had the biggest smile plastered on her face, her eyes wide and full of want. "Making a hole!"

The next neon arrow that she nocked charged up slowly, her energy weapon channeling a large ball of mana at the arrow tip. Zephyr's words were hungry as she loaded the ability in, and Artorian zipped to be behind her rather than in front of her, sweeping a few clever chickens that knew the value of flanking out of the way. "Staravar Beam Cannon."

The macro-battery meant for ship-to-ship combat pulled up its sleeves and neatly slotted itself into the ball of built-up mana. Ready to party!

"Fire!" The release of the arrow fired off a *bwaaaaamp* that cut through the air. Rather than a bright neon arrow, a ten-meter tall by ten-meter wide beam carved a path through the feathery horde. Trying to swarm and swallow Master Sunshine whole with sheer numbers was a great tactic, when one did not jump beak-first into the air fryer. With Artorian and Zephyr as of yet unharmed, what kind of damage these chickens did was a mystery for now. They would likely find out the moment they got utterly overwhelmed, and the damage numbers ceased to matter.

Artorian could only guess that Zeph had overheard the banter of what his Loved by Mana character trait did. Once he resumed the vanguard position, she made no effort to keep him out of her Staravar's firing line. On the upside, his trait ate the portion of her attack that moved through his space, and funneled that energy into fuel for Lucia's shields as they got hen-pecked. This left him topped off, with a clear path to advance, and a much crispier set of targets to sweep!

"Heavy Ordinance: Infinite Flurry!" Zephyr's attack to back him up was followed by the continuation of the musical hard style beat. Her next arrows slammed into the wall of feathers to keep beating it back after making the path, the both of them rushing for the gate so they could regroup in the dungeon.

Zephyr felt the drain hit her before they made it, and finally succumbed to proper teamwork as she noticed that her arrows were doing a lot less than she liked. "Administrator, I need ten minutes before I have another Staravar, and I am not dealing damage with anything else! My hard style flurry repurposed to crowd control is keeping the chickens at bay, but I am pushing them, not pulping them. I am too low level for Vanaheim! My highest attribute is maybe two-hundred!"

Artorian loved the information, able to work with that as he mowed through vampiric chickens with his broom. Displacing them clean out of Zephyr's path hadn't been difficult to begin with, but practice made it easy. He wasn't doing any noticeable damage either, but he was clearing the crowd and getting where he needed to be as the cluckening dissolved into a furious mass of feathers around them.

Being chased was going to be a constant new factor to deal with, so he might as well start coming up with solutions. So far, the Boom Shaka Laka broom was handing him a clean sweep! "Keep hen-pecking them right back! Whatever piece of the sea is closest, you slap them with physics. Killing these mother cluckers may not be the best solution. You just keep up behind me as I start pouring on the speed, and yell when that becomes a problem. We can be chased by the waves of flock all day long if we can stay ahead of them. If you have an idea on how to handle this, I am all ears!"

Zephyr was ready for this very moment.

Her aim swerved behind her so she could curtail the chasing sea of cluckery with a continuation of shots, the beat dropping hard and fast as her arrows landed with audible success. Her steps then used the resulting sonic waves as footholds to propel herself forward and keep up with the Administrator. "I have the best strategy!"

Artorian needed no preamble, only the plan. "Give!"

Zephyr cackled, and called upon a most ancient warcry and ritual as they both crossed the threshold into the dungeon, madly dashing deeper.

"Leeeeeroy Jeeeeenkins!"

CHAPTER THIRTEEN

Sunshine punted another clucking cuckoo violently, doubting anything good would or could come from that warcry. Leeroy Jenkins was most definitely not a plan. Snagging a mother clucker out of the air to beat another mother clucker out of the way with it, Artorian put deciphering the dungeon design second, in favor of putting extra distance between himself and the feathered sea first.

A quack of a prompt had to be addressed first.

Uack.

———

Violent fighting style unlocked: Devastating Disrespect.

Unlock requirement: Beat a guy with another guy. We suppose chickens count too.

Mana color: Carmine.

Effect: Devastating Disrespect is a fighting style meant to entertain more than it is effective. Each maneuver, skill, and ability in this fighting style functions as some kind of experience gain multiplier.

Description: Face tank that pesky damage. Let the enemy know their efforts were absolutely negligible and pointless. Even their mother slaps harder than that.

Special: *"Is that all you've got?"*

———

Was Vanaheim his curator now? What happened to Incursus? The realization that Incursus had been left behind on Zephyr's aft deck hit him far too late. *"Oh no*! Our chelonian castle!"

"I've got him!" Zephyr missed Artorian's ear with her main neon arrow by a mere two inches, making him duck and flinch. The other eight successfully skewered a unique vampiric chicken to the wall, pinning the bothersome cluck in place like a butterfly to a collection board.

Her barrage of bowyery did an excellent job at crowd control, allowing Artorian to focus on sweeping the path as Zephyr overshared, informing him exactly how safe Incursus was. "Secured in the balcony!"

Artorian had too much decency to think of the very pleased turtle nested securely in a High Elven balcony, but his alternative stunk. Especially when he saw what happened to the pinned mother clucker.

The gothic aesthetic of these darkest dungeon walls were one of his least favorite types. They were sticky! Made of blackened, hardened, throbbing, unpleasant looking Casu Marzu cheese. He did his utmost to ignore the walls when they shifted, surrounding the pinned victim.

Artorian even specifically looked elsewhere when that chicken's call of distress went muffled. He did not want to see the cluck consumed into the Casu Marzu, whole and uncooked. There a small chance he'd seen lots of tiny things wriggling around in the wall, but Artorian staunchly refused to pay that detail any mind. This place was bad enough, and a higher Perception would only have driven him to madness.

He'd never considered that a low attribute could be helpful

in certain instances. Luck may not have been his strongest statistic, but it appeared that he still had the stuff in spades.

Glad to not notice the details for once, he shoved the prompt in his pocket, made a positive noise that Incursus was present, and used the Perception he did have to follow and track the deep bunny-paw indentations. The footprints were easy to read in the... admittedly fleshy-looking floor. Another detail that he didn't want to think about. The floor had *give* to it, like a thick carpet. A thick... meaty carpet.

Artorian hated this dungeon; it ticked too many of his bad boxes. Without the Cleaning Aura, he would be outright miserable from the smell. Or the spores. Those sneeze-inducing menaces were so thick that they hung in the air like puffy spring pollen. Then there was the dreaded namesake. While the area at the entrance gate had some ominous lighting, this dungeon was dark as pitch.

Zephyr's neon glow provided the only local illumination as she barely, but successfully, kept the gobbling masses at bay. That dim light put a hamper on his Glitterflit tracking speed. At least where Ember had been was obvious. That traversed ground had been reduced to scorched wasteland. She may have had the right idea. "I don't know if I want to clean the whole place, or burn it to the ground."

Genius struck him. Prompts provided illumination! "Incursus. Throw open as many of my screens as you can. I need light!"

The chest-bundled turtle eagerly did so, though Artorian once again wondered if seeing more was better while down here. On the bright side, the winding dungeon paths were easier to see, Lucia's paws smoother to track, and some information he otherwise would have missed hung at the forefront of his peripheral.

The not so good news was that the paw-print tracks took a vertical nosedive down a truly unpleasant-looking hole, so actually reading them would have to wait. But prompts that included the titles *'Devastating Disrespect'* and *'Glorious Overkill'* would turn his frown upside down. Particularly some words that would bring a tear to his eye if they meant what he hoped they meant. *Maneuver: La Chancla.*

Artorian made his choice as he dove into the hole. Corkscrew running down the wall, he felt and heard the unforgivable squelch beneath his feet. That was the last cheesy straw. He kept up with the tracks that had also seen fit to wall-run down the well as he added a snappy comment, then reached for his brooch. "Definitely burning it to the ground."

With a press to the communicator that still didn't need to be pressed, Artorian was in no mood for further unpleasantry. One day he would delve into the land of thinkery of where he'd picked that odd habit up from, but today was not that day. "Lucia, we're going down the… shaft. I'm going to pretend that this is a shaft and ask no questions. Do you have the ball boy? We are being chased by a sea of vampiric chickens and have gotten ahead of them, but—"

A Glitterflit paw-clap resounded through his brooch, followed by a matching flash of light further down the shaft.

"Never mind! Found your light. Coming in with the Cleanse!"

Artorian wanted to say he hard-landed and handled the impact like a pro, but the floor had so much of that unpleasant give to it that he only felt a shudder go up his spine. He settled for catching Zephyr who had—with utter guts and gusto— jumped right down while still laying down covering fire. She hadn't even bothered to look down, entirely focused on sending a hail of arrows up and out of the well to any clucker trying to follow. "Get soooome!"

Zephyr's call made Artorian's echolocation flare. He could see the outline of the well shaft, and the general design of the space around him without needing to look. This made it exceptionally easy to catch the High Elf before she hit the ground, and redirect where all that velocity was going. Tapping into a movement and fighting style that the system hadn't seen fit to properly slap onto his character sheet, Artorian flowed as water and moved like the wind.

Altering her momentum by throwing the High Elf down the hall did nothing to deter the endless flow of neon arrows. With Zephyr now ahead of him, Artorian vindictively chose to be terribly unskillful with his footing. He broke the floor out of spite, and caught up to an arrow-blasting Zephyr as she gracefully turned her momentum-powered toss into a clean stride.

Her continued trek was seamless, her movements uninterrupted as Zephyr copied Artorian and flowed like the wind, retaining her image as the picture of grace.

High Elves were made of cheats!

She was doing that in heels.

Heels!

Breaking into the room where Lucia was unleashing a heaping of Southern-Style Bunny-Fu, Artorian instantly loved what she'd done with the place. Bright shields both kept the hissing vampiric minions at bay and the arena of choice well lit. Though, rather than a flock of feathers, she appeared to be fighting something else. Her paw-clapping was generously applied to a floating, accursed, hanging wall scroll that she engaged with maximum vengeance.

Lucia howled out her dissatisfaction and disgust for the things. "I hate charts! They are grudges made physical."

Momma Bun unleashed protective mommy mode when the chart lurched too close to Hans Jr., beating the floating scroll into submission like an ornery Faith Foundry patient that wouldn't stay down. Or a Heavenly being a pain in the grass.

After chasing down the child, to whom this had all been a most wonderful and exciting game, the momma bun activated a full-on rage-phase. All to the misfortune of her current enemy, as Lucia tumbled into a mid-boss encounter with a most despised enemy. As was par for the course, Team Sleep did not stumble into boss encounters. Boss encounters stumbled into Team Sleep, and were promptly put to sleep.

Artorian took the scene in one detail at a time.

First the good news!

Hanging via a glowing choker that appeared to be a repurposed shield around Lucia's neck, Artorian saw Hans Jr. safely retrieved. Acting as a makeshift jingly bell, the excited and clapping child within knew only glee. Unsurprising, as the babe had a front row safety-seat to a full-sized Glitterflit unleashing momma-murder on the deserving chart-type enemy.

Lucia unerringly struck with the full force of her rail-paws. Each impact was both a lightshow and reason not to get into her line of clap. Once the wall-scroll was crippled and crumpled, she held the chart by the curls of its edges and engaged a combo move that could be chained into itself.

Father Richard would have been proud, as the attack came straight out of the Holy Falcon-Captain's playbook of Smiting.

"The knee! The knee! The knee!" Lucia mercilessly and repeatedly slammed her knee into the chart's over-worded contents. All the while blaming the chart for being a wasteful time sink that detracted from actual patient care.

To end the combo with bonus damage, a consistent set of hypervelocity paw-strikes slapped the chart into pieces. Lucia defeated her hated foe so utterly that the mid-boss suffered conflagration before fading into particulates. As far as Lucia was concerned, all to escape its well-deserved suffering. Her foot kicked at the fading, misty remains. "And stay out!"

Several of the particles attempted to reform into a brand new chart, but made the blind mistake of doing so next to Artorian. Who disrespectfully flicked the budding monster back out of existence.

Ding!

———

Maneuver discovered!
Maneuver name: Flick.
Style: Devastating Disrespect.
Effect: Disrespect a foe by using minimal effort in the pursuit of their

defeat. An opponent defeated by a mere flick will earn the user double experience points from that specific kill.

———

More prompts were ready for him, but they had to wait.

A problem that wasn't the flock of fury on his tail required immediate solving. On one hand, he had flicked particles and killed a monster that the Amalgamation Pylon was busy bringing into existence. On the other hand, according to Truesight? He had hit an illusion. What he saw, that the rest of the group did not, was a small rat pacing back and forth in the middle of the room, holding up a plain wooden sign.

The sign simply read 'Scary Enemy.'

This could not wait. "Lucia, can you put up a shield blocking off the path behind me? I have a new priority problem and need a minute."

"Shell Shock!" Lucia instantly shot up a paw, erecting a luminous, girthy barrier in the form of a turtle shell that blocked the path Artorian had come from. In addition, this barrier blocked off all surrounding paths, and bumped everyone present up an inch. The shield enclosed the group while reshaping itself to form a cylinder, at which point Lucia dropped her paw. "I needed a breather, Kit. Good call! My heart rate has been a beating drum ever since I began the chase. Apologies for not responding over the brooch, I heard you both coming with ease after Zephyr laid down the music."

"I call it wub-step. I step on the wubs. They're a great source of acceleration." Zephyr, in full agreement, slumped down on the ground alongside the momma bun. Blowing out heavy exhales, her barrage was at an end for now. She waved both her hands as her wrists were sore, and checked her flagging mana bar. "That barrage wasn't going to have held up much longer."

She did not have the stats to be here, but that, sure as High Elf honor, wasn't going to stop her. "Heard you were the origin of that particular trickery, Administrator. I like wubs! I will be learning the cultivation version as soon as I can, if I don't master the technique here."

Artorian politely nodded, accepting their words.

Hans Jr. clapped gleefully in his ball of safety, oblivious to the danger. His eyes were wide and hungry for more spectacle. A spectacle currently occupied by the horde of chickens flooding in against the barrier's walls.

To Momma Bun's exceptional credit, her shields held the tide, and held the line. That this was one of the skills she had, Artorian did not know. What he equally did not know was why the rat with the sign had sat down with them. The critter had put said sign on the floor, pulled a sandwich out of an unknown hammerspace, and started munching as if it was breaktime.

He pointed at the rat. "Am I the only person who sees the danger mouse?"

The party looked, did not see what he did, and shot him the appropriate odd facial expressions. Artorian thought that sufficient. "That's unfortunate, but interesting. I'll figure this out in a hurry so we can get to Dawny. I mean Ember. Abyss, I'm doing it again."

CHAPTER FOURTEEN

Pushing a prompt out of the way so he could engage in conversation, he accidentally made the prompt think that it was the screen's turn. As such, the prompts related to the topic he touched all jumped back in front of his face, shining bright while stubbornly remaining front and center before his eyes.

Ding!

Maneuver discovered!

Maneuver name: Flick.

Style: Devastating Disrespect.

Effect: Disrespect a foe by using minimal effort in the pursuit of their defeat. An opponent defeated by a mere flick will earn the user double experience points from that specific kill.

Maneuver discovered!

Maneuver name: Glorious Overkill.

Style: Devastating Disrespect.

Effect: Experience multiplier. Eliminating an opponent without flourish will only ever reward ordinary amounts of experience. Gloriously Overkilling an opponent will multiply the experience gained. By a factor equal to the number of times their maximum health allotment was met. If an opponent with five health is eliminated with the use of five damage, you will be allotted normal experience. If that opponent is eliminated with the use of ten damage, your experience gain will be doubled. If that opponent is eliminated with fifteen damage, your experience gain will be tripled. Twenty will quadruple your gain. Twenty-five will quintuple your gain. The only determining factor is the maximum health of your opponent.

Note: This maneuver can be combined with any other maneuver, as it is a matter of style, and styling all over your opponents.

————

Maneuver discovered!

Maneuver name: La Chancla.

Style: Devastating Disrespect.

Effect: Ranged weaponry is not your enemy! For each opponent you backhand and fade to black, your experience points will stack! All your Disrespectful maneuvers will function regardless of your opponent being eliminated at range or in melee, so long as you are responsible for the killing blow. In addition, all eliminations achieved outside of melee range will always have their experience values doubled.

Note! Additional multipliers will increase the experience multiplier by one, rather than the multipliers multiplying each other. That's too much scaling, and math.

————

Special effect unlocked!

Style: Devastating Disrespect.

Special: "Is that all you've got?"

Effect: When all damage of an incoming attack is received, but entirely ignored, the user gains a stack of Menace. Menace grants the temporary buff: Menacing. For the five seconds of this buff's duration, two effects will occur. One, the user will appear menacing and frightening, especially to the attacker. Two, any damage dealt will have its physics effect doubled, allowing even a minor attack to have much greater impact.

Special: If combined with Flick, Menacing's enhanced physics effect will be quintupled instead. If combined with both Flick and Glorious Overkill, the effect will be increased even further, to the tune of a full category.

Note: A category still means times ten, Artorian.

———

Artorian chuckled.

He wasn't sure who was making these particular prompts, but he glanced over them, and went ahead to clear them. The illumination dropped just a touch from the loss of screens, but that was fine.

Ding!

———

Notice!

Personal Pylon Hold at 25% capacity.

You have used one-fourth of all available Pylons currently in your allotment.

———

Good to know, he supposed, even if he sort of wanted to see the overall number. A quick check on Lucia's cylindrical shield proved that her Shell Shock spell, if it was a spell, successfully held back the sea of chickens. Including the other creatures that had gotten mixed up in his ever-ongoing taunt effect. The rat only he could see appeared to be unaffected? How interesting.

"Good information." Hopefully this would help the rest of his team. "Speaking of."

Artorian squeezed his brooch. "Emby, we're in a safe spot, and as soon as we're all topped off on mana, we can beeline it straight to you. How goes your eternal war, dearest? I admit I'm feeling somewhat overwhelmed by what I'm surrounded by, even if Lucia's barrier is muffling the sound."

Ember's voice soothed him like a crisp spring morning, wisdom flowing as fresh dew. "Ships don't sink because of the water around them, darling, ships sink because of the water that gets in them. Don't let what's happening around you get inside you and weigh you down."

She paused in her reply, and must have looked around before answering his question. "I won? I think I won. Unless all the enemies are where you are."

Artorian checked his surroundings as well, finding that statement to be painfully truthful. "Likely! I'm actually not certain how we're getting out. Any chance you can come to us? There's a lot of chicken here that needs to become rotisserie. Also, I am getting the strangest skills and maneuvers. Have you ever heard of Devastating Disrespect as a fighting style? Those prompts keep pouring in."

The squee across the brooch made Artorian tug his head away and wince, as Ember developed several new ice cream flavors of excitement. "I made that one! The experience multiplier based on style? That's me! Though, it's very violent. I'm not sure that style fits you well, sugar, that's all red mana and…"

Her reaction ended with ominous growling. "Oh, I see what's going on. **Violence** and **War** are having another little interference bout. Remind me what your class was, honey bun? I'm on my way to you, stay put. I'm bringing the heat."

"Status." Checking his screen when his character page popped up, he confirmed what he thought he remembered. "That would be Violence for the class, and Ultraviolence for the specialization. Didn't you have something with War? This sneaking suspicion you raised is starting to make my nose tingle. Do we want to do something about this, or roll with it?"

"We're going to do something about it, alright." The

amount of growl in Ember's tone was far more concerning that the tingle in his nose, but given she was on his team, he didn't feel as concerned as he likely should be. "Sugar? There should be a chicken in the horde named Achilles. Find him for me? There needs to be some killies."

Artorian instantly felt bad for this particular chicken. He hadn't even found the clucker yet, and that poor bird's fate was all sorts of sealed. "Will do, dear, see you shortly."

Ding!

———

Notice!
    You have mail.

———

Opening the prompt while remembering he had a rat to talk to, Artorian's smile grew threefold. His face hurt from smiling, at least, for the contents were truly precious.

———

Player Blanket has sent you an item.
    Item: Plain stick.
    Description: A stick that Blanket found. He wanted you to have it.
    Message from Astrea: Blanket is jealous of Voltekka's cleverness, and is adamantly following in Tekka's footsteps. Paw-steps? Claw-steps? The stick is the test to see if sending you equipment works, because Blanket has succeeded in itemizing himself as a living gear. I can send the set to you anytime, but remember, Grandpa! You'd wear Blanket. If you get hurt, Blanket gets hurt. Are you going to let our Blanket get hurt?

———

Artorian grinned from ear to ear, instantly filled with ideas for version four of his Eternia character. "No-Hit run is a go! Why care about one HP when the point is to never get hit? That would work great with my original 'No' style. More goals!"

A confirmation chime from his prompt controller made its telltale ding, followed by one from an actual system prompt.

Ding!

———

Quest notice!

You have been offered the quest: Soulsborne.

Objective: Complete a No-Hit run in Eternia.

Bonus: Complete this quest with the Glass Cannon trait applied to your character.

———

Artorian smashed accept, even if he wasn't set up to even begin that quest right now. The system was trending in the right direction! This was an excellent gameplay incentive. He was still at rock bottom as far as immersion was concerned, but this was an excellent path to good times. He liked it. Another!

A happy noise from Zephyr pulled his attention away. "I got another trait!"

Artorian and Lucia both turned, expecting her to elaborate, which the High Elf gladly did when provided attention. "The trait is called Lightshow. Every time I hit an enemy with one of my arrows, it gains a DoT called Glow."

She leaned toward the Administrator, winking in amusement. "That means damage over time."

He rolled his eyes and his wrist, wanting her to explain.

Zephyr stifled her giggles and continued. "Each arrow that hits applies a stack of Glow. Glow deals one damage for five seconds, ticking once per second of its duration. If another arrow hits an enemy that already has a stack of Glow, the damage and duration compound. So Glow would now do two damage a second for a duration of ten seconds. Or nine? If it took me a full second to get another arrow on target, I'd always lose a tiny bit of duration as the damage piles on. I can shoot nine arrows a second with Neon Sails. If all of those pin the same target, that's nine damage a second, for just over a minute and a half. That's great!"

Artorian had to agree, with Lucia nodding on the same sentiment. That stacking tick damage was pretty good. Lingering damage over time on an enemy you had to stop attacking for a bit could be very useful if you had to cut and run, which they were certainly doing. "We should find you a Gnome named Metro to keep a tally of all your ticks!"

He then turned to the rat when the rest of the team got absorbed in their goodies. The rat that seemed to have gathered that one of the players could see him. The sneaky danger mouse attempted to tip-toe its way out from the premises, only to walk nose-first into the same wall keeping all the gobbling and related clucking out. "Now, onto the rat race. Hello, little sign-holder. Why don't we have an innocent chat?"

The rat replied by throwing its wooden sign at Sunshine's forehead, which thunked off harmlessly as the shield ate the single point of damage the sign dealt. This confused Lucia to no end as she hadn't seen anything attack Artorian, yet her shield had clearly been hit. "What?"

"Handling it." Having taken and tanked all the relevant damage while remaining unharmed, the Menacing buff popped into activity, fueling and enhancing Artorian's diplomatic entrance as he replied with a truly villainous grin. "You shouldn't a' did that, danger mouse. You shouldn't a' did that."

The rat squeaked in fear while pressing itself to the inviolable barrier as the ominous figure loomed ever closer. Its small arm extended while chirping in a futile attempt to keep the major villain at bay. Artorian appeared all sorts of frightening to the rat, as the Menacing buff hammed up its effect like a Bard solo-strumming a lute. The Nightmare Fuel tag added by

Brother Moon, visible to the rat, wasn't doing Artorian's attempt at gentle diplomacy and conversation any favors either.

To the rat, there was no Sunshine here. Only Dreadshine. Rapid shrieking followed as Dreadshine leaned down low, his voice a whisper filled with doom.

"Tell me *everything*."

CHAPTER FIFTEEN

One fainted rat and many answers later, Artorian had more screens than he wanted. He had not expected to uncover not merely the rabbit hole, but a full-on warren of rat-related problems. With one old name in particular sticking out like a sore thumb. "Abyss, Pag. What did you do this time?"

The answer was already found, floating in a screen before him. Artorian merely didn't want to accept the information, knowing he was going to have to deal with it. He'd already been asked to assist with the Amalgam Pylons. That this task would be a sooner rather than later problem was gaining clarity.

He stuck the Amalgam assault in queue after Yuki and friends, but expected this problem to be one he'd get called in for. What had Cal said about shoving Pag into the bottom of a volcano again? That suddenly seemed like such a good plan.

With Lucia still trying to sneak a peek like the curious bun who wanted to get her sniffer in trouble, he turned the screen so she stopped needing to be stealthy about it. "I think Pagacco is calling himself the Great Rat Maiden now? Ten Old World gold says there's a maid outfit involved, otherwise I don't know what this means."

Name: The Echeese-iarchy.

Government: Theocracy.

Mantra: The goal is to become a big enough problem that someone solves my problem!

Rule 1: Worship the Great Rat Maiden. Be not a maidenless rat.

Rule 2: Non-rat-things count as food.

Rule 3: Non-rat-homes count as shelter.

Rule 4: Expand everywhere.

Rule 5: Exploit all natural-things. If it glows, and you can eat or drink it without dying? Do so.

Rule 6: Never question if inventing something is a good idea. If it kills non-rat things, it's good!

Rule 7: Never fall for the same trick more than once!

Rule 8: If your enemies throw wave after wave of disposable minions at you, you must answer in kind.

Rule 9: If at first you don't succeed, return with larger hordes.

Rule 10: Always be the problem, never the solution, except to the Great Rat Maiden and your fellow rats.

Lucia didn't know the person mentioned by name, and couldn't connect the dots. Her ears drooped lopsidedly in confusion.

Artorian knew he'd have to explain, but didn't particularly want to do so right now. "We'll get to that later, Momma Bun. This is more of a me problem, unless I get to bring backup into the Pylon Holds. I'm not even certain if game abilities work down there. With Pylons as touchy as they are, I expect there to be some rule changes."

Noot.

Brother Moon was trying to get his attention again? Had enough damage not been done? Artorian reached for the cheese-colored screen that appeared in the orb of information around him and picked it out from the line up.

———

Message from: Vanaheim.
It is inconvenient to talk with these prompts, there are limitations.
Can I send you a messenger?

———

Artorian kneaded his brows and forehead, felt a small thundercloud gather over his thoughts, and pushed accept because he wanted Ember to get here so they could all get a move on. Then again, this is what Administrative life was always like. Detours were the swiftest path to get where one was going. "Sure, Moon-moon. Send me someone, so you can get off your fondue plate what you need to get off your fondue plate. My itinerary remains with Tisha and Decorum, before we book it to wherever Yuki is."

Noot.

Expecting another screen, Artorian looked around, but found no new yellow interloper after the existing message became particulate. Instead, in the middle of Lucia's cylindrical shield with them, there stood a black and white speckled cow with a pope's hat on its noggin.

A holy cow. Ridden by a very moody, string-cheese arms-crossed Elemental. Even without a face, the Elemental was giving all the signs about being unhappy with its reassignment.

Lucia yelped, leaping to hide behind a nervous-looking High Elf when her ear picked up that someone was being sent, only to find that particular someone had completely ignored her shield, and had arrived in their midst. "Abyss!"

Zephyr had drawn her bow, arrows at the ready as her eyes flicked back and forth between the messenger and the Administrator. "Don't shoot the messenger? Do shoot the messenger? Shoot the messenger a bunch? Ventilate and make holy?"

Artorian blinked, held up a finger to pause Zephyr, and said the magic word. "Inspect."

Artorian barely got into reading the prompt that came up before devolving into a bout of laughter, his hands pressing to his knees. "Pillow Breaker the Cheese Elemental, and Holy Cow, an actual Holy Cow? What's next, a cheese banking system for all your cheese-based currencies?"

Pillow Breaker raised a yellow tentacle to assault Sunshine with a pun, as he had been planning and plotting to do for a while now. He got as far as overhearing the comment on the cheese banking system before that idea fully consumed his synapses, the ideals of punnery shoved onto the backburner, trying not to devote synapse time to how it had been relegated away from final boss, and into the role of spokesperson. Not that he could act against the great will of Brother Moon either way, but the change of expectations stung.

No, stung was not a great word here, that could be a cheese-related pun of some kind instead. Pillow Breaker would think on this more and pun-ish his original foe!

Forming a voice box so it could converse, and more properly assault his original opponent where he was weakest, Pillow Breaker tested some words. The Cheese Elemental spoke with a nasally tone, not quite getting inflections right as the Elemental inhaled like a bagpipe before speaking like an accordion. "Allo allo."

Artorian's first thought was that if any of the musicians were to see this Elemental speech, they would fight over who got to play him like music first. Poor guy. That was a lot of short ends of the stick kind of draws. "Hello, Breaky, I see Cal got you and gave you some interesting additions? I'm curious. Have you ever even held a pillow? I'm looking at your character information, and there's some contrivances here."

The Cheese Elemental cocked its version of a head, still trying to form itself into something mostly resembling a human shape. Having an up close and personal example helped. "Non. Je n'ais pas seen, or held, this pillow."

Procuring his Faith Foundry pillow from his storage bracelet, Artorian thought it worthwhile to try actual diplomacy for a change. Rather than the more popular, recently applied kind. He stepped in, attempted to play nice, and handed Pillow Breaker the pillow. He wanted to see if the elemental would actually break it.

Accepting the soft item between cheesy tentacles, Pillow Breaker learned to rein in the sticky quality of its tendrils. Otherwise, the pillow was difficult to handle. Turning the object over a few times in confusion, understanding did not dawn until Breaky squeezed the fluff and gasped. "It le squish!"

Repeating the squishing motion several times while enthralled with the little object, Lucia and Zephyr both sighed in relief. Breaky turned the object over several times, inspecting, prodding, and compressing the fluffy thing. "Mais sapristi! Qu'est-ce que c'est, this magical contraption? Surely, this inno-cent, little, soft curd cannot be responsible for injuring me. She is so soft! So gentille. I must know her secrets."

Artorian slapped his knee, all smiles and laughter before he reared up and drew in a deep breath. His face stopped being red before he rested his hands on his hips. "Ahhhh, I needed that. Breaky, I think that we are in the same boat, and we have greater powers trying to thrust us into roles that we are not meant for. I am not focused on violence, but the class seems to be entertaining. While you, now that you are holding one, are clearly no pillow breaker. Your Pun-isher class completely gave away who is meddling on your end. Unless the lack of nooting indicates that Moon-moon is desperately hiding behind a corner while sweat pours down his face."

Artorian had a look around just in case, but if it had been Moony, then Vanaheim wasn't giving it away this time. Not that it was difficult to hide in the sea of clucks still thinking they could face-smash through Lucia's spell.

They really weren't letting up.

The Elemental considered the form of the pillow, then its own. Through its synaptic memory, Breaky recalled the memo-ries of a Penguin that had visited Cal and Tim, sneaking into the forbidden space that a Penguin was not supposed to get into.

Cheese cared little for barriers. Why fight a boss fairly when you could lob projectiles over a wall where it couldn't get to you, killing that boss without it having any hope of getting to you? The way of the cheese was all about using cheap or low-quality tactics to win. Exploits were fair game!

This made Breaky respect that an item that shouldn't have been able to damage him had done so. Rather than the event being a drive for vengeance, the Elemental saw the pillow in a new light. "Oui. Mon anger must be misplaced. Le petit pillow is not something I can be upset at. This ruins my blind reasoning for wanting to dramatically appear moments before your demise, and ensure it."

Artorian wasn't certain how to feel about that tidbit, and thus changed the narrative. "You seem to be more of a detective to me, cheesy. I can probably conjure a new name for you, if you're interested. I can't help but feel you're more a seeker of truth. The truth, however ugly in itself, is always curious and beautiful to seekers after it."

The Elemental considered this, then nodded as even more of a humanoid shape developed. Breaky appeared to be leaning toward the frame-shape of Tim, rather than the beanpole qualities of Cal. "Dis moi this name, idea man."

Artorian was working through the speech oddities, but could understand the Elemental well enough. How could he help, here? A slight tweak of the narrative? A nudge in a brighter direction? A name beginning with a P would be perfect. Ideas struck him, and the performance flowed forth with enthusiasm. "Poirot. Detective extraordinaire. Punisher to all who believe they can cheese the rules, and mold their way past you in their blatant disregard of these rules."

This notion was an instant affront to Breaky, who kept the pillow tight to what had become a chest and sizable stomach. "Quoi?! Only that which is cheese is allowed the Way of the Cheese. There are fools who do this?"

Artorian raised a hand, admittedly guilty.

The Cheese Elemental got off from his high cow, pressed one makeshift fist to a hip with the pillow pinned, and used his brand-new arm to stick a finger high into the sky. "Non! This will not do! I still have reason to chase you, Sunshine man."

Artorian could only smile. If all he accomplished here was side-stepping a boss fight that he didn't want to have right now, he would call this change a win. Ideas on how to further redirect Poirot were already forming, but for now this would do.

He wanted to believe that he was not one to shoot the messenger, even after the messenger had made clear that it was an assassin. "Certainly! Though, I would prefer you do it as a person, rather than as a tool. I am to encourage minds to chase their dreams and to do what they love. Or discover what or who it is they love. That you are a supposed enemy of mine is of no consequence. If I can cultivate love within others? Then there is no difference from that effort, and cultivating love within myself."

The Cheese Elemental's character sheet updated, and Artorian made calming hand motions at Zephyr that it was likely fine to drop the pointy end to the conversation. The Elemental renamed itself to Poirot, and gained the Detective profession. His Intelligence attribute also shot up by a whopping twenty points, while a Nixie Tube lit up above his head. "J'ai une idée. A new belief."

Intrigued, and dismissing that there was other material to get to, Artorian leaned into the lightbulb moment. "Do tell."

Poirot developed a tiny cheesy mustache, of which he smoothened the edge upward. "A new profound belief of mine is that if you can induce a person to speak to you long enough, on any subject, sooner or later they will give themselves away. I feel the little gray cells beginning to manifest. Life is found in order, and method. I have discovered that the pursuit of revenge is rarely a good idea. Wisdom befalls me. When one looks their most innocent is when they are up to something."

Stars filled the developing eyes of Poirot, the Cheese

Elemental detective, as great truths assailed him, and his speech gained clarity. The detective's mind wandered ever further away, negating the purpose of why Poirot had been sent over by Vanaheim in the first place. "One cannot argue with a point of view."

When Poirot began mumbling to himself as the knowledge streamed in, Artorian turned his attention to the cow. One threat down, one possible threat to go. "Now, hello there? Can I safely assume you're the clever sort as well?"

The holy cow's retort of *moo* proved otherwise, but it would never be said that Artorian hadn't tried or provided the benefit of the doubt. Lucia and Zephyr both giggled as the young Administrator shrugged, and scratched the second threat off his mental list. "I tried."

CHAPTER SIXTEEN

Noot.

———

Message from: Vanaheim.

My attempt at using a messenger as a proxy has failed spectacularly. Are you still mad at me? Please don't beam out another whole section of my realm. I've had to get a Wisp named Scotty involved.

———

Artorian read the yellow prompt, and sighed. Brother Moon really was trying, and trying mattered. "Tell you what, Moon-moon? You go fix up Demeter's Dream, since you broke it and gave me the big first scare in the first place, and we'll call it even. I will figure out this Taunt, you patch up my napzone. I fetch my friends out of your depths, and we get on outta here. Sounds good?"

Noot.

———

Message from: Vanaheim.

I would like that very much. I will move from my spatial orbit and go mend your Demeter's Dream. I am out of messages after this, please do not hurt me too badly. The dungeon location is precariously close to sensitive bits.

———

Artorian laughed, slapped his knee, and felt a bit better about life. "I'll call that progress in the right direction."

He took his brooch and squeezed it. "Honey, I was expecting you to be here by now. You okay?"

Only static returned over the connection, making Artorian lose his mirth and turn a slight shade of pale. "That's not good."

Poirot snapped from his musings, attention diverting to Sunshine. "A mystery? Poirot loves mysteries."

The Elemental then remembered a segue that he was supposed to explain, and couldn't be stopped from divulging the information until it was done. Regardless of how bad a time it was. "Per the cheese banking system, it's best to keep cheese of all varieties in a dark, cool, and airy space. Not too humid or cold. Wrapping your cheese does wonders for longevity, and cheese paper is always the go-to recommendation."

No matter how much Artorian tried to divert attention, Poirot could not be deterred from the topic of cheese. "Cheese should be allowed to breathe. Preventing the cheese from drying out, or becoming too humid and sweaty, can all be accomplished by good wrapping and thoughtful storage. Once you've broken into a new cheese, keep it contained in a sealed box. A useful way to ensure a long lifespan for your cheese is to add a sugar cube inside your container. The sugar will absorb excess moisture, and prevent the cheese from sweating. This will sustain the value of your cheeses, allowing you to bank them for later with greater success."

Artorian shot Poirot an incredulous look, which finally snapped the Elemental out of it. "Ah, oui, le mystère. We are looking for the lady of many fires, oui? Mon synapses tell me that she has been affected by the spores, and is fighting enemies she believes to be there. She cannot currently hear you, but with her setting the world on fire? The spores cannot fully take control of her either. We still have a chance to reach her, mon ami! Though, Poirot cannot help you fight. Nor does Poirot know how to get through the sea of unprepared rotisserie that you must wade through."

"Easy." Artorian touched his own shoulder, rolling his arm as he provided a simple solution. "More violence."

He then looked down at the rat, and had an idea as he recalled some game mechanics. Particularly his bout against the Steamlord, and some exclusivity rules regarding challenges. Non-challenged foes couldn't interfere during a challenge, right? With a free arena? That was worth testing. "What did the danger mouse call me again? Dreadshine? I'm going to lean into that persona and see what I can come up with. I'm rusty on Ember's wading through war as if breathing the freshest of air, but I am certain that I can put on a good show."

Artorian turned his gaze to the momma bun, his plans unfolding as he made them. "Lucia? I'm going to be distracting all the opponents. As soon as you drop your shield, hustle and bustle with Zephyr and get to Ember. She needs that Veracity."

Lucia used her large ears to mimic a salute, already grabbing Zephyr with her mouth to throw the High Elf over her Glitterflit shoulder, ready to nyoom.

With his team all set, Artorian spoke to his deductive new friend. "Poirot? Thank you for coming, but you better get to safety. If Moony needs you to stick around so we can talk, please feel free, but do keep in mind that you are in the splash zone. There is a risk of rain."

Poirot considered these words, and formed his first smile

before getting back onto the Holy Cow, preparing to meander on out. "I listen to what you say, and I hear what you mean."

Artorian nodded appreciatively, crossed his arms, and addressed the enemies affected by his Taunt. "I, Dreadshine, seek Achilles. I challenge him to a duel."

Drums rolled and rumbled to the tune of scientific triumph.

The gobbles, honks, and screeching died down as all the noisy cluckery paused on the other side of Lucia's barrier. One of the overcrowded corridors cleared, revealing a single chicken in warrior's attire. Taking center stage, the feathered fowl shot both wings into the air to accept the challenge.

Artorian believed to have both found Achilles, and proved that challenges worked the way he thought. Taunt or not, a one versus one was better than a one versus everyone. At least, for the moment. Somewhere during the duel, he was going to need to figure out how to tackle the crowd. Ember's mention that the chickens would merely come back on defeat had not been forgotten, but he was a master of odd victory conditions.

That should be a system skill.

Still, this success allowed him to ham up his performance, and save Ember some revenge time. He should have asked why Achilles was slated for a fate of the killies, but that could wait. Striking a pose, Dreadshine adopted an aggressive martial stance as he mocked the chicken while Achilles accepted his challenge. "Your free trial at living has ended."

Artorian's second assumption also appeared true, as the cavern system around him bent and stretched to form an arena, widening and creating more space for their challenge bout, just as the space in New Haven's courtyard had altered to fit the scene.

He felt the moment when it arrived. "Bun! Bolt!"

Lucia dropped her Shell Shock barrier and blitzed out of the large chamber while it was still in the midst of expanding, her light-lines trailing behind her. The provided illumination began to drop precipitously as Artorian quickly found himself alone. His prompts were doing little to fight back the encroaching dark. He felt that using prompts, while viable, was not how he wanted to go about this. He required the key component that separated a villain from a supervillain. *Presentation*.

If he was going to put on a show, and buy time for Lucia to both find and get to Ember, he ought to make it flashy and make sure he was keeping everyone's attention. He thought of something, smiled, and cocked his head. "So. Are we using your music? Or mine?"

Achilles clucked at him while keeping both wings raised. The cluck paraded around the midst of the arena as if he were champion, and favored to win. As the favored, he thus called the tune of the music, clucking for a song with a *buh-gawk* that didn't seem to fit his theme at first glance. Regardless of that, the stringed instruments, congas, guiro, and maracas of 'La Distancia Para Un Duelo' set the stage nicely.

With the music chosen, the rooster stroked its wattles in counter challenge. If the cluck could speak, that detail wasn't being revealed. Even as the continuation of the music betrayed that there was more to the chicken than first assumed.

Dreadshine squinted at the bird. The tempo and tone of the song were akin to a blade unsheathing. So he wouldn't make the rooster wait, and gathered what he needed to win. Artorian loved his information, so information he would have. "Inspect."

Ding!

———

You have encountered: Achilles Agrippa, the Raging Rooster.
    World: Eternia.
    Realm: Vanaheim.
    Region: Darkest Dungeon.
    Terrain: Dungeon.
    Circumstance: The Oof.
    Local event: Official Duel.
    Unique properties: Heroic Entity.

Racial template: Vampiric.
Species: Chicken.

———

Detected Trait: The Cluckening.
    Detected Skill: Rooster Martial Arts.
    Detected Skill: Hyrule Hatred.
    Detected Skill: Kill That One Specifically.
    Detected Skill: La Verdadera Destreza.
    Detected Ability: Wing Shield.
    Detected Ability: Unconventional Javelin.
    Detected Ability: Lance-a-lot.
    Detected Ability: Heavy Spear.

———

Protection: Resistance to Cold.
    Vulnerability: Weakness to Fire and Melee.

———

Attack 1: The One True Peck.
    Attack 2: Feather's Rapier.
    Attack 3: Moonlight Armament.
    Attack 4: Moonlight Spurs.

———

That all seemed to match up with the earlier inspection into the sea of feathers. Nice to see some consistency! With a heads up on his opponent's arsenal, his own could be tailored appropriately. This fight would be engaged in close range, with fist meeting spur, and blade meeting blade.

Artorian rolled his shoulders, settling his martial stance as he let his screens wink out one at a time like a countdown timer.

Achilles appeared to grasp the intent behind this action, readying himself as a moonlight glow developed across his beak and spurs.

The last of the Taunted dungeon-foes settled into the stands when the last of the screens winked away, eager to see their targeted enemy be pecked to death by a true Champion of the Cluck. As the last screen blinked out, the world descended into darkness.

Leaning into the role of Dreadshine, Artorian's center came alive with a heartbeat of light as he called out his opening move. Artorian played no games with his opening maneuver, and brought to bear a brand-new source of illumination. "Voltekka."

A flash of light revealed the completed setting: a darkest dungeon's dueling arena, filled to the brim as Achilles crowed in response to the threat. Agrippa charged, surging forth to begin the bout with The One True Peck. The one peck to end it all. A death-beak that would circumvent the need to use any Verdadera Destreza arts at all.

Used to being challenged, Achilles Agrippa wanted this bout over quick. There were roosts to visit! Heroic tales to sow. Moonlight to shape into an ever-increasing arsenal of weaponry. Why the Moonlight arts worked so flawlessly on Vanaheim—even underground—he would one day uncover. For now, he savored its convenience. Agrippa would have the first blow, and taste the succulent worm of dawn as instant victory followed. He had come for the Taunt, but would stay for the adulation as the crowd trilled to cheer for him!

"Effect Cosmetics. *Villain.*" The growing white and green glow ahead of Achilles altered as his foe spoke and revealed his hand. The morphing armor coating his challenger adopted an onyx black and carmine red color scheme. Culminating with a dangerous hum, the visor on his opponent's full plate protections shone intensely with an imposing crimson sheen. The sigil of a roaring sun burst out behind the armor's back as it finished forming. A sun that adapted to the new color scheme as well, adding to the menacing flair as Dreadshine grew to the size of an adult human.

Voltekka released a metallic rumble when the morphing was complete. The lines on the seamless plate protections—where seams ought to be—gained thematically correct carmine illumination that reflected ominously against the darkened armor. A detail that was accentuated particularly well as he rose up, and widened his arms in preparation of a violent hug. Claws extended.

Adding to the flair, the Voice of the World released a klaxon call. A hanging prompt forming above the middle of the arena that hovered in place.

————

Challenge!
  Achilles Agrippa, the Raging Rooster.
  VS.
  Dreadshine, the Nightmare Fuel.

————

To the unlearned crowds, this was truly a match between Hero and Villain. The great Moonlight of Agrippa, versus the one who dared rattle their roosts.

Entirely serious, Artorian was going to make sure he could win the war before he played with his food. Achilles, about to enter melee range as the bird twisted in mid-air, planned to land the killing strike like a pickaxe blow hewing down from above. What terrible showmanship.

Dreadshine deemed the outcome to be otherwise, and vanished from his position with a crackle of red electricity. His voice was modulated, slightly more metallic. "Archimedes."

CHAPTER SEVENTEEN

Achilles Agrippa's One True Peck hit dirt. What should have been a one-hit-kill failed to land on his suddenly missing opponent entirely, as the fated foe appeared behind him with an unpleasant zap. Unpleasant, for several reasons. First was the dread. The dread of having missed his attack, losing sight of his opponent, and yet being intimately aware that the reverse was not true.

Second was the failed resistance check against a Minor Stun. One second of nonactivity didn't seem like much in the grand scheme of things. When the back of the neck bristled from an impending impact, one second was a lot when one could no longer prevent what should have been a panic-fueled dodge. Getting socked clear in the back of the skull was a bad time on any day. Being punched in the back of the skull while already beak-pressed to the ground felt like being curb-stomped by a building.

The crowd's jubilation turned from enthused chirping and supportive *buh-gawks* to a drawn out and breath-hissed *buh-kowwwwwwwch*.

Accompanied by a truly nasty egg-cracking noise, Agrippa's

head was planted deeper into the dirt, to the tune of a whole lot of damage. That there was no dirt in the Darkest Dungeon, and the ground was made of something slightly worse, didn't receive consideration time.

In short, the peck was missed. The stun hit home. Agrippa's face hit the floor. Agrippa's skull was punched deeper into said floor. The world got very dark. Concussion took up residence. Damage was tallied. *Ow.*

Eight-hundred free damage from Shunpo wasn't a lot, but it still stacked onto the actual single-hit beating he'd taken. His vision swam, but luckily for Agrippa, there was nothing to see.

From Artorian's perspective, he Flash Stepped out of the way of the dangerous peck. He appeared behind his charging opponent who thought they could end it quickly. He clocked the rowdy rooster in the back of the noggin. All sensible steps.

The ground fractured under the impact of his punch, burying Agrippa a good foot and a half under the springy dungeon ground. The act reminded Artorian of planting a fence post. Only Agrippa's spurs and feet were visible as they stuck out of the hole, but Artorian took no chances and Flash Stepped back a good fifteen feet so the chicken couldn't spring any nasty surprises on him.

Sk-boom!

The hole that Agrippa had been staked into utterly exploding certainly counted!

When nought but feathers and burnt fondue rained down, Artorian squeezed his brooch. He was a touch confused, having expected a whole lot more from the duel. There was no way Achilles was dead already. No way, and that explosion was very odd.

The boom had been identical to one of his old Critical Hit effects, but he no longer had that specialization. Granted, the duel didn't seem to be over since the crowds weren't accosting him. He still needed to do something about that. Were there any mental effects more potent than the anger they were deriving from the Taunt? Later, later.

He considered the crowd staying put as good a measuring stick as any. "Incursus? I know I asked for no damage prompts, but how hard did I just slap this chicken? There was an explosion, and I don't know where it came from."

The soothing clickety-clacks instantly filled the gap in music. Earth-toned screens with green text appeared and filtered information in line by line. Incursus had custom colors now? The custom colors were great! "Love the tree-theme with your prompts, Castles!"

K-chink!

K-chink was a new noise. Was it Incursus's new prompt sound? Artorian would find out the hard way, pulling the tree-themed prompt closer to give the damage information a quick gander. Something had gone wrong again, and given the battle music both sprang back into activity and was getting louder, he didn't have too long to run the numbers.

———

You have hit Achilles Agrippa, the Raging Rooster, with Unarmed Melee Strike.

Damage Type: Kinetic, Melee.

Impacts: 1.

Strength Damage: 1,600.

Physics Damage: Disabled.

Special: Voltekka's offensive trait, 'First Blood,' provides an automatic Critical Hit on the first successful damage dealt in combat.

Critical effect 1: Explode on Hit.

Critical effect 2: Double Damage.

Explosion Damage: 0.

Components affected by Explosion Damage: 10.

Total Explosion damage: 0.

Updated Total Damage: 3,200.

Enemy Weakness: Melee.

Weakness: A four times modifier in an unfavorable direction.

Updated Total Damage: 12,800.

Sneak Attack!

A Sneak Attack deals double damage, and is calculated independently from Critical Hits, and Weakness modifiers.

Attack of Opportunity!

Math unavailable.

Final Damage: 25,600.

Multiple errors detected.

Escalating errors.

————

Artorian dismissed the prompt as Agrippa burst from the hole like he'd taken off via trampoline. Landing on the stable edge of the exploded open hole, the chicken looked decidedly crispy at the edges. The mystery of the boom would wait… for about two seconds, as another prompt arrived so fast it slapped Artorian across the head.

Peeling the screen away, Artorian looked at it for a brief moment before needing to throw it away and engage in combat. He'd field test the new ability instead!

————

Ability gained!

Ability: Brilliant Behemoth.

Style: Risk of Rain.

Rank: Novice.

Cost: 1% Determination.

Activation: Once per Unarmed Melee Strike.

Range: Melee.

Effect: All the user's attacks create short-range, cone-shaped explosions, dealing damage equal to 50% of the player's Constitution attribute. This damage is considered Explosion damage, and will be tallied per body location struck.

————

Notice!

Due to a Pylon routing error, you have been assigned the ability Brilliant Behemoth.

The Critical Hit routing, which attempted to utilize a specialization that you currently do not have, has been discovered. The delayed explosion problem has been mitigated with the assignment of this ability. To recover original functions, please reinstate your prior specialization.

———

"Moonlight Spurs!" Agrippa struck first as the music commenced anew, a blade of Moonlight extending from the rooster's spurs before he leapt, spun, and struck! The chicken's voice was surprisingly melodic, fitting extremely well with the theme of the music. "Heavy Spear."

"Moonlight, you say?" Artorian leaned into the villainous role of Dreadshine once more. He looked the part. Cal wanted him to play the part. Maybe the idea to be a player character villain in Eternia, to make sure he wasn't one outside of Eternia, had merit. He could Flash Step away, but no. No, this was a duel! Duels required blades. Extending his armored arm, he enclosed his grip around empty space. "**Pride**."

The rainbow claymore formed into his closing grip, its multicolored properties extinguishing while adopting the shape of a broken blade. Artorian would meet mettle with mettle, the soft silver moonshine budding in Polly's hilt changing to a dark carmine. "Tsukiyomi Series. Excalibur Style. Mordred's Rise."

Rather than a serene silver blade of moonlight extending from the broken portion of the claymore, an ominous *pizouwww* resounded instead. The dark, carmine red claymore blade rose at speed with a blackened light trail as Agrippa moved in. Blocking both incoming silver spur-blades and fending them off with a feat of strength, Dreadshine stood his ground.

The act flung the rooster away with the same arm-swing that had blocked the rooster's dual spur blades. While the ground crackled below his armored feet, Dreadshine had not budged from his position.

Artorian hammed-up his performance, allowing Voltekka to have fun and modulate his voice further. The dino acting as equipment thought this was all fantastic, and was having a great time. The additional metallic growl in Dreadshine's voice became ever more menacing. "Is that all you've got?"

The villain lowered his blade. Then lifted his open hand to make 'come hither' motions at the surprised chicken, mocking what Artorian had determined to be one of the many students of the True Moonlight Rooster belonging to Master Jin of the Earth Vein.

The disrespect! The gall! The audacity!

Achilles Agrippa felt his fluff ruffle and feathers bristle. Such insolence! He would brook no such insult! Direct strikes had proven fruitless, jabs found no purchase, and he had been bested in strength. Agrippa had no choice. He would have to use the full arts of La Verdadera Destreza against this unworthy villain.

Agrippa glowed with faint silver as he leaned into the skillset. The technical hallmarks of the Destreza system were specific, and all began with the visualization of an imaginary circle between the opponents. To conceptualize distance and movement. The rooster had believed he would be able to skate by with his support skills, and had eschewed the main teachings.

No more!

The rooster would remember his lessons. The most important distinction between Destreza and other methods of fencing was the technique's approach to footwork. Linear footwork was to be eschewed. The Destreza doctrine taught that advancing directly on an opponent was a poor method. Instead, Destreza specialized in off-line footwork to either the right or left side, gaining a more favorable angle of attack before striking the killing blow.

Supplementing this style was the reminder that the cut could be as useful as the thrust depending on the situation. One should adapt their weapons accordingly. If blades found no success, then blades were not what Agrippa should be using.

The crux: remain out of the opponent's reach, while remaining within your own.

This would prove difficult with the Moonlight Spurs. They were thus abandoned as he enacted the lessons, and unknowingly taught them to his foe. Profile the body to increase reach and reduce target area. Advance from the side. Control the opposing weapon. All this was feasible. All Agrippa had to avoid was a carmine claymore on the villain's left side. A villain that had arrogantly chosen to stop dodging.

"Moonlight Armament." Agrippa lost the spur enhancements, but prepared for a new weapon. He surged through the sky via a swift set of side-to-side hops that were joined by short bursts of speed. To delude the opponent, and sneak within striking range while staying far away from that claymore. The rooster successfully breached melee range on the villain's unarmed right side, formed a javelin of moonlight silver in his beak, and struck while craning his neck so the tip would pierce at a downward angle. "Unconventional Javelin!"

"**Sorrow**." Unlike Polly, who had needed a moment to check some logs and make sure all was kosher before adopting the villain vibe and suggesting a thematic attack, **Sorrow**, as an ex-demon of the Garuda type, had no such qualms whatsoever. It was instantly happy and on board with the plan as the monstrous black katana formed in Dreadshine's main hand. **Sorrow** rubbed its metaphorical fingertips together, locked eyes on honey pie, and felt hungry for an easy indulgence. Pink flame that resisted the carmine call ran purely down the edge of **Sorrow**'s blade, rather than cause the usual full-on flare. The intelligent weapon was more than happy to reward the user for the use of this particular theme by not causing the usual drain, nor claiming the dues and costs.

As far as **Sorrow** was concerned, this was delicious, and it wanted more. **Sorrow**'s pink flames also caused Artorian's damage to count as both melee and fire, which the soon to be chunk of kebab was not going to like.

"Disappointing." Dreadshine was simply faster than Agrippa. That fact had nothing to do with technique, and everything with raw attributes as the downward swing from the armored villain cleanly separated the rooster's head from his body. All before the tip of the moonlight javelin plinked against Lucia's shield for a measly couple hundred damage.

Lenity took a scratch, and that was all.

Releasing the claymore and returning the weapon to his storage bracelet, Dreadshine turned with such finesse that he snatched Agrippa's severed head from the air. The rest of the rooster's burning body *pflunked* against the ground as Dreadshine earned his five second buff.

Artorian had his Nixie Tube moment.

He knew what kind of feeling overpowered anger, and held the head up to the crowd. Stricken with horror at the sight, Dreadshine once more hammed up the performance while letting his visor glow bloody and bright. The single stack of newly gained Menace infused him with the uncanny ability to apply the scariest version of diplomacy. "Are you not entertained?"

CHAPTER EIGHTEEN

The crowd was mortified. Silenced by menace and fear.

Artorian thought this just might work! Until a loud shimmer of flickering shield-light stole that hope away. The beheaded form sprang up, performing some incredible capoeira-esque movements. When Agrippa's body lurched up from the ground, the silver javelin vanished from Agrippa's beak and reappeared between his feet. Feet which had angled to kick the javelin up into Dreadshine's thigh.

Lenity took far more than a scratch. A painful four-thousand damage stabbed out of Lucia's well-applied protections. Artorian took no direct damage. While he gained another stack of Menace, he didn't understand why his opponent wasn't dead.

A quick stomp pinned the body of Achilles to the ground. That didn't appear to stop the writhing of the rooster's headless form, nor the angry glare he was shot from Agrippa's severed head. He was missing something. The music was still going, so there was clue number one staring him in the face again. "Inspect."

Scanning down the entries of Agrippa's character page, Artorian's eyes landed on the Vampire template. That template seemed to differ between different vampires, or at least wasn't properly consistent. El Mosco's version had been something of a shield flavored as armor before damage could be dealt. While with Agrippa, damage was dealt just fine.

The oddity? After slapping the cluck with over forty-thousand damage, the rooster still wasn't dead. Severing something's head should make it dead.

Hadn't one of the Dwarves explained this to him outside of the game? Kellen and McShane? The detail was that their weak point was the heart. Nothing else. Just the heart. If it had the vampire tag, throw the usual conditions and weaknesses out the window. Given how his damage tally prompt had treated the weaknesses as if they very much did matter, and that El Mosco had been El Killed several times already, maybe the crux of the matter was to damage the weak spot before they would die? The lore from the Dwarves could be out of date.

Solution? Brianna's favorite. Stab.

Before his stacks of Menace expired, Dreadshine flipped the black katana upside down. With a brutal stab, the flaming pink edge cut right through the wing shield that Agrippa hurriedly tried to put up. **Sorrow** ignored the shield, and sliced deep into the rooster's heart. An act that made the katana very happy.

Artorian could hear **Sorrow** giggle as the mind in the blade clapped its hands together, wiping an imagined tear away out of sheer pride. Seeing a hero turn villainous was just so beautiful. The li'l ones growing up was always such a touching event.

Purely to show its appreciation, **Sorrow** added its Wintercourt flower-lei around Dreadshine's neck. The colors clashed, with Dreadshine's armor being all ominous black and imposing red, while the lei's flowers were a very frosty set of blues. **Sorrow** didn't care about such minor details right now. Graduation presents were a must!

The katana, overly helpful, reminded Artorian with pure

feeling that the Freedom of Mind Skill boosted speech. He should use it with his stacks of Menace!

Artorian was uncertain how to feel about **Sorrow** having this much autonomy, and a personal inventory. He put the blade's actions on the backburner and held up Agrippa's severed head like a skull of Yorick. It was performance time.

Crushing the rooster's skull in his grip now that the creature should hopefully be killable, Dreadshine's carmine faceplate curled into a wicked smile. The vampiric chicken released its death throes upon losing its singular condition-protected hit point, and turned to ashen dust.

Dreadshine then turned to the crowd, both arms raised palms up as he returned **Sorrow** and the lei to the bracelet, taking the advice to apply the speech boost from the referenced skill.

Dark and ominous, the villain repeated himself. "Are you not entertained?"

Pained silence was his answer as he paced the arena, his upturned palms making continuous 'come at me' motions to anyone willing to jump down and face him. "Will no others respond to my Taunting? Are you all… too chicken?"

Pained silence continued as the crowd looked cowed. Seas of chickens that would have assailed him purely from the Taunt effect instead remained rooted to their seats. Geese and other fowl appeared on the edge of deciding whether the twisted furl in their feathers was worth the engagement. Geese cared nothing for fear, but they were far from their roosts, and there was nothing to be gained here. They'd merely get killed.

The villain knew the vampire secret.

As far as the crowd was concerned, that downward stab into Agrippa's heart had done far more damage to them than it had to Agrippa. Agrippa wouldn't agree, but Agrippa was dead for now, and didn't get much of an opinion. The accuracy of the strike. The knowledge that this was the way. The cold, emotionless, mechanical precision of the response.

No. Even the geese decided that today was not the day.

Dreadshine dropped his arms, turning to leave the arena in the same direction that Lucia had bolted, seemingly disappointed by the crowd's cowed response. "Pity."

K-chink!

Artorian accepted the screen from Incursus as the prompt came in with its pleasant green text. Another damage prompt? Another damage prompt. He would need to tell the turtle that his request had been more of a one-off, but he wasn't going to begrudge the turtle for wanting to help. "How hard did we hit?"

———

You have hit Achilles Agrippa, the Raging Rooster, with **Sorrow**.
Damage Type: Kinetic, Melee, Fire.
Impacts: 1.
Strength Damage: 1,600.
Physics Damage: Disabled.
Sorrow Damage: 800.
Updated Total Damage: 2,400.
Enemy Weakness: Melee, Fire.
Weakness: A four times modifier in an unfavorable direction.
Weakness is applied twice for a times 8 modifier.
Final Damage: 19,200.

———

Artorian was a little confused on why he got that prompt twice. The contents were identical. "Ah, once for the decapitation, and then again for the heart-stab. That makes sense. All this together... I slapped Agrippa for exactly sixty-four-thousand damage total? That's a lot of damage. That can't be right. Doing such heaps is convenient for me, but I'm not certain that it will lead to good gameplay experiences for others. That resistance and weakness multiplier needs to be toned down. I'm happy to zip through the game, but if this needs to be done in groups, then a bit more struggle would be appropriate. Something has to give for the sake of balance. I doubled my damage from a crit, a sneak attack, and then a whole heap from the weakness calculation. Maybe the lesser versions need to be more common? These are big deeps."

The confirmation chime from his prompt controller played, prompting Artorian to nod as he crossed the threshold out of the arena, happily not accosted by the Taunted sea of chickens behind him. Other things might still be after him, but the visible threat was resolved! "Tekka, armor off. Save that power source for the next bout."

Reverting to the size of a teenager, the seamless plate armor turned to particulate. All of which was absorbed directly into Artorian's sternum. He squeezed his brooch as he fell into a jog, squinting as he began to run out of light. "All done on my end! I need some light source ideas. Lucia, I'm heading to you via floor prints. Did you find Ember?"

The explosive, burning cascade of Abyss-fire going off on the other end of his communicator confirmed that before Lucia put the truth into words. "Sure did, kit! She can't distinguish friend from foe anymore, and we have been running *away* from her since finding her. Don't follow my tracks, go straight down. Just go down! There's a bottom level to this place. According to your new cheesy friend Poirot that has decided to tag along with us, we know Decorum is down there as well. He's done most of the work for us."

Artorian had to skid to a halt when the darkness became too much. "That's great, Momma Bun! Also, your shield saved my bacon, but I can't see. Cleaning Presence is keeping my environment spotless and safe, but that won't help me if I slam into a wall. Ideas?"

Zephyr came to his rescue, speaking through Lucia's brooch. "Do you have any equipment or attacks that make light? Doesn't need to be constant light!"

Artorian threw up his character page, the minor light barely enough to see that he was in a tunnel. He still didn't want to use the game prompts for illumination, but at least he had the option in the pocket. Didn't **Sorrow** emit pink fire? On that note, didn't **Pride** do the same with moonlight? "My friends make light! Zephyr, you're a genius! I'll meet you all at the bottom. I don't know how I'm getting down there yet, but I'll be there. Cleaning Presence should help clear up some of Ember's addled state, and then Lucia can slap her with a Veracity."

Laughter erupted from his brooch, which he was happy to hear before closing the connection. Artorian called his guardian torches. "**Sorrow, Pride, Compassion, Explosion**. I need light!"

The four unique weapons surged forth from his bracelet and hovered around him like excited wolves, each flaring their power to provide a reddish hue of light in their own special way. Save for **Compassion**, as the Albion Principe was wholly confused on the carmine thematic. The geometrically perfect blade stopped in place, then turned to Artorian as if to say, 'What the Abyss? What's all this? Why all the villainy? This is not how we do it, old man!'

Artorian, quick to agree, fixed that right away. "Effect Cosmetics. Trans Am."

All the carmine red and onyx black colors clicked over to the new theme with the tug of a lever, allowing snow white and celestine blue colors to overtake the prior options. **Compassion** was far happier with this, but **Sorrow** paused in place to pout. Artorian could feel the katana's disappointment and outburst of 'Awwww…'

Pride and **Explosion** both seemed undeterred, happy to play torch while hovering in a circle around one of their favorite people. **Sorrow** and **Compassion** glared at each other, both of them choosing to battle it out by seeing who could provide more luminance. **Sorrow** flared his flames as much as he could without a user to sap emotions from, their coloration unpleasantly white. **Compassion** did the same as their musical staff did its best to glow blue.

Pride easily outperformed both of them, Polly puffing their metaphorical chest out while all set to lead the way. Artorian could feel **Explosion** laugh in the cadence of a Dwarven grandmother, and instantly got emotional as he got his hopes up. He didn't want to ask. Being wrong would hurt so much. Being right would make him break down and cry in place. Asking had to wait.

He inhaled firmly, steeled himself, and broke into a jog as the blades all surged into formation around him. Their combined glow provided him with illumination equivalent to a fresh daybreak.

T'was enough!

Zipping through underground gothic architecture, Artorian had the chance to see many of the sights entirely unaccosted. Ignoring the construction material, of course. Cathedrals were once again popular in design, as were catacombs. He ran past fake ceilings that pretended they were a sky, graveyards, twisted temples, and places with odd names that he didn't know what to do with. There was a floor dedicated to a dilapidated ancestral hamlet, a cove floor, and a ruins floor.

Those were easy.

Then there was a big arena for a boss fight that seemed to have been roasted before his appearance. Artorian saw some burnt popcorn, but no sign of what the boss could have been.

Zipping along, the arena was followed by a weald floor, which was a word that he did not know the meaning of. The warren floor made sense when he figured out that it was for swine and swindling rather than rabbits, given that all of the item drops appeared to be cured bacon.

He made certain to abscond with some.

Then there was a whole section of nothing but fancy court-yards, a farmstead, some broken circus bits, and finally, a floor that appeared dedicated to a single road. Or, at least, that was where he got stuck.

The road floor didn't make sense, but it didn't need to make sense. The important bit was that, much like the prior floors, there were certainly more and more ways to go down!

During this trek, he'd even seen the aftermath of a scorched earth policy. The telltale sign that Ember had been by, which made choosing the right way down all the easier. He was certain that he was catching up to Lucia as the sounds of heat-based explosions could be heard in the distance, and felt via hot gusts of wind. The smell of fire coming out of the ground had become so thick that it was getting through his Cleaning Aura.

Which was also a good sign. Sort of.

Good that he was going the right way, bad that the smell was so strong; his tools weren't handling the effect properly.

"I need more speed." Artorian said the words without much thought when no pathways leading down showed up, but he agreed with his own statement. A Nixie Tube flickered to life above his head, followed by a scheming smile. "I did say that I was going to field test Brilliant Behemoth, and I do recall something about effects that come out of my hands also being able to come from my feet. Time to see if it was the socks!"

Leaping in the air while on the dungeon floor dedicated to the lone road that didn't appear to end, he gave the ability a whirl. "Brilliant Behemoth!"

K-thoom!

His next footfall planted as any other, then exploded from the ground with force as he propelled himself forward using the might of the great boom. Instant success! Artorian loved it! Once again, he had braved the skies and found a way to go vertical. T'was inevitable! "Yippee! Again!"

K-thoom!

Leaping rather than running, Artorian laughed as he loved that this worked. Each boom-step no longer gained a benefit from his Hypermobility skill, but *eh*! With Brilliant Behemoth serving as propulsion, he also wasn't trying not to damage the ground in the first place. He sang out his jubilation. "I missed intent-based goodies! I missed them so much! This is my toast. This is my jaaaaam."

Each footfall was joined by a delightful boom, as Artorian copied what Zephyr had called wub-step. "I step on the wubs!"

K-chink!

Artorian opened the prompt from Incursus right away when the missive rolled in. He was in a great mood as he made progress to several objectives all at once. "Talk to me, terrific turtle!"

―――――

Would you like to learn the skill Wub-Step?

―――――

"Absolutely!" Artorian smashed accept, and his explosive steps turned melodious. His running gait was accompanied not by a bang, but by the consistent deep thump of, *nn-tss, nn-ts, nn-ts*. Artorian adored the improvement, making word-noises along with his speedy run that matched the home-made music. "Yeah! Boots and cats and boots and cats and boots and cats."

K-chink!

―――――

Skill gained!

Skill: Wub-Step.

Rank: Novice.

Effect: Wub-Step allows the user to step on soundwaves, and use them as a valid source of footing. These Wubs can come from music, explosions, enthusiastic vocals, or instruments. If it makes a soundwave, you can step on it. How much force you can apply to the sound waves for propulsion depends upon the rank of this skill.

―――――

Outstanding! "Excellent! I like Wub-Step. I like it a lot."

K-chink!

Artorian opened the next prompt right away.

There is more. Would you like more?

Artorian was in the right mood for skill gains, very much entertained.

"Absolutely! Gimme!"

CHAPTER NINETEEN

K-chink!

———

Notice!
    Brilliant Behemoth has improved from Novice to Beginner.
    Would you like to customize Brilliant Behemoth's improvement now?

———

Artorian saw no reason to wait.

All he was actually waiting for was a piece of specific landscape. The next waypoint or marker that signified that he could go down to the next floor. With the ground shaking now and again from one of Ember's attacks, he knew he was close to the bottom. Otherwise, those tremors would have moved farther away by now. His Taunting was still active, but either all the enemies were dead, or the story of the scary villain was overpowering the need to come accost and bother him. The villain tactic likely only worked for what was behind him. That put his money on either Decorum or Ember having torn through the lower dungeon populaces.

Either way, win! "Yes! Gimme!"

Before the prompt could populate, **Explosion,** the Assault Nagamaki, surged ahead of him. Speaking with flashes and pops of nitroglycerin, Artorian laughed as he didn't speak boom-boom fluently. The mental nudge on the other hand, was far easier. "You want to add your input on how to improve Brilliant Behemoth? Of course! Have at it!"

The Nagamaki twirled in delight, the text of Brilliant Behemoth updating without Artorian's input.

K-chink!

———

Notice!

> *Brilliant Behemoth has been improved to the Beginner rank.*
> *Improvement choice: Activation condition simplification.*
> *Populating results.*

———

Ability: Brilliant Behemoth.
> *Style: Risk of Rain.*
> *Rank: Beginner.*
> *Cost: 1% Determination.*
> *Activation: Once per strike.*
> *Range: Melee.*
> *Effect: All the user's attacks create short-ranged, cone-shaped explosions, dealing damage equal to 50% of the player's Constitution attribute. This damage is considered Explosion damage, and will be tallied per body location struck.*

———

"*Oooh*, I see!" Artorian was a happy camper with this level up. "Now this ability can be used when I swing or throw weapons. Thank you, Grandmama!"

His stomach twisted when he realized what he'd said.

He didn't want to know.

To be proven wrong would be devastating.

K-chink!

———

Artorian had no control over the prompt that opened right next to him. He likely would have closed it instantly due to how he was feeling, if the prompt wasn't bright pink and glowing. While *k-chink* was certainly Incursus's new prompt noise, the contents were not his. Or not solely his?

The information within did not clickety-clack or filter in slow like the other prompts. Rather, the prompt was filled with simple black text that outlined the weapon's game-based entry.

An entry that was changing, as the Nagamaki learned more about itself when a sympathy connection locked into place. Artorian felt his heart drop and live in his stomach until the text of the weapon's material rolled over and updated.

He grit his teeth, and bit back the tears.

———

Name: Explosion.
  Shape: Nagamaki.
  Prefix: Assault.
  Suffix: Returning.
  Full Name: Explosion, Assault Nagamaki of Returning.
  Material: Soul of Ephira Mayev Stonequeen.
  Rarity: Legendary.
  Damage Type: Kinetic, Melee. Explosive.
  Damage: 50 – 500 Kinetic.

Special Quality: El Kabum. Nitroglycerin (boon). Nitroglycerin (bane).

Explosion is an incomplete concept weapon in the shape of a cavalry-slaying Nagamaki. Made from the recovered soul of Ephira Mayev Stonequeen, a beloved Dwarven leader from the Old World known as Grandmama. As a living weapon, Explosion can choose whether its wielder is immune to its effects.

The Assault prefix doubles this weapon's original base damage of 25– 250, but eliminates this weapon's ability to block, or use any protective maneuvers.

The Returning suffix allows this weapon to be recalled to the hand of whoever the weapon so chooses.

The Nitroglycerin (boon) special quality passively helps the wielder deal with high-stress situations. This boon relaxes the blood vessels and increases the supply of blood and oxygen to the heart while reducing its workload.

The Nitroglycerin (bane) special quality causes all kinetic damage dealt by this weapon to be dealt again as explosion damage.

The El Kabum special quality causes a colossal explosion that turns all numerical damage dealt into physics damage. This feature can only be used once per week, and multiplies the base damage before the conversion calculation by one-hundred.

Note: While this weapon is immune to physics damage, the user is not. This weapon is able to detonate El Kabum anytime it wants, so long as the special quality is off cooldown.

Try not to get on Explosion's bad side? You'll end up over there, over there, over there, some bits over yonder. You understand.

———

System Note: All Legendary weapons, including rarities above, are living weapons of some variety from the moment that there is a mind present. All living weapons are granted Autonomy of Movement and Costless Wisp Flight.

———

Inner turmoil struck him. Unlike with the other three flying swords, the mind within the Nagamaki was woefully incomplete. Artorian knew intrinsically when the blade became introspective, and felt familiarity to the listed name. Yet the Nagamaki clearly did not know who Ephira was. Except that it liked the name.

Artorian needed memories.

Memories of Mayev.

What he knew of Grandmama, and how he knew her, was utterly inadequate for his sudden need and drive to mend this situation. Inhaling sharply, he felt his muscles tense. The Determination metric on his character sheet caught white flame.

He knew where to get memories of Mayev.

"No more waiting." They were with the sister she had been with for several years. The same sister who currently couldn't tell friend from foe. "We're going down. We're going down, right now."

He extended his hand for the Nagamaki, knowing how he was going to accomplish this feat. If there was no convenient hole in the floor? They would *make* a convenient hole in the floor. "Ephira!"

The Nagamaki snapped into his open hand like the hilt lived there, home with family. Artorian instantly added to the creativity as he used the Brilliant Behemoth explosions to spiral-run up into the air. Wub-Step kept him going and brought him higher and higher without losing pace, until he was at the ceiling and could go higher no more.

Once there, he spun in place, and aimed his throw straight down. Artorian's form grew and bulked with muscle as the motions of the throw were performed. Barely keeping up with Artorian's visualization of the self as the game attempted to adapt, he was, for just a moment, the muscle grandpa from the alpha run. A glorious beard spilled forth, his form ablaze with Determination's white flame. He roared as Voltekka, and threw the weapon like a spear from Odin.

A moment of poetry struck him. "As rods of Iridium drop from the high heavens, so I do send thee. El Kabum!"

The non-Euclidean space of the road floor—meant to keep its occupants trapped, regardless of which cardinal or ordinal direction they traveled—shattered outright. The entire floor was backhanded completely out of existence. The grand explosion ripped all the clever runic script straight out of the walls and ground, destroying the encoding outright as the ceiling of the bottom-most floor went up with a glorious *ka-bang*, and a depth-crushing wave of pressure that plastered everyone to a ceiling, floor, or wall.

The physics damage eliminated all the happy numbers in Lucia's Lenity shield instantly. The indiscriminate boom glued him to the ceiling, and took a big bite out of his actual health bar. Artorian could not bring himself to care for the harm, his mind focused, and objective clear.

Once released from the pressure wave keeping him glued against the ceiling, he verbally recalled Ephira while the other three weapons flew back to him on their own volition. Artorian lost his muscle Grandpa means, but hadn't noticed he'd gained them in the first place. Once more sporting the physique and shape of his prior Teen-torian self, he fell into action.

With the brand-new gaping hole in the floor, Artorian quickly had eyes on Ember. As the brightest flame and light source one floor down, she was easy to spot. Decorum and Tisha were nowhere to be seen, but he did find Lucia, Zephyr, and... the bards? How had the troublemakers made it down here? Never mind. He found them in a corner, all tucked away safe and sound in one of Lucia's protective barriers. The Glitterflit herself had a burned cotton ball tail, but otherwise appeared unharmed. Exhausted from running, but otherwise unharmed.

Ember appeared to have been fighting something, but that something was now extraordinarily dead after taking the combined force of a diamond uppercut from below, and an El

Kabum from above. Whatever had been between those two forces was now particulates.

Of note, Ember was the only person and creature present in the floor below still solidly on her feet. El Kabum had turned everyone else into a plastered sploot, shield or not. Artorian thought that was notable. "Why is the girl I love so incredibly scary? I am not a masochist."

Ember's face turned up to spot him when he spoke. The green spores hanging around her, and the alteration of her eyes to match that color, gave away that she was not herself. What could have also given it away was that she was in his face a mere second after.

Her fists swinging for the fences.

Or his face. Which she hit with an unarmed strike.

For six-thousand something damage. *Yeowch!*

Artorian smashed into the far wall, and had to instantly put effort into recovering and using explosion-sourced Wub-Steps to get out of Dodge, because Ember was right on him a mere half-second later again. Her attributes far eclipsed his, and he knew exactly what that fight was like when performed from the other end. "Voltekka!"

Voltekka morphed over Artorian in a hurry, who was wall-running while conjuring his win condition. He was never, ever, ever, going to win against Ember in anything that resembled a straight up fight. Maximum grandpa cleverness was a go! Let loose the cheese-wolves of war! Shenanigans were knocking at the door.

At least he was in the right place to be ridiculous.

He pressed his fingers against his armored neck, compressing the brooch. "Poirot! I am sorry about your dungeon. Chunks are going to go missing!"

The Cheese Elemental laughed through Lucia's brooch. Thinking that comment was hilarious, since Sunshine said it after the devastation was already here and ongoing. "Ce n'est pas mon donjon! This is not my dungeon, but I will tell the big cheese."

Artorian considered that checkmark applied, and his bases to be covered as he moved onto practical solutions. "Lucia! Shield me when you can! I'm going to steal the tactics my prior opponent should have put more focus into using, and not cut corners. I'ma try to keep Emby close enough to keep her within my Aura radius, but not close enough to get me Le Killed. Lantern me!"

"On it!" Lucia's swift response through the brooch brought him incredible comfort. Unlike the fists and feet of fury breaking holes into his surroundings. Ember was expertly destroying the gothic architecture walls as he was chased down like a thief in the night by a person-shaped volcano. "Lantern on its way! Bad news update! Aura's a great call, but it's also all you've got for the distance game. I will never get close enough to paw on a Veracity, and she already wrecked her Lantern. Astarte will flash-fry me into a bun-flambé. I can hunker with the crew, but that's all I can do until we get that Lantern to you."

"*Joy!*" Sunshine oozed sarcasm before needing to focus when the environment lit up ever more and got scorching hot. How had she seen him so fast? Why was there a white mane of white flame all over him? "Well, blackest night just turned into brightest day. Let's play!"

His weapons did their best to float near him, but even they had to dodge Ember's raging rampage as she laughed loud and held back not one matchbox worth of fire. If more fire could do, then more fire would do! On the plus side, the Pyroclasm that freely flowed out of Ember as she hurled ability after ability at him provided a plethora of illumination! "This place is going to be renamed to the Kiln Dungeon at this rate."

His rear was hot, hot, hot! But at least he could see. "I need defenses! Incursus! Show me the prompts of the three other swords! Maybe one of them has something! That twenty percent damage mitigation from Tekka is only going to go so far, and why is my Loved by Mana trait not working? I'm getting roasted!"

K-chink!
K-chink!

Incursus had Artorian's shell and played him some confirmation chimes.

Turtle power and help was incoming!

CHAPTER TWENTY

K-chink!

———

Name: Sorrow.

Shape: Katana.

Material: Soul of Urcan.

Rarity: Legendary.

Damage Type: Kinetic. Melee. Fire. Mental.

Damage: The average of the user's Wisdom and Dexterity attributes, split between the mundane and magical damage types.

Current Damage: 800.

Specified Damage: 400 Kinetic. 400 Fire.

Special Quality: Sorrow.

Sorrow is a concept weapon in the shape of a man-slaying katana, made from the Soul of Urcan, a Savant-class Garuda-type Demon from the Old World. As a living weapon, Sorrow can choose whether its wielder is immune to its effects.

This weapon represents the physical manifestation of Sorrow. This katana alights with pink flames that eat away its wielder's emotions, visual-

izing the feeling of deep distress that originates from the loss of something precious, dear, or loved. Sorrow can create greater amounts of flame, determined by how much the wielder loves others, sapping away an equivalent amount of emotional energy in doing so. This action turns the wielder's appearance grayscale, leaving the wielder's decision-making process entirely reliant on cold, hard, logic.

Touching, wielding, or being struck by this weapon afflicts the recipient with a stack of Sorrow that lasts for one minute. This effect makes the recipient feel sorrowful for the duration of the stack, drastically reducing their willpower, drive, and combat capability.

The Sorrow special quality occurs on hit, and ignores all armor, shields, and magical protections that the blade comes into contact with. Damage from this weapon is not subject to damage reduction or mitigation of any kind. This effect supersedes other effects that would directly contradict this special quality.

This weapon can be parried or deflected, but not blocked.

———

Sorrow had changed since he'd last seen the entry! Notably, the rarity was now set to Legendary instead of Dani. Was that an improvement, or a downgrade? Artorian was never going to ask. Playing evade-the-apocalypse, he determined Sorrow was not the right play here, and moved on to the next prompt as Incursus worked hard on the clickety-clacks.

K-chink!

———

Name: Compassion.
  Shape: Albion Principe.
  Material: The concept of suffering.
  Rarity: Legendary.
  Damage Type: Kinetic. Melee. Sound. Mental.
  Damage: Charisma attribute.
  Current Damage: 200.

Special Quality: Compassion, Paladin's Righteous Smite, Zither.

Compassion is a concept weapon in the shape of an Albion Principe, made from conceptual energy stemming from the emotional plane. As a living weapon, Compassion can choose whether its wielder is immune to its effects.

This weapon represents the physical manifestation of the feeling that arises when one is confronted by another's suffering, and feels motivated to relieve that suffering. While compassion literally means 'to suffer together,' it is the actions taken to relieve another's suffering that define compassion.

Touching, wielding, or being struck by this weapon afflicts the recipient with a stack of Compassion that lasts for one minute. This effect instantly obliviates any recipient that is anathema to the concept of compassion, such as Old World Demons.

Non-anathema recipients will instead take Mental-Stun and Mental-Shock damage equivalent to their lack of compassion, which affects selfish, self-centered, and narcissistic minds with substantially increased effect. Minds who value the wellbeing of others, over that of themselves, will receive this weapon's special qualities instead.

The Compassion special quality applies a stack of Bolstering for the duration that this weapon is held. Bolstering acts as a deterrent against an ongoing negative effect, diminishing or negating that negative effect for the duration of the stack.

The Paladin's Righteous Smite special quality causes this weapon to deal double damage against the selfish, self-centered, and narcissistic. Those who care not for others shall know the wrath of Compassion.

The Zither special effect is controlled entirely by the weapon. As a true concept weapon, Compassion is able to do far more than ordinary weapons without needing the use of Weapon Ignition. Fully sentient and sapient, Compassion is able to play the zither according to the musical notation listed on its staff, which it can shape and alter freely. The more the weapon plays music and dances around you, the more Compassion likes you.

While the Zither music plays, Compassion deals double damage.

Striking an enemy in tune to the music of Compassion's Zither triples damage instead.

Note: Weapon Ignition will cause a unique interaction.

Unlike with other weapons, where their latent and hidden abilities are unlocked, Compassion will instead undergo humanization. Once this occurs, please refer to Compassion as a She rather than an It. This individual's personality will consist of her special qualities, which still have room to grow.

———

That was a big one! Artorian would have to reread that hunk of a description later, but he'd gotten the gist of it. He successfully ducked out of the way of the literal armory that Ember was unloading in his direction. Mostly.

Skipping a step and falling, a hail of Damocles arrows trimmed his hair. Impromptu visit to the fire-barber aside, he still didn't have the means to do a whole lot. Compassion was great, but no good against a laughing, manic, having-the-time-of-her-life Astarte. If he had to close the distance and enter melee range, that might as well be handing her the win. Artorian was a jester in that arena, and Astarte was the entire royal court. "More! Incursus, I need more!"

Incursus shadow-boxed and took some quick breaths, instantly diving back into the system.

K-chink!

———

Name: Pride.

    Shape: Claymore.

    *Material: Polly, a Parrot bound to the Law of **Pride**.*

    Rarity: Legendary.

    Damage Type: Kinetic, Melee, Radiance.

    Damage: Double the user's Intelligence Attribute.

    Current Damage: 400.

    Special Quality: Moonlight Greatsword. Complete Rainbow. Tsukiyomi Series Moves. Ex-Calibur Style. Aura Blade. White Light Majesty.

    Pride is an incomplete concept weapon in the shape of a broken clay-

more, made from Polly, a Parrot. As a living weapon, Polly can choose whether its wielder is immune to its effects.

This representation of **Pride** *as a concept is modified by Polly's interpretation of the concept. While* **Pride** *encompasses more than what this weapon mirrors, Polly is focused on the punishment of excess pride, and the balance of having just enough. While Polly is able to instill* **Pride**, *they have opted to eschew the mental damage type and tag.*

Polly has opted to use Intelligence as its damage modifier, for the reasoning, "The more one understands about **Pride**, *and how it is affecting themselves or others, the more potent I shall be."*

The Moonlight Greatsword special quality is a passive, thematic power boost. As a broken claymore, Polly begins combat incomplete. If exposed to moonlight, or light that is reflected from anything with the orbital body moon tag, then Polly instead begins combat as a Moonlight Greatsword, counted as its base form. As a Moonlight Greatsword, Polly's damage is improved by a step to triple, rather than double, the user's Intelligence attribute.

The Complete Rainbow special quality is Pride's first upgrade level. When held, Polly can be provided a constant source of energy to mend its broken form, adopting the full breadth of a claymore's acumen with spectacular rainbow colorations. In addition to being fashionable, this improves Polly's damage multiplier by a step, similar to that of the Moonlight Greatsword.

If both Moonlight Greatsword and Complete Rainbow are active, Polly will become a Rainbow Greatsword, dealing five times the user's Intelligence attribute as damage.

The Tsukiyomi Series Moves special quality provides the wielder a unique set of combat maneuvers that may be used freely so long as Pride is held. Including: Lakelight Legend. Fallen Pride. Mystic Lake. Mordred's Rise.

The Ex-Calibur Style special quality provides the wielder a unique fighting style meant for two-handed weapons. During the use of this style, the blade can act as a shield until it is time to strike with great conviction. While you use Pride as a shield, you may use this weapon's static damage value as block. During the use of this style, you will have access to all your shield, tower shield, offensive defense, and walking wall maneuvers.

The Aura Blade special quality allows the wielder to directly pour mana into Pride, creating a silvered blade of light that grows larger and longer as more and more energy is invested into the blade. This energy will be expended when Pride is swung, but will deal additional damage based on the new size of the weapon.

The White Light Majesty special quality is unique to this weapon, and can only be activated by the weapon itself. When engaged in combat to strike down one with excessive pride, the White Light Majesty musical score will play, providing an end-of-formula damage doubler to Pride's Intelligence attribute base calculation. Meaning that if Polly is in Rainbow Greatsword mode, you will be dealing ten times your Intelligence attribute as damage, rather than the listed five times.

———

Incursus turtle-high-fived his help, and finally got to the last piece of the requested information that Sunshine had asked for.

Artorian had not provided any commentary to Polly's entry, but he had instantly called the claymore close, and was using the large silver blade as a mobile tower shield.

K-chink!

———

Information: Astarte, Goddess of War, uses the heat energy metric, not the mana energy metric. Her heat gauge begins fully loaded, and is expended as she uses abilities. Her energy regeneration method occurs via a calculation based on her Charisma and Constitution attributes. You may wish to run faster.

———

Artorian Flash-Stepped and dive-bomb-dodged out of the way of Astarte's cluster grenades, as she'd gotten wise to the silver sword-shield in her way far too quickly. The well-over one-hundred and change hovering super-caltrops that doubled as mines did not exist on his planned itinerary, so he had to Wub-Step through the field pretty darn carefully.

Duck and weave, duck and weave! "Run faster? No celestial feces joke! I don't even have time to look behind me to see if she's in range. When do my Auras improve in rank? That's been active non-stop!"

Incursus observed the sky-splosions from the world below, his balcony position one of great comfort. He could look up and see Artorian saving his own bacon by a mere hair every single time that Ember threw out another haymaker. Or a fire-whirl-wind filled with contact-grenades. Or a named ability that Sunshine had to chain Flash-Step away from.

He considered it an impressive feat to survive that endless downpour, but the key appeared to be to keep moving. Lucia had skated by with speed, shields, and all the cover that was now mostly rubble. Artorian had to do the same thing mid-air, through a questionable application of physics, without shields.

Go, Sunshine, go!

When Artorian mentioned the Aura, Incursus thought that odd. Those should have gone ding by now. He nudged the Pylons with a foot, and instantly got feedback that Cleaning Presence was at the Apprentice rank already. Some reference Pylons must have not gotten the memo, because he had gotten no memo.

K-chink!

———

Cleaning Presence improvements available: Two.
Improvement direction requested.

———

"Range!" Artorian learned the hard way that the remaining cover was a joke. Astarte's 'Longinus' charged lances pierced right through dungeon walls, 'Apollo' accretion arrows did area of effect damage, and the 'Ramsey' volcanic self-proliferating great-axes julienned any and all cheese they passed through. What was that thing she said about people surviving her for ten minutes? Abyss that! He would rather fight ten Halcyons for a fifth specialization over one Astarte. She wasn't even using equipment anymore! "Everything in range, Incursus, because I am in her range and she is not in mine!"

Incursus snapped to it, upgrading the Aura to measure in radius instead of diameter as the first slotted improvement. For the second improvement, the dungeon bumped the measurement metric up from one meter to two meters. Easy and quick. He fired the update off to Artorian so Sunshine could use the better tool, and succeed where Agrippa had failed.

K-chink!

———

Aura: Cleaning Presence.
    Rank: Apprentice.
    Special Qualities: Aura, Clean.
    Shape: Orb.
    Description: A field emitting a constant cleaning effect, centered on the user.
    Output: Two meters in radius of cleaning effect per percentage of maximum energy bar invested.
    Note: You may only have one Aura type effect active at any given time.

———

"Got it!" Artorian felt the improvement rather than needing to read it, because the accursed Aura turned off when the update hit him. Reinvesting his entire Determination bar, he chanced a look over his shoulder. The wild animal chasing him was playing with her food, but thanks to the improvement to his Aura, Ember was now in range!

A great thing to discover.

Unlike the discovery of pain when a charged lance went through his left foot and threw off his entire running cadence, trashing his in-progress escape plan. A loss that allowed for all the other burninating death already pointing his way to unpleasantly become far more on target. "Lucia!"

"Won't make it!" The words spoken through his brooch weren't initially understood when Momma Bun threw them at him. He could see the Lantern that would allow Lucia to put a shield on him from long-range hurry over to him, but the Lantern had barely crossed half the needed distance. "Dodge!"

To dodge, unfortunately, was no longer in the cards. There was no way that he was surviving a second lance to the anything, but that was a secondary problem. That single charged lance still accosting his foot had stabbed him for a little over ten-thousand damage, before Voltekka knocked twenty percent off.

Followed by a bonus eight-hundred against the physical damage of the stab thanks to the armor's inclusion of Iridium, and another eight-hundred against the fire damage of that same stab thanks to the Silverwood. The Mithril in his armor, on the other hand, had that pesky weakness named Ragdoll. That weakness, when struck, pulled Sunshine along with the physics of the lance as it yeeted him off course.

Much like a chicken from earlier, that got him solidly pinned against the wall.

In no mood to choose between being consumed by the already moving Casu Marzu, or taking a full pyroclastic arsenal to the face, Artorian was left with scant choices. He could gamble on **Pride** pulling him through with block, gamble on Archimedes Flash-Stepping him out of the pin without that doing more damage, or do something truly stupid.

Had there ever been another choice when that third option appeared on the table? Surely, the people watching this spectacle unfold already knew what he'd choose. Artorian thus fed them what their hearts desired, and said the first of many magic words as he stared down the incoming rain of arrows and assorted weaponry that blotted out the sun that was Astarte.

A risk of rain indeed.

Narrowing his eyes, Artorian made the observing crowds cheer. "Cowabunga."

CHAPTER TWENTY-ONE

"Effect Shaping, Voltekker!" Artorian ignored the mouse-scream that came from his environment, but he had probably given Vanaheim some kind of trauma related to the word. Unsure just how compact he was going to get a ten percent fueled Voltekker, nor certain if it would annihilate the self-proliferating axes being hurled his way, he accepted the madness and let rip. "Wall!"

Sunshine's armored shoulders opened to roar out the copper and hunter-green colored damage, Voltekka delighting in the use of his creation. Unfortunately, Voltekka did not understand that this particular use of Voltekker was not meant to drain the armor's entire energy supply. The dino was happy to dump the category damage modifier into the ten percent attempt!

Who needed protection against a rogue fire soul? Clearly not Artorian. What even was damage mitigation? Didn't need it. Throw it to the wind!

The good news: rather than a country-spanning conical blast, Sunshine did get his wall. T'was a nice wall. Beautiful corners. Lush green glow. Pleasant copper edges. Girth. Everything that one might want from a wall.

The bad news: the wall was not small, and wasn't fooling Artorian. "That's a cube!"

The effect-shaped Voltekker did swallow up the weapon stockpile hurled at Artorian, but it also swallowed up his allies, the general environment, and got a smidge too close to Vanaheim's sensitive bits for Brother Moon's liking. Half an inch wasn't a lot of distance, but to Brother Moon, who was paranoia-laughing in the highest of pitches? Half an inch of grace had him *hoooo'ing* in a goofy, nervous sing-song tune.

Any more scares like that and Brother Moon would find religion. Or make one? Something related to the girding of loins, and the grace of surviving close calls. The church of cheesus, perhaps? It was a gouda start. Alternatively, accepting the premade one by the Pylon Rats could be brie-lliant. He already had a Holy Cow, and had stolen all the relevant bovine statues and artistic bits from the Niflheim Realm. Echeese-iarcy? All of Vanaheim's currency was cheese anyway, so why not. All hail the Echeese-iarcy.

Artorian would have sat down with Moon Moon had there been the time, but Astarte appeared in his face like a roaring comet once more. The Voltekker had dealt serious damage, but Ember had clearly not cared. If anything, the enthusiasm of her combat hunger had increased. Laughing and on fire like a Von Degurechaff, she gripped Sunshine's armor by the shoulders and kneed **Pride** hard in the block value.

Voltekka's depleted armor shattered behind the sword-shield, and the bruised claymore had to retreat to storage when its blade snapped and broke. Turned to particulate, the suit forcibly returned to Artorian's inert core as he yelped and saw stars from pain.

In addition to smacking Artorian out of the mantle of white flame effect, the physics of Ember's knee blew him clear through the wall he'd been pinned against. His form was freed from her grip as his body snapped back to Teen-torian proportions, making Astarte wildly miss the roundhouse kick that followed up. There was likely a reason he got bumped up to adult form while Tekka's armor was active, but he had zero spare crackers to think about that burnt-toast topic right now.

On the bright side, the heatwave from the missed kick pushed him further. There was no longer a lance through his foot, and he was no longer being assailed by an armament arsenal that saw him as a fish to filet.

On the dark side, he'd lost his light sources and the world was now very black. Falling fast, he was also pretty sure that taking a power-knee to the stomach had crunched his health bar. In comparison, he was convinced that Ember knew she hadn't confirmed the kill. Already, she was beelining at him for a follow up strike.

If the laughter hadn't given that away, Emby being the sole light source in the new cavern certainly did. A gothic cavern that held all the dungeon mobs that hadn't wanted to enter the next room. The reflections from their eyes was a sight to fear, until one saw the fear in their eyes. At a glance, the general consensus of all the chickens, aberrations, undulating cheese-shapes, and figures too vague to make out, was a very firm 'Nuh-uh.'

None of them were willing to deal with the flaming diamond that was Astarte, no matter how much that aggravating Taunt from Sunshine kept trying to draw them closer. Unfortunately for the masses, Astarte momentarily considered the peanut gallery to be of greater threat than the falling star.

Much less green in the gills, and seeing that she was surrounded, Astarte copied her Sunshine and went nova. She even laughed out the word she recently heard. There was a big smile on her face as raging solar heat burst from her being in a massive spherical pulse. "Cowabunga."

Artorian yelped, but couldn't look away.

"Gotcha!" Lucia's voice cut through the fire and flames as her Lantern slammed into Artorian's chest before the solar burst reached him. A blessed spell followed from Momma Bun as his arms instinctively clung to the item, slowing his rapid descent. "High Lenity!"

High was not a modifier that Artorian had encountered yet, and he certainly didn't know the activation conditions for the affixes and suffixes, but the instant helping of shield in his heads-up display did wonders for his mental health and wellbeing. No, no, he messed that up. Mental wealth and hellbeing? Yes, that. Much better.

A front row seat to an entire cavern of dungeon mobs being turned into roast peanuts wasn't new, but that didn't make it unimpressive. Many attempted to flee, most were stuck due to his Taunt, and some accepted the death with open arms and maddened expressions.

This place was messed up.

With the chaff separated from the wheat, and the entire field very much on fire, a building-sized bone-based mid-boss broke free from the barn and lurched out from the wall. He spotted Ember happily hurling cataclysm after cataclysm at it, but something was off with the mid-boss.

It wasn't solid? No, it was another one of those odd illusions. Flickering his Truesight, he saw a plank hauling butt. Squinting, he spotted the rat attached to it a moment later. Sure enough, the rat was holding up a sign with 'Eldritch Bone Horror' scribbled on.

Retuning his sight to see what Ember did, Astarte was in the process of beating back the cavern-sized illusion that attempted to strike where she was weak. With tentacles made of teeth.

Mmmm.

Uncomfortable.

Artorian was directed from that discomfort by a sudden tension in his Silverwood bracelet as it was struck several times by objects he hadn't been able to spot. When he checked, the remaining swords had appeared in his inventory.

Having not fared particularly well against Astarte's solar flare, they all chose to check out of the engagement, lest it be their last one. That was a shame; he would have loved their company for longer, or their Costless Wisp Flight to save him from a hard fall. "I miss sword surfing. Flying swords should be all the rage."

Another spell from Lucia cut through his thoughts. "High Prosperity!"

The instant tick of positive numbers into his upset red health bar caused relief. Stealing that relief away was the reminder that he was still falling, and the impact against the ground was going to hurt. Wub-Step might break his legs. He could go left or right, but not up, so that changed nothing. Archimedes didn't allow him to hard-stop momentum, so even a bump of fifty meters only meant that he would be falling at terminal velocity for another fifty meters.

Not ideal.

Voltekka was snoring, the blades were out of commission, and the shield was only going to eat up so much damage. The lance not being in his foot didn't mean that he suddenly didn't have a hole in his foot, which made wanting to use it difficult. He hadn't expected the psychological hurdle to be what did him in with Freedom of Mind around, but that was the ticket he appeared to have punched. Rather than crackers and toast, Artorian developed a new disappointed swear word. "Rats."

The sudden stop didn't hurt as much as expected. He'd squinted his eyes shut while holding tight onto the Lantern that was doing a good job of making him feel like his fall was slower. Respawn was going to be so annoying. He was going to have to make the character all over again! He was tired of it! At least death didn't appear to hurt?

"Sugar? Why are you squeezing your face with your face? You look like you just ate twelve lemons." Astarte's voice made him peek open an eye. A most beautiful girl with wild, flowing hair, and the most gorgeous eyes had caught him. In languished descent, the radiant, diamond angel of warmth held him by the shield and the front of his pajamas. Unlike his pajamas, the Lenity shield bent and twisted around her fingers. The shield was not liking her hold one bit as the protective number value began to plummet. "Why don't we put you down."

Relief accompanied the feeling of solid ground under his feet, even if his knees were somewhat wobbly and weak. "*Ahh...* sweet, sweet solidity. Are you back, dearest?"

"Did I go somewhere?" Ember cocked her head, clearly confused before pressing her spare hand to her hip. She ignored the firestorm raging above her that consumed the bodies of the fallen, including one very crispy sign-holding Rat. When Lenity shattered in her grip, she thought to let go rather than reminisce. "*Hmm.* I must have. I remember getting foggy? Lots of fun enemies to fight everywhere I went all of a sudden."

Ember narrowed her gaze, still completely on fire. "I remember a great time, but no real details? I remember feeling like I was getting violently scrubbed in a bath every time I was near this one particularly pesky fly that wouldn't let me swat it. Then I was throwing fire at some bone creature that needed a few molars broken. When it suddenly vanished, I noticed you were falling when you got all bright and shiny. So I dropped what I was doing and caught my boy."

"Glad to have you back, dearest. When you're feeling tiptop? I have something important to bring up. Nudge me?" Artorian sighed in relief again as Ember turned off her fire, though not before his pajamas gained new burn marks.

"Of course, sugar." Sticking purely to her Diamond Body ability, she tried to wipe the scorch damage away as her boy talked, but only made the smudge worse.

Artorian thought the growing smudge to be pretty funny. He wondered if he could keep it? Like a small trophy. Could he exclude a detail from his Aura? Might as well try! Feeling the strength in his legs return, he squeezed his brooch. "Momma Bun? Team's back together. Outstanding timing on that shield."

Lucia did not share his good mood. "Kit, we are under attack. Can you two hurry back? That green roar of yours took almost all the happy numbers out of my stationary shield. I cannot recover any of it right now; I am *tapped*."

Before he could say they were on their way, Ember threw him over her left shoulder and shot towards Lucia, the persistent smudge abandoned as it was go-time.

"Vongola Style: Burning Backdraft." A corona of heat and flame surrounded her as she crashed through matter like an asteroid that had confused the difference between stop and slow down. Ember instead opted to speed up, and convinced the environment that it needed a much better reason for existing if it wanted to stay in place. Complete with ludicrous sing-song lyrics as she barreled her way through barriers. "Move, Abyss. Get out the way. Get out the way, Abyss, get out the way."

Shoulder-bashing all obstacles out of her way with her diamond form, she answered Lucia using Artorian's brooch. "Be there shortly, bun bun! What's the big blue meanie look like?"

Lucia snarked out one of Ember's favorite answers, her mood dampened by wet gnawing noises in the background. "Flammable, and like they go squish."

Ember cackled, and continued the juggernaut power-train as her boy clung to her for support, Lucia's Lantern stowed under his other arm. She then addressed a rogue thought in her head. "Were you saying something about nine-tailed foxes, sugar?"

Artorian didn't follow at all. "No? What made you think I did?"

Ember crashed through a thick wall and into a multi-legged thing that swiftly had a new hole punched through the center, allowing them both to burst forth from the chest and trek on. "Memories are coming back. I thought I heard you say Kyuubi? That's a nine-tailed fox."

Artorian grasped what she meant, but couldn't mentally keep up with the physical travel. At least Cleaning Presence kept any of the insect-gunk from sticking around. "Oh, no dear. I said cube. That thing with the shape and the corners."

They could both hear the bardic troupe and Zephyr laugh through his brooch. Hans, Meg, and Oak were never going to let him forget this, because Meg threatened him with horrible circumstances. "Did you just say 'that thing with the shape and the corners'? We're making a song about that, Grandpa!"

Artorian groaned out in defeat as Astarte hard-landed on whatever multi-mandible mutant was trying to get its mouth around Lucia's shield, turning the centipede-looking thing into a flaming pancake before it turned to particulate. There was some pop up about defeating a Greater Thousand-Armed Scolopendra Subspinipes, but that was thrown by the wayside.

Artorian was far too mentally stuck on the bards making songs. "Oh, no. Not *that*. If there's anything worse than this dungeon, it's probably that."

To this detail, the Dire Mushroom managing this dungeon paid precariously close attention. Glade, the dungeon master, rubbed his mycelium together. Mad Dungeon Disease might have been banned, but there was always more. An embarrassing song from bards did more harm than the Shamblers and horrors? That strangely matched the information about puns being abhorred by at minimum one member of the current adventuring party.

You don't say.

Say more!

The suggestion for 'Kiln Dungeon' had already been a revelation by itself. The title alone brought ideas, and a road for the future. That the current dungeon had been wrecked by this party was irrelevant, the Glade only cared for the darkest circumstances. This event was not a setback.

This event caused room for improvement.

Surely, higher-powered players would be coming back to challenge him? This Team Sleep proved that his current designs were insufficient! Yet, the mightiest of them had been made to turn on her compatriots. Shields had kept his spores at bay, which, in retrospect, seemed fair. Though, then there was the mobile mop. That accursed janitor and his incessant need to be clean, who appeared to have a villain mode? Intriguing.

Feed me more, Seymour.

More.

Artorian whined, and Lucia slapped everyone with fresh shields. Already tapped, that act exhausted her so much that it caused her to bunny-sploot and bury her face between her paws. She was still in the fight, but she needed a minute. When Artorian began to lament more about bardic songs, the party laughed, the dungeon laughed, the floor laughed, Astarte blew up the floor. All in all, good progress.

Plus, a way down!

Decorum was now within reach.

CHAPTER TWENTY-TWO

Decorum paced on the bottom most floor of the Darkest Dungeon, bright wisps of air hanging around him providing scant illumination.

The large Liger stopped pacing to look up at the brand-new skylight in the ceiling when it appeared with a bang. He snickered with laughter when his brother appeared head-first through the hole like a ceiling cat and waved at him. Ember joined and also waved, followed by a very large rabbit nose that sniffed but couldn't wiggle through properly. The hole was swiftly made larger as people began tearing away at it.

"Brother!" Shifting into the shape of the stately, well-dressed human, Gomez raised his arms in greeting. "Come down! There is nothing here, and I require aid. I have been bamboozled! My Tisha. My heart. She is not here! I am woeful, saddened beyond words."

Unlike his compatriots, Artorian could see the rat with the sign sitting in the middle of the empty room clear as day. The wooden plank it held said 'Bad,' plain and simple.

"Well, that's not a good sign." Saddened that no-one else thought that funny, he sighed as the entire troupe held onto

Ember like a bundle of scared cats. The fire released from her feet controlled their descent until she was able to let them all down, her flight problem long solved. Hug-laden reunions aside, with Hans utterly fawning over Hans Jr., Decorum's problem was easy to spot.

To everyone except Artorian, there was nothing here.

Basic architecture notwithstanding, the entire floor was empty. The odd support pillar and angled strut here and there, sure, but no Tisha, no castle, no Howl, no boss encounter. Just a bored rat holding up a sign, and something being wrong with the background. The sign could have at least said 'under construction' or something similar. For the first time in a while, Artorian grumbled at his Perception score.

He knew something was out of place, but couldn't place what.

"She was here, brother. I know she was!" Gomez resumed pacing, his tone once more upset. "The smells are correct, but there is no wind. No sign of my dearest hellion. I am confused. This dungeon has confused Decorum. Confounded me! I shall have vengeance! Magic missiles shall be cast into the darkness, and in the direction of yowling shall I chase my prey."

Artorian scratched his hair, then pointed at the wooden sign. "Alright, now I really must ask. Does nobody see the rat?"

Lucia and Zephyr had kept quiet when he'd interrogated a piece of vacant floor last time. Strange stares told him plenty, but Hans appeared personally insulted. He was plenty visible! Artorian shook his head. "I will take that as a no."

Walking a few paces, he had a moment to wonder what was so strange about the background. It was crooked? Sunshine punched in the direction of the rat. "Brilliant Behemoth."

Sk-boom!

The rat and sign both went flying from the resulting explosion, death occurring in slow motion like a knock out fatality. When the sign clattered to the ground, Artorian made a happy sound as the background de-crookified itself. When the makeshift cardboard panel crudely painted to look like empty floor space fell over, the bottommost floor lit up with twinkling shells and corrupted coral reefs, revealing the rest of the room to be a final cove level.

As the cheap stage prop fell, they could all spot Tisha bound and asleep in some glass coffin, wedged against the prow of a broken shipwreck. They also found the boss encounter! Which included one very oversized, tentacled menace that Artorian was worried he recognized. Particularly when it introduced itself with a flourish of familiar seashell weaponry.

"Unexpectus?"

With a rising *scree*, the red menace raised a sharp implement in each of its tentacles, brandishing the spikes used as weapons as the sensory illusions faded. Larger in size or not, the Octopus still spoke with that same nasally, holier-than-thou tone. "How dare you expect me! I am Unexpectus, of the Red Ink-quisition! You have fallen into my trap, my ancient enemy! You shall—"

The sound of a fist beating into Unexpectus's face and mouth silenced the giant Octopi as Astarte took to the field with a lack of patience. Once the Octopi saw Orcas swimming around his head, Astarte squeezed Unexpectus by a tentacle and started mercilessly laying into him with the full, flaming arsenal of martial arts at her disposal.

Artorian had never seen a three-hundred-combo move performed in mid-air before, and Unexpectus had clearly never been on the receiving end of one. The shuddering, repetitive booms of sound barriers being broken was nothing new, but Astarte finishing that combo within eight seconds was both spectacular and impressive.

Fire roiled from her mouth. "Shut! All of this because of you? You pain in my bonfire! You let the lady go this instant, and the beatings will *lessen*."

Unexpectus leaked ink, and Astarte threw him on the ground with a wet clap, crushing corrupted coral. Artorian heard the red Octopus mumble something along the lines of 'that doesn't mean stop,' prompting Astarte to snatch him by the beak and slam Unexpectus left and right onto the ground with rapid repetition. "Don't back-talk me, you invertebrate insult."

As Unexpectus attempted to fend off Astarte with futile effort, the others all piled in and joined the fray! Artorian got out his broom once the Ink-quisitor was a prone, flattened pancake. Laying into the Octopi with repeated overhand swings, the rest of the crew ganged up on the boss and started the encounter by kicking him in the sides.

Zephyr nailed the red boss with neon arrows from above, Hans taught Hans Jr. how to beat a man with a lute, Meg stabbed high-frequency vibration blades into Unexpectus's suckers, and Oak was making Brucible Lee noises with each pink-smoke-coated kick.

Gomez and Lucia had both sped to the glass coffin instead, having chosen other priorities as they tried and failed to either destroy the coffin or get the glass lid to open. The sight was comical until the Octopus released a defeated *huerk*, and turned into particulate.

Sad, rusty trumpet noises arrived accompanied by old confetti.

Pwaap.

———

Congratulations!
You have defeat many floor. Such end boss. Wow.
Good job you!
Get out.

———

The prompt fell to pieces like it had been held together with bad tape and only one screw, offering neither rewards nor further explanation. While the crew cheered that this meant they were done and could leave, Artorian hurried over to the glass coffin, hoping the lid problem was a matter of strength. Why Lucia was patting the bottom of the coffin as if it was an upturned jar that just needed some love, he wasn't going to question.

"Brother, scoot!" Gomez slunk out of the way so Sunshine could get his child-sized fingers into the gaps that his adultier adult of a brother was having problems with. Gomez was good at humanization, but stress was making the big claws come out, and that wouldn't do for fine mountain-climber finger-work. Finding an easy spot that was sadly coated in Octopus goop, Sunshine put one foot against the prow of the wreckage and heaved with a loud *hnnnnn*!

The glass coffin croaked like old wood, but budged! "Decorum! This thing is trying to snap back shut like a clam shell. I think I can get it open, but you're going to need to be quick! Emby! I'm tearing the coffin from the housing and I'm not gonna have the leverage to pry it open if it does. That needs more strength than the tug-of-war I'm having against this coffin. I need help to beat this euphemism. Stabilize!"

Ember and Lucia both rushed to grip the coffin by the top and bottom, counterbalancing and providing leverage so Artorian could keep pulling as his arms began to show strain. What kind of gimmicked box was this that one-thousand, six-hundred strength wasn't getting the job done with any semblance of speed?

The wooden creaking noise getting louder was dangerous. Artorian knew he could do it, but just like overtaxing his strength as a normal person in the real world, the effort was going to cost him. "Gomez! I'm going to pull really hard and expend my arms. Get ready in three, two, one!"

K-crunch!

"My heart!" Tisha was in Decorum's arms faster than the wind could turn treacherous on the ocean seas. "I have you, my most beloved Abyss. Your Gomez is here."

Artorian let go of the coffin that snapped itself shut, yowling while doing a dance that involved pained arm flailing. That entire endeavor had hurt! On the bright side, Tisha, while still unconscious, held her Gomez. Her arms slunk around his brother's neck out of the sheer feeling of safety that he provided her. He'd forgotten if she was some kind of bat, or reverse mothman, but that was irrelevant. Love had won the day, and he felt empowered.

Victory. Glorious victory.

———

Quest Complete! Arcoplex.
  Congratulations. Wholesome finish!
  Objective: Rescue Tisha. Complete!
  Bonus Objective: Help Decorum rescue Tisha. Complete!
  Reward: 200 Adaptive Pylons.

———

Artorian hollered, regardless of not knowing if he still needed Adaptive Pylons. He hadn't seen a number for them yet. Still, more was better! Ember was trying to pry the glass coffin free for use as a new bashing weapon, while Lucia hopped to mending duty.

Artorian thought his arms had become gelatin from how noodle-y they'd become. Any more limber and he could be served as pasta at the Crème de la Crème à la Edgar. At least Cal wasn't paying attention, otherwise he'd have gotten the noodle-arms skill or something.

A fresh shield from Lucia with another Prosperity slapped on top did wonders for his ailing health bar. Veracity, as always, helped with the lingering other debuffs, such as the noodle-fication of his arms. He had feeling back in his fingers within no time at all, and sighed in great relief. "Anyone who doesn't self-heal needs a healer on the team. That should be one of those game rules, along with DPS types getting dumped on."

Lucia paw-rubbed his head. "It was, kit. Do you need the whole performance to happen all over again?"

"No, I'm good. Thank you. If I want the addendum, I will go see Master Roberts the Ruminating myself. I already have a puddle-trip planned, and must remember to bring pistachio-flavored ice." Artorian stood there to ponder as the gentle petting turned into momma-fussed grooming as soon as Lucia spotted the burn marks on his pajamas. "I do, on the other hand, want to see Yuki before this always-on Taunt bites me in the butt. Zephyr, are you good to ship-mode us out of here?"

Zephyr looked over from checking her own character sheet, smiling wide before nodding. "Sure can! Just need a path. Are you going to make us a hole?"

Something about the expectation behind that question made Artorian uneasy. If he was getting a reputation for being careless, that wouldn't do. He didn't see Poirot anywhere, but maybe the detective was hanging around. Or, perhaps, he wasn't around because Moony had gotten more messages to use? "*Hmm.* Moony? Are you listening? Your messenger is missing, so I figured whatever he needed to tell me was no longer important. Do you have a way out for us, or is it game-required that we leave the hard way?"

Noot!

———

Message from: Vanaheim.

That will not be required. A path is being created, regardless of the complaints by the dungeon core of the sub-area you are in. Glade can throw a fit, but I'm glad to see you go.

I am about finished putting Demeter's Dream back together, and you have company waiting. Please feel free to leave as soon as possible, at your earliest convenience. Do not feel pressured to come back. Please let nobody convince you, either.

In expectation that you might, I have booted the rats out of my Pylon Holds, even if I am keeping their Cheese-iarchy. I have uncovered some old logs relating to reputation depending on how good one has been to cows. You have a most interesting score that will be remembered. Have a nice cycle, cheese be with you.

––––––

True to his message, as the yellow prompt closed, a path immediately began to open in the ceiling that led all the way out. The way could easily accommodate a full-sized luxury yacht.

Artorian nodded in appreciation. "I think I finally understand what those strange red Hedgehogs were talking about all the way back from the alpha run. This is *Da Wae*. Or were they Echidnas? It's been so long."

"Ready!" Artorian turned to look over his shoulder as the whole crew was boarding Zephyr in her fancy High Elven yacht form. She called out using a porthole to speak, and that was plenty to get everyone moving.

Once aboard, they had to push Gomez and Tisha to the main cabin the moment that Tisha woke up, as neither of them could stop flirting or fawning over one another. When Artorian was inspired by their open affection, he shot Ember a wide smile, only to get her hand slapped onto his mouth.

"Don't even think about it!" Beet red and lightly fuming from the Elven ears that were turning a hot shade of orange, Ember stared him down, proactively preventing him from starting a whole litany of honey-laden words that would make her melt on the spot. "You be good to me!"

Unfortunately for Ember, she was in the presence of several bards, all of which were keeping an ear out for this most delicious of gossip. Hans, of course, to his own detriment, could not be stopped from making mistakes. The seasoned bard laid down his comment like a playing card. "Oh, he'll be good to you, alright."

A mistake that was sure to haunt him through many a desert, as Ember's slow head-pan made both him and Hans Jr.

adopt identical expressions. Raw concern and the clenching of booty. A smile curled on her lips as a pleasant idea struck Astarte, her words oozing with sweetness. "Zephy? Gorgeous?"

Zephyr, of course, snapped to attention at being called. Like any other High Elf, she also instantly sunk into the compliment like a giddy schoolgirl. "Present, and thank you! I have been putting so much effort into sprucing and detailing work. This filigree doesn't make itself! How can I be of assistance?"

Ember's eyes remained locked on Hans. "I need you to go fast. Exceptionally fast. I have wet, dirty laundry to hang from the aft, and it needs a good shaking to get the stains off. Maybe the bards can make a song out of the screaming."

Artorian wondered for a moment if Soni had ever told Ember that she would make a very good Demon. A thought quickly replaced by the ponderance on if he should do anything about that. Best to start late than it was to never start at all.

Still muffled, he spoke anyway. "Sugar?"

Ember turned to look at her boy, her anger for the bard conflicting with her affection for her Artorian. She released his mouth, but clearly still wanted to punish Hans.

"If you hang Hans out to dry…" He gently patted her hand. "Then you can't hold me in Zephy's fancy lounger, and I'm probably about to pass out again."

Artorian had meant the idea as a jest, but the acceptance that he wasn't in top shape acted as a kick in the shin to the system. An entire barrel of negative status effects dropped on him. Including a need for sleep, overexertion, using a Voltekker, and a litany more, as if having remembered that getting stabbed should come with a cost. The wound in his foot might be healed, but Artorian had still gone through an entire dungeon in record time.

Speedrunner or not, the suddenly wobbly Teen-torian looked like he was going to be forced into another nap. Ember had her arms around him before assumption became reality, and his face slumped into her chest with a dull thud.

Ember dropped a daring finger in the direction of the

bards, who were all giggling uncontrollably at the sight. "Not. One. Word."

She then growled at Hans, but a further slumping Teentorian shifted her priorities. "*Hmph*! Another time. Momma Bun? Please come pick up my boy and give him a once over. Zephy, cool those amplifiers. Take us out slowly. Dock in Demeter's Dream."

"Aye aye, Cap'n!" The sails of the yacht moved to salute Ember at the crow's nest. With an easy lift, Zephyr sailed the crew out of the Darkest Dungeon, and Vanaheim altogether. Artorian was the only one who did not see a horde of Cheese Penguins wave them off with white napkins as they breached the surface.

Brother Moon was happy to see them go!

May they never return.

CHAPTER TWENTY-THREE

Ding!

———

Victory!
> *You have completed: Darkest Dungeon.*
> *Rewards are being tallied.*

———

Ding!

———

Victory!
> *You have destroyed: Darkest Dungeon.*
> *The dungeon has been remade with the influences of your party!*
> *New dungeon: Kiln of the First Ember.*
> *New monster template developed: Ashen.*
> *Rewards are being tallied.*

———

Waking to both the sound of the prompts, and the strong scent of bacon that Artorian half-remembered handing over mid-slumber, he blinked the sleep away and lounged out on Basher fluff into a big stretch. Glitterflit fluff gave Alpaca fluff a run for its copper. Could he get all his clothes made from this stuff? How did Bashers trade? Headbutts? The lights that get knocked out of people? On that note, hadn't he passed out in the dungeon? "Anyone up?"

Sitting up to a surprising amount of silence, Sunshine fist-ground the remaining sleep from his eyes. Tuning his ears, he found a whole bunch of people snoring around him as Lucia's gentle breathing raised and lowered him. Alright, that explained the lack of voices he'd been expecting.

Some people were in odd places, like they'd fallen asleep mid-task. That instantly worried his sniffer, as the tingle in his nose screamed that this was somehow his fault. It was a sleep-related incident; clearly, this was him.

"I have no Sleep powers?" Artorian pondered out loud when the realization hit him. "How can this be my fault?"

Checking his character sheet, he slapped his forehead and sighed. "Never mind. Someone has been putzing around with my ability entries."

Working his way down fluff mountain to take the bacon off the fire, he began munching away. Always make time for a good snack! Taking a more detailed look at his prompts, he'd figure out what Eternia had flubbed this time. Pylon flares and failures were nothing new. Noting that the change was in Aura, rather than abilities, Artorian shrugged and pulled up the cause of what had everyone a-snoring like fatty C'towl. "*Oooh*, several new toys!"

———

Aura: Field of Sleep.

Rank: Master.

Special Qualities: Aura, Sleep.

Shape: Coin.

Description: A coin-shaped field emitting a constant sleep effect, centered on the user.

Output: N meters in radius of cleaning effect per percentage of maximum energy bar invested, N meters in height. Where N equals the numerical equivalent of the Aura's rank.

Equivalents: Novice, 1. Beginner, 2. Apprentice, 3. Student, 4. Journeyman. 5. Expert, 6. Master, 7.

Details: Field of Sleep may be resisted via a Hearts and Minds Save, which is calculated from the average of a resister's Constitution and Willpower scores. For every threshold that they beat the user's Force of Will function by, the resister regains one step of waking, up to four steps, at which point they are immune to the Sleep effect.

A threshold is considered fifty points.

Note: Auras in the Eternia beta are being reworked to operate on the 'Force of Will' function. This function takes the average of the user's Charisma and Wisdom attributes, as they represent presence, power, warmth, and the ability to apply those concepts.

Note: You may only have one Aura type effect active at any given time.

———

Doing some napkin math on how hefty of a coin that would be, a seven-hundred meter radius effect was nothing to sneeze at. Overall, nice to have. "I should expect to see deja vu cats. They're changing things again. What's this other one?"

———

Aura: Pressure.

Rank: Master.

Special Qualities: Aura, Pressure.

Shape: Cylinder.

Description: A field emitting a constant pressure effect, centered on the user. Improving the rank of this Aura grants more control over which targets you may exclude from Pressure, and improves what actions you can take without preventing the actions of others. At the Novice rank, all targets in your radius are affected by your Pressure, forcing the world to a standstill if you move.

Pressure may be resisted via a Perseverance Save, which is calculated from the average of a resister's Strength, Constitution, Willpower, and Luck scores. For every threshold that they beat the user's Charisma attribute by, the resister regains one step of mobility, up to four steps, at which point they are immune to the Pressure effect.

A threshold is considered fifty points.

Output: N meters in radius of Pressure effect per percentage of maximum energy bar invested, N meters in height.

Details: This Aura may cause damage with the addition of intent. This Aura will deal N times Crushing damage equal to the user's Charisma score, where N equals the numerical equivalent of the Aura's rank. This damage is reduced by a quarter, down to none, for every threshold that a resister can prevent.

Equivalents: Novice, 1. Beginner, 2. Apprentice, 3. Student, 4. Journeyman. 5. Expert, 6. Master, 7.

Note: You may only have one Aura type effect active at any given time.

Note: If this is your only Aura, it is active by default.

———

Artorian half-contemplated complaining, but settled on eating more bacon while doing the napkin math on that one. "Two-hundred times seven is a clean fourteen-hundred. Then that gets cut into four chunks of three-fifty damage each, depending on how many thresholds get through? Not bad. Wish it told me what the tick-rate on that Pressure damage was. Once per second? Once per minute? Once?"

The confirmation chime of his prompt controller played, making him drop the topic and move on. Goodies were good, freebies were not. He was steadily gaining the opinion that if he had to build the support structure and people network for specific goodies to be available to him, that he wanted to build it. Give him all the infrastructure. All the scaffolding!

He squinted at the mended ceiling of Demeter's Dream, suspicious of the ability creator's motives. Was this all some elaborate plot to make him sink his teeth into the value of all that which goes slow and steady? That lesson was unnecessary; he was a professional at leaning into the support structures to make advances as a cultivator. Taking dangerous, life-threatening steps to get there? Sure! So long as it was his own life he was risking.

For all his many loved ones? No. There would be steps, places, and people. If he could crack down on the lethality rate of a cultivation step by as much as a percent, he would happily go all Lenore on the system in question.

Wanting to get a screen out of the way so he could get to exploring, Artorian tapped the glowing quest prompt as the entries cleaned themselves up until only three remained. One of them did not look familiar, and he did not remember ever picking it up. In line with the goals, yes, but he'd never accepted this one from a system perspective.

————

Updated Quest: Lair of the Far Squid.
  Objective: Visit Señor Louis. Make a friend.

————

Quest: Soulsborne.
  Objective: Complete a No-Hit run in Eternia.
  Bonus: Complete this quest with the Glass Cannon trait applied to your character.

————

Quest: Friends and Fraternity.

Objective: Rescue Yiba Su Wong from the Alfheim remnant. Complete.

Objective: Rescue Paladin Yorn from the Svartalfheim remnant. Complete.

Objective: Rescue Rip and Tear from the Asgard asteroid belt.

———

"I'm going to have issues with whoever stole the agency from me, but at the same time I'm impressed that behind-the-scenes people got a quest spot-on for once. I still don't like quests. I stick to my to-do lists like snow sticks to mountains. Handled one avalanche at a time. This gets a pass, even if I clearly got help." Artorian checked to see which Aura was active. He noted it was the sleep one. Ticking that off in favor of the eternal clean, he moved on to checking his surroundings. One by one, to-do tasks vanished from his checklist. Patriarch Yiba Su Wong and Paladin Yorn, now both old and withered in their ancient age, were slumped together over a plate they had both been trying to steal the last miniature sausage from.

Both their forks were stabbed into the culprit.

Good to see his old friends again, asleep or otherwise.

The bards were all slumped around a fire, flopped over their instruments. That was going to leave some nasty indentations on their faces. Served them right. Getting up to meander, he found sheafs of paper scribbled with lyrics. The title read, 'That Thing with the Shape and the Corners.'

Promptly throwing every last scrap into the fire without any remorse, he spared no effort in tracking down every last scribble and feeding the scraps to the flames. That monstrosity was not seeing the light of day!

Scouring the atrium of his current locale allowed him to discover a snoozing Ember one room over, with one arm each wrapped around the necks of Tom and Valhalla. With their armors coated in fist shaped pock-marks, it was easy to deduce what happened here. Tom had been made to wear a set, likely for his own protection. Artorian doubted the man was big on armor otherwise.

This atrium looked to be an armory of some kind, so this scene made sense. Meandering on, he encountered several more known faces. In the kitchens, Yuki was dead asleep while neatly tucked into one of Tim's arms, who was out cold and snoring for twelve. "Tim sleeps from his own system's Pylons? That can't be right; something else is afoot."

Artorian just about jumped out of his skin when a previously still shape next to the ovens moved without notice.

"Oui, I agree, mon ami! Poirot's little gray cells tingle at this most pleasant mystery." Snapping to the dark corner of the kitchen, Artorian's Perception kicked in to spot the rotund, jolly-looking humanoid in a rather nice gray suit while holding a monocle. Done with his inspection, the rotund man with a most excellent tiny mustache snickered in gentle laughter, then tapped the side of his nose as he walked into view.

Poirot, while a Cheese Elemental, had easily and quickly figured out the human shape and mannerisms. Particularly Artorian's. Surely that would bode well? "Come, come! Poirot wishes to show you the piece de resistance of this mystery. Poirot is having a great time! Is this usually the case with your surroundings? You shall find me hot on your heels, chasing you down the rivers of time, hasty or otherwise! Perhaps I should nickname you Captain Hastings? That is most amusing."

Poirot laughed a jolly laugh, but Artorian wasn't sure how to feel. "Come, Hastings!"

He did, however, follow the rotund detective back into one of the halls connecting to the atrium, where Poirot leaned over Deverash Neverdash the Dashingly Dapper, and poked the Gnome with his walking cane. Dev had clearly passed out mid-explanation, but no other body was on the floor that gave away which poor soul he might have been lecturing. His pointer finger was still extended in the classic 'and another thing' pose. "Et voila! The reason for le mystere."

Artorian scratched his head. "Dev is the reason why everyone is asleep?"

Poirot rolled his head disparagingly, as if the real reason was obvious. "Mais, non! Plunder his pocket!"

Artorian was more interested in why he was being relegated to the task of going through his friend's pockets. "Why haven't you done it if you're so sure?"

Poirot pulled up his nose, and set his monocle. "Non! Poirot does not know where he has been. Poirot still needs gloves. White ones. Snug fit. Thin leather with fluffies on the inside. Mais pas à mon fingertips! There the leather should be thin, so Poirot may pick up the little details carefully. Cleanly."

The detective then drew a deep breath, and smiled like he was in the Celestial realm. "*Ahh*, mon céleste, the world is never as good as it is when you are around, mon ami. Le monde, c'est frais! It is fresh. It is clean. C'est parfait. It is perfect. Not a dust bunny to be found to stick to me or cling to my skin. It is art and beauty, this, Poirot says, is truth. Cleanliness is next to godliness."

Artorian wasn't about to naysay Poirot. If this was how the elemental cheese was choosing to develop, he was sure as Abyss going to let the creature. There were worse alternatives than a neat freak, and he wasn't exactly against preaching to the choir when it came to cleanliness. He rifled through Dev's pockets, and found a miniature Pylon that looked to attach to some greater contraption based on the cut. The crystal was shaped like an open dinosaur mouth, and the neck portion was clearly designed to lock or slot into something larger.

"I don't like where this is going." Artorian stood up and held the miniature Pylon up to some light, trying to ignore that Poirot got so close that the detective's nose was pressed to his own. "Poirot, would you like to hold it? You don't need to shove your big nose into my personal space like that, and I barely have any to begin with."

"Non!" Poirot instantly rebuked holding the unknown

object of questionable origin. "Poirot does not even possess a napkin to accept it!"

Artorian shrugged, wiped the Pylon against his pajamas since his Aura had undoubtedly cleaned them by now, and held the piece up. "Inspect."

———

Warning: This is an O.o.P. The words 'Oop' and 'Oops' happen frequently around objects such as these. Handle the Object of Power with care, or you won't live long enough to pronounce the S.

Item: Amplification Pylon - Focus Lens Prototype.

Production Name: Auric Dynamo #42.

Game Name: Dyno-Mite.

Material: Erinite Synthetic Pylon.

Rarity: Unique.

Special Effect: Toggle, Bypass, Unstable. Critical Catastrophe.

Costs: 5% of an energy bar's maximum.

Cooldown: None.

Toggle: This item may be used either as an Object of Power, or as a Component.

Unstable: This object may blow up on use. Chance unknown.

O.o.P. Effect: When activated, Auric Dynamo #42 will link with the closest Aura in activity, and amplify its output using the Bypass special effect. Bypass allows an Aura to cause one threshold step of success to take hold regardless of the resistance applied, preventing a resister from being immune to the Auric effect. A resister may prevent up to three steps of threshold against an Aura with this improvement, but not the full four.

Component Effect: Auric Dynamo #42 is considered a crystalline focus lens, and can be slotted into a medium or heavy Light Fusion Beamer. Erinite as a material will cause the resulting beam to be green, and deal earth damage of the energy type. Earth-based energy shielding will thus fully rebuke a beam of this type, as per the shielding rules. While green beams are the brightest, they are not the strongest.

Warning! Adjacents will interact. Opposites cancel. Like reflects like.

Always read the entry of your components, and always check the method of delivery on your Focus Lens.

Material Limitation: Erinite can handle an energy influx of 500 energy per use.

Delivery Method: This Erinite Focus Lens releases ten short range beams in a conical manner, with each beam dealing one tenth of the invested energy. Beam range is limited to thirty feet before automatic dissipation.

Warning! This Focus Lens is unoptimized, and will cause double the heat accumulation on use. Never fire a Light Fusion Beamer holding this component without slotting a Gelid Heat Sink, Rime Rack, Fimbulwinter Cartridge, or Permafrost Round, depending on your beamer's chassis.

Warning! Critical Catastrophe item. If this item goes boom, you and everything around you are going with it.

Artorian had no idea what kind of hornet's nest this kind of word salad was going to get him into, but he was sure curious. Better set some priorities before he fell into another hole. "First, my shark boys. Then, Louis, the Rats, and the Amalgam. Lastly, New Haven."

He held his chin. "I have a funny feeling that I'm going to need a Light Fusion Beamer, and that I'm definitely going to be in the Pylon Holds in order to round out this adventure. After which, we slap a storm, and then I think I'm done with the Eternia game for a while. The whole point was to get away from it all with Ember, and instead, I am once more in the thick of it. I'm finishing this, getting my people home, and hanging up the towel. I have cultivation and a life to get to."

CHAPTER TWENTY-FOUR

Artorian looked at Poirot when his ears picked up familiar fussing, the newly minted man deep in consideration for the order of events that the young Nascent Being had laid out.

The big man looked like he was on the cusp of asking questions, but stopped himself to ponder more instead. When Artorian stored the focus lens and pushed his hands into his pockets, Poirot had formulated his confusion. "You do *not* care for the power. Non. Neither do you lean to the violence you are assigned. Poirot has seen a number of players 'testing the waters,' before Poirot was Poirot. However, my dear Hastings, now that Poirot is both detective and punisher? Poirot has doubts about the direction of his life."

Artorian thought that concern was both common and simple. "Ah, I wish I could go Grandpa-mode or something before answering that, because it's not going to sound very genuine coming from the voice of a young'un, but I do have the resolution to that worry."

Poirot perked up in both surprise, and unexpected relief. "Oui? Then you must go 'Grandpa-mode,' and tell Poirot."

Could he do that?

The form followed the measure of function in Eternia, and appearances were mostly cosmetic with a flavoring of intent and perception. "Honestly? The person who has the answer to whether I can do that or not is napping at our feet."

Ding!

———

Quest Notice!
  You have been offered the Quest: Grandpa Mode.
  Objective: Go Grandpa Mode.

———

Artorian thought that amusing. Was his prompt controller trying to express a sense of humor? Sure, why not. Accept!

Some gentle shaking later, and the well-dressed Gnome snapped upright with bleary eyes. "Don't touch my sprocket!"

Blinking away the dream, Dev ground his fists into his face and grumbled as clarity dawned. "Sunny? What are you doing in my workshop? The **Law** for Procrastination will get to a node! Eventually. My chart…"

Clarity might need some more time, as Dev looked around when he couldn't point at his chart. His continued stream of consciousness was prevented from finding new steam when there was suddenly an enraged Lucia in the hallway, her paw charged and ready to lay destruction upon any chart in the vicinity.

She wasn't awake. Her eyes were clearly still closed, but her facial expression and pointed ears betrayed the murder-ness just fine.

Artorian salved the situation. "No charts here, Momma Bun. You killed it."

Pleased, the large Glitterflit curled right back up on the floor, none the wiser that there had never been a chart in the first place. Her soft snores were the key sound they all paid attention to until those snores gained in strength, and Dev carefully continued. "Note to self. Move a certain workshop farther away from Basher noses."

The detective leaned over the Basher, but knew better than to prod the chart-murdering fluff with his walking stick. "Poirot is enamored by the complexities of these relationships."

Chuckling, Artorian pulled the focus lens back out of his storage bracelet and held it in front of Dev's nose. "Speaking of noses. What is this thing and how did it put everyone to sleep?"

"It did not." Dev was quick to poke a finger into Sunshine's knee. "You did. This made it worse. As to what that focus lens is? Easy! About to explode anytime someone uses it. If you want more on focus lenses, just follow the sound of Cal's mad cackling. On second thought... No, don't do that. You'd be better off finding Soni and One-Stone. Feel free to hang onto the amplification pylon, my tests with it are already concluded. Nap-success is great success!"

Artorian looked at the object with concern, and pocketed the object into his storage bracelet before it could decide to blow up on them at random. "Nap success is great success. Will everyone wake up on their own?"

Dev brushed himself off once on his feet, but on realizing that Sunshine had his favorite Aura active, he chose to instead let the field work its magic. "Your nap-time Aura makes people sleep as one normally would. It's not like the Sleep damage I've been trying to develop on your behalf. Loved the idea! Nonlethal damage resulting in a nap? Gentle, yet direct. I should likely get back to that, unless you have questions?"

Artorian could delve into several topics, but ought to keep it curt, or he'd sink into the storm and end up at the workshop for a year. "I need some kind of Grandpa Mode. I don't like slamming the Deity lever, and even when talking to my grandchildren, a gentler form would have been better."

Dev crossed his arms, face twisted in consternation and thought. "It'll take one of your achievement rewards, but Appearance Cosmetics could work just like Effect Cosmetics.

Yes, I think I can make that work. Though, my time will cost you two other Abilities I need tested. Do you need it soon?"

Artorian laughed, not having a problem with the cost. "Dev! You genius! I was worried if it was possible, and here you are telling me it's done. When it's convenient, my friend. There's a comfort that the accompanying physique brings, regardless of how much enjoyment I have tromping around as Young-torian."

Proud and flushing, Dev coughed into his fist and looked away. "Of course! I am a Gnome extraordinaire! I also forgot entirely what I was doing before my nap. I'm not sure why I'm here anymore. Please give me some space? I'm going to Bifrost back to the workshop."

Poirot and Artorian both backed up, watching a beam of rainbow light slam down from above. The beam carved a pattern onto the ground, and then whisked Dev away when the light pulled back. The runic pattern left in place was physically carved into the floor, but Artorian wondered if the new hole in the ceiling was going to become his problem. Some floor art could be brushed under the rug. Then again, it didn't rain here, did it? "Sunroof."

Poirot questioned Artorian with a look, but a few glances between the hole and the man made him tap the side of his nose in understanding. "Oui. Sunroof."

Quickly squirreling themselves away, Artorian got the expected notifications from Dev. The costs his friend mentioned arrived before the requested tool. Dev had likely jumped into his fancy chair and started work on it with a mad-Gnome smile on his face. Gnomes may not rule, but Dev certainly did. What a fantastic Gnome he was.

Ding!

———

Class gained: Lumin Lord.

Lumin Lord is a class dedicated to the usage of Light, Radiance,

Resplendence, and any related elemental magic. This class may further evolve into a more potent aspect of its current form. Namely, Lumin Lord into Radiant Lord, The Radiance, or Resplendent One.

This class is considered a base class, and is designed for use by an area boss or above.

Skill gained: Effortless Shaping (Light).

Effortless Shaping allows the user to use their powers to shape their element, in this case Light, into any shape that they can imagine. This can be used to form weapons, imagined shapes, abstract thoughts, and so on.

Effortless Shaping negates the fabrication and manipulation costs of Light Shaping.

Ability gained: Light Shaping.

Light Shaping allows the user to convert their energy into Light, and related states of matter. Note that Light is not a state of matter, it is an energy. Light does not occupy space, has no mass or volume, and is therefore not considered matter.

Solids, liquids, and gasses are available for the purposes of shaping.

The effects and attributes of Light Shaped matter are equivalent to the amount of energy invested into the creation. These values will fluctuate depending on the focus and intent of the user. A created blade can easily be made to deal more damage, but without thought as to durability, will shatter on contact.

No numerical values are available for this description. This ability requires testing.

Ding!

Specialization gained: Wub Warrior.

Wub Warrior is a sound-based melee specialization, focusing a front-line combatant into the path of adding sound to their strikes. This specialization may further evolve into aspects that use other forms of energy, the functions of waves, or the transfer of energy through physical means.

—————

Skill gained: Effortless Shaping (Sound).

Effortless Shaping allows the user to use their powers to shape their element, in this case Sound, into any shape that they can imagine. This can be used to form weapons, imagined shapes, abstract thoughts, and so on.

Effortless Shaping negates the fabrication and manipulation costs of Sound Shaping.

—————

Ability gained: Sound Shaping.

Sound Shaping allows the user to convert their energy into Sound, and related states of matter. Note that Sound is not a state of matter. It is energy. Sounds are produced by vibrations. Note that it is easier for sound waves to pass through solids than through liquids, because the molecules are closer together and more tightly bonded in solids. Similarly, it is harder for sound to pass through a gas than through a liquid, because gaseous molecules are farther apart.

Solids, liquids, and gasses are available for the purposes of shaping.

The effects and attributes of Sound Shaped matter is equivalent to the amount of energy invested into the creation. These values will fluctuate depending on the focus and intent of the user.

No numerical values are available for this description. This ability requires testing.

—————

Ding!

Item gained: Class and Specialization Respec Ticket.

This ticket removes a player's current class and specialization, and all related features.

This ticket allows a user to select a new base class.

This ticket allows a user to select a new floor-tier specialization.

Usage: Rip in half.

Dev gave him the best toys. "Now this is a good way to get abilities and tools. In trade for something else. I actually need to do something to obtain the goodie. That's much better!"

His brooch hummed, Zelia's voice chiming through. "My Dreamer? Does that mean you would be willing to try something of mine? There is a function I would like to see applied."

Artorian was surprised to hear from Zelia, but was instead worried about how she'd known when to add to the conversation. "Are you still watching me? I forgot that was going on. I can test your gimmick, Zelia. As for cost… What's the verdict on the game show interactions? Any chance I get to hear from these ardent fans of mine more directly?"

Dwarven laughter cracked wide open through the brooch's connection, prompting Artorian to look around. Hang-drum music pealed as the Dwarves were merry, accentuated by the rushing of waves in the background. Where was their point of view located? Trying to spot the denser than normal glob of energy that his audience was looking from, Artorian squinted as he couldn't locate the darn thing this time. Normally he just knew, but his Nascent Being sense was coming up dry. Was a new gimmick in play? He'd find it. Or was this his lowered Perception kneecapping him? Probably that.

Zelia cleared her throat and personal giggles to answer him. "Yes, my Dreamer. Though there is much more to it."

A smugness entered her speech. "We are developing an

interface to interact with commentary, though I will warn you beforehand about the crassness. A particular Heavenly has arrived outside of the expected order, and immediately threw himself into the project."

The smugness doubled, warning Artorian that nose-tingling notions were afoot. "Shalom of **Discord** sends his jubilant regards. That mensch has a fanciful sense of humor. He has been going on and on that it will be a place where your fans can come ask questions, request things they'd like to see, and come slap down errors they believe to have found through their journey of observing people play the game. More eyes on the prize improves the whole pot, unless they all add salt."

Zelia's tone returned to its normal secretarial self after making a point of the schemery that Artorian had definitely picked up on. "May I provide you with the goodie?"

Artorian ran his fingers through his hair, then shrugged. There was nothing he could do about this ploy in progress, so he may as well roll with it. "Please do, Zelia."

The connection closed in coordination with the *ding*!

————

Skill gained: Kinetic Flow.

Rank: Novice.

Kinetic Flow provides the user with the abstract understanding of the mixture of Might and Magic that goes into kinetic movement. The user is able to manipulate these forces to some degree, based on skill rank.

————

Ability gained: Telekinesis.

Description: You know what it does, my Dreamer.

Output: Try it.

————

Artorian wondered if he'd been bamboozled. There was a lot of giggly chaos in this orderly prompt, because it was nebulous and uninformative. He was going to have to puzzle Kinesis out the hard way, and it was probably one of Zelia's favorite little toys along with Portation. He should keep his mouth shut or that would get slapped onto him as well, and he had enough to test as was.

First things first. "I should talk to Emby before I tear up and use this respec ticket."

CHAPTER TWENTY-FIVE

Artorian and Poirot made their way back to the armory, where the snoozing sight had not changed. Poirot was intrigued as to why Sunshine did not wake Astarte in the same direct way as Dev. Then the detective recalled that this was the same girl who had beaten a dungeon to a pulp with propane and propane accessories.

One did not wake the queen of the hill like a boor.

Not sure how to approach without getting kicked in the chin, Artorian instead took in his surroundings a bit more. Perhaps there was a clue of convenience. Walking the perimeter with a curious Poirot in tow, Artorian stopped at some manual that laid on a shield rack. He picked the handbound work up and flipped through the manual, eating up the information easily enough. "Carian Grandeur. Seems to be the mana manipulation version of something Polly can do. Big energy sword gets bigger. Then swooshidy-swooshes. Simple enough. Enhance currently held weapons, or create magical greatswords. *Mhm, mhm,* all basic."

Putting that one down, he picked up the next one he saw. "This is a bit more interesting. 'Exceptionally Many Bolts of

Electrified Radiance,' or E.M.B.E.R. for short. This honestly might go well with the new class I picked up. I should read this in full."

"No!" Tom and Valhalla were thrown to opposite sides of the room as Ember shot up from dead sleep. They hit the walls hard and woke up in crumpled heaps. The impacts were an irrelevant detail compared to the beatings they had both been getting beforehand, and both chose to stay down for more naps instead. If Ember knew they were awake, she might call for round two far faster than they wanted. "I'm still working on that!"

"*Ohohoho*, are you now?" Artorian smiled like a fox and ran for the door, holding the manual high over his head to commence an improvised game of keep-away. "I am going to read every line! I fleeee!"

"Boy!" Waking up in a hurry, Ember snapped at her troublemaker and chased him right out of the door. Tom and Valhalla tactically chose not to move a muscle as they were saved, a curious Poirot coming for them with his walking stick. "Gimme that!"

"I refuuuuuse!" Artorian cackled and gripped the book with Telekinesis, pretending to stumble and toss the book on high when Ember was right on him in no time at all. "Oh no!"

Ember launched from the ground and dove for the manual, which took a sharp left turn before she could get her hands on it as Artorian was already running another way. The book returned to his grip as the boy laughed and laughed, having a great time. "Never mind! Safe!"

"Vongola Burst!" The fire and flames from Ember's hands and feet made Artorian's cleverness moot pretty quick. The warrior woman opted for instant air-superiority with her pending victory in all matters of speed. "Gotcha!"

She wrapped her arms around her Young-torian's chest from behind, lifting both him and the book high up into the air as she flew off with him. "Gimme that!"

Artorian looked over his shoulder, grinned from ear to ear,

and giggled dangerously. "You can't take objects out of my half of the bracelet, can you?"

"Boy, don't you dare!" Before she could snatch the manual out of his hands, the book vanished altogether, appearing in Artorian's side of their shared inventory. Ember felt the item slot into place through her bracelet. She stopped her flight and hovered, her arms squeezing as her hands formed claws. Her following words were more of a stifled groan rather than a reply. "*Mmmmm!*"

Cheeky as could be, Artorian held his foxy smile. "I'll give it back to you. Small price. Very cheap."

Ember glared death and fire at him. "Gib."

Artorian instead pointed at his cheek, poking the spot. "Small one. Right here."

She growled loud, her throat boiling. "Are you extorting me for kisses with my own book?"

Artorian gasped loud, his hand pressing to his sternum. "What? *Me?* I would never."

Glaring, Ember cocked her head as she puzzled the situation out. It would be so easy to just… drop him. Something he'd said didn't add up, and he wasn't the type to hold something over her. Wait a minute…

Holding up a hand, she pulled the book from their shared storage space just fine, then beat him with it while fussing. "You incessant fox! You tricked me! We can get items out just fine, we just can't place things in the other's section!"

He snapped his fingers. "Crackers. So much for my clever idea."

"Shut up." Ember stored the book, grabbed his chin to stop his head from making any motions, and smooched him on the cheek. "Don't do that! You'll see the manual when it's done. Next you'll tell me you almost read Carian Grandeur too."

"*D'awwww.*" Flushed and purring like a kitten, Young-torian squirmed adorably, his small legs kicking like a shy boy having received unexpected affection. "That was so sweet! I liked that, dearest. Though, the other one I already read. Nice and simple, easy to understand."

Ember flushed bright red, looking away. "Yes, well, nobody saw me, so whatever."

Artorian bit his lip. There was no way he could say anything about Zelia keeping tabs on him, and there at minimum being an entire tavern of Dwarves watching them. Lots of bets and money had likely just traded hands. Why did he feel like he'd just made Zelia rich?

A question for later. Emby would throw him into orbit with a scream if she found out right now, and turn the entire Coast of Rica into scorched scrapland. Or Nidavellir? No, Artorian had heard beach sounds in the background. His Nascent Being sense was going off and making him think of fancy drinks made of protein and whey, and Dwarves referring to each other as 'bro' while flexing. Those dwarves would get forcibly evicted, he'd be to blame, and everyone would know.

Lucia's voice cackled gleefully through the connection, having woken up from all the noise erupting from her own brooch. "Oh, darlin'. Everyone saw that. Everyone."

Turning beet red, Ember pretended that wasn't true, and chose not to address it. Momma Bun was just poking her in the ribs. Yeah. Innocent prodding. The Glitterflit was trying to get a rise out of her and turn her cheeks ever more red than they already were. That did not stop Lucia from failing to stop her giggles, all of which continued to erupt through the brooch.

Ember flicked her communication device with a huff to turn it off.

"Wait, you read Carian Grandeur?" Ember snapped back to the topic the moment her embarrassment faded. "Did you get a pop up?"

"I did not." Artorian shook his head, pointing at one of the waterfalls because it was a nice view from all the way up here. "Just read that big sword go woosh."

She clicked her tongue. "*Tsk.* That means it's incomplete. Making manuals is hard."

Artorian wondered about the completeness of the book, and if that was necessary. "Pretty sure I could do it without a system skill? Speaking of."

Making the respec ticket appear, he held it up for her to see while she held him high in the sky. No longer being teased, Ember's grip turned less deadly and threatening as she adjusted her hold for comfort. She wasn't going to let him fall. Not for that.

Artorian gave the golden ticket a wave. "I received new class and specialization options from Dev for things to test, but I would lose the Violence ones. Figured I'd ask first, since you're the one the Heavenlies are messing with. There was a mention that I would lose related skills, but I don't think I have any. Do the maneuvers count?"

"No, they do not. Rip it." Ember's verdict held no hesitation at all. "Rip it now. I will happily pick up your current class and specialization. I actually can't have them while you have them, and it would do me a lot of good when I run into those two Heavenlies again. I know they're going to be in the game. I know I'm going to find them. I know there will be diplomacy. Lengthy, *lengthy* diplomacy."

Artorian tore the ticket. *Rrrrip*! "Done!"

Ding!

———

Notice!
 You have lost your class!
 Violence has been removed.

———

Notice!
 You have lost your specialization!
 UltraViolence has been removed.

Notice!

Your character sheet cannot tally further changes without a new class being slotted.

You have pending entries for a class and specialization.

Would you like to slot Lumin Lord as your base class?

Would you like to slot Wub Warrior as your specialization?

"Yes to all." Sunshine tapped yes on all the prompts, then flashed a bunch of colors in swift succession as his body updated to the new system settings.

As Artorian worked administrative tasks, Ember flew them over to the waterfall her boy had pointed out, wanting a closer look at the venue herself. A thought struck him. "Say, a little late for this. What was the story with Achilles Agrippa? I put him in the ground, but I'm not sure I knew why you wanted to bury him."

Ember copied Lucia and didn't stop herself from laughing, slowly spinning above the waterfall to enjoy the moment. She took the time to drag out the adorable slow dance, twirled to the sound of rushing water. "That snooty chicken! I heard him boast that he wasn't merely the greatest rooster under the sun, but that he was the greatest rooster above the sun. A true lord of war. The sun thought that was very funny, coming from crispy chicken wings, and I thought that **War** might have had an influence."

Her grin broadened and turned wicked, Ember enjoying the thoughts of delicious rotisserie. "When I saw him briefly in the dungeon, I knew my chance had come to strip away an agent of that influence. I got preoccupied instead, but I'm glad you turned him into kebab. I'll want to hear the whole story when there's time. Give me the short version. Landing now, plant your feet."

Artorian did as told, planting his feet when she put him down on solid rock. With its big waterfall, nice greenery, and good rocky ground, the venue was romantic and great for a date. Artorian found that very promising. "The story is interesting. Tried out the villain mode thing. It has its time and place, that's for sure."

"It is! Have you seen mine?" Ember turned on a coin, her mood chipper and excitable as she bounced on her toes. Utterly distracted by the new topic, all attention to the venue got shoved off the boat.

Artorian pushed doubt on a prompt that wasn't there, realizing that his sneaky plans to be sickeningly sweet were going to have to wait. "Didn't I see it already?"

Ember shook her head as she crossed her arms, certain that he had not. She'd told him about the possible fifth specialization thing, but not her villain mode. "You've never seen me in the new Orbital Armor, hon. Watch."

As her boy went to sit on a rock to pay attention, Ember pulled a familiar-looking trick out of her pocket. Flicking her Silverwood Bracelet, Ember equipped a Morpher in the form of a pendant. A pulse of ruby light flared from the gem slotted in the center of the object before the familiar sensation and thrum of an Armored Core coming alive followed suit.

She winked at him, before grinning wide. "Karakum."

CHAPTER TWENTY-SIX

Orbital Armor was not what Artorian had expected.

He would serenade the virtues of a good robe on a hill, but he knew what plate armor was. Full plate not being too much different, you just added more metal. Seamless armor had been a surprise back in the day, but having spent enough time throwing Henry and Marie around, that too had begun to feel like an ordinary sight.

Seamless armor was slightly larger than full plate overall, but still retained the rough confines and dimensions a person ought to sensically have. That one's size was flexible when represented by the Eternia system was slowly starting to make sense. A careful, well-calculated modification for a seamless fit, matching a general kinesthetic sense of the world while one was of the new size.

Orbital Armor cared nothing for this subtlety.

Orbital Armor was meant for an Abyss-blasted Titan.

Forget the concept of a small size discrepancy. Karakum's Armored Core allowed Ember to become a full-on, raise the roof of the heavens and hold the planet on your shoulders, Titan.

As a lattice of Ruby and Iridium surged over Astarte's body, she quickly grew in mass and volume. Once fully covered, the gemstone armor buckled and adapted into the shape of an Asura as four extra arms and a scorpion tail burst from the humanoid shape. The Ruby Titan roared and woke the world, its multiple sharp black slits for eyes leading only into the depths of a black hole.

She was so massive that Ember could easily fit the mesa Artorian sat on between her hands, and chuck the entire brick into the glass window of space. The visual was what sold it.

Ember could chuck the mesa into space without going Titan mode, but there was something about the awe of it all that made the belief a forefront thought, rather than a fact that had to be recollected. Titan-Astarte smirked and winked as she towered high above, her six arms spreading in the universal 'come at me' gesture.

Artorian gawked. "Why wasn't she using *that* for her fifth specialization barrier thing? Forget the fancy arena of the sun and nine-tailed fox trickery. Just throw that madness at someone, it would do fine!"

Astarte wouldn't break the freshly fixed ceiling of Demeter's Dream, but she could! She ran her fingers over the ceiling to show Karakum's new power off. Using a Dungeon Core instead of a Beast Core as a Morpher's foci came with perks!

Posing cute in her oversized armor, she waved down at him with minimal movement. This still caused gusts of winds to whip past his ears before she doffed the Ruby, Asura, and Scorpion-themed armor set. Returning to her prior youthful size, the Orbital Armor turned to particulates and swirled into her pendant.

Smug as a peach, Ember grinned from ear to ear and plopped her butt on the rock next to Young-torian, whose jaw was still on the ground somewhere. "Told you!"

Leaning over when he didn't reply, she pressed her fingers to the bottom of his jaw and helped it shut. "Didn't even use the color picker skill either. Effect Cosmetics? Yes, that."

"That's incredible!" His arms shot up when he regained his faculties with the shutting of his jaw. "I want one! That thing was huge! Why bother calling it Orbital Armor? Just call it Titan Mode. Everyone is going to want one! We're going to need to set aside a whole Dungeon Core for a realm devoted to these, so people can play Attack on Titan as a Titan."

She laughed, poking him in the chest. "That's between you and Tekka! I'm sure he can do it, but it's going to take time and effort."

Artorian snapped to his feet. "Tekka! We have a new project, m'boy! First, Grandpa Mode. Then, to the stars!"

Ember thought the sight was hilarious and laughed louder, jumping up with him and punching the sky. "To the stars! Ad Astra!"

They clasped hands, and three-bounce-jumped in a circle while chanting Ad Astra over and over, getting more and more excited about going to the stars one day. When Artorian tripped, Ember laughed, caught him, and squeezed her boy to her chest with a soft purr that escaped from her throat. "I love having you in my life, my most favorite silly boy."

She then squinted at her surroundings, looked around as if to murder anyone that might be nearby, then leaned down just a bit and pressed a finger to her own cheek. "One is okay."

Young-torian beamed, copied her move from earlier and steadied her by the chin, then sweetly and slowly took his time to kiss Ember's cheek as her face turned pink. Ember quickly pressed a finger to his mouth as he moved back, some steam coming out of her bright red ears. "Not yet. I don't want to hear it yet."

Her boy merely held her hands, his cheeks equally coated in a pleasant hue of pink as she released his mouth. "However long it needs to be, dearest. However long it needs to be."

Ember huffed, crossed her arms, and blew away a strand of red hair that had curled into the middle of her face. "Hush!"

Artorian laughed, and sat back down to not torture his sweetheart. "You're lovely. Your armor, though, is the definition of imposing. Mine is all speed and sleek agility, but yours is power, power, power. Do you even need more of it?"

He had meant the question in jest, but Ember's face turned to stone. Something had shifted in his dearest, her physical form adapting. Ember's age slowly altered to that of a girl about to leave her teens. Then into one of a clear adult. Then into a serious and mature powerhouse cultivator. Ember's red hair shifted as the ages ticked, gaining ancient purple hues at the root and orange-yellow details at the tips.

Before a stunned Young-torian stood Dawn, the Incarnate, in all her radiance. Her adult voice was both tense and serious. "Always. There will always be someone or something that is more powerful than me, and it will always threaten the happy life that I want. When the time comes that it runs into me, I will either be the reason it runs away, or be the reason I couldn't protect my family that day. I will always seek power. I will always keep climbing the cultivation stages. Until I am at the ceiling, and only an act of the heavens could possibly take you away from me. Then if they do? I will instantly be there to break down their door, and get back the soul I adore."

Dawn wrapped her arms around her Young-torian's head, protecting him from unseen forces, and plagues unknown. "I'm not doing this without you, honeybee. You are either here, alive, and thriving, regardless of what form that takes. Or you are not, and then I will burn the entire world down."

She inhaled with shuttered breath. "This will serve a message to any and all that might glance at our local sphere. That the howl from this sector of space comes from a vengeful and cruel **Sun,** collapsed into a black hole, hunting down all those responsible."

Artorian attempted to protest, but Dawn refused to let go. "I will break every Tower. I will crack every node. I will chew every concept and consume all there is in every galaxy. So that when not even entropy is left, I will collapse into the last and brightest star, and bring existence back anew. With the burning reminder that treating **Love** with scorn will get them all the pointy end of my horn. They can do it again, and do it better, or I will be back to claim them all a second time. A third. A fourth. Until I wake in a galactic span that reminds me of you. A universe filled with your affection. A reality that I no longer want to burn down."

Dawn rocked her boy left to right, her face pressed into the top of his head to hide the wet stains on her cheeks. Her hair silvered as her voice faltered. Wrinkles marked her cheeks as she aged like a mortal. Grandma-Dawn held her most important person tight as her heart rate pounded in her ears. "Then, and only then, will I stop crying."

Artorian refused to wait on any sort of system prompt or assistance. The moment was here, and the system could deal. He poured Determination into his intent, forcing the Pylons to action. He grew in muscle, bulk, and height as a pink energy hummed around him.

A splendiferous beard that braided itself grew into place, coming into being as his larger and older arms surrounded his dearest. He lost the hair on his head, but Artorian did not care as his game body shot through the years purely to hold Dawn tight, and hide her face against his scorch-marked pajama shirt. Rather than rip, the clothes, fueled by Determination, grew with him as a blazing solar sigil flared out from his back.

In his most soothing and grandfatherly voice, Artorian the Elder held and rocked his most sunny soul. "I am here, my dearest, most beautiful fire soul. I am here."

The Ancient Elven Lady clung to her boy, now old and grandfatherly. She swallowed loud, but melted into place and lived in the embrace as she processed the anger and inner turmoil. Safe in the only place that could ever be safe.

Artorian kept his muscled arms around Dawn, protectively holding as much of her back as he could. The amount was insufficient, and when he looked up, his swirling eyes spotted the blob of denser than normal energy that gave away where he was being observed from. Rather than chastise or condemn this flagrant breach in privacy when it had been necessary, he spoke a name. "Blanket."

The order was less a command, and more a calling. Blanket, the house-sized Sugar Glider, dive-bombed into Eternia, hurled Artorian's way by an entire team of Wisps that handled import tasks. With a rampant *piiiii* and wide-open wings, Blanket orbital-dropped on Artorian and Dawn, swallowing both up in fluff, warmth, softness, and protection.

Blanket had been called.

Blanket had dropped everything he was doing when Zelia had suddenly been there, her clawed hand extended as she hid her face behind a fan. Her silver irises burned with expectation as she was set and ready to take the Glider exactly to where he needed to be.

Blanket knew his oldest, and most sacred task.

Blanket defends.

Blanket protects.

Balled up in darkness and Sugar Glider fluff, Artorian and Dawn both heard the Beast hiss at the blob of denser energy. Blanket chased the onlookers away before even considered uncurling from his charges.

In the snug darkness, Dawn held her boy still, as Artorian had not let go. She ground her face into his shirt and mumbled, her voice cracking. "Terrible day for rain."

Artorian pet her head, running fingers through her eternally soft hair, regardless of what color it was. "Terrible day for rain. So rude of the weather. I have good news, though?"

Dawn wiped her face again with a sleeve. "Give me something to think about instead. You mentioned something important for later? Just tell me now."

Normally, he would protest. This time, he pulled a weapon from his storage bracelet and eased the Nagamaki into Dawn's arms. "Your sister needs you, and she has come to visit. A small part of her, at least. The part I expect that could be salvaged from the deep void, though she does not have what she needs to be whole again. I lack the memories she needs. Only you, Hadurin, and Mo have those."

Dawn just about teared up again as she felt the familiar spirit in the weapon, and clutched the handle. Pressing the long handhold against her cheek, her finger squeezed to cope as a second wave of emotions hit her right after the first. Yet, this was better for her. If there was to be a battle, she would meet the challenge on the field.

Emotions were no different. "Mayev. My sworn sister."

Blanket opened up just enough of his wadded up fluffy protections to stick his massive nose into the conversation. First sniffing the problem out, and then attacking Dawn with the tip of his tongue to clean her up because the Momma-fire was sad. Momma-fire wouldn't be sad long, Blanket was here! There would be snuggling, and cheering! He knew the locations of all the best honey and berries. Even where Lunella kept the pie!

The Sugar Glider chirped loudly when Dawn protested. Grinding his nose and head in the fluff pile, Blanket was determined to be of help until Dawn couldn't take it anymore and weakly laughed. "Okay, okay, you living pillow of worry. I'll be alright. Many thoughts were holding my heart hostage. Get your wet nose out of my hair. If it wasn't for my Artorian keeping the world clean, I would be a soaked rag. Nose out. Nose out! I need to talk with my sister."

Uncurling like a good boy, Blanket instead rested his massive head on Artorian's bald noggin. The old man chuckled, but didn't mind. Artorian held the silver-haired Dawn, while Dawn held the sheathed Nagamaki tight. Her eyes closed as she communed with the blade as she checked out from the local environment, her mind entirely elsewhere.

Artorian controlled his breathing.

This was fine.

This was just fine.

No matter the glare he was getting from a single prompt hanging in the air. A big, serious one that only showed one word on its entire fancy screen.

Tim had not enjoyed that determined stab to the Pylons.

———

"Ow."

———

Artorian did not mind that one. Tim would be fine. One little forced system ability or skill for an appearance fix was hopefully no big deal. His plan to do it properly had been curtailed. The second prompt that showed up from Tim, on the other hand, was far more frightening.

———

"I'm telling Yuki."

CHAPTER TWENTY-SEVEN

"Oof." Artorian remembered that he was supposed to talk to Yuki about The Oof. Just because that always-on Taunt wasn't heckling anything here didn't mean that it wasn't still going off non-stop. "Whelp, Grandpa's going to get an earful."

Blanket licked his bald head in confusion, but Artorian guffawed at how adorable that was, and used the fabled Telekinesis purely to scratch the top of the Beast's fluffy head. Blanket devolving into happy noises and coos was most excellent. Surely, there was no better use for that fancy power than this. To grab your hot drink from far away. To scratch that spot on one's back that was always just out of reach. To pet the good boy. This was obviously what TK was meant for. TK was a nice shortening. He liked that.

For a moment, the world was peaceful. Soft fluff to lay on. Pleasant waterfall noises. The occasional chirp of a bird. This was pleasant. He wanted more of this. Artorian's big nose turned to the interference of unwanted sound. Of course he wasn't going to get any peace and quiet. Of course.

Sure enough, one of Tim's **Order** gates materialized nearby. The Kings and Castles black and white design of the bishop piece that arrived on scene was eye-catching, even before it opened at the front like a drawbridge. He expected Tim, but the cold wind flowing forth changed that expectation as Yuki strolled forth from the short-lived gate. She gracefully skated over floor-forming ice to be near Artorian, coming to a stand-still with a sharp, ice-scraped stop of the heel.

When their gazes met, her rigid posture was both stern and flawless.

Yuki inhaled deep, and sighed as she took in the sheepish Swole-torian's expression. The frozen-kimono-clad lady of ice and snow regarded him with her usual flair and unimpressed mannerism, judging his predicament. Her voice and tone were both cold, as always. "As a fence is meant to stop people who are on the fence, you will not deter someone who is determined."

That was not the scathing icicle to the kidney Artorian had been expecting. Was… was Yuki taking his side? Over Tim? Was the world ending after all? Again, for the fifteenth time? Honestly, he'd lost track at this point, and who knew how many he'd missed. He'd somehow missed the famous real-world-ending Moonfall, so why pretend otherwise?

Yuki tilted her head, taking out a small notebook that could spell doom for anyone. Nothing was as powerful as a story in the right hands. Well, a few things, but Yuki could certainly convince one otherwise. "I'm going to look the other way on this, my Dreamer. I was woken rudely, but enjoyed the opportu-nity for the nap. I have a question, a concern, and a statement. Which would you like first?"

Artorian blinked, having expected a verbal stabbing. Reaching for his beard, the relief of it being there helped him pick the most worrisome option first. "Concern?"

Yuki flipped several pages in her tiny notebook, freeing one of Zelia's brooches that was being used as a bookmark. She had clearly been informed, and informed thoroughly. "Why do you need my Silencing abilities, when you could easily solve your Taunt problem via the use of your Administrator title?"

Artorian looked dumbstruck. He blinked, vaguely felt his vision lose focus, and moved his hand without thinking. Calling up his admin privileges and pulling on his Administrator lever, a welcome prompt appeared, followed by the appearance of a Wisp in every color of the rainbow, for a total of seven Wisps. One each in the rough ranges of red, orange, yellow, green, blue, indigo, and violet.

Yuki laid a look laden with expectation on him, so Artorian decided to say hello. "This is pleasantly unexpected. I don't suppose one of you would be able to help me fix a problem with an ability?"

The Blue Wisp promptly hovered closer, a tendril moving free for the Wisp to salute. The lack of verbal response was going to add on some difficulty, but Artorian wasn't going to be unhappy about having help for this one. "I have an ability called 'The Oof' that won't deactivate. I need it not to do that."

The Blue Wisp saluted a second time, then turned into a flat prompt screen. A screen that populated with the information in question, before the ability entry changed before Artorian's eyes to something far more satisfactory. An Aura entry!

Womp womp.

———

Aura: The Oof.
Rank: Apprentice.
Special Qualities: Aura, Taunt.
Shape: Orb.
Cost: Free.
Activation: Toggle.
Range: Between one meter and one L, or 33L.
Effect: Taunts all enemies within the listed range, calculated as a radius. Taunt makes all enemies aware of the taunter's position, and they will favor attacking the taunter over other targets, unless the other targets are too opportune to be ignored.
Note: You may only have one Aura type effect active at any given time.

———

Artorian loved several things about this entire interaction. One, he didn't have to mess with the Abyssal screens himself. Two, this Wisp had a fantastic grasp on how he would have wanted to fix it, and did so in record time. Three, he could talk to the Wisp, instead of grumbling to himself about the difficulties. Four, custom notification sounds! "Why thank you! That is most helpful."

Updating his character, the blue screen promptly returned to being a Blue Wisp, who got back into his spot in the arch of rainbow colors, position five out of seven. Checking his sheets, Artorian lost an ability entry, and confirmed that he'd gained the Aura entry instead. "Much better!"

Artorian, also feeling better about life while holding onto Dawn, turned his attention back to Yuki. Yuki was intently studying the silver-haired, grandmotherly version of the Solar Incarnate. A sight she had never expected to see. "She is here physically."

Artorian nodded to Yuki's direct statement. "Mentally elsewhere. She's safe in my arms, and if this helps, she's welcome to be home in them anytime. There was a question and a statement? Question next, if you'd like me to choose."

Yuki remained focused on Dawn as she spoke to the Administrator. "Was there no other way to do this now except stab Tim?"

Figuring she was talking about Grandpa-mode, Artorian apologetically shook his head. "The moment came before the plan to do it right, system-wise, occurred. I must meet the moment when it comes, lest it pass me, and pass me by. To my great, eternal regret. I asked Dev, and I'm sure he'll have something for me that will allow me to switch back. I bet leaving the game with this stature will be problematic in some sense. Youngtorian still needs to go through life the slow way out in Cal."

He adjusted his grip on Dawn as she shifted to lay on him

better. "Honestly? I'm glad that dumping energy into the system still works. I try not to use the hidden tricks, but necessity called. The game comes second for me, and I'm looking forward to wrapping this beta round up. I'm being given lots of interesting tools and toys to try, but Light Shaping by itself could be a whole book."

He tilted his head in ponderance. "I think for the game experience to work for me, I may have to start at the bottom like everyone else. Otherwise, I may as well just play boss characters or Administrator. I'm hoping to hand off all my abilities and skills to some students? Someone else could get far better use out of all the goodies I've garnered. Perhaps during the trials when new people have a go at Eternia?"

Yuki nodded with closed eyes, accepting that he'd at least tried to consider Tim. "I find comfort in your grasp of the gentle transition, and enjoy your thoughts of delegating your tools. This knowledge does not all have to be written in your story. Others may write their own, and give attention to that which you could not. I will speak to Dev about a more gentle method of form control. If he doesn't beat me to it. Now that I have taken in your current predicament, that brings us directly to my statement."

Not about to argue, Artorian replied with a half-smile when Yuki upturned her palm. The colorful beach-attire clothing covered in palm-tree shapes that Yuki pulled out of nowhere looked oddly familiar, making Artorian squint and lean forward. "Hold the pie. Why do I know that design?"

The cold lady smirked far too ominously for the clothing's existence to be a good thing. "The Dwarves from the Coast of Rica deeply and truly enjoyed your performance in your bout against Henry and Marie. Particularly while under the capoeira effect of **Celebration** and **Rhythm**. Brasilia and Bellini greatly influenced their beach-heavy party styles. They made you this set, though they sized the set for, and I quote: a muscle-Grandpa. A Swole-torian. A Gains-torian. Sir Lift-orian. The

Beefcake. Mr. Tough Love. Welcome to relaxation cultivation. Sip the coconut."

Was he supposed to be proud, or cringe horribly?

Fifty-fifty? Do both at the same time? "None of that sounded like a statement, madam."

Yuki proceeded to lean into the wide-open trap she had laid, with Artorian stepping right into the middle of it. "You will be using this as your attire. There will be no complaints."

Artorian looked up to Blanket for help, but the house-sized Glider was shaking his head left and right that he was not getting involved in this, lest he be turned into a large sorbet. A sensible choice. Excellent wisdom. Unfortunately, that left Artorian in the lurch. "I'm going to pretend that it's part of your 'looking the other way' fee, Yuki. I'll make them happy, but it lacks something."

Yuki wasted no time holding up a brand-new set of stylish sunglasses. "Worry not, my Dreamer. I would never let a story develop without sufficient material. Particularly when I am keeping track, and writing them down."

Artorian sighed, running a hand over his bald head that had cleaned itself free from Beast saliva. "About that, is now a good time to voice an odd concern?"

Yuki raised a snowy brow, but rolled her wrist for him to keep speaking. She placed the clothing set, glasses, and accompanying footwear down on some green foliage that was starting to show signs of fruit. The Demeter grapes grew between bushels of lavender, with part of the plant entangled around a rusted dory. A shame for a nice spear like that to be reduced to decoration. "A side thought, with you placing the clothes, is that I miss Artifacting. I'd have loved to turn that stabby stick into something nice."

The Yellow Wisp moving in front of the rainbow-arch congregation caught his attention, but he held up a finger. "One moment. I'm glad about what you moving means, but one madness at a time or I'm going to lose track of my thoughts."

Yuki sagely nodded at this wisdom, before Artorian

addressed her. "Am I doing all right? Am I in danger of meandering into Wandering Sun territory? Are people upset?"

The well-dressed **Kenopsia** cultivator raised her hand, a throne of ice growing and freezing into place before she sat. Folding one leg over the other, she held her own hands and looked at the sky to consider. "I believe I understand the spirit of your question, rather than the phrasing. So I will answer the spirit, and let yours be at ease."

Artorian was once more surprised at the response, but leaned in for what she had to say. Leaning back in her frozen throne, Yuki pressed some of her fingers to her cheek while resting her elbow. "Ups and downs are normal. Not all life is endless, constant action. Not all happens while at rest. You have some fans in the stands that are vocal about your adventures lacking a coherent plot. I see that originating from a lack of understanding per where you've come from, and a lack of grasp of where it is you're going. To me, both are clear."

Her off-hand clicked nails against the icy armrest. "There are some worries that you get sidetracked too much, but those people fail to understand that all you do, my Dreamer, is get sidetracked. You love people, and will go to great lengths for them. You take strolls to smell the roses, fall into a narrative that you stick your nose into, and work with the life that comes from it. Some of these people return to help you in their darkest hour. Some only ever live in the background, but remember you fondly. There is nothing wrong with this."

Remaining silent, and doing his best to get onto her track of thought, Artorian pet Dawn's resting head as Yuki spoke. "In Eternia terms, you have turned people that could have been end-bosses into the closest of friends. Purely because you are who you are. Because you chose to love them, instead of kill them. Because you care more about helping a person, than solving their problem. To love someone long term is to attend a thousand funerals of the people they used to be. This problem is especially potent for those of us who are eternal, because while our faces may remain the same, what is behind that face may not."

She pointed at him, but without derision or judgment. "Your face changes. Your age changes. Most importantly, Artorian, who you are at your core does not change. To many of us for whom that cycle swirls in the opposite direction, this is a blessing in disguise. You are a lighthouse in unknown waters. Firm and steady. Your arms open, your smile wide."

When she laced her fingers on her lap, the world around her had gone quiet. To give credence to her words. "Not all situations can be a Henry and Marie, a Barry and Ghreziz. In the course of your life? The shortest route to your destination is made of detours. Your side quests, deemed unimportant to someone else, turn out to be main quests that went unseen by those with different priorities. Do not be concerned by these priorities that others may have of you. Pay no heed to the direction another wants you to take. Ignore the brook and babble of the fans that watch you from Cal. Care only for the direction you would have taken without their influence, and walk proud and strong across that frozen lake."

She smirked, just a little. "Polly knows you could use more Pride."

The broken claymore pushed itself from Artorian's storage bracelet purely to form a moonlight fist and shake it at Yuki, before retreating to the safety of the warehouse.

Pressing her fingers to her mouth to stifle her amusement, Yuki still formed a highly unusual smile. Unusual because Artorian wasn't used to the sight. He wasn't sure if he ever would be, but politely listened as Yuki wrapped up her answer. "You can't please everyone, my Dreamer. Do not try. You cannot save everyone. Cope as you can. Someone will always nitpick and find something wrong with the flow of another's life, their decisions, take your pick. Ignore them. You touch hearts and heal minds, and those hearts and minds are better for it."

Tapping her lips, she shared commentary that had been overheard. "Apiculteur, that Wood Elf, and currently self-proclaimed Mead Magus, said this: 'Artorian refuses to be king, no matter how many yearn for such a rule. Not because he is incapable, but because he cannot stand the thought of someone falling through the cracks, when it's his responsibility to take care of them. Artorian would rather be wandering around, ready to catch those people.' I thought that was both sweet, and accurate."

Yuki was done, but clearly had her thoughts still stuck on something. Artorian, being Artorian, gently prompted her to vocalize the thought. "Please do feel free to vent your thoughts, Yuki. I don't mind. I'd love to ask how you are doing as well, but I have the feeling you're not in that kind of mood."

Yuki paused for a beat, but gave Artorian something to work with. "I am not, though I am well. I wish to return to watching Fuyu No Arashi's progress, though I am not bothered regardless if my creation ends up winning or losing against New Haven. Lenore is doing admirably, for now."

Artorian appreciated that she took the moment to share. "Thank you, Yuki. You had a worry?"

She nodded, letting the thought free. "There was some mumble-grumbling on the Task Manager. What he was. Where did he come from? There were complaints from the crowd that there was no lead up to his existence, but Api successfully surmised that the Task Manager was a kind of Master Pylon. A naturally grown, intelligent Pylon meant to keep all the synthetic ones in line. Tim created it to offload a lot of his responsibilities, but that Task Manager was corrupted by lingering whispers from Barry. Some of the gossip I hear is strange, but that one stuck with me. Not all villains have visibility. Not all heroes are heroic."

She then squinted at the distance, her tone sour. "Then, of course, there is *Pag*."

CHAPTER TWENTY-EIGHT

"Pag is coming up too much for my liking." Artorian held his beard, wondering if he needed to shift priorities. "Something about the Pylon Holds? Moony mentioned it as well."

Yuki's sour tone held. "He is the reason that Amalgam Pylons are more common than they ought to be, has infiltrated several holds like the rat he currently is, and is cackling his way through multiple invasions of ratkind. Believing that by holding the Pylons, he will hold all the power there is to hold in the game."

Artorian had to rub his forehead. "*Pag?*"

Having been in the same boat, Yuki merely nodded with forced patience. "Pag."

"*Mmphrrow!*" Grandma Dawn rose as if from a nap cut short, shoving the Nagamaki into Artorian's hands. She got up like a stretching cat straightening its tail, walked off indignantly, and stole the show by catching fire. Reducing herself to a heap of ash, Dawn rose anew! Rising as a phoenix from the crumbling flames. A younger Ember rose and stretched without a care in the world, brushing the soot from her being once she was up and running.

Blanket instantly slammed his wing down, preventing any unruly onlookers from getting any ideas before new clothes could be provided to the soot-coated lady. Soot did not count as clothing. Artorian's Aura, wholesome as ever, thought only of the bath it needed to provide, and therefore did as Ember sorted her own clothing problem.

Ember, whose priorities were far from the concept of decency, had first pressed her hands to her hips before realizing what Blanket was chirping at her for.

She pulled new clothes from the Silverwood Bracelet that snapped back into place on her wrist, adding to the prior conversation without missing a beat. "Pag has been a pain in my butt since the days of yore, and I think he picked the Pylon holds because we can't use powers there. Not safely. Any ability-use done that close to the source codes will make many booms. The wrong vibration can nova an entire hold, and there's hard rules against energy meter use. If we can get our hands on Light Fusion Beamers? That's the way to go. Pylons bounce beams from these things away."

Walking around Blanket's wing in her prior youthful form as she fluffed her carmine red hair, Ember sported a very pleasant-looking orange cheongsam that looked to be of clear Dark Elven make. The outfit had Brianna written all over it, and Artorian and Yuki both gave gentle applause when she performed a few modeling spins.

Ember then power-walked to Artorian and looked him up and down with indignation. "Too old! Fix it. Match me!"

Artorian reared his head back and roared with laughter. "*Hahaha*, I can't!"

Rising from her throne, Yuki dismissed the icy creation and allowed the sculpted seat that was left behind to begin melting. "That is my cue to go check on our crafty little Gnome."

The slam of a Bifrost punching the ground made them all jerk and stagger as the sound it made was akin to metal twisting. Deverash the Gnome became visible when the rainbow light receded, his tiny frame holding a praise the sun pose. "Have no fear! Gnomes are here!"

He then shoved a finger to the sky after dancing by doing a fanciful twist. "K-pow!"

Artorian's character screen opened by itself, the system giving him a wonderful update. Complete with another delightful, funky new system noise. Like a spring being far too excited about what it could do. The game or its controllers were making them to be silly at this point, but Artorian thought it amusing. Did he have a favorite yet? He should pick a favorite system prompt noise. Gold medal so far was either on the clickety-clacks, or... honestly? Quackbang. He got a kick out of Quackbang.

Poing!

———

Notice!

Race upgrade: Rejuvenescence.

The potential of the Nascent Being blooms beautifully, as a wellspring of all that is new. Rejuvenescence allows a Nascent Being to revert its physical form to a younger state of being. This effectively allows a Nascent Being to be functionally immortal, if they so choose.

———

Notice!

Race upgrade: Potentia.

The form suits function. Function suits form. The great hidden potential of a Nascent Being is unknown, allowing them to shift into a state of greatest prowess. This may be reflected via a chance of age, musculature, or other yet unknown factors. Potentia allows a Nascent Being to grow into stages of adulthood, bolstering physical maturity.

———

Artorian whistled loud. "That's a big pie slice, Dev. Functionally immortal? There's no way that's fair or balanced. The other thing is basically Grandpa Mode, and that does place a smile on my face."

The Gnome shot Artorian the stink eye. "You'd think so! You'd reeeeally think so, but no! We've had functional immortality in Cal for ages, and barely anyone has made the kinds of leaps and strides that would be assumed. Amount of time alive does not equal the amount of time devoted to a particular type of growth. *Rejuvenescence* doesn't give you the infinite growth you think it's going to give you, and Dawn has had a working version for far longer as is."

The fancy Gnome spun on the heel of his shiny, black, and expensive-looking shoes. "Speaking of, oh grand lady of the hot flames. Are you ever going to tell Cal that you figured out the Phoenix problem long ago? He's still stuck at Molotov Cockatiels."

Ember laughed, shook her head no, and crossed her arms. "Mine!"

"Then I know nothing." Throwing his hands to the air, Dev didn't even try to pursue the matter. He did take several steps to the left before politely making a motion at Yuki that he was getting out of her way. "Apologies for the rushed entrance, but I needed to deliver that quickly, and Tim was hoping you'd be back soon, Kiki."

Ember and Artorian both shot Yuki a look at the nickname used, but she was an unreadable statue of ice. Dev then spotted the frost throne, and should have probably kept his mouth shut. "That looks like a civil engineer designed it."

Cupping a hand next to his mouth, he whispered in the direction of his friend. "That means it's ugly. You need architects to make things pretty. Especially city layouts."

Artorian drew in a deep breath, but pressed his lips together tight and released a sound that made Blanket worried, but made Ember understand that he didn't want to comment for worry and fear of redirecting Yuki's wrath. Ember, on the other pyre, told Dev what he needed to hear. "You should be running."

Believing that to be a silly notion, the dapper Gnome was about to extoll the virtues of his opinion. The sudden drop in temperature made him dive into his own Bifrost. The rainbow light came down, snatched him up, and carried him away.

Yuki gave a light, extremely polite bow to the Administrator and the Solar Saintess, then excused herself with a prim and perfect skate-slide into the same Bifrost floor-carving. The rainbow light came down, snatched her up, and carried her away. The cold and eerie atmosphere vanished with Yuki, which allowed Grandpa-torian to flop-fall down onto Blanket and release his held breath. "*Pfffff*... All these years, and I still get nervous."

Ember thought that very funny, but pointed to the rainbow array of Wisps still waiting on him. Artorian looked, then remembered he'd asked about Artifacting and the yellow one had moved forward. "Right. I'm a little frazzled at the moment. Please feel free to Artifact that dory spear as you see fit. I will be deactivating my Administrator functions, but thank you all for being here and making this old man's life a bit more convenient."

He gave them each a polite nod, which became very silly after the seventh head bob. Cranking the title lever, the seven Wisps all bobbed in unison, then popped out of sight. "Pleasant to know that works as it does. I feel some lingering embarrass-ment for not having thought of using the Administrator title, but that's what I get."

Artorian motioned at his Potentia and Rejuvenescence prompts. "You wanted a Young-torian, dearest?"

Nodding quickly and with repetition, Ember's preferences were clear.

"Rejuvenescence." Glowing bright with the purest of light, Artorian's grandfatherly form diminished and condensed, melting away as a figure of luminance, before the palettes of normal skin tones and hair colors returned to the prior Young-torian form that he'd been running around with this entire time.

Check one. Bald chin, fluffy hair! Excellent.

Check two, voice. "Testing, testing, one, two, three."

That was his younger voice again alright. Standing and stretching, he offered Ember back the Nagamaki. "Works as intended. On with the show. Sugar, what were we doing again?"

"You're starting with stowing Ephira. I've done what I can, but she needs a nap, and then she needs to go see Don and Hadurin." Ember paused her train of thought when she spotted the colorful clothing that Yuki had brought. Clothing that currently no longer fit her boy. "Well, I'm not that flippant. No matter how much I'd like to see that sunrise, pink-to-orange gradient, Dwarven beach getup, on my most favorite longbeard."

Artorian had no such qualms! He snatched the clothes, and tried the other race upgrade right away. "Potentia!"

Returning to the same luminant person-shape, Artorian increased in size, quickly and easily returning to the full form of Swole-torian. Dressed in the new digs as a bonus convenience!

Check one. Bald head, fluffy beard! Excellent.

Check two, voice. "Testing, testing, one, two, three."

That was his grandfatherly voice again alright. "I love it. I love it a lot. Works like a charm, doesn't hurt, is quick, and rife with potential for mischief!"

Ember's Elven ear twitched at that last detail. "What?"

"What?" Artorian shot her a gleaming, forcefully innocent smile that showed far too many teeth for the claim to hold weight or water. He posed magnanimously in his Dwarven beach attire, and really wanted to cause trouble at the Coast of Rica. Before Dawn blew it up, or he was otherwise blamed for the mass eviction of all 'bro' type Dwarves to... Svartalfheim? Probably Svartalfheim.

CHAPTER TWENTY-NINE

The sudden arrival of the Drums of Ganja-Tai made both Ember and Artorian look around for the musical source. Spotting a brand-new glob of observation energy, Grandpa whisked the stick that Blanket had sent him through the mail from his bracelet, and chucked it at the unwelcome glob. "I'm having none of that. Blanket! I choose you!"

Blanket instantly hurled himself after the stick with a *chiiii*!

An odd *vwop*—that sounded far too close to a Teleport for it not to be one—absconded with Blanket as the Sugar Glider vanished from Eternia. Based on the sudden screeching that erupted through his brooch, Zelia appeared to have been mid-progress on some shenanigans in a Dwarven tavern. Shenanigans that had been thwarted by a rogue Sugar Glider and a wee stick that Blanket was now breaking said tavern to find.

"Get em, Blankie." Artorian flicked his brooch so the sound would stop.

Checking himself while in the new attire, Swole-torian did some light flexing, then tried to reach for the solar sigil that was still stuck in a hover pattern behind his back. "Alright now, what's this thing? Isn't this part of the armor? Why's it out?"

Rifling through his screens, he paused at his inventory prompt. "Dawn of the Deep Soul, a sunrise beach-attire clothing set. Gradients of pink to orange. Has a counterpart called Dusk of the Deep Soul, a sunset beach-attire clothing set."

Ember squinted at the horizon, pulling that very set out of her bracelet. "I was wondering what this orange to purple gradient clothing set was for! It covers so little, though the frilly skirt is cute. The cutouts are nice. More tactical movement potential. This bundle was hurriedly shoved into my hands, but there was no explanation. This attire is meant to match? I like that! Beach adventure!"

Checking the details on the clothes, Ember grumbled, needing to stow the swimsuit right back into storage. "My getting older and younger cycle isn't as convenient as yours. I may have to wait to wear it. It's sized to my adult shape, not my teen shape. What a lump of coal."

"Rejuvenescence." In a flash of light, Artorian returned to being Young-torian, though the clothes had swapped themselves out for his burned pajama set. "That is… not how I was expecting that to work. Rejuvenescence and Potentia will size my existing clothes up if I don't have an alternative, but will swap them out if I do? Huh."

"I am not one to complain about convenience." Ember sat, her gaze leveled at him as if delivered over the rim of glasses. "Are we having a pleasant date, or…?"

She stopped talking when the glob of observation energy returned, both of their gazes flicking towards the intrusion. Ember glared, the heat in her vicinity rising. "The date will wait. I think I have a new venue in mind. A nice, empty, deserted beach. Not a Dwarf in sight for leagues."

The blob quickly made itself scarce after spitting Blanket back out, but it was too late. The damage was done. The massive Sugar Glider face-planted onto the mesa, looked up with the stick in his mouth, then shifted into a Sugar Glider the size of a child's hand and skedaddled over to Artorian. Making himself right at home on Young-torian's head, he sped off once more when Artorian took the stick and chucked it all the way to another mesa.

Blanket took off after the stick like a Gnomish rocket.

Ember exhaled fire, her hands opening and closing. "Honey? Run me through events or things we can do? Excluding bringing Ephira to Nidavellir. I am postponing the planned visit. Don's nudge during the Crème de la Crème was already on my nerves. My tea kettle is making an unhappy sound. Hadurin has less of my ire, having cleverly kept to himself, but I'm dangerously close to stepping into the age-old Elf-versus-Dwarf feud."

Glad to provide alternatives, Artorian ran through his planned stops while counting on his fingers. "A serious talk with Poirot about life and purpose. Fetching the sharks from the Asgard Asteroid Belt. Finding Señor Louis and making a friend to scratch off a quest. Pag and the Pylons. For which we need LFB's, and to possibly see Soni and someone called One-Stone. Then, lastly, backhanding the chill out of New Haven. Then we go home? Maybe I can cultivate without going boom? I'll go where I'm needed, but if I'm no longer needed anywhere, there is a small ocean of things I'd like to do. I'm already incapable of being in all the places I want to be."

Instead of getting to do any of that, a muscular man dressed in the gaudiest reds and yellows fell from the sky. Accompanied by a royal klaxon's *pwaa-waaaamp*.

The first thing properly visible after his dusty impact with the ground was a pompadour so large that it stole the entire show. It also stole the rest of Artorian's train of thought, when what was clearly going to be a pain in the keister introduced himself. Worst of all, the newcomer did it in an annoying song-song style. "Perrrrr-fec-tion is here!"

Flicking a comb free, Artorian and Ember watched in disbelief as the impressive specimen groomed his impossible pompadour. Surely such a persona was meant as a stage play. No person would willingly smile at them in the same way that a bar patron looked at their last beer when trying to seduce the glass into refilling itself.

"All hail with breath bating, Gaston the expectorating!" Spitting powerfully, Gaston the Gaudy posed.

His massive teeth gleamed as he adopted a stance meant to receive endless adulation, with his shoulders squared and chest puffed out. His boot stepped on a stone that he was clearly pretending to be a stump, while one muscled arm flexed up, and the other muscled arm flexed down. "There is no es-cape from Gast-on! I herald my wake by klax-on!"

Ember asked Artorian questions with expressions, but Young-torian put his hands up with a shrug. "I have no idea, sugar. Is Odin teaching classes on haughty and heinous behavior now?"

Ember turned away from the unwelcome addition to their quiet little getaway, ignoring Mr. Pompadour entirely. "Cultivation is still going to be a no-no, darling. Eternia is building you up artificially, so you don't suffer the explosive side-effects of trying it in Cal. The tethering issue didn't magically fix itself. If you want to truly and properly cultivate again, we'll need to be out of Cal. If you want to be a proper Mage without being reliant on Cal, you'll have to make that transition while not in a Soul Space. Your Mana may be hanging around like a worried wolfpack, but they're all good boys."

"Do not ignore Gaston!" The man made mostly of pompadour swung with intent to sock the small girl in the cheek, for having the cheek to speak over him. None interrupted Gaston! She appeared neither perturbed, nor about to do anything about it.

Gaston's powerful fist struck an immovable object, halting his angered rush as polished knuckles hit an open palm made from constellation light that grabbed his hand.

Ember inspected her orange stiletto nails, altering them to be just a touch sharper without bothering to look at the mismanaged miscreant who'd thrown a haymaker. "Sugar?"

Cosmic-torian turned to his dearest, linked into his full

fierce Deity mode. Unlike last time when his Divine mode had turned grandfatherly, this time the constellatory form had remained youthful. His Young-torian voice was mostly unchanged, gaining a bit of holiness as spice if one was paying close attention. Fierce Deity mask or not, the majora of his cadence went unchanged. "Sweetheart?"

Ember squeezed her hand into itself so hard that her knuckles turned white and popped. "I understand that Gaston is angry because you're muddling with the system he's specifically tasked to oversee, but I am in a bad mood."

She fluttered her eyelashes. "Break him for me? Just a bit? No holding back."

Cosmic-torian smiled at her adoringly, then squeezed and crushed Gaston's hand into a shattered wreck of broken bone shards and twisted meat. The girly scream that followed went ignored. "Ah, the things I do for **Love**. Of course, precious."

Gaston had much to say, great grievances to air in lyrical form, and many complaints to lever. Gaston, the magnificent specimen, got as far as a yelped scream. Pulled in by his shattered hand, Cosmic-torian stepped into the forward motion and replied with a haymaker of his own. The cosmic punch cracked Gaston's head, sending the burly man's legs straight into the air from the momentum and spin applied.

Rather than letting go of Gaston's arm—which broke with a snap, crackle, and pop—Cosmic-torian instead stomped Mr. Pompadour's face into the ground, breaking it with a rock-shattering thunderclap and shoving the sing-song-savage down a full foot. "Alley-oop! Is that enough for you, hon?"

Ember sighed wistfully, her expression dreamy. "I love that about you, hon. Even having freshly given up the Violence class that would have grown from this, you're not afraid to express your priorities."

Cosmic-torian released Gaston's mangled hand, tapping into Effortless Light Shaping to downwards-kick the girly-screamer with a beam of light, cracking the interior of the mesa while burying the pompadour with a small earthquake. The interloper ended up crumpled and shoved several hundred feet down into the limestone's crags.

A whimpered, non-melodic 'ow' floated back up through the cracks as Artorian turned off his Fierce Deity mode, sitting down next to his dearest and accepting her hands in his. "Of course, Dawny. He wasn't welcome, was clearly here to stir the pot, and this put a smile on your face."

He winked like a fox. "I may be a good soul most of my days, but sometimes you need to snap a raider's neck. Or twenty. Anyone who comes out and swings for the fences to the tune of Jasper, Odin, or Zeus's playbook? We know that problem is only going to be solved by throwing hands."

Gaston's voice gained strength from the crack in the limestone. "The mage man is in melee! Why is the mage man in melee? This is against the rules! Where are my Task Managers? The one true way is by discovery through gameplay, not minmaxing via mechanics. Gaston calls foul play!"

Breaking free from the ground looking no worse for wear, the immaculate specimen flexed his previously mangled hand open and closed. Physically, Gaston looked completely unharmed as he flicked his comb back out to fix the style of his pompadour. "You cannot hurt me, cheating child. Only Gaston is allowed true perfection! The ways of Thaumaturgy and Fleshmancy are Gaston's, and Gaston's alone! The rest of you ought to be penalized properly for even attempting to reach my grandeur. You are eschewing the proper order of things! It is Gaston who sits at the top. Only Gaston is to be perfect, with flawless attributes. The rest of you are beneath Gaston!"

Artorian held his face and didn't want to say anything as Polly pulled themself free from his bracelet in the shape of liquid moonlight. Purely to pull up their metaphorical sleeves. The Parrot in sword form then got upset when it wasn't **Pride** that was at work here, as this was an **Envy** battle. Begrudgingly, Polly made the 'I'm watching you' motions and slunk back into the bracelet as Artorian translated for Ember. "Found the midboss."

About to break out into song, the gaudy muscle-man entered his pose of accepting adulation and got as far as uttering one more sentence. "My power comes from a Titan!"

Astarte silenced this claim, her claw clamped on Gaston's face. Those burning orange nails squeezed his mouth shut as her heat and fire utterly boiled over. "I'll kill your Titan next, Mr. Gelatinous Grime."

The species-mention made Artorian flicker Truesight. Sure enough, Gaston was no human. Though what creature possessed a perfectly square shape for a shadow? He didn't know. That was a new one, unless Gaston was a Gnome in another funky new die form. Plausible, but unlikely. Dawny would have just called Pompadour-man a Gnome if that were the case. What was a Gelatinous Grime?

Artorian didn't like the initial thought he was provided, and made sure his Cleaning Aura was cranked up to full blast. "Please don't let Gaston be a slime. Or an ooze. Though it would explain the schmooze."

He shook his head. The time for details was over. Gaston slapped Ember, and that was the beginning of the end. Astarte turned into a volcano, and away went the little details of the pleasant venue as she took the majority of the mesa with it. Her outrage flattened the entire top surface of the limestone landscape into a Budokai Tenkaichi ring as her personal Pressure Aura flared.

Bubbly brooks turned into vapor from the heat, plantlife shriveled to become particulate from the pressure, and the waterfall packed its bags to go on vacation to another mesa. Their current mesa decided it would salute the scene and turn into a perfect cylinder. With pretty little hatch-mark cross-shapes on the arena floor, because it was important that all squares make a circle.

"Gaston is immune to your fume!" For his muffled comment, Mr. Pompadour ended up hurled across the arena floor like a stone skipping fifty times over a particularly good lake, with Astarte boiling in place as a localized furnace.

She was mad, but flung several of her screens open. Her teeth remained grit as she spoke. "He. Stole. Traits. I lost Free from Gaston, and Experimental Attributes."

Seething, her burning gaze slowly turned to Artorian. Her voice turned sweet, but her smile couldn't succeed in its attempt to look innocent or non-threatening. "Honey? Can I see your Villain Mode? If I fight now, I will break everything that Moony fixed, and far faster. I want to do this myself, but I have a Titan to settle a score with, and finding the right one requires some menu work. I think that—like a certain roasted Task Manager—Gaston is cheating, and there is no victory condition until I can strip his power source away from him. So that has to be my focus. Can I work to the sounds of a healthy smackdown?"

Young-torian pressed his fingers to his lips and blew her a kiss with the wave of his hand. Tapping into both segments of Effortless Shaping, he pulled on the most basic of alterations to his environment. If he was going to show off to his sweetheart, and provide entertainment to take her upset mind from things? Then he would make sure that there was a show, laden with presentation. "Then it will be my great pleasure to introduce to you—my most important darling—Dreadshine. The Nightmare Fuel."

CHAPTER THIRTY

Artorian mentally checked in with Voltekka. The Teslasaur's response returned pain. Through the visual of teary eyes and a sobby, bulged out lower lip, Tekka looked back at him like a child that had fallen from a seesaw. "Do you want me to leave you out of this, my boy?"

Tekka had been kneed hard, but stiffened his expression and wiped the wetness away from his eyes. The energy in his Armored Core was negligible, and Tekka still needed serious naptime, but he puffed out his chest anyway. If Artorian needed him then, by the chompiest of chomps, Tekka would be there.

Artorian placed a proud mental hand on Tekka's head. "Then let's put on a show."

Channeling Effortless Light Shaping, the natural arena lighting around Artorian shifted, centering entirely on him like a spotlight.

With the arena prepared, he fueled Determination into his Armored Core, but the effort did not seem to have the intended effect. The suit of seamless plate enveloped Sunshine's youthful form, but the feeling of dynamic energy within the Armored Core didn't change at all. At most, he was giving Tekka a lease on activation time, but Determination did nothing when it came to replenishment.

Oddly thematically fitting? Determination could keep you going, but it wasn't going to mend wounds or fill an empty stomach. Speaking of thematic changes…

"Effect Cosmetics. *Villain*." The current Ad Astra glow of Voltekka armor altered. Rather than the friendly snowy whites and celestine blues, an onyx black and carmine red color scheme bled over his being.

Culminating with a dangerous hum, Voltekka's slitted visor shone with an imposing crimson sheen. Adopting a low pose so it could get full attention, the sigil of a roaring sun freshly burst free from Artorian's back. The sigil was far larger and more intense than the lesser version provided by his beach attire. Adapting to the new color scheme, the carmine sun added to the menacing flair as Dreadshine grew to the size of an adult human.

Voltekka released a metallic rumble when the morphing completed, the adult-sized warrior rising up with his arms wide. As Dreadshine shifted the local illumination to dampen and darken, the lines on the seamless plate protections—where seams ought to be—gained thematically correct carmine illumination that bloomed with ominous glow, allowing only the lit-up segments of Voltekka to be visible within the confines of the mesa's arena.

The alteration to area lighting felt effortless to Artorian, the change done mostly by feeling. These effortless abilities he needed to test were going to come in very handy for a whole lot of things.

Adding to the flair and summoning several more observers, the Voice of the World released a horn call. A cube formed above the middle of the arena, the hanging prompt hovering in place with the same information presented on all sides.

———

Encounter!
   Gaston the Matchless.
   VS.
   Dreadshine the Nightmare Fuel.

———

Excellent. The stage was ready, his opponent was picking himself up, and the first sprinkling of flair had been thrown out as confetti. The warrior was ready, now for the armaments!

"Incursus." Dreadshine's metallic villain voice rumbled as he pressed fingers to his collar, compressing the communication brooch. "Give me some information to work with as it rolls in."

Releasing the brooch, Dreadshine clicked off his Cleaning Presence. A different Aura was needed for a good show. There was no need to further taunt the pompadour, and he didn't want to fade the Gelatinous Grime to sleep. Dawny needed something for her nerves, so Dreadshine cranked up the Pressure while retaining his 'come at me,' arms-wide pose.

The area around him compressed as gravity doubled, then tripled, then quadrupled, and kept going. This visually manifested around Dreadshine as tiny black lines that were pulled down to the ground before being further pulled out of the air above. Artorian mentally toggled everyone except Gaston to be counted as exclusions, so the effect wouldn't flatten them. Dawny would be fine, but if Blanket blindly rushed back, the Glider needed to be fine as well.

Incursus's personalized clickety-clack prompt sound chimed with grace.

K-chink!

———

Aura use: Pressure.
   Alternative name: Reiatsu.
   Ticket resolution: Pressure Damage is tallied per second.

Ticket closed.

———

Excellent. Time for the weapons check.

Ephira? Out of commission. No Nagamaki.

Sorrow? Out of commission. No katana.

Compassion? Out of commission. No Principe.

Polly? Out of commission. No claymore.

Rats.

Archimedes? Good to go.

Broom? Can vroom.

The O.o.P? Let's O.o.Not.

Voltekker? *Haha. No.*

This meant he had fists, fighting styles, the Brilliant Behemoth, and shaping.

Plus one more thing, he supposed.

"Attention on Gaston!" Gaston reintroduced himself to the fray with a flying haymaker, employing insanity. As he was trying a second time that which didn't work the first time.

Dreadshine reacted by testing a new toy. Raising his armored gauntlet, Artorian visually appeared to squeeze air with his armored claws. Gaston *hurked* loudly as he was stopped in place by an unseen force that violently grabbed him by the chest.

"I'm trying it for you, Zelia." Reading the kinetic flow, Dreadshine leaned into the Kinesis ability.

Altering his hand-claw to form two outstretched fingers, Dreadshine rapidly and disparagingly thrust them toward the arena floor. His kinetic grab took Gaston with it as he floor-smashed the Gelatinous Grime in humanoid shape. He added as much force and pressed down as hard as he thought he could, which was proving hard to measure. Kinetic flow needed more ranks.

A clever idea occurred. If he could use Kinesis to touch his opponent without being in direct melee range, that meant he could strike them, couldn't he? He could step on sound, so sound could be struck. How much of a leap was raw force? Keywords mattered. "Brilliant Behemoth."

Sk-boom!

Dreadshine felt the need for some insurance, channeling Effortless Sound Shaping to slap both an explosive and percussive show on top of the kinetic shove. The expected girly scream might as well have been music, which reminded Artorian that this component was so far missing from the performance. He should really stop spending so much time around bards; they were influencing him. The consideration reminded him to use rhythm. He had never become a competent musician, but Artorian did so very much like his percussion.

Holding up his hand and about to snap his fingers, Dreadshine altered the light in his immediate darkness to pulse in strobes. Matching them to the beat that he began to tap out with his foot, before he dropped the bass. "Three, two, one, *Wub*."

Sk-boom!

The finger-snap mixed an explosive, sound-based cavitation bubble directly above the floored Gaston, mixed with a Brilliant Behemoth. Effortless Sound Shaping then took that initial bang from the behemoth, turned it into a follow-up Wub, and finished that combination off with another Brilliant Behemoth. The explosion of which served as the starting point for another finger-snap, repeating the process.

Sk-boom!

Each time Dreadshine snapped his fingers, he also appeared to have moved closer to Gaston, the strobes in his vicinity masking normal movement and only showing segments of Dreadshine's current location. Segments that only appeared in matching unison to the dropped beat of the wubs that kept punching Mr. Matchless repeatedly into the floor.

Gaston tried to get up, of course.

While the Pressure damage was not worth paying attention to, the lockdown effect was far more difficult to handle and mitigate. Keeping a humanoid shape cohesive at all was a task and a half, and the kinetic grip on his chest that kept him pinned down wasn't helping. Piling concussive and explosive damage on top of that did not help matters, nor Gaston's chances of getting back up. That was not what irritated Gaston to no end. The damage numbers so far, he could ignore. The method in which this cheating child of an opponent was approaching him?

Unacceptable.

Each time Dreadshine was visible, the accursed annoyance dared to do it in style. Each moment of visibility, before the finger-snap that made the boom go boom-boom, was accompanied by a full-on pose. Dreadshine phonk-walked toward him with all the time in the world, posing like some kind of Spiritual Summon user that liked to stand in place and look menacing.

How dare he take the spotlight from Gaston like that? That center-stage light belonged to Gaston. That physique belonged to Gaston. How dare anyone style on him with such irreverence? Style belonged to Gaston! The narrative would be his! His and his alone!

That was when Gaston realized that the explosions had stopped. Looming and menacing, Dreadshine was there. Leaned over and bent at the hips, that glowing visor drilled its sight into a very misshapen Gaston. He felt the fear in his pompadour when the uncaring villain spoke without feeling. "My, my. You really are made of ooze. I wish to know more, Ivan. *Inspect.*"

"Authority." Gaston expectorated his rebuttal before the rude monster could finish casting his inspection. Snapping back into person-shape, a limelight clung to the gaudy man. An unpleasant sheen that gave Artorian a prompt he didn't like.

K-chink!

———

Inspect blocked.
Creatures with Authority cannot be inspected.

———

"Well, well. Would you look at that?" Dreadshine clapped his armored hands together. "Well played, well played. That smells like Task Manager cheese to me. Unfortunately, Gaston, I have had my fill of cheese. Now stand up, so I can knock you back down."

K-chink!

———

Damage tally.

Damage dealt: None.

Target's 'Gelatinous Physique' racial trait makes Gaston the Matchless immune to physical and kinetic damage.

No damage from either Concussive or Explosive sources was tallied.

———

Not even explosion damage had gotten through? The prompt held no information for why neither Brilliant Behemoth nor the Wubs had caused any harm. Surely the boom-booms and boom-boom accessories weren't counted under physical or kinetic? Or was he getting the meaning of kinetic wrong? Either way, no reason to dwell. The system said no, so he would find something new that the system couldn't say no to. Then make a show out of it.

Dreadshine was the Nightmare Fuel, and so would fuel Gaston's nightmares. He'd already adopted Astrea's sick beats, so why not dip deeper into that portfolio?

Gaston turned out to have another nasty surprise ready for Artorian as the Gelatinous Grime reconstituted. "Would you kindly…"

Artorian felt a sudden tension and paralytic sensation attempting to assail him. A terrible feeling. One that caused more bad memories and the resurfacing of some old trauma, rather than any direct effect.

Gaston stood up to shove his own face to be right in front of Dreadshine's faceplate. His expression was far more villainous than what Artorian had managed, as if both experiencing rapture, and the tasty meal that was envy being fed. "Obey?"

K-chink!

———

Freedom of Mind has blocked an attempt at mind control.

———

Gaston expected that to be the end of it.

No foe ever came back from a 'would you kindly.' One of the many reasons never to let an opponent see your statistics or capabilities was that it allowed them to circumvent those powers. Or make plans in an attempt to. Gaston despised giving out anything for free, or giving out anything at all. All that was best would belong to Gaston.

Believing himself to have won as the lighting effect in the arena reset itself to normal, he muscled through the Pressure effect now that the kinetic hold was gone. The man-shaped Gelatinous Grime with deep ties to Task Managers then smiled wide, and slapped Dreadshine in the face. "I'll take that."

Observers gasped.

On impact, Gaston stole away the traits Free from Gaston and Experimental Attributes, resetting Artorian to have an even distribution of seven hundred and fifty points in each attribute. An evenness that annoyed Gaston, as it prevented him from penalizing the child playing dress-up.

Gaston then had a wonderful idea! The child had come all dressed for an occasion, and the other annoyance that had stopped accosting him was still observing the tussle. The walking volcano had no idea that Gaston had already won! Her hands were buried elbow-deep in layers of screens. "That one cares for you, yes? How good of you to come dolled up. A man has to look his best when it's time to get married. Or buried."

The pompadour then opened into a giant mouth filled with teeth. A mouth that smiled hungrily as Gaston talked from the sensible place where speaking should happen. "Any last words, legless little bard? I did so enjoy taking your mobility from you. *Hmm?* C'towl got your tongue?"

Gaston could not see Artorian's equally frightening smile behind Dreadshine's faceplate. Gaston should really, really not have touched any ability that existed in the realm of attacking his agency. There were worse ways to make an enemy out of Artorian, but that one? That one was high on the list. Time to pay the piper.

"Is that all you've got?" Dreadshine delivered devastating disrespect to a suddenly frozen and terrified opponent, salting the dish with a helping of humiliation as Artorian gained his stack of Menace. "Flick."

CHAPTER THIRTY-ONE

A flick by itself did little. A flick at seven-hundred and fifty strength wasn't a flick as damaging as one from one-thousand six-hundred strength. That mattered none when the physics of that full-power, strained hand-motion multiplied its physics output by five.

Was the flick going to do damage? *Nah*.

Was that the point? *Nah*.

Gaston went hurtling into the distance with a bruised forehead as Dreadshine calmly talked on as if the man was still standing right in front of him. "Once one realizes that being a celestial feces smartass far outweighs any of the repercussions? There is no turning back."

Artorian then looked down just enough to see the still-rooted legs of Gaston standing in place. Exactly where the false humanoid had left them. One of the legs formed a mouth and, as if that wasn't creepy enough by itself, unleashed a spell from the foot. "Grime-a-geddon!"

An explosion of sticky, caustic ooze burst like an overfull balloon right in front of Dreadshine. The caustic slime melted whole slabs of limestone and caused near-instant rivers of smoking divots. The pool of ooze crawled along and hissed against the stone, streams of acidic vapor forced into the air. While rapid, this continued until the sides of the mesa gained new holes where the acid ooze had tunneled, allowing the slime to pour out as if from a latrine.

The other leg, still standing, laughed as it formed its own mouth. "Gaston always has the last laugh!"

Dreadshine bent down extra low, blocking out the natural light so the glowing carmine visor almost pressed against the eyes that formed at the top of the Gelatinous Grime's leg. "Gaston is very funny. A real laugh. Any more of this, and I won't be able to hold myself back from laughing at you, Mr. Comedian."

K-chink!

———

Trait: Loved by Mana, considered the spell Grime-a-geddon to be amusing. The mana of Grime-a-geddon has been subverted. You have gained a temporary shield that provides Least Resistance against Acid damage.

———

Dreadshine's voice growled with heavy metal, the local illumination dampening and darkening once more as the second stack of Menace tacked on top of Artorian's first. "Tell me another joke, funny man."

The Gelatinous Grime's goopy leg-eyes bulged as the villain continued, an obvious mirth entering the vocal pattern. "No. Allow me. It's a short joke, but a severe one. Told in one word."

Dreadshine made sure to enunciate. "The joke is: Gaston."

Fuming with rage, Gaston blew up. "Grime-a-geddon!"

The second verse happened identical to the first. The arena took massive acid damage, new divots, and limestone remodeling. Due to the latrine paths existing already, on the other hand, the effect was far more short-lived. The majority of the ooze simply drained away as Dreadshine stood a little straighter, optics trained on the distance as he felt his body reattune with his statistics.

He was at ease with the seven-fifties across the board. He knew what those felt like. There was a familiarity present, and his flexing hands found a quick balance between strength and kinesthetic sense. A discrepancy that told him just how awful min-maxing had been.

Dumping all those points in the physical statistics had been idiotic for him, even with the Free from Gaston effect. This strength, while lessened, was far more 'his.' His to control, his to fine-tune. This body felt more like home than the forced skewing that had been the case a short while ago.

Even without the forced penalties, the evened-out statistics felt right.

His sight adjusted, his senses equalized, and his movements were natural.

They felt natural, which he decided was more important.

As he gained a third stack of Menace, Incursus pushed him a just-in-case prompt.

K-chink!

————

Trait: Loved by Mana, considered the repetition of the spell Grime-a-geddon to be boring. The mana of Grime-a-geddon has been subverted. Your temporary shield has improved in quality, providing Lesser Resistance against Acid damage.

————

Artorian was pretty happy that least and lesser affixes were starting to make an appearance. That was far better balancing than the instant uses of normal resistance and its associated four times multiplier. Some movement in the background was definitely happening, and he would bet gold on the armor values having changed. No damage from a point-black attack? The mana? Sure! The residual acid effects? That should have done something.

Dreadshine rolled his shoulders, deciding that if Gaston was going to muck around with immunities, he was going to choose not to care about so far succeeding in the Soulsborne Quest. Ah, no. He needed the Glass Cannon trait for that. Another time.

First, some good old sing-song vicious mockery. "Where is that boo named Gaston? Wait, what, who is Gaston? No one knows anything about… what is the name again? Some rube that gassed on? He's exceptionally skilled at evaaaa-porating. Yes, that's the guy, the matched one."

Dreadshine slow-clapped in clear insult, the sing-song tone traded for monotony and dry wit. "One little tap and he flicked right off. The man was a soggy wet match, I could only scoff."

"Shut!" Gaston returned to the arena by leaping from far away and landing back into the destroyed ring. Fully formed, and once again dressed in flawlessly gaudy yellow and red soldier coat with matching vest. "Up!"

The pompadour had gone back to normal, but Gaston looked worse for wear. A bit haggard, one could even say. *Tsk tsk!* "Only Gaston is flawless! All your splendor shall belong to me. Matchless Grime, all is mine!"

That last part turned out to be an ability activation, but Artorian at worst felt a momentary tug. As if his character sheet was being referenced by the system, rather than any sort of attack originating from Mr. Pompadour. That made his nose itch. That workaround had Task Manager written all over it. "Inspect."

K-chink!

———

Inspect blocked.
Creatures with Authority cannot be inspected.

———

Artorian had forgotten about Authority, which was his own fault. Then again, he did not particularly respect Authority. He was downright irreverent on his best day, particularly to people who put any effort whatsoever into trying to convince him that they deserved it. That was not how respect worked. A lesson that, perhaps, he was going to need to knuckle-sandwich feed to the Gelatinous Grime. The creature took no damage. Alright…

Dreadshine's carmine light thrummed when an idea struck. "Tell me, Grimy. You feel fear. Do you feel pain?"

Gaston winced, refusing to answer. Silence told Artorian plenty, adopting a stance that Gaston had not seen before, the fighting style clearly meant for some kind of hand-to-hand combat.

Fighting off both the unworthy threat and the persistent Pressure effect that was starting to become very irritating, Gaston tried to turn the tide in his favor. The Aura was not worth paying attention to damage-wise, but remained irritating. "Gaston now has your physique! Your mind! Your luck! All of your attributes are now Gaston's attributes. You can at most cause a stalemate, but that means you cannot win, and Gaston cannot lose. The Statue of the Platinum Angel stands defiant! The Cloudsteel Kirin sees to that."

Dreadshine glanced over his shoulder, ignoring Gaston entirely. "Darling? Was that useful to you?"

The stationary bonfire that was Astarte replied with a volcanic smile and excited nodding. "Thank you, sugar! I couldn't find a Titan related to a Gelatinous Grime, but I immediately found the entry for Cloudsteel Kirin, and where it is. I have now also found the Titan, which is pretending to be a Platinum Statue. I'll be back soon, okay? I need to teach a Titan the melting point of a certain metal."

She pressed his fingers to her lips, and blew him a burning kiss. "Thanks for the cheer-up show, honey. You can put him in the ground now."

As Astarte blasted off to the stars with heat and rage, Artorian mentally tallied a victory point. Awarded to Poirot. The detective was onto something with his mention of 'keep them talking.' "Voltekka? That's enough. You get to rest."

On wobbly legs, and the last of his tail strength, Voltekka formed a claw into a loose approximation of a fist. He raised it to the sky like an all-mighty god that did not, would not, and could not quit when the chips were down. Even if he passed out on his feet like that, and the seamless full plate turned to particulates.

"Effect Cosmetics. Off." Returning to normal colorations as the armor swirled into his chest, Young-torian fell a short distance as his size shrank. He landed easily enough, then bounced on his toes.

Gaston burst out in laughter. "You weaken yourself? Purely because your precious little onlooker left? Are you going to take up planting like she suggested? You'd make a poor farmer, child."

"Weaker?" Sunshine gently tilted his head to the left. "I don't need to see your character sheet to know that you're about to have a bad time. Incursus? Could I get that in Comic Sans, please? There were so many funny fonts in the prompt language library. That one feels so... fitting."

Gaston wasted no moment and attacked the child with a flurry of rapid punches and jabs that blurred out his arm movements. Now that the child was no longer in armor, acidic damage could be dealt far more easily. With the stolen and copied attributes, emptying out Sunshine's health bar would be a total breeze! Gaston even yelled out a noise with each strike, his flexible arms bending and twisting oddly under the Pressure effect. For a reason Gaston had not sussed out yet, that effect was far more potent. The reasons were irrelevant. Acid Punch time! "Ora ora ora ora!"

Eating the damage and not budging an inch, a mane of white flame erupted from Artorian's skin. As he let his Determination roil, the white fire coated him. Raising a hand, he effortlessly snapped a slipper made of hard light between his fingers —a chancla that was smoothly coated in a warbling field of finely tuned sound—creating a brand-new weapon that would wubbilate an envious wacko.

Particularly when the slipper also caught on white fire, and music related to hopes and dreams began to play from the sky. Gaston stopped punching when his hands turned into molten goop, forced to back off. "What did you do, cheating child? You should be out of health by now!"

Artorian popped his neck by rolling his head and flexing his back and shoulders. "The lady said I could bury you. That means I no longer have to put most of my effort into putting on a good show to cheer up someone important to me. Even if a mere smidge, there was a smile on her face before she left. That smile means the world to me, Grimy. A pleasure and heart-felt warmth that can only come from the happiness of another, and I live and thrive from the happiness of others."

Artorian's form lost physicality, and gained constellations as Gaston took a calculated step back, regardless of all the stacks of Menace expiring. That awful, oppressive energy feeling was back again. The same one that had stopped his first haymaker cold. "You did some research on me, Grimy. You didn't do enough research on me."

Gaston winced, understanding arriving at the same moment that Astarte found her soon to be dead Titan. "It was not a joke. You are an actual Divine. You have Divine mana! No wonder you are not dead yet. The Divine modifier alters energy into something of another category. Just using that stuff around people will cause harm and oppression. I knew you were a tyrant! That tale rings true!"

A part of Jotunheim going supernova sent such a shockwave through Eternia that, space or not, Demeter's Dream shuddered as a whole. Cosmic-torian beamed as the earthquake struck. "That I am a tyrant is true, and there's my cue!"

He pontificated on how to bury Gaston, his voice leaning towards the grandfatherly, regardless of his appearance. He was drawing wisdom from experience, after all. "I was thinking of combining Pantheon Style into Dreadshine's kit, which left me wondering what kind of beat down would be appropriate for a Fierce Deity. Swole-torian should be all about Tonfas. Growing up the first time, my life was one with the Mauling Phoenix styles, and that should stay that way. I have unleashed ballistae from bows, torn armies asunder, and talked enemies into defeat. My Grandpa Mode feels like it belongs with my denial methods of the No Style, which leaves me to think that as a Divine, I should focus on what's important to me in this role. *Education.*"

Cosmic-torian locked gazes with the Ooze. "The lesson of the struggle. The necessity of both blessings and curses. The value of what one learns from suffering. Good people are made from hardship. Children should get to be made of hope, and play without regard for reality. Societies should get to be made of dreams, and grow from the values they prize."

Gaston bravely ran away as Artorian gently tossed and caught the chancla. "I care about helping people succeed in their struggles. To survive them as they claw through the ages with their own will, defying both fate and expectation. As a game Divine, this is passively reflected in my health regeneration boon."

Sunshine reached back in preparation to properly throw, aiming at the speedily fleeing Gelatinous Grime that thought moving in a zig-zag was going to help. "Actively? I'm more of a smiter. I meddle. Education Style: Urtu! Sharing is caring!"

Gaston had no hope of ever dodging that white flame chancla. Guided by kinesis, the spinning slipper twisted through the air with all the power of a grandmother's backhand. Gaston might have been immune to kinetic damage, but Radiant and Fire had not been in the cards. Particularly not when combined together into Radiant Fire.

Gaston had no idea who Urtu was, or that it was important that Urtu was the Heavenly of **Holy Fire**. That did not make getting smacked by a very disrespectful slipper better as the humanoid form of Gaston turned into a sandwich-schmear of

paint speckling. The pattern of what was left of Gaston sprin-
kled out across limestone ground, in the loose shape of water
that had been thrown from a bucket to land wherever it may.

Kept down by the no longer opposable Pressure wave, now
that he was no longer protected by several external system
factors, the Gelatinous Grime whimpered out another non-
melodic 'ow.'

A most lesson-filled sound that floated back to Fierce Deity
Cosmic-torian, along with the chancla that returned to his
constellation grip with the use of some basic kinesis. He was
getting the hang of that as he began to stroll. "Excellent. Now, I
need you to go ahead and reconstitute, Gaston. I remember
something about... What was it? Ah, yes. A man has to look his
best when it's time to get buried."

CHAPTER THIRTY-TWO

With the snap of his fingers, Cosmic-torian swapped out the Pressure Aura for his Cleaning Aura. The smoky, acid-heavy environment quickly mopped itself up, leaving behind a clean limestone arena. "I'll do you a courtesy, Grimy. Any last words?"

Reconstituting into the shape of an extremely haggard human specimen of excellent physique, Gaston, understandably, expectorated. "This is why I like Beasts over Humanoids. At least Beasts grasp the concept of 'enough.'"

Cosmic-torian continued his stroll, using the side of his foot to scrape some loose limestone gravel back into a divot. "Funny, that. According to one of my swords, you're basically made from **Envy**. Color me intrigued either way, Gaston. Tell me more."

Before the Gelatinous Grime could, another swat of the chancla clapped the man back into a floor-schmear. The strike was out of character, but it also cut away the sass.

Forced to reconstitute again, the more humanoid Gaston staggered this time. "Beasts rest when they are full and sated. They don't hunt without need, and don't endlessly hoard like your kind does. You say that you will be satisfied once you have enough of something, anything. Then when your kind has that amount, suddenly they change their mind. I could give a human infinite resources, and they would ask of me another infinity of resources. The conclusion is easy. Humans don't grasp the concept of 'enough,' so why bother giving them anything at all? Gaston will take it all! The Beasts don't need it. The Humanoids don't deserve it. Only Gaston deserves it. Nothing will ever be enough for the likes of you!"

There was no point in refuting or arguing. Only the walls would hear it. Artorian honestly thought that a bit sad. A lesson into human greed, sure, but that held up poorly as an attempt for a spare-me speech. Regarding Gaston with emotional understanding, he paused in front of the Gelatinous Grime and sighed apologetically. "I know."

The Divine patted the slick pompadour with his left hand, a steady ball of light building and charging up in his right. Gaston did a good job with his appearance, but basic touch ruined all the magic. Gaston felt like wet ice, without the cold. "Unfortunately, Grimy, that changes nothing about you being the one who crossed lines that they shouldn't. If you want to dedicate your life to making sure people trying to cheat on their numbers get their comeuppance?"

On reflection, that was commendable, though had to come with a lesson. "You know what? Go ahead. You want to make sweeping changes and punish people you don't agree with based purely on your opinion, and zero input from anyone stuck in the system?"

Artorian *tsked*. "This is what's going to happen."

Sunshine gripped Mr. Pompadour by the false hair, rather than gently patting the creature. A blade of pure hard-light in the shape of Compassion's Albion Principe then plunged through Gaston, and erupted clear from his back. "Carian Grandeur."

K-chink!

———

You have hit Gaston the Matchless with Carian Grandeur.
    Damage Type: Kinetic, Melee, Radiant, Fire.
    Impacts: 1.
    Strength Damage: 750.
    Radiant Damage: 750.
    Fire Damage: 750.
    Enemy Weakness: Fire.
    Enemy Immunities: Kinetic, Melee.
    Weakness: A four times modifier in an unfavorable direction.
    Updated Strength Damage: 0.
    Updated Radiant Damage: 750.
    Updated Fire Damage: 3,000.
    Updated Total Damage: 3,750.
    Carian Grandeur, Charge 1: Damage increased by 5%.
    Carian Grandeur, Charge 2: Damage increased by 10%.
    Carian Grandeur, Charge 3: Damage increased by 15%.
    Carian Grandeur, Charge 4: Damage increased by 20%.
    Carian Grandeur, Total Charge Damage bonus: 50%
    Calculated Charge bonus: 1,875.
    Final Damage: 5,625.

———

The light-shaped blade had a beginning, but no end. Like a ray of light that broke through gray clouds. Thematically nailing the Gelatinous Grime to the sky, Artorian allowed his white flame mane to flare, now that he had grasped that the mane was linked to his determination. "My dearest made a good point. You cannot step on those who are more powerful than you and disagree with you. You'll only end up trampled, unable to do more than die on your hill."

Artorian waffled on that point after stating it. "Well, you can try. Sometimes you can succeed. Overall? It's a fool's gambit, but you and I are very different kinds of fools, Gaston. Until you learn the difference? You don't have what you need for an uprising. Sleep tight."

Before Gaston could get another word in, Artorian unsheathed his sword from the Ooze's chest, and swapped his Cleaning Aura out for Field of Sleep. Gaston critically failed his Hearts and Minds save, knocked out instantly. With a fluid follow up motion, Sunshine thematically beheaded the gaudy gutpunch.

K-chink!

Coup de grâce!

A coup de grâce is a more extreme version of a sneak attack. A sneak attack is a strike that occurs without the opponent knowing where the attack is coming from, while unable to take action against it. A coup de grâce is a sneak attack where the opponent has no hope of preventing the attack what-soever. Such as by being asleep, unconscious, or completely restrained.

A coup de grâce adds a 0 at the end of your total damage.

You have hit Gaston the Matchless with Carian Grandeur.

Damage Type: Kinetic, Melee, Radiant, Fire.

Impacts: 1.

Prior Total Damage: 5,625.

Coup de grâce Final Damage: 56,250.

Glorious Overkill!

Experience awarded: None.

Artorian didn't hear it, but observers applauded.

The grace of Sunshine's divinity today was that Gaston died while at rest. A painless end for the particulating Gelatinous Grime. He'd be back, but he'd be back more cautious. Or, perhaps for the third time, would try the same thing again when it had proven to not work the first or second times.

K-chink!

Warning! The unexpected removal of two traits has destroyed the Growth Pattern reference pylons connected to your Silverwood Bracelet. You have lost all your Growth Modifiers.

"That's fine." Artorian dropped his cosmic effects, having learned something new about the Divine modifier. Going cosmic—or Divine, he supposed—altered his energy metric in a way not reflected by the system. That going Divine could harm bystanders was a good tidbit to have. He'd dive into that when he could devote time to the whole Divine aspect of the game, which was certainly not right now. He should go pick up Ember, and the boys. Was it worth trying to fix the character sheet losses?

He'd think about it, letting the active effects of Determination ebb away. The Carian weapon and white flames both doused as he called for assistance. "Zephyr."

Artorian checked his character sheet as the High Elven yacht took off from Demeter's Dream's central landscape feature. Carian Grandeur was still nowhere to be found in his ability section, regardless of his ability to conjure the effect.

Glancing to Zephyr's approach, the large aesthetic block of well-carved structure that served as housing looked rather nice from all the way over from the mesa. Well, arena. There wasn't much mesa left. No, no, no. A mesa simply meant flat-topped mountain or hill. A wide, flat, elevated landform with steep sides. The arena still counted!

"Incursus, show me a concise update of the simplest basics." He didn't need to see the stats. Seven-fifties across the board, no gimmicks. No reason to pull up that information or have it narrated to him. Repeating the exact same thing nine times in a row was grating.

K-chink!

―――

Name: Sunshine
Character Level: 1
Race: Nascent Being
Class: Lumin Lord
Specialization: Wub Warrior
Profession: Janitor

―――

Base Values:
Hit Points: 7,450.
Mana Pool: 7,500.
Mana Regen: 187 / second.
Stamina Pool: 7,450.
Stamina Regen: 375 / second.

―――

Adjusted Values:
Determination Pool: 14,950.
Determination Regen: 562 / second.

―――

Artorian had completely lost track of how any of that stacked up against realm averages, but he shrugged at the thought. "I'll fix what's broken. I'll test what's needed. I'll learn what the actual averages are the hard way. I'll start on Midgard with the rest of them, and figure it out. Eventually I'll hit a realm where I begin to struggle, and then I can start being clever and considering the power scale."

Now what was going on with his Pressure Aura? He'd expected that gimmick by itself to keep Gaston pasted to the floor, but the Ooze had been pretty fine. Cheatery, maybe? He'd test it on something else. How much damage was that doing now anyway, with his attributes back to baseline? "Master rank seven times... Charisma?"

K-chink!

———

Pressure Aura DPS: 5,250 Crushing Damage.
Crushing Damage is considered Kinetic.

———

"Thank you, Incursus." Artorian closed the prompt, and made a slight sad face when he did the napkin math on Archimedes. No, wait, he was getting his numbers wrong. Five percent of his energy bar was currently about... seven-fifty? Seven forty-seven? Okay, that was still not nothing. Given his current strength, an in-the-face teleport equated to essentially a good punch in the mouth.

Brilliant Behemoth did half his Constitution value. An easy three-seventy-five, counted per location. In other words, if he could use percussion, he should use precession.

Ephira's damage fluctuated, but went boom. Strength of seven-fifty, plus a dice roll somewhere between fifty and five-hundred. Damage per smack ebbed and flowed between eight-hundred, and one-thousand, two-fifty. Not bad.

Sorrow's damage was static. The katana split damage half and half between Wisdom and Dexterity. Three-seventy-five Kinetic, three-seventy-five Fire. Plus seven-fifty Strength for even more kinetic slap. A thousand, five-hundred all around. Also not bad.

Compassion counted straight Charisma on top of straight Strength. A thousand five-hundred all around again, a nice, even balancer to Sorrow. Still not bad.

Pride had stacking damage, but Artorian was only going to napkin math the minimums. Or try to. Strength of the usual seven-fitty, and double Intelligence. That was a very tasty one-thousand, five-hundred floor to tack that Strength damage on. Two-thousand, two-hundred and fifty damage per smack was the best of the bunch so far, when not looking at all the special effects.

Creating moonlight likely wasn't going to be very difficult for a Lumin Lord, to activate Moonlight Greatsword. Providing energy was almost a guarantee, so there was the Complete Rainbow step, and... was there one more?

No, the rest was all about block value, and the damage stacking maxed out at the Rainbow Greatsword step, at five times Intelligence. Given his Strength and Intelligence were the same, he'd just napkin math Intelligence times six. Same difference.

Young-torian whistled at the four-thousand, five-hundred damage per smack. Polly knew how to party! "I'm not going to play favorites, but currently the moonlight is speaking to me. Ephira has to go home, and the emotion weapons are dangerous just to hold."

Zephyr was about here, so he checked the O.o.P. "Oops indeed. I don't want to use this thing. I'd rather find out how to put a normal LFB together and then play with customization."

Double checking, he made sure Cleaning Aura was on rather than one of the others, and stowed all of his screens. Brushing off his pajamas, he waved when the High Elven yacht pulled up. Patriarch Yiba Su Wong and Paladin Jorn were both present on her deck, excitedly swinging their arms to greet him wildly with clamor and noise. Artorian nodded with his hands on his hips as Zephyr set herself down, and lowered the boarding ramp. "I like having friends."

CHAPTER THIRTY-THREE

When Artorian learned it would take over eight hours to get to the Asgard asteroid belt, he spent two hours catching up with Yiba and Yorn before he passed out in his chair. After having repeatedly assured his friends that he was fine, and not tired at all. His snores were great traitors. By the time he woke up, they had been at the belt a while, and neither Yiba nor Yong were to be found.

Based on loose banter that he could pick up like spare change, he'd missed an entire other mid-boss battle. Waking slowly, he caught the back-end of some joke that the Asgard asteroid belt was a reverse sheep. Because it was shortened to Aab instead of Baa like a proper noise, and it bothered people that the Aab didn't have a proper acronym.

When conversation shifted to putting the belt first, Artorian checked out. He didn't even know who the voices belonged to yet, but with Echolocation trying to paint him a picture, he decided that he wasn't awake enough for it.

From his laying-down position, he sussed out that Zephyr had docked somewhere. The nearly complete and encompassing view of empty space, with chunks of realms floating through an unfathomable distance, didn't help with his footing. The chunks of Asgard and the joking at least gave him a rough idea of his immediate location, but that wasn't enough.

Some glancing around allowed Artorian, who was far, far more bundled up than he remembered being, to spot a Milliways sign. Where were they? Some restaurant at the end of the universe? The place had a massive dome, and flashes of light continuously went off within. Different colors of flashes, which nicely broke up the monotony of not knowing which direction was down.

The sound of heavy footsteps making their way up a boarding plank turned Young-torian's head. His pillows went flying as he saw heavily armored sharks make their way onto Zephyr's deck. "Rip! Tear! My boys!"

The two sharks in Doom Slayer armor, coated in more war scars and odd weaponry than any reasonable person wanted to involve themselves with, both stared at him. The sharks shared a look. That their visors covered their expressions did nothing to hide their abject confusion. Who was this random child?

Having freed himself, Artorian prepared to beeline towards the boys, only to be stopped by Gaston, who chose that moment to fall out of the sky like a most unwelcome interloper with a fully restored pompadour. "Perrrrrr-fec-tion is here!"

"No." Artorian's patience jar was empty. Multiple colored lights blinked into being above his head as his arms fell. Lights that grew into full Wisps, who held formation in a rainbow pattern. "Potentia."

Light-flashing into the form of the beach-attired grandfather, Rip and Tear both fangirled and screamed in the highest of pitches as their hands shook next to their heads. Recognition had dawned! They had no recollection of the kid, but they knew Sunny just fine!

Before Gaston could find the steam to get going, Grandpatorian loomed above him, and stared the human-shaped Gelatinous Grime down. "Why, Grimy? Why are you limited to purely inductive reasoning? Is this going to keep happening?

Was the lesson poor? Do you need a firmer back of the hand to throw your cheek into?"

Gaston pressed a gaudy hand to his puffed-out chest, having bountifully recovered from looking haggard. "I am the eternal, the mighty, the one and only Gaston! I am important to the system, a true connoisseur of balance. You, Grandpa, are a mere—!"

"Administrator." Artorian cut the Ooze off and snapped his fingers. Saluting in unison, the Wisps fanned out around him. Expecting one of them to be addressed now that the Administrator lever was flipped, they circled Gaston ominously. "And not *an* Administrator, Grimy. I am *the* Administrator. I don't appreciate your Abyss, don't have time to deal with it, and won't deal with it any further. I am not your entertainment, and you are not in my league."

Gaston gasped and backed up a few steps without realizing he did so, sputtering indignantly while unable to find the right words for a rebuttal. The sudden array of weapons that heavily armored sharks aimed his way made the words extra difficult to find.

"Poirot?" Artorian asked his environment just in case, but was very glad to notice the rotund, well-dressed detective of the little gray cells slink out from the ship's innards like a shadow in the night.

The plump man smiled, studied the circumstance, and smoothed the tiny edge of his mustache. "Monseigneur Hastings?"

That was plenty for Artorian, who leaned into the detective's nomenclature. "Monseigneur Poirot. Could you please escort Gaston back to his assigned location, so he can do what he is good at? After which, if you could thoroughly investigate him for abuse of power, that would be *delightful*."

"Poirot would be equally delighted to do this." The detective tapped the side of his nose, sensing the potential for great cheese to be involved. He then steepled his fingers, and provided the Administrator some other good news on the side.

"Je suis prêt. I am ready. Also, I no longer need a speech from Grandpa-Mode. Poirot has sniffed it out by observation. The answer to what to do with Poirot's life is easy! I must find what makes me happy, and do that to my delight. Or, I must find that which I am good at, and bend it to my profit. Poirot has received an older lecture on Ikigai from the Synapse-record. C'est most helpful, Monseigneur. Merci."

Artorian replied with a grateful nod, but did not receive the floor as Gaston felt utterly insulted now. Between the disrespect, being treated like a mere cog, and people speaking over him when only Gaston should be on the soap box? The Gelatinous Grime felt bruised on the ego. "Gaston shall not be spoken to like this! Nor spoken over! You cannot make Gaston do anything!"

"Wisps?" Artorian, in full upset Administrator tone, coiled his arms behind his back as he leaned forward to eke a glance over the rim of his sunglasses. Glasses that fell low on his big nose. "Please add Gelatinous Grime, Ooze, and Slime of all kinds to the list of effective targets that are attacked by Cleansing Presence. I need to wash Gaston's mouth out with soap, and make a point that his appearance will be met with a scrubbing that Shai-Hulud would approve of. While we're on the topic? Add Mosquitos of all kinds. I consider it a public service."

Circling in place, the Wisps figured out who was doing what, and supporting who. Artorian had figured out three of them as of now. The blue Wisp tackled abilities, the yellow one seemed to have Artifacting power, and the green one that freshly moved out of formation could alter his Aura. As the Wisps got to work, Artorian didn't skip a beat.

He addressed the bothersome slime directly while Gaston was trying to do something other than huff and puff indignantly. "You need to learn when you've been let off gracefully, or you'll learn the lesson of what happens when you keep irritating opponents that don't belong in your playbook. I wanted you to learn what kind of fool you were, and you failed. Failure comes with repercussions, and not a slap on the wrist and a '*ha-ha*, that's just the way it is now.' I don't want to be bothered by you, and sure, while I am not inclined to tell other people what to do with their lives, neither will I sit idly by when education proves to be necessary."

Artorian glared death and menace into Gaston, who shrank away under the Administrator's furious gaze as the man-shaped slime began to register that this had been a terrible idea. "Goodbye, Gaston."

The Gelatinous Grime got a finger up before being scrubbed out of the area in a sea of soap bubbles and the sounds of violent drowning.

Clapping his hands together, the Administrator looked up to the Wisps and pointed at Poirot. "Please take him to wherever that Grime ended up, and give him some investigative permissions. I was going to be lax about the whole Task Manager thing, but if it's Task Manager and friends that are preventing this game from being run as it needs to, then it is time to give some people the broom and get to sweeping. I want a report made on anyone that is intentionally breaking things, or going around trying to break the game from working as it needs to. If a report exists at all? Send Poirot after it to confirm the information, and if those values line up, send whoever is responsible for tearing weeds out by the roots and replace the person, place, or thing in charge."

The rainbow arc of Wisps all saluted him as one, winking out one at a time as the violet one sped over to the detective. The violet one handled permissions? Good to know. The violet Wisp vanished with Poirot in tow, leaving Artorian to inhale deeply and grumble to clear his head as he turned off his Administrator lever.

The sharks had wisely waited for that whole short-lived encounter to blow over, their Light Fusion Beamers lowering now that the enemy of Sunny had gotten its teeth violently brushed. A fate that both the sharks were intimately familiar with. Tear considered asking for a checkup, but the piece of sturgeon that had been stuck cleaned itself up due to being within Artorian's Cleaning Aura. Rip and Tear sighed with great relief, that same Aura giving them both a full once over, regardless of their armor.

The pause in greetings had allowed more people to show up, resulting in the sudden culmination of a quest being resolved. Followed immediately by another when he spotted Soni in moth-form. Who was standing next to a much older, white-fluff-coated moth with slightly crooked glasses, and an equally crooked glint in the eyes. That moth must be One-Stone, and Artorian felt kinship. Here was another sharp-nosed troublemaker! He should introduce Father Richard; surely nothing could go wrong.

He gave his prompts a gander as he processed that news of his planned events had gotten around. The people who he needed to interface with had self-gathered for his convenience. The heads up to Ember must have had people listening in, because this was most helpful. His habit of talking out loud was perhaps not such a bad one!

Uack!

———

Quest Complete!
   Quest: Friends and Fraternity.

———

Quest Complete!
   Quest: Go Grandpa Mode.

———

Remaining Quests:
   Lair of the Far Squid.
   Soulsborne.

———

Rewards!

———

The bottom of the rewards prompt falling out made Artorian hold his face. The screen disintegrated into glass shards before his rewards could be shown, but at this point, a functional screen would have been a reward by itself.

Rip made consoling motions, but didn't move from his spot when Artorian held up a pausing hand. "I don't wanna know. I am stuck on why the Quackbang prompt sound played, more than I am the prompt breaking. I blame Pag."

Artorian controlled his breathing, and spoke to the environment. "Quacky, are you here? Is it urgent? I'd like to catch up with my boys and meet their friends."

Uack!

The glasses-wearing, white-feathered duck knew to stick to the Old World's language. As the time before, Alfred Jodocus Kwak—Quackbang, to his friends—adjusted his red scarf and straightened the clipboard under his wing. The flat tone of the duck was the same, complete with the droll and dejecting clipboard reading.

Quackbang cleared his throat, and got to it. "*He-hem.* I quote: When Artorian actually bothers being an Administrator, please go bring this over. No, not that part. You don't have to write that down and narrate it. You did, didn't you? Why is it that we can make a thousand of you without a hitch, but nothing better than a Molotov Cockatiel? Never mind. Just tell him: When you actually want to be the Administrator proper, please come let us know, we could use the help. Until then, we heard something about you wanting to tackle the Amalgams? Please do. We are close to making the game work as intended again, but that rat problem needs to go. Cleaning duty for the Janitor? Please and thank you."

The duck turned a clipboard page. "P.S. We have figured out the linkage issue, and can move your Pylon Bank over to a fresh batch that doesn't have the Task Manager's self-destruct features. I think you call it version four, but on our end it's more likely going to be version one of a set of batches that you can jump between. One for Admin work, one for being a player, one for being Dreadshine, and one for other world boss needs. We don't know what to do with your Deity thing yet, there's no real need for an Overdeity yet, so thanks for being alright with sitting on the backburner."

A second page flip followed. "We all got a kick out of Dreadshine, and Cal is smug as a peach. Though also believes the horror dungeon utterly failed. The kiln dungeon's prior version had lots of overt threats, but no slow or insidious ones that came back regardless of what you did to them. No sense of something creeping ever closer. That'll get refined. Keep at it, and please try to have fun. We find the feedback useful, and your prompt controllers are diligent. There's a small treasure trove of junk we have to give you, but honestly, if you wanted to glance over them and throw the entire lot into the recycler? We would not blink twice."

Alfred moved the clipboard back under his wing. "So ends the statement, and my task. Jodocus Quackbang, out."

Uack!

Poof!

CHAPTER THIRTY-FOUR

Artorian suddenly had too much on his plate. "That's too much for handling all at once."

Soni put her hand up. His hand? Her hand. That new moth form leaned far too much to the feminine, and the voice that was used did not at all reflect the odd little bat that Soni used to be. Progress? Progress! He'd been indirectly warned that people were changing, based on how he didn't.

Soni the motherly Moth-Mageous now existed in full form and fury! Her brand-new voice was gentle, forward, and full of warmth. "We can wait, Administrator. We may be chronically early, but One-Stone and I only just got here. We need to have a sit and go over some of the latest progress reports. Material processing is as dull as it is thick."

She pointed one of her fronds at the sharks in their presence, both of the boys having altered their poses to praise the sun as the Auric scrubbing felt divine. There was nothing like a good bath when they'd been out of the water for far too long. "Rip and Tear have been our field-testers, along with Corrupt and Rupture. Those two are still in the Pylon Holds, testing the latest designs against an endless supply of theocratic rats."

Artorian chuckled at the happy shark noises, then returned a nod. "That would be good. Please make yourselves comfortable. Zephyr let you on, so I assume all related paperwork or politics that needed to happen have already happened."

Soni happily claimed a soft surface with her butt, and checked out by pulling up a tome of prompts labeled 'Materials Processing: Corruption Effects on Cores.' That was going to be a heavy read.

Artorian gave a polite nod to One-Stone as the Moth shuffled up to also find a seat, holding out a hand to the overfly fluffy Mothman. "Mr. One-Stone? I hear you're one of the people I need to speak to about LFB's."

The older Moth laughed, throwing his head back, then marched right over and powerfully met Artorian's grip with his own. No shyness was to be found whatsoever in old One-Stone.

The older Moth spoke with the most pleasant and quirky accent that he dipped in and out of. Very orderly and efficient. "Ja! Mein Strahlung Project. So good to make your acquaintance, Herr Administrator. Ich bin Science-Moth One-Stone. Ze joke is that if I had two to knock together, I vould split ze Essence between them und cause ze explosions. Please, call me Professor, und I would appreciate it if you did not call ze project by the beamer name. Ze prototypes are a disaster."

Artorian returned a laugh of his own, and shook the Moth's hand hard and well. He could work with that. "Make yourself comfortable, Professor. I will be with you as I am able. You know how it goes. Endless work."

One-Stone momentarily looked miserable. "Preach to ze choir. Caring for my Kleingarten and eating my Stullen while I touch some grass keeps me sane."

The Moth reared up to launch into a heavy lecture, then looked over Artorian's shoulder and promptly backed off like he needed to punctually arrive early elsewhere. One-Stone shrugged at the sight. "Tja, nothing to be done about that, but I shall not be in ze blast radius. Ze light in ze brain is ze only one I wish to chase. Toodeloo!"

Artorian of course turned to look as One-Stone dove behind Soni for safety. He found a prompt hanging in the air that was so laden and thick with color and rampant energy that it looked primed to burst and blow. Just needed two rocks.

The Administrator squeezed the bridge of his nose. If that prompt went bang, he wasn't dressed festive enough for the party. "That looks like it's for me."

He waved the prompt closer, and tapped the lock icon on its surface. If it blew up in his face, he would probably be fine. Instead, he got an outpouring of trash dumped on him in the form of loot. A pile so large that he was buried under the refuse.

Ding!

––––––

You have encountered: Aberrant Pile of Loot.
Please designate any loot that is not to be recycled.
Format: Weapon name, Weapon type, Weapon effect, Weapon fluff.

––––––

Thunderblade - Zweihänder - Small chance to stun.

Epée du Monde - Epee - A fencing blade with a nature-themed circle attack.

Mooncleaver - Cleaver - Leaves glow trails.

Silver Tongue - Dagger - Damage increases with Charisma. "May your blade be as sharp as your wit."

Thorn - Dagger - Creates thorns that grow from the wound.

Boomerang - Boomerang - It goes boom when you say it rang.

Flying Pan - Bladed Frying Pan - This weapon has the weight of a frying pan and the utility of a throwing knife. When thrown, its weight decreases by three quarters.

Confusion - Spear - When you try to stab with the spear, the spearhead moves to a random point on the shaft. Yes, even the spear is confused.

Spearmint - Spear - The blade leaves a lovely aroma when it cuts.

Dragon's Tail - Fire Whip - Causes scorching burns.

Decorating Bow - Bow - When an arrow is fired from this bow, it is replaced by a decorative bow which wraps around the target.

Distraction Blades - Twin Daggers - On failed Wisdom check, the target is distracted. To distract an idiot, see left blade. To distract an idiot, see right blade.

Dance Club - Club - On hit, the target gains the need to party.

Shield of Exception - Buckler - When the shield of exception is struck, it will take exception, and strike back.

Alright Sword - Sword - Not as good as a great sword, but it's alright.

Staff of Bleeding - Mage's Staff - When mana is channeled through this staff, blood starts flowing through the gem at the top. More mana means a stronger blood flow. No, we don't know where the blood is coming from, we just roll with it.

Cursed Shield of Destruction - Shield - When an attack hits this shield, the damage dealt is doubled. Why would you do this to yourself?

Hammer Time - Hammer - When the hammer is used, it causes all movement in the local area to stop for one second.

Skull Cap - Skull Cap - Any strikes to the head cause extra damage, as if they were striking the skull directly. Note, it only works against the wearer of this cap.

Apex's Bite - Bastard Sword - Once this weapon has cut a person ten times, it will summon a spectral wolf to bite the target.

No More Mr. Knife Guy - Knife - This knife can only be used once per person.

Fifty-Two Pick Up - Deck of Cards - Creates a storm of razor-sharp playing cards. Very messy, protect your fingers.

See You Next Fall - Hammer - Anyone struck by this hammer is likely to trip.

What's the Point - Sword - This weapon will miss one-hundred percent of the time.

Blue Wail - Flail - The biggest flail in the land, smells fishy.

Cross Bow - Bow - This bow is just really angry.

Cestae of Sepsis - Bladed Cestae - Every cut inflicted by this weapon will inflict a different variety of poison damage.

You Will Die - Dice - A twenty-sided die which deals damage to a struck target, depending on which number is facing upwards after it stops moving.

Morning Star - Morning Star - Whoever wields this weapon thinks it's morning.

Ace of Clubs - Club - Only deals damage on the first hit of a combat.

Blade of Grass - Sword - Causes grass to grow in the cuts made by the blade. Extra effective against dirt.

Dicey Business - Sword - Dice stored in the hilt of the sword determines the number of cuts per hit.

A Pick Me Up - Ice Pick - When used, the user gains the effects of caffeine.

Void Caller - Warhorn - Blowing this horn causes a void portal to appear, sucking everything within a hundred feet into the void. Hope you can run fast.

Horn-et - War Horn - When blown, a swarm of hornets is released.

Weeping Willow - Bagpipe - When this bagpipe is played, people will stop and weep at its bittersweet tones.

Bag-Pipe - Flute - This instrument can be used as a storage device.

Sword of Banishment - Broadsword - Anything touching the blade when mana is fueled into it is banished. Yes, that includes the handle for it.

Across Bow - Crossbow - When fired, the weapon stays with the bolt, but the bolt travels the distance it otherwise would have anyway.

Were-pon - Swordbow - This sword turns into a bow under the full moon.

Yeet Grenade - Flask - When this item detonates, everything within a ten-foot radius gets thrown in a random direction.

Where-pon - Dagger - Teleports away when you put it away.

Shake-spear - Spear - When hit, the target temporarily becomes more proficient in writing, but the wielder gets the shakes.

Blade of Mercy - Dagger - This dagger won't kill the target, no matter how much damage is dealt. Repeated applications still hurt.

Plague Doctor's Mask - Mask - Increases poison damage dealt, and improves health restoration caused.

Fear Me, If You Dare! - Rapier - Greatly increases Dexterity if the blade is wielded with fearlessness, or when you face death.

Cheese Slice - Sword - You won't find a gouda weapon than this one. It's made of cheese, and there's Stilton more damage it can cause.

———

Rather than read further, Artorian tapped the recycle prompt and placed it on the floor. Getting out his broom, he swept every single item into the bottomless hole it produced without bothering to read any more of the entries. The many, many more entries. "I want none of it! Into the hole you go! I have science to get to, and rocks to bang together."

CHAPTER THIRTY-FIVE

Rip and Tear were broken free from their sustained pose of praise as Artorian wrapped his Swole-torian Grandpa arms around their Doom Slayer helmets. "My boys! Good to see you."

Ding!

Rather than a pleasant reunion that involved adorable spinnies provided to small children, another outpouring of trash was dumped on him. Once more in the form of loot. In no time at all, Artorian and the boys were buried under a pile of random weapons.

You have encountered: Aberrant Pile of Loot.

Please designate any loot that is not to be recycled.

The Sharks and Artorian all broke free from the pile rather than letting the narration play from the hanging prompt. Artorian instantly got his broom back out to fuss and shovel piles of weapons back into the bottomless hole, while Rip and Tear each snuck some armaments into their back pockets. No reason to let stab-quipment go to waste.

———

Mora Puukko - Shank - Finish Him. All death blows made by this weapon cause the wielder to become mute for one minute. Showing Mora to a shop-keeper lets you leave the shop without paying. Only works on shopkeepers lower level than you. In reality, every weapon shares this buff.

Noita - Wand - On cast, there is a one in one-hundred chance to be Noita'd, and die from a seemingly avoidable cause that you totally saw coming. You still die.

Kirves - Axe - Disarming strike. You lop the guy's limb off. No arms means disarmed, right?

Ukko - Wand - Contrary to popular belief, this is not a casting focus. Run up to a guy and stab them. No need to learn spells. You do learn the spell: Stab, regardless.

———

Artorian may not care too much about what weapons did, but the Sharks had been going through gear like toothpicks at a seafood buffet. When the second pile was all cleaned up, Artorian sat, and missed the convenience of a good robe.

More prompts blinked in his peripheral vision, wanting his attention. "Prompt controller? I really want to get to One-Stone's Strahlung Project. What are the utterly crucial prompts I need to see and tackle? Everything else has to be later. I want the pew pew. I want to see Louis, Pag, and Lenore in that order. Then I want out, and see the blinding fluff of a soft pillow."

The prompts reorganized themselves, a scant four moving to be within his field of vision as the rest all winked out. He tapped one, and resolved to get through this quickly.

Ding!

———

You have lost the Title: Roaming World Boss Duo.

———

Ding!

———

You have gained five new Pylon Banks.

You may swap between these banks depending on which role you are fulfilling.

    Bank 1: Sunshine.

    Bank 2: Dreadshine.

    Bank 3: Roaming World Boss.

    Bank 4: Deity.

    Bank 5: Administrator.

———

Ding!

———

Your current Pylon Bank has been set to: Sunshine.

This Pylon Bank is considered a Player Bank.

Death will cause the loss of experience, but your character will respawn after a few days. The loss of this experience is correlated to the loss of some memories. The memories lost are tailored so your continued time in Eternia occurs more smoothly, improving your overall integration score. This will lead to a higher immersion value.

———

Ding!

Your current Pylon Bank can be reset to a fresh character. You may also take this opportunity to activate the Glass Cannon trait, permanently setting your health to 1. Activating this feature will reset your values and acquired tools. As a running iteration, you will receive several import choices in the New Game Plus menu.

Would you like to run this task?

Artorian shook his head. "No, but if you could set me to Dreadshine's Bank for now, you can begin preparing the Sunshine Bank for the overhaul, without my character being immediately affected if something goes wrong."

The confirmation chime was music to his ears. He watched a scant few entries in his character sheet update. A fate far better than watching a rolodex spin itself to pieces. The prompts all closed, allowing Artorian to reposition himself and sneak a peek over Rip's armored shoulder.

The Shark had repositioned himself into the circle with Tear, Soni, and One-Stone. They were going on and on about numbers and component failures. Grandpa-torian stuck his nose in. "Is this a good time to pick up a beam thingy, and a related explanation?"

The Sharks made room, and Artorian happily plopped himself between them, his arms swinging around their necks. Rip and Tear both leaned in heavily so Artorian could do that in the first place. They were both larger than him, but the endeavor clearly wasn't a problem. Their wagging Shark tails gave that away very easily. Zephyr adored this, and altered her deck so they could all sit in a circle on some good fluff. Their local environment reshaped into a recessed pit where they could all lean and lounge.

Some squabbles were exchanged for who was doing the

explaining, and after a lost game of hand motions, One-Stone was designated.

The old Moth excitedly rubbed his fronds together, his multiple hands stacked with prompts. "Oh zis is so gut! Where do I even begin? Ah, ja! Ze coolant! One of ze many components that makes a Light Fusion Beamer. No coolant? No Strahlung. Unlike a bow, LFB's do not need conventional ammunition. Zey need to stay frosty."

Laying one of the prompts down, One-Stone tapped the screen so a model popped up. Five images of increasingly larger, odd-shaped weaponry floated in a big circle. Artorian thought them to be misshapen crossbows with crystal chunks tacked on, but remained open-minded. This was going somewhere.

One-Stone began with a primer. "Many complicated terms exist that you may get lost on, Herr Administrator. So I begin with this: a Strahlung is developed to solve a problem, but not a problem zat exists in ze Soul Space. Cultivators are, without knowing techniques, repositories of energy. Ze higher und more potent a cultivator, ze more that zey zemselves are made of energy. While ze loss of zis energy hampers cultivation, techniques already cause zis, meaning zat vhat is important is having ze means to continue living. Rather zan always focusing on advancing ze ranks. A dead cultivator does not advance."

Artorian knew this quote. "A dead DPS deals no DPS?"

"Ja!" One-Stone slapped the table. "You have attended ze lectures of Herr Roberts ze Ruminating? Wunderbar! Zis shall save me so much time."

Artorian thought that funny, and did not interrupt as the happy old Moth did as professors tended to do, and lost themselves in the swing of the lecture. "Based on ze growth of younger cultivators in ze Soul Splace."

One-Stone stuck his tongue out and sputter-spatted a few times, then tried again. "Soul. Space. We have come to a few conclusions. Techniques are difficult to learn, whereas Aura shielding is simple by comparison. LFB's raise ze value of having ze correct shielding, or otherwise having ze component zat allows you to circumvent your opponent's shielding. We have had an exponential increase in external cultivators, and zat brought in ze need for new weaponry when ze disembark day comes. Internal cultivators can punch their way through problems. External cultivators cannot."

The Moth tapped the side of his left frond like it was his nose. "Ze overseer may want everyone to be Mages, but one must plan for the contingency of zat not happening."

One-Stone's accent swung high and low as he did his best to keep his language steady. "There are six sizes…"

The Moth coughed, hurriedly correcting himself. "There are five sizes of Strahlung, or LFB. They differ in weight, and the size of components they take. The size of the component must match the size of Strahlung. You cannot plug a medium lens onto a small frame."

After glaring at Rip for a strong moment, he dropped the accusation. Rip knew what he did. "Each Strahlung is modular, and can be divided into the following pieces: the chassis, or the frame. The coolant, so it does not explode on use. The power source, which is either a Beast Core, a Mana accumulator, or a cultivator. The affinity focus, which determines the color of the beam and the Essence type used. We've also called this a converter before? Then finally, the focus lens, or whatever we end up calling the method of expression. Some frames come with space for a utility slot, but we haven't figured out what goes there yet."

That seemed plenty sensical so far, so Artorian gave a polite nod, and rolled his wrist for One-Stone to continue. "From smallest to largest, the coolant involved goes as follows."

The Moth motioned to the first hovering image. "Cold Clipazines slot into the smallest model. That chassis is easily held in one hand, and as it is the smallest, it is also the most economical to use. Has the least power, but you can give it to an F-ranker and expect a last-hurrah to actually do something. The effort may kill them, but it's the only model you can even try that stunt with at that rank."

Tear leaned in to move the model, showing the next LFB as the Professor professed. "The second smallest, which has slightly more kick to it but still only needs one hand, takes Fimbulwinter Cartridges. Best suited to D- and E-rankers. An F-ranker doesn't have enough Essence to even fill a charge and make the fusion ignite."

Artorian let go of his boys, and crossed his arms as he followed the lecture.

"The medium-sized Strahlung must be held in two hands, and uses Gelid Heat Sinks. C-rankers will be very at home with the medium model. Also because the D- and E-rankers can't hope to lift it. Not well, at least."

Tear moved the image again, tapping his favorite model as One-Stone cracked on. "The large-sized Strahlung must be held in two hands, and possibly rest on the shoulder. C-rankers *can* use this, but we're sliding our toes into Mage territory. This chassis uses Rime Racks."

One-Stone rubbed his fronds together when they got to the second to last one. "The Super-Strahlung cannot be picked up unless one's strength is, frankly, very silly. Zese are so large and ridiculous, zat they are almost always single fire. We have developed Permafrost Rounds for this model, but since zey are so hard to move, we have not really had chances to know if zey work. Super-Strahlungs are usually stationary. Rank needed? Mage or more."

Scheming and trying to hide information on the last one, One-Stone hushed conspiratorially. "Ze last one? Ist eine Über-strahlung. Very secret. Tell people you are going for the Super-version."

With a powerful wink that fooled nobody, One-Stone snuck that prompt away. "As I vas saying. Super-Strahlungs are usually stationary, or need to be mounted on something very serious."

Artorian had flashbacks to using a ballista as a bow. He had to try this. When testing new goodies, why opt for the lesser boom? "I'm very serious."

The group looked at him as if he had made a joke. Soni was the first to laugh. "You are anything except serious, Administrator. Though I know that gleam in your eye, and I was there for the first-hand use of going wild with Ikaruga. I strongly remember shooting Hel-cows off the Vanaheim bridge in order to keep Alfheim secure. So if you want to try? We'll let you. I know that you have the Mage statistics."

"All I'm hearing is a good time, with beeg dakka." Artorian brushed off his shoulders, his smile widening to concerning proportions. "I like dakka."

One-Stone clapped his hands together as he shot up from his seat. "To ze laboratory!"

CHAPTER THIRTY-SIX

The yacht didn't move one inch at One-Stone's proclamation.

Indignant and defiant, the lightly dressed High Elf leaned in the doorway with a precariously raised, carefully curated eyebrow. Zephyr didn't listen to anybody save for a very select list of exceptions, of which One-Stone wasn't one. He was allowed aboard, but if he thought that he was going to be giving any orders, she would see some Moths get thrown in front of her keel.

The older Moth kept his vim and vigor, but was internally sweating when the boat didn't move. "Und ze please, und thank you?"

"You're adorable." Artorian fought back a snort, but smiled as he got up. He gave himself a once-over with his Cleaning Aura just to feel the scrubbing effect, and then let go of his Grandpa-Mode. "Rejuvenescence."

One flash of light later, Young-torian strolled toward an indignant High Elf in his Faith Foundry pajamas. Ember's hand-printed scorch mark had been successfully retained, which Artorian was pretty pleased about. It was a silly little mark, but he liked it. "Zephy, do you know where this laboratory they're talking about is, and are we actually waiting on anyone else? I know somewhere along the itinerary, we have to pick up Ember. If you happen to know where Señor Louis hangs out, I'd like for that to be an interim stop. I have a related quest that involves meeting the man."

Zephyr's sour expression quickly changed to rosy and sweet as the young Administrator walked up to her. Gracefully sinking to a knee so she was at eye level, she held her cheeks and chin with both hands. Zephyr was downright bubbly in her reply. "I do, we're not, and of course we can make a detour! I was also told that the Lady Saintess will inform me when she wants to be picked up, but that she may not have time before we need to route toward New Haven. She mentioned gardening, and planting Titans to ensure a bountiful harvest?"

The High Elf squinted at the starry sky. "Something about burying rocks and putting people in the ground? Either way! I know the location of both the Far Squid, and the laboratory. Milliways is a temporary stop in the Asgard asteroid belt that will be dismantled when the realm gets restored."

She pointed at the restaurant and party palace in question, the Milliways dome still flashing colors. "Decorum and Tisha have disembarked here, along with my currently disbanded bardic troupe. They wanted to stay, and did mention you were invited if you had time. They expect you not to have the time. The place sounds like fun all the way from the dock, but I can't really be in two places at once. Body or not, I'm the boat."

Artorian nodded, satisfied. "I will let them have their happy reunion. I sadly do not have the time to socialize freely just yet. Thank you for the correspondence; you're wonderful, Zephy. Are you doing well? Do you need anything?"

The question hadn't been expected. Zephyr's expression turned complicated, then cleared up as she shook her head no. "While there is far too much I might want, given that I am still a High Elf, and lean dangerously towards decadence? There is little I *need*. I'm of the opinion that my needs currently prioritize making certain that I am seen as valuable and useful, before hierarchies get upended on Exodus time."

Artorian suddenly had very different problems. He held his small hands behind his own back, and frowned in thought. "You make it sound as if people will stop being cooperative with one another as soon as the door to the Old World opens up again. Are there things I need to know?"

Tilting her head, Zephyr poorly hid that she didn't want to say anything, but relented with a nod. "There likely is, Administrator. Though that information doesn't need to be handled at this very moment. There is a time and place for non-Eternia difficulties, and while you are here, I wouldn't mix the complications."

Artorian returned a nod of his own, then wet his lips before pruning them back and forth with a grumble. "*Mmmm.* Politics. *Great.*"

Kneading his forehead, he threw his hands up to mentally toss the topic. "It has to wait. Can we see Louis, then drop by One-Stone's laboratory? I'd like a Strahlung put together so I can go spelunking. I'm not a great cook, but fried rat is on the menu."

Zephyr rose gracefully, pressed her arm across her stomach, and replied politely with a succinct bow. "I will not be accepting that on my yacht's menu, Administrator, but I follow the sentiment. I shall set course for the Lair of the Far Squid. The journey will likely take several hours, so please make yourself at home."

Vanishing inside to sneakily undo her Elven form so she could focus on being the ship, Zephyr undocked herself from the mooring and calmly listed into a gentle orbit. Lights blinked in a variety of colors from the side of her hull, signaling to the Popeye harbormaster enjoying a nice can of spinach that they were vacating the berth. The harbormaster whistled twice through his pipe, and waved them away.

Returning to the recessed sitting area, Artorian considered tackling the politics now, but shook his head. That debacle really had to wait. There would be endless tasks and problems, and he could personally only do so much. Delegation was the name of the game! "Alright, is there anything else I need to know that must be explained, rather than shown? I want to see and feel the differences in LFBs rather than get a lecture."

Soni produced a Noisy Cricket from her inner pocket. "This is the smallest version of an LFB. One handed, tiny, packs a surprising punch for anyone not an F-ranker. In Eternia terms, you can pick this up and use it the moment you have a mana bar, regardless of stats. Is it going to do a lot? No. Does it work? As reliably as One-Stone randomly falls asleep."

Artorian glanced at the older Moth, expecting a rebuttal of fury. He found only snoring. The old Moth had a book covering his face, which was clearly going to hide that fact. Soni moved two of her hands toward One-Stone to show the example, while holding out the Noisy Cricket to Artorian with the fourth. "Told you."

Taking the tiny, near weightless beam weapon, Artorian turned the object over a few times. The light fusion tool was so tiny that it easily fit into his considerably smaller than normal hand. "That's not what I expected."

He aimed the Noisy Cricket off the bow of the ship, but aside from the crossbow-like triggering mechanism, he could not puzzle out how this was supposed to work. "Do I pull the bolt-release? There's not much to this thing."

Rip and Tear both rapidly crossed and uncrossed their arms while shaking their heads. Soni nodded sagely as if testing the trigger was of no consequence. *Hmmm*, to go with the reformed demon, or the trusted good boys? That win went to the Sharks. He placed the Noisy Cricket on the table, to the great, slumping relief of both Rip and Tear. He wasn't being told something, and since Soni clicked her tongue and looked away, there would likely have been a spectacle. "Not here. In the lab."

Soni recovered the Noisy Cricket, a small metal stick with a plus sign at the tip screwing open the delicate components. Pointing to the handle, she poked the cold white brick located in the handle. "This is a Cold Clipazine. There was a big argument between a clip and a magazine that many people simply didn't grasp, so we mushed them together and never looked back. Not that it's difficult. A clip holds coolant cartridges together to make them easier to load. A magazine is a container that feeds coolant into the frame during discharge. This part does both."

Soni grit her teeth, her fingers pressing together out of strain. "Not. Difficult. Just like the colors. The colors are supposed to make it easier."

Artorian glanced at the armored-up Sharks, who had not removed a single piece of gear. Maybe there was water in their suits or something. Rip and Tear both bobbed their heads at this follow up, as even they liked the use of colors. When Artorian pressed them for information with a look, both poked at their helmets, shook their heads, then pointed at Soni.

Soni tapped one of the Noisy Cricket components when she had the Administrator's attention, her metal stick moving along as she addressed the other pieces. "In this chassis, the coolant goes into the handle. The core goes in the back, the converter goes in the middle, and the lens goes at the front."

Her metal stick poked the core, the *tink* of which woke up One-Stone. With a large nasal breath, the book went flying, and the Moth had to pretend like he'd been present all along. "Ja, I am here! Was ist los? What's going on?"

Soni chuckled, and poked the visible component of the opened up Noisy Cricket a few more times. "Going over components and why the colors matter. Do you want to lecture? You love to lecture."

One-Stone took the metal stick when it was offered, then pushed up his fluffy sleeves. After some hushed words from Soni that allowed One-Stone to catch up, he nodded with wisdom and eased right into the related explanation. "Ze smallest model uses a micro mana accumulator as a core. Beast Cores and Dungeon Cores are too big to slot, and trying breaks the chassis.

Ze problem? A micro mana accumulator uses untyped Essence, and pouring untyped Essence through a lens *melts* ze lens."

The old Moth tapped the converter in the middle, which looked to be an aquamarine gemstone. "As a solution, we add converters. These are affinity-type gemstones... or... ze other way around? The gemstone determines ze affinity type, but the conductivity can vary wildly even within a gem's own peer group. Both ruby and scarletite give you fire, sapphires and fluorite give you water, taaffeite really likes air, while emeralds and erinite lean to earth."

Artorian was following so far, but made finger-swirls to get some details. "Do those actually do anything unique?"

The professor was glad to teach. "The elemental ones are nice und stable, especially all the water and earth affinity gems. Earth affinities help ground the weapon and increase stability, which means your beam goes where you aimed it to go. Meanwhile, water affinity gems don't create nearly as much heat. Fire does more damage but creates even more heat, and air affinity gems increase the effective range of your beams, but thin them out. For the outliers? Topaz for Celestial, and good luck for Infernal. Kiss your stability goodbye with those last two."

Artorian dropped his hand while nodding. Those were useful goodies.

One-Stone held up some of his favorite pretty rocks that he kept tucked away for... reasons. "When sourced through gems, Fire beams are red with orange flecks. Earth beams are green with brown flecks. Air beams are yellow with light blue flecks. Water beams are deep blue. Celestial beams are gold. Infernal beams are a dark purple. As a rule of thumb when you don't know what a gem might give you? If ze color matches ze affinity, you are going to winny."

He smiled wide, expecting that his incredibly fine joke had landed exquisitely well. "Nein, nothing? Tough crowd. I shall continue. Converters solve ze problem of ze energy source destroying ze lens. Lenses can only channel so much juice, and overdoing it turns your perfectly good LFB into a perfectly good missing hand."

Artorian thought he knew why the Sharks had told him not to fire the Noisy Cricket. He had intended to channel his personal mana pool, or equivalent, into the weapon. He'd never even thought to let the Noisy Cricket draw from its own internal energy supply. That was just not how he handled equipment. The thing would have blown up his hand? *Joy.*

Soni clicked her tongue when Artorian's expression betrayed that he'd figured it out. Artorian would remember that jest for later, even if he would probably have been fine. "Does the converter have to be a gem?"

One-Stone waved his hand dismissively, more of his wonderful accent bleeding into the conversation. Rather than fingers, he held up a whole hand for each point. As he had four of them, Artorian figured the Professor had four statements. "Nein, but it helps in the majority of cases if it is a gemstone. The higher purity the converter, the better. There's some energy loss from using any converter, with lower purity having higher losses. Losses happen for any steps between the power source and the means of expression. Converters are worth the losses to get typed Essence into the lens in order to keep the lens from blowing up. *Haha!* Trust the Cold Clipazine to handle the heat from the converter inefficiency."

One-Stone's fronds drooped conspiratorially. "Corrupted gems that are not made from Essence at all also cause some interesting reactions, and are in some cases better? Dangerous for the user, though. Very dangerous."

He cautiously tapped the converter component. "Even when compared to opal, which is one of the very few gems to provide Infernal-typed Essence? There are some materials, like arsenopyrite, chalcanthite, cinnabar, und torbernite, that you truly do not want to get near. Fantastic und devastating output? Ja. Likely to kill you for pulling ze trigger? Ja. For safety, stay away from heliodor, though nobody will tell me why. Und try, really *try* not to use opal or diamond. Infernal cannons are technically against rules from ze Council of Geneva."

"Diamond?" That one didn't fit in the list, making Artorian frown and lean in to inspect the chassis. "Why is diamond a problem, and why was this tiny tool so incredibly heavy for its size?"

One-Stone tapped the frame that all the components were housed in. "Treated osmium. Safe. Stable. Can withstand ze internal forces. Ze downside? *Heavy*. As to diamond. Ja, very potent, very powerful. Ze multiple affinities? Very difficult for ze majority of lenses. If ze Strahlung isn't tuned to a very specific, single affinity? Then ze tool does not work very well. By which I mean, two stones are suddenly involved."

One-Stone didn't have to make the explosion sound effect with his voice and hands, but the sight was comical. "If you want to use ze diamond converter? Then you better be using a diamond lens. Und good luck getting one. Additionally? The more affinities are involved in conversion, the more expensive the drain on ze core. If you put a diamond converter into ze Noisy Cricket? It could never fire. Zere is no micro mana accumulator that can hold enough charge to ignite the fusion and create a beam. Even if you did from an external source, there isn't enough osmium in this frame to contain that output. You will melt through all your coolant, realize you don't remotely have enough, and bang!"

Artorian rubbed his forehead, and fished the prototype lens from Dev out of his pocket. "What's this thing, then? It has text in here that makes me think it's also a converter."

One-Stone's eyes lit up, two of his hands making grabby motions. "Look who has returned home! Number forty-two, you little scoundrel! Where have you been, you dangerous noodle. I thought you would have turned some poor test pilot into a crater by now."

Artorian unhappily handed the lens over, likely having been intended as said to-be-cratered test pilot. Soni and Dev were conspiring. He could feel it in his big nose that people were wanting to use him as a guinea pig since he could likely live through the explosions and tell the tale. Learning shields from Lucia got moved up the to-do list.

He momentarily checked out while One-Stone fawned over the lens and spoke to the object like a long-lost child, getting snug and cozy between the pillows. "That's enough mechanics for now. Wake me when we get there."

CHAPTER THIRTY-SEVEN

"We have arrived." Artorian woke to Zephyr speaking in dulcet tones. The cadence was wrong. Her voice was too calm, deep, and trance-like. Her lights flickered, erratic and not sequenced.

He sat up with a strong push to free himself from the pillow bunker. Someone had played the game 'how many pillows can we stack on Artorian without the pile falling over?' Whoever had won, it hadn't been Young-torian. "Zephy, you alright?"

The reply from Zephyr was unsettling. "We are Unbound. The solar winds blow across our skin. Hyperspace sings in our ears. The universe unfolds around our thoughts."

Perplexed and concerned, Artorian freed himself entirely from the pillow tower of Babel so he could move around and take in his updated surroundings. An eerie feeling accompanied their location. They were far, far away from the realms and asteroid belts.

Artorian could squint and see them in the distance, but where they currently were was almost entirely composed of starless void. The black. Where were the Serenity Bees when he needed them? The creeping, eerie crawling over his skin intensified when he found the Moths and the Sharks asleep. As in

Demeter's Dream, they appeared to have conked out mid-task. Some screens were still flickering with life, their tasks pending in the midst of prompts and confirmation menus.

He checked his Auras, but found the option still set to the scrubby one. Whatever had made the crew cast off to sleep land this time? It hadn't been him.

While Milliways had been difficult to place due to only having asteroids in the vicinity, and the concept of down was hard to pinpoint, here, the matter was worse. Zephyr was blindly lilting in an aft-over-head spin. Had it not been for the utter lack of stuff to compare that spin to, his stomach would be suffering similar twisties.

He was the only one awake. "Ominous."

A shake to the shoulders accomplished nothing. The Moths didn't budge, and the Sharks were out cold. He pulled up their information, and clenched his jaw at the same debuff they all had stacked up. "Space Madness? Hundreds of stacks of Space Madness?"

Shivers shot up his skin. The black had moved. Like an oily snake under the surface of water, causing a hint of a ripple. He felt the debuff try to take him, but Freedom of Mind backhanded and punted each stack off and away from his own character sheet like a possessed, singing goalie. 'Block, block, block-block, block, block, everybooooody block!'

Artorian pulled up the location, and tapped the prompt to get confirmation.

Ding!

———

Location: Lair of the Far Squid.

———

No time like the present for some good old diplomatic dice. He was in the right place, regardless of how stifling and alone that place might feel. "Señor Louis?"

Space coiled.

Rather, the thing space was doing in order to move likely didn't have a word in the lexicon yet. The area around him didn't feel like it was twisting, or bending, or tearing, or conjoining. If he had to describe the feeling, it was the uncanny impossibility of watching a crumpled piece of paper become flawlessly flat and whole again. The big hurdle was not one of detail, but one of scale.

When scooping a piece of earth from the ground, one has a good sense of how much ground they have compared to the size of their hand. A shovel gives ten times more, and a wheelbarrow ten times that. A mound could be ten times the size and amount of earth stored in a wheelbarrow, and a hill could easily be ten times the dirt stored by a mound. This was all sensical to place and scale. One could compare themselves to a hill, walk it, survey it, and compare oneself to it.

A mountain was more difficult to compare oneself to. Here, we enter the problem of conceptual values, such as an absurd amount of coin that could never reasonably fit into a single room. The mountain could be scaled, but the mountain was vast, treacherous, and made of more ground and dirt that could reasonably be measured. From there, a mountain range was as unfathomable as a single mountain, and the concepts blended together. One was clearly greater than another, but the distinction was nebulous and hard to keep between one's mortal fingers.

So when a planet uncoiled from the black, in the mantoid shape of a necro-morphed being of bone and tanning oils, with all of its organs externally visible? Scale, unlike detail, was difficult to describe.

Protected by Freedom of Mind, Artorian was looking at a cross between an eldritch entity and a necromancer's wet dream. Three horse skulls began the head of Señor Louis, fused together at the base. One skull pointed ahead, while the other two pointed out to the sides. A crown of bone sheathed a visible brain, while an underpinning set of horns curled out below the triple skull. Which connected to the rest of the eldritch being's form by an eel's body that served as a neck and spine from nose tip to tail end.

Loose bone protruded from this eel frame, showing biological madness. Visible sinew and pulsing organs the size of landmasses bulged and pillowed, coated in protective carapace and chitin that flowed as if fins were operating underwater. Tentacles of glowing violet pushed from its back, and arms in a variety of designs and sizes came adjoined in pairs down the mantoid's frame.

Artorian almost had to ignore the insectoid wings and ocean-sized scythes from everything else going on with this creature. The size and scale had his mouth agape, and only a skill was protecting his eyes from bleeding at the sight. "What. The. Abyss?"

The eldritch being of bone and sinew ceased uncoiling at the mention, the space around it still unspooling more and more of the eldritch bone-horror's form. Then, beyond belief, the planet-sized mantoid *tsked* him. When Señor Louis spoke, Artorian heard the words directly in his brainpan. His ears were of no use, and Freedom of Mind looked at him like a fawn pinned in bright lights. The skill had no idea how to block Ultimate Telepathy.

Señor Louis lurched closer, but to Artorian there was no visible difference. The eldritch mantoid was slightly larger as it spoke with words stolen from the original Agrippa. How tasty that brain had been. "Órale! Do not accuse Señor Louis of being related to that dreary pit of muck."

Artorian blinked, having no idea what to do. He pulled up his tried-and-true playbook, and shifted straight into wise, grandfatherly responses, regardless of being in child-mode. "Oh, my apologies. Hello? Are you Señor Louis?"

This must have amused the eldritch thing of unfathomable size and power. Señor Louis replied with a gurgle-y laugh. "Si! Hola. Cómo estás, cabrón?"

Artorian blinked again, having no idea what to say until Señor Louis followed up. "Ándale! You wake Señor Louis. Speak, before you are a snack."

At a complete loss on how to speak to a critter the size of a planet that could enjoy Brother Moon as a chew toy, Artorian did the next best thing. He pulled up his quest log, tapped the related entry, and whisked the prompt toward Señor Louis. The prompt's flight time took a long moment, but the craning of a neck combined with the blue prompt growing severely in size said plenty.

Señor Louis read the prompt, an event that was followed by Artorian's head filling with booming laughter. Guttural, wet, throaty laughter. Señor Louis gave the mortal a moment for the echoes to die down in his skull before speaking with improved amusement. "I know you know, shiny mind. You are the Vovô that Brasilia and Bellini are so fond of bragging about."

This time when Señor Louis moved closer, the change in scale was severe. From far away, anything could look small. When that something small surrounded the ship you were on, that was a more difficult sell. When one part of that far-away being moved closer, it became unfathomably larger. Like a mountain-sized eye that pushed in for a closer look. When that particular eye was one of the smaller ones. "You are tiny, for a Vovô."

Artorian swallowed, but considered that his cue. "Potentia!"

A flash of light later, and the beach-attired grandfather found himself standing on Zephyr's deck. He felt horribly mismatched as a sunglasses-sporting beach-goer in the depths of space with an eldritch bone-monster uncomfortably close. "Señor Louis finds your choice of appearance... appealing. Señor Louis shall join you."

Artorian had no return to that, but saying 'no' seemed like one of those really bad Kings and Castles moves. He mentally moved a piece, and would see what the opening would get him. "Welcome aboard?"

A wrenching of space squeezed the eldritch horror down

into a pool of protruding bones and fleshy black sinew. A pool that condensed itself into a five-by-five space on Zephyr's deck. Señor Louis coalesced and coagulated into the rough shape of a person, complete with oversized black sombrero, and a matching set of beach attire. In darker color choices, but similar nonetheless.

Lucky for Artorian, between seeing the changes in Poirot and Gaston, this was the third time he'd encountered an individual in recent times that had undergone this kind of transformation. So some semblance of sense, as weird as that was, was found. "Welcome to Zephyr, Señor Louis. I don't know what your type of proper greeting is, but would a handshake do?"

A glowing tentacle wrapped around his hand and arm, squeezed wetly, then released and retracted. Artorian didn't say a word until Cleaning Presence scrubbed clean every last sticky spot. "Charmed."

"Encantado? Si. Me gusta eso." In humanoid form, complete with sombrero, Señor Louis was tall and fair. Long and dark curly hair accompanied slightly olive-tinged skin, though it took Señor Louis a decent amount of time to get the hands correct. Knuckled mini-tentacles were an effort in absolute precision, and the concept of a thumb was baffling as a limitation. Why bother with thumbs when you could have multiple, fully prehensile hand-tentacles? "Como esto?"

Señor Louis looked to Artorian for basic movements, who opened and closed his hands in example of how the muscles worked and where the bones were placed. Details that Señor Louis discovered with some intrusive, sticky prodding that Artorian was biding his way through like a tense teakettle. This was nothing. This was fine. This was manageable. Confused but friendly eldritch-critter beat out obtuse and loud, bothersome pridemongers.

Señor Louis needed helping.

Odin needed belting.

He was trying to make a friend here. Friends helped friends, and Señor Louis had not proven to be hostile, regardless of the relentless eerie feeling that still clung to his skin. Like something was still not right with his surroundings. The blackness of space felt off, even without Señor Louis coiled up in it. Something else was here, and very well hidden. Truesight kept telling him that he was seeing something in the black, but without other colors or shapes to discern what, black on black gave him nothing to work with.

At least space didn't suddenly surprise him with a gleaming white smile. That might have killed him on the spot.

Once content with touching Artorian's face like a blind man trying to see, Señor Louis ended up with a spectacularly handsome face himself. One joined by dark eyes with purple irises. Artorian thought the look aesthetically pleasing, but very discomforting. Particularly when he tried to look Señor Louis directly in the eyes.

His Truesight kept flaring and trying to be useful, but the entire background changing to include the outline of a world-sized mantoid necro-morph was difficult for the brain to handle. He repressed the inclinations where he could. Whatever else Truesight was trying to tell him wasn't getting through, regardless; he may as well stop the headache before it got worse.

Artorian felt a good chunk flustered, but put his best foot forward. "Shall we move to instructions? I mean, introductions? I am Artorian, but I go by Sunny, or Love. Or, if we're using the game names, Sunshine. Vovô was something an eccentric new friend of mine called me."

The awfully pretty man that was never going to pull the wool over Artorian's eyes clasped his hand properly this time, regardless of no handshake being offered. Trying the handshake again for a round two, Artorian deemed the attempt to go much better this time, purely due to lack of a sticky component.

Señor Louis was happy. "Si! I am Señor Louis, El Portero. The Gatekeeper. Good to meet you, Vovô. I, too, wish to be an eccentric new friend."

Artorian was never going to look this gift horse in the mouth. "Then it is good to meet you, my new eccentric friend."

Ding!

Quest Complete!
Quest: Lair of the Far Squid.
Objective: Visit Louis. Make a friend.
Reward! You now know the location of a very important secret place, which acts as a surprise tool that will help you later. Gift horse. Mouth. Don't do it.

Artorian was going to say nothing about the prompt reading his mind, and swept his arm out to the deck. "Shall we walk and talk? Oh, and if you could stop breaking the minds of the crew? That would be very friendly of you. Zephyr doesn't know which way is up with whatever effect you are creating. Space Madness is serious juju."

Señor Louis spun his sombrero and clapped his hands, enjoying the function of basic physics. Accepting the request, he pulled the lever on one of the effects that came with being a cosmic space horror. "Si, Vovô. We walk, we talk. I am enamored with these 'legs' that I am using. They could be tentacles!"

Artorian nodded, understanding this was going to be a difficult conversation that spiked between questions from a five-year-old, and knowledge from an ageless thing. "They certainly could be, Louis, they certainly could be. Have you encountered the idea of 'gravity' before? Fascinating stuff. Really hammers home the need for a well-designed bone and muscle structure."

Señor Louis loved the topic of bones and muscles, and Artorian could feel that truth in his twin hearts. Or see it in the bright sparkle of those purple irises. The reply from the eldritch horror in human form bordered on seduction. "Vovô? Speak to Louis."

CHAPTER THIRTY-EIGHT

Zephyr recovered to the gentle pat-pat of Grandpa-torian's hand on her fancy golden-filigree balustrade. He walked along the outer edge with Louis, brushing across the banister and tapping out the odd ditty with his fingers. Percussion did remain his favorite, and the top rail made pleasant, dull, wooden thuds in reply. Señor Louis had been quiet for a while, lost in thought about the purpose of a vestigial tailbone.

Artorian could tell when Zephyr returned, greeting her as the drunken aft-over-stern maneuver stopped. "Welcome back, Zephy. Take some pleasant breaths? You're going to be alright. The Cleaning portion of my Aura may only keep your floors shiny, but the Cleansing half does scrub that debuff right off. You'll be right as rain soon enough. Take us home?"

Her voice, thankfully, was groggy but back to normal. Bubbly High Elf beat out the terrorizing, dull, and droning Bentusi alternative.

"Home? Yes. Home is a great direction." She stabilized her prow, and pointed her nose back toward Eternia's galactic center. The solar sails opened wide and neon engines flicked on, but no fine-tuning of the course occurred. "Which home was that again?"

Artorian paused from his sauntering stride. "Right. Let's do One-Stone's laboratory, then if you could take me to Pag, or wherever the Pylon problem is? That would be the plan."

One-Stone shot awake, pretending to have been in the conversation the entire time. "Ja! Hans! Get ze flammenwerfer. Roast ze rats! Bring ze delicacies to ze cold place, und stuff them into Stollen. Feed ze world. Ze plan is foolproof!"

Artorian wasn't sold on the nutritional value of rat. Still, sometimes dumb ideas had merit. How was New Haven doing on the ol' food stocks? Weren't they rapidly depleting their supply due to a hot influx of new players? He turned on his heel, shooting his words right back to the older fluffy white Moth with matching energy. "Yes! Great idea, Professor! They will become supplies, and we will feed the world! To the laboratory?"

One-Stone was on his feet and on the table instantly. A thematic bolt of lightning cracked in the background while he held one hand high above the rest. "To ze laboratory!"

Zephyr, this time, did correct her course and flared her engines to get going. "One way trip to lightbulb city, coming right up."

One-Stone rubbed his fronds together, tantalized by the prospect of more scientific progress. "How exciting. Ah, Herr Administrator! Which laboratory division do you wish to sniff around in? We have two."

Artorian didn't get enough information out of that query. "What are they?"

One-Stone wondered how to explain, and settled for asking the question that every light-seeker had to ask every morning. "Are you trying to achieve greatness, or are you trying to avoid disappointment? The divisions are named Reason, and *Reeeeeee*. Not respectively. Because I put them in ze wrong order. They are ze other way around. Because... Ja."

The Administrator buckled with laughter when One-Stone

got flustered over a minor language hiccup. The choice was easy! "Oh, it's gotta be the goblin warcry. We must go fast and break things. Puzzling out why is for people smarter than me. Besides, who wants a Super-Strahlung made out of *reason*? Slap some bits and bobs together, hand it over, and point me at the target. Then you can bet glowy lights on what is going to explode first. The target, or the Strahlung!"

Artorian copied One-Stone, creating explosion sounds, and matching hand motions. The Moth loved it and cracked up, only to be glared at by Soni. Who still had a small mountain of reasonable paperwork waiting in prompt format. Begrudgingly returning to work after getting off the table, One-Stone stone chewed his way through requisite paperwork.

The Moth rubbed his forehead with his fronds. "I am a smart man, but I am not a clever man. Thank you for not poking at ze loose scaffolding."

Artorian commiserated. He knew that pain. Best not to get in front of it. "I would call myself the opposite, Professor. I am not a smart man, but I am pretty clever."

He'd lost track of Louis, who had kept pacing, but standing in place long enough would loop the Señor. Leaning on the banister, Grandpa-torian tried to enjoy normal ship-related events, which was when he noticed that they were missing. There was no wind to blow over his skin or through his hair.

No scent aside from the yacht-approved mixture of yellow tulips and pink peonies that were popping up across the vessel stood out at all. He'd either scrubbed the rest away, or there had been nothing to scrub. No salty seawater. No ocean breezes. No gull squawks. No children sputtering on faces full of sand. None of the sounds of life were present aside from the fussing with prompts and humming of neon engines. He roughly remembered hanging around the planet's orbit in Dawn's deep-sea armor in the past. That same silence and lack of sensory noise ate a bigger chunk out of his well-being than any overt threat ever had.

Should he even go to the lab? He could ask for the tool and

mosey straight to Pag. Artorian shook his head, and recounted to himself some grandpa-wisdom. "You don't put your nose where it belongs, you put it where it matters."

When Louis caught up to him, the man lapped him and walked right on by. Artorian looked over his shoulder, expecting a dramatic stop and turn, but no. Louis was off in his own world, and Artorian understood that well. The Señor would find him when the Señor wanted to find him.

That left him with a prime opportunity! More catching up with the Shark boys! Pushing away from the yacht's edge as the wooden banister began to bloom with more peonies, he took the moment to praise Zephyr first. "Love your nature's touch, Zephy. Very good and well done. Do they glow in the dark?"

Zephyr's reply was delayed. Clearly from a mixture of excitement and eureka. "They're sure going to, now!"

Chuckling gently and nodding to himself at a good deed well done, he patted the edge of the boat and sauntered his way over to the boys that were still snoozing away. On second thought. He liked putting people to sleep, but he didn't like waking them up. Let the boys sleep. One look at the Moths helped determine that he didn't want to bother them or break that conversation up, but as the conversation lived in the realm of smart, and not clever, he would wisely keep his nose out.

He was smart in the ways of the person, and the cultivation, but all this math stuff? It could miss him and he wouldn't miss it when it did. Did this give him some of that extremely rare and vaunted... what... what was it called again? Free... free thyme? Like the herb? No, free time! Yes, yeeeeees, that was what it was. Elusive little thing.

He stood there and had no idea what to do. "Have I been so swept up in the flow of things that my head just went utterly blank at the attempt to think of something to do that I wanted to do, that isn't work related? This white canvas is terribly bright."

"Herr Administrator." One-Stone easily snatched up Artorian's attention, which behaved like a piece of flotsam floating on the waves. Though if the Moth was going to ask anything about the prompts with base, added, increased, and more damage on them, Artorian wasn't going to be of much help. One-Stone might as well be asking him about Grommets and related Wallaces. "Do you remember if Essence had will all by itself?"

That left turn was a lifesaver.

"Philosophy! My field!" Artorian pulled up to the conversation faster than a seagull could steal part of a forgotten sandwich. He abandoned free time, and chose academics. "In general, any energy that we as cultivators have encountered lacks the very capacity, or the 'thing,' that allows it to make independent decisions in the first place. Essence, Mana, and the like, might have inclinations or ways that it is 'more likely' to go. I doubt that's different in Eternia, if you're developing tools meant for Cal or the outside."

Soni pitched in with agreement. "Energy, by itself, cannot be Julie. Nor can it do the thing without an outside force. Sunny's personal oddities where his Mana enjoys proving him wrong? That is the outlier of outliers. Artorian proves that it can be the case that Essence and Mana act otherwise, but he also proves the case that in nearly all other circumstances, it just doesn't do that. The Administrator is often used as a guidestone to reverse engineer a 'normal' or average value. Because if you run the numbers and you end up at Artorian? Something went wrong."

Should he be... proud? Insulted? Artorian wasn't sure.

One-Stone scratched some text on the prompt that he was stuck on, distracted by his problem. "Ze feces of celestial. I was hoping that corruption und related materials could... Nein. Never mind. Corruption cannot solve my intent problem purely because it looks the other way und crosses its arms like a feisty teenager."

The Moth procured very familiar-looking documents. Artorian's old corruption notes! They lived! "You made ze original notations on the workings of corruption, but working with that variation of Essence seems unfeasible. Anything other than purging it from a system, either swift or slow, seems to be a fool's errand."

Artorian leaned over to steal a glance at this corruption prompt. The cultivator business was in his wheelhouse! So the question was on intent, not materials? He'd comment on both. "When it comes to Essence doing anything, or being moved to act? That corruption counts as an outside force is just a really bad stroke of un-luck for all things cultivator-y. Cultivating with corruption doesn't really work, because that's trying to move a solid in a system meant for a liquid. You'll gunk up the tubes, clog up important valves, and *huerk*! There goes your cultivator. The same is likely true for materials. You add corruption to an Essence object? Same difference. You're going to gunk up that object and change how it works from the inside out."

He waffled on his explanation, even if being able to shove unwanted corruption into Beast Cores was both a blessing and a curse that he wasn't going to get into right now. "I say liquid, but gas is more appropriate for what a cultivator's internals function on, and even that isn't nebulous enough."

Upturning a palm, he found it surprisingly easy to shape a light model of a person. "Physical space in a body isn't occupied by the majority of a cultivator's funky juju. Neither your cultivation technique, nor your meridians, are physically present. There, but you can't open a person up and find them. When C-rankers infuse cells with Essence, that's when nebulous energy starts becoming more physical. Until then?"

Artorian dismissed his person-shape into that of a glowy cloud. It was a cute cloud. He gave it googly eyes. "Essence breaks down 'what you think something is made of' to a state of matter that I think can better be described as particles of potential and change that make up the very foundations of a universe."

He separated the cloud into shapes and objects, but ultimately, those things were all still made of clouds. "Concepts, matter, stuff, and things, all come together from the tiniest of nothingness. Until you have something, and that something keeps clumping on and on until you have us and everything in it. Corruption is the part of that energy that doesn't want to change anymore, and thus doesn't. Cultivators only really function with the variant of that energy which does, or else they will get turned into stuff and things. Much like this cloud."

One-Stone held his face with four hands and two fronds, deep in thought. "Pushing energy through corruption should still work fine, conceptually."

Artorian stole the Professor's prompt since it was unattended, needing to know more of where this conversation was coming from in order to grasp where it was going. He was losing the thread and One-Stone was not giving him much to work with. "Ah, I see. Yes, Essence can move through items made of corruption, so long as they are conductive of Essence. From what I recall? There is still a difference between a basic rock, an Essence rock, a rock made from Essence, a corrupted rock, and a rock made from corruption."

He slid the prompt back over and moved some line items. "Examples would likely help. In order for the easy ones: a basic rock is a pebble, an Essence rock may as well be a Dungeon Core, and rock made from Essence is easily described as a gemstone."

Turning the prompt page, Artorian cleaned up the disorganized notes as he went. "The corrupted versions are the same in concept, but differ in material and their effect. Different input got you a different output."

Pleased with his meddling, Artorian returned the prompt. "That may be why all these explosions listed are related to pushing energy from a mana accumulator through a converter that has something to do with corruption."

The Administrator tapped the bottom, which showed a nicely segregated list of what had gone boom versus what hadn't. "Compared to a converter that doesn't use corruption, those seem to work fine. You're getting bigger damage numbers because more energy is needed to make the end result pew in the first place. Not because there's a conversion issue. The converters just can't handle the load and blow up."

The Moth flicked his fronds back and forth between the adjusted prompt, and his notes. His four arms shot up in the air; the change in format had been such a small thing, but it made such a big impact to have all the same data collated together. "Eureka! This was so simple all along!"

Artorian thumbed his nose, a tiny bit smug. He wasn't smart like One-Stone, but putting the right information in the right order was a breeze. Finding which information needed to move? Now that was the right question, and the right question was Artorian's strong suit. "You actually had it all along, Professor. If you look here, you will see that your notes were accounted for."

He tapped an underlined segment where One-Stone had gotten frustrated. "Now, if you meant using corruption as the power source, that's a realm of madness I don't tread and don't know how to operate in. I can't bottle lightning. I have seen physics do some strange things, but I am not the person to ask for how to replicate them. You won't get anything intent-driven out of corruption-affected objects, and you can't make it do something it wasn't already going to do."

One-Stone glared daggers at Soni, recalling events that he did not wish to recall. "Ja. Ze intent-driven versions of the Strahlung were... *exciting*."

"We learned not to cross the streams." Soni fluttered her eyelashes, innocent as a peach. "The ghosts learned not to meddle, and got put into time out. Which is a very lovely, very well sealed, striped yellow box. It all worked out in the end."

Artorian thought that anti-ghost fusion beams sounded pretty handy, in the unlikely event he ever needed one. He remembered the tale of 'Moon's Haunted' quite well. "Do those have a name too?"

Soni clapped her hands together as if that joke could be seen from a league away. "Ghost-busters!"

CHAPTER THIRTY-NINE

Zephyr and Soni both thought the same thing as they saw the white-fluffs get into it, lose track of their topics, devolve into ever wilder tangents, and yell '*what do you mean*' at one another in ever more dramatic ways. Particularly as they waded too deep into the knowledge base of the other.

The old ones were adorable.

All the finger waving, accusatory pointing, table-slapping, and opinionated warring on the smallest, dumbest details that nobody in their right mind would both take a stand on. Yet here these two old coots were, throwing themselves on hills purely to sprawl over them like cats on a heat rock to yowl in complaint.

By the time they arrived at One-Stone's lab, the Goblins of the Green Plain—or the GGP for short—had been waiting at a hastily constructed berth. A berth that looked so rickety, Zephyr hadn't been sure she even wanted to land. A piece of the empty green plain would probably have been safer than that Jenga tower of bamboo that had run out of the will to live.

The GGP waited for the noisy ones to disembark, heard more bickering about the disembarking process, then eventually began to leave when the white-fluffed ones took too long. This was the Land of *Reeeeeee*, not the Land of Reason! There were things to test and mistakes to make.

Only other Moths remained by the time One-Stone and Artorian descended the boarding ramp with their heads pressed together, their fingers pointedly waving as they both talked over each other at the same time like it was a national sport. A sport that One-Stone was winning on account of having more fingers.

Artorian considered that some blatant cheatery. His Shark boys each grabbed him by a shoulder once on grassy green ground. The startled Administrator snapped from his entertainment as they did, the mind wrenched back to the task at hand. "Hmmm? What is it, my boys? Oh, we're here? We're here! Wonderful. No dallying then, straight to the components! I want to slap a Super-Strahlung together and do as a Goblin does!"

The approving calls of *reeeeee* in the background were far more motivating than they should be, as Rip and Tear both had to try to stop Artorian from hauling himself off in the wrong direction. He had no idea where he was going!

One-Stone composed himself from having an absolutely stunning time in a good old yelling match. Always pleasant to do with a highly acknowledged peer that understood the value of letting the rampant thoughts out through a good shouting session. Did the arguments have a point? Absolutely not. Has it been great to have the equivalent of an academic pillow fight? Absolutely yes!

The plain turned out to be the lab.

Artorian had expected a building, or Gnomish organization, or underground Dwarven bunkers, or Dark Elven obfuscation. The Moths cared for none of that, opting instead to expose as much of their Alfheim grounds to the sun as possible. Something about basking in the great glow of unreachable enlightenment.

Artorian chose to say nothing about the 'praising the sun' poses anytime a local experiment seemed to go well. The

Goblins instead took flying lessons, the *boomy-booms* far more frequent over in their neck of the woods. That... likely used to be actual woods. He could tell where the goblins had shacked up as, instead of grass, they were all walking on wood chips like it was hammered cobble. Or that the tables were made of what hadn't become compressed flooring. Either way, he made his way over to the Moth side of things.

The Moths also had tables. Laden with a great variety and spread of models, pieces, and related components that they were still in the process of organizing. The frames for the weapons themselves on the other hand, laid on the grass in neat, spread-out rows. Some of them didn't seem to have moved in a while, likely because they were too heavy? How heavy was a chassis made of Osmium anyway? Couldn't be that bad.

Rip and Tear had to go before Artorian could pull up his first inspection prompt. They both tapped their helmets, and made swirly motions with their hands. Artorian figured they needed to change out the water in their suits, and gave each a squeeze hug before waving as they headed off to a nearby lake.

Artorian inspected the silvery hunks as Soni joined him. One-Stone had been pulled away to a group of other Moths, so Soni served as the explainer. "You can pull up their information like prompts. That's a big reason why we're doing this in Eternium instead of Cal. The Eternium versions are a lot easier to handle, with there being an energy regeneration metric. Better for testing. Once we have combinations that work, these models will go to Cal, where we figure out how to work them efficiently without all the game backing. Once we have efficient models, a few will be selectively approved for exodus use."

Artorian puzzled out the need. "Do we still have that many non-Mages in Cal's soul space? His efforts to push people into Magehood has been a grand endeavor, but I expected that endeavor to be mostly successful. My Lunella and Wux should be outliers."

Soni crossed all four of her arms in the multiplication sign.

"Not the case. Cal certainly succeeded in pushing everyone who had the will or ambition to breach that rank, but there are many who didn't meet… I'm going to use the word qualifications, but the people who didn't make it by now disqualified themselves. Lu and Wu are a discussion case for the example of people who flat out said no."

She tugged at his bright pink sleeve, and made 'come along' head motions so they could get started with prompts at the smallest model. "Cal did all he could to make cultivation as painless as possible, but it's public knowledge that you have to do the majority of the process again once you're out. Where it will not be painless, the Essence will not be bountiful, the environment will not be safe, there will be no supporting infrastructure, no government to speak of, and no superpower having your back while you go through the process. All of that assumes you have no prior or outstanding obligations to anything or anyone else. Children, in particular, tend to move people's minds."

Artorian grumbled in pained understanding. "Just because you can learn the methods in Cal doesn't mean you can replicate them out in the real. If you even meet the bar for learning what you need in the first place. Not all people are cut out for all tasks. I remember. That conversation was around the time I was informed that Beasts won't be able to Humanize outside of Cal. Or perhaps not without significant effort."

Wanting to break up that conversation, he motioned at the bucket of water that Soni had stopped next to. "What's this then?"

"The water of measurement." Soni dramatically bent low and motioned at the bucket, losing Artorian entirely. What was the point? Was there another bucket in the bucket? Was the water not water? He looked at her for guidance, or hoped the jest was a joke.

Soni's face flattened when she didn't get a chuckle out of him. "It's a liter of water, in a bucket with no real weight. The question of how heavy Osmium is was written all over your face, so I assumed that the first time you got an explanation, it wasn't enough. Pick up the bucket."

Grandpa-torian thought this was a really odd joke if it was a joke, so he picked up the bucket. "That's certainly a bucket, and that does seem to be water. What about it?"

Soni's amusement dropped away. "How much does a liter of water weigh?"

Artorian hadn't the foggiest. "You can skip to your point."

That, Soni could work with, even if the cause was the confused expression on his face serving as the payment that the chuckle hadn't provided. "If I tell you a weight, what's that going to give you aside from some number that makes no sense? Everyone can get a liter of water with fair ease, pick it up, and roughly feel what that liter of water weighs. In numbers, one liter of water has a mass of almost exactly one kilogram. Or about two point two pounds."

One-Stone shouted from afar to amend that verdict. "When measured at its maximal density, which occurs at about four degrees Celsius, ja!"

Soni didn't blink at the interruption. This was normal. "Comparing what things weigh to how many liters of water you're holding is really handy for Moths. It also lets you throw a bucket of water at them from time to time, like this."

Taking the bucket from Artorian, she hurled it towards One-Stone, who darted out of the way before pointing and laughing at her like a small child. "*Ha-ha*! Miss!"

One-Stone took the second bucket of water straight to the face, thunking him down to the ground as he held his nose.

Artorian's head snapped back and forth between the attacker and defender, confused about only one thing. "Where did you get the second bucket?"

Soni chose not to reveal this trade secret. "Out of the first bucket."

Nodding as if that was raw truth he wasn't going to argue with, Artorian motioned at the Osmium frames. Soni gladly picked up the thread to explain where this was all going.

"Osmium is a lustrous, silvery metal. It is the densest metal known to the public, and is unaffected by water and acids, but dissolves with molten alkalis. We work with Osmium while it's in a liquid form, and each liter of Osmium weighs about fifty pounds, or twenty-two and a half kilograms, rounded down. The stuff is *heavy*, and we haven't had the chance to scale down in materials to see if anything lighter works, because that's an efficiency issue. Here we're at the stage of does it work or not? It doesn't need to be pretty."

Soni nudged a Noisy Cricket chassis with her foot. "This little monster, tiny as it is, took a fifth of a liter to mold and make. One-fifth of a liter of Osmium, when finished, weighs ten pounds. This tiny, meant for a children's grip, F-ranker toy, weighs ten pounds. That's about five water buckets, and five water buckets for something that small is a lot. Most people with F-ranker Eternia stats need two hands to pick the thing up, and it has a *nasty* kick when fired."

"Is it supposed to?" Artorian picked the Noisy Cricket chassis up like a paperweight. "I could dance this thing between my fingers like a coin. That's all from attributes?"

"No. Beam weaponry isn't supposed to have a kick, *at all*." Soni scowled out her distaste for not knowing why the Noisy Cricket kicked like a mule. "They correlate... somewhat. A real Mage is obviously not going to care what things weigh; they pick up multiple tons worth of objects with ease and don't blink. Getting a mortal to do that? That gets you a different perspective, especially with the rule of 'no such thing as Mages' in Eternia. You're always going to feel like a mortal or a C-ranker here. The numbers do what they can to facilitate, but only the Wisps and their secret projects that I can't wriggle my fronds into have the real numbers."

She shot him a look full of suspicion. "Have they told *you* the real numbers?"

Artorian smiled his most innocent smile. He hadn't a clue, but he wasn't going to tell her that when he didn't know the secret of the magic second bucket. "I don't know Abyss."

The Moth rolled her fronds instead of her eyes, but the body language hilariously matched the intent. "Inspect the Cricket already. Once we go over all the frames, you can see why a Super Strahlung has been such a problem. Then you can giggle and slap it together with matching components. Then I will be most happy to show you right to the Pylon Holds where Pag is being the snootiest problem. I can't stand the whole 'maidenless rat' shtick, and I am siiiiick of Amalgam Pylons. We got the random spawns to stop, but the giggly little nuisance is trying to make more of them."

Artorian *hmmed* derisively. "Well, we can't have that, now can we? On with the show."

Soni agreed, pulled up her own prompts, and momentarily left Artorian to his own devices as she was flagged down by another Moth. He was inspecting inert pieces of Osmium. What was the worst that could happen?

CHAPTER FORTY

"Incursus, you still with me?" The Administrator received blessed clickety-clacks.

"Excellent. Inspect." The magic word worked as intended, to the tune of mechanical background typewriting. Artorian got a slew of information as he walked down the rows and repeated the word a few times to get multiple prompts up and running. "Easier to compare them all that way."

K-chink!

———

Item: LFB Frame.
  Size: 1 - Least, Tiny.
  Material: Treated Osmium.
  Name: Noisy Cricket.
  Variant: Standard.
  Coolant: Cold Clipazine.
  Coolant Slotted: None.
  Core: None.
  Converter: None.

Lens: None.
Weight: 10 lbs.

———

Artorian saw that major portions of the information were all the same. Without components, there was a lot of dead space and overlap. "Incursus, could you exclude information that repeats? I know it's made of Osmium."

K-chink!

———

Size: 2 - Lesser, Small.
Name: Kīkōhō.
Coolant: Fimbulwinter Cartridge.
Weight: 30 lbs.

———

Size: 3 - Average, Medium.
Name: The Standard.
Coolant: Gelid Heat Sink.
Weight: 90 lbs.

———

Size: 4 - Heavy, Large.
Name: Ludere Launcher.
Coolant: Rime Rack.
Weight: 270 lbs.

———

Size: 5 - Ridiculous, Stationary.
Name: Schwerer Gustav.

Coolant: Permafrost Round.
Weight: 810 lbs.

———

Artorian nodded at the information, then snuck a glance at One-Stone who was pointing at a hunk of Osmium poking oddly out of the ground with far too much purpose. While at the same time trying really hard not to make it obvious. Ah, yes. Secret model number six. "Inspect."

———

Size: 6 - Überstrahlung.
Name: Yamato.
Coolant: Heart of a Frozen Star.
Weight: 2,430 lbs.

———

Why opt for the lesser boom? Clearly, he was going for the big one, assuming he could lift it. How many water buckets translate to two thousand five-hundred pounds? Too many? Too many. Doing it anyway! "Incursus? What's the weight of that last one in the other measurement type? Can I even carry or pick up that thing?"

K-chink!

———

Converted weight: 1,102 kilograms, or the same number of water buckets.
    Note: OSHA's lifting limit for an average human adult is 50 lbs, for what it's worth.

———

Eternia beta carry weight calculation: Per point of Strength, 5 lbs of weight can be manipulated or moved. That statistic is considered your total encumbrance value. This value is divided into the following categories: light load, medium load, heavy load, and overburdened. Not accounting for lifting, dragging, or pushing.

The light load threshold is considered active while a player operates under one-third of their encumbrance value. A light load means you are unencumbered. A player suffers no movement, stamina, or other endurance-related penalties while operating within the light load parameter.

The medium load threshold occurs between one-third and two-thirds of a player's encumbrance value. A medium load halves a player's speed, causes all actions to cost double Stamina, and halves Stamina regeneration.

The heavy load threshold occurs once a player breaches two-thirds of their total encumbrance value. A heavy load drops a player to ten percent of their maximum movement speed, prevents any movement-related techniques, causes all actions to cost five times their listed Stamina cost, and cripples Stamina regeneration down to ten percent of its current value.

The overencumbered threshold occurs anytime a player is over their maximum encumbrance value. This may result in failing to pick up an item, dropping an item instantly, being crushed to death, or taking constant percentage-per-second health damage until they are no longer overburdened. A player may force movement, but being overburdened causes all actions to cost ten times their listed Stamina cost, and cripples Stamina regeneration down to nothing.

———

K-chink!

———

Dreadshine's Strength value: 750.
   Total Encumbrance value: 3,750 lbs.
   Medium Load: 2,500 lbs.
   Light Load: 1,250 lbs.
   Minimum Überstrahlung Weight: 2,430 lbs.

Expected additional weight from components: 300–400 lbs.
Expected final weight: 2,800 lbs, rounded high.
Expected encumbrance while operating: Heavy Load.

———

Artorian held his chin, secretly trying to optimize that back down to a medium load. What was causing all that component weight? "Incursus? If I forgo a power source. No Beast Core? How much weight can I save? A converter and a lens can't be that heavy. Even if I'm looking at a fifty-pound block of quartz."

K-chink!

———

Information: Majority of added weight comes from coolant, rather than any of the other components. A power source, converter, and lens all tally in at 10 lbs per size category. Foregoing the power source is possible, but having it present eases the regulation with the converter. I would suggest including all components. Size six core components weigh approximately 60 lbs each, optional or auxiliary components currently not included weigh the same. One unit of coolant begins at a weight of 0.6 lbs, and multiplies by three for each size category you go up. Making a list.

———

K-chink!

———

List: Coolant weight per category.
    Note: The amount of usage in a unit of coolant is determined by its rarity. Unless modified, each LFB can hold one unit of coolant.
    Cold Clipazine - 0.6 lbs.
    Fimbulwinter Cartridge - 1.8 lbs.

Gelid HeatSink - 5.4 lbs.
Rime Rack - 16.2 lbs.
Permafrost Round - 48.6 lbs.
Frozen Heart - 145.8 lbs.

———

List: Coolant uses per rarity.
   Trash - 1.
   Damaged - 2.
   Common - 4.
   Uncommon - 8.
   Rare - 16.
   Special - 32.
   Unique - 64.
   Artifact - 128.

———

K-chink!

———

Information: With only core components and a single unit of coolant, additional weight tallies in at 325 lbs. Adjusted final expected weight: 2,755 lbs.
   Result: Heavy load.

———

Artorian saw no way around that particular hurdle. Medium load was off the table, meaning that when he pulled the big cannon out of his pocket, he wasn't going anywhere after he did. Then again... did he have to move with the cannon out? Couldn't he pull it, fire it, pocket it? Learning how to refill or reload the coolant currently sounded like the most difficult portion of the problem. "Incursus? Since I'm… stuck in heavy load anyway… what can we tack on to make that Über-strahlung more interesting? I know I asked you not to repeat information, but I did see the word 'variant' on that first Noisy Cricket. Does that mean these frames come in different flavors?"

K-chink!

―――――

Information: All LFB frames, components, and related pieces come in a variety of qualities and rarities. This includes different effects with different modifiers and values on all these pieces, such as differing implicit values, affixes, and suffixes. No two components, even if identical to other core components, are likely to have the same modifiers on the gamified item. One amethyst converter may increase coolant efficiency. Another amethyst converter may give no efficiency at all, but increase beam or penetration range. The values are random per component, and no wiki has been compiled as of yet for which creation processes cause what effects.

―――――

Severe grandfatherly beard-stroking followed. His big nose was tingling, and his eyes were full of wonderful mischief. "So you're telling me… that each component, by itself, can be an *Artifact*?"

K-chink!

―――――

Information: Correct.
  Would you like to see the variants?

―――――

Artorian rubbed his grubby little hands together like a raccoon preparing to feast. "Oh, yeeees."

CHAPTER FORTY-ONE

Incursus snuck Artorian a few goodies that he could delve deeper into if he felt like it, while Incursus compiled all the information on the LFB variants. The first of which was turtle-themed. Incursus was clearly not biased.

Artorian didn't mind one bit. People, Dungeons included, getting to express more of themselves was an upside. This was positive growth. More!

K-chink!

Strahlung: Devastating Turtle.
 Special Quality: Shelling.

Strahlung: Tolerance.
 Special Quality: Paradox of Tolerance.

While he liked goodies, Artorian wasn't sure what to do with such sparse entries. He tapped the bottom most thing just to push something.

———

Special Quality: Paradox of Tolerance.

The paradox of tolerance disappears if you look at tolerance, not as a moral standard, but as a social contract. If someone does not abide by the terms of the contract, then they are not covered by it. In other words, the intolerant are not following the rules of the social contract of mutual tolerance. Since they have broken the terms of the contract, they are no longer covered by the contract, and their intolerance should not be tolerated.

Effect: This Strahlung deals no damage against individuals who have not strayed from their social contract. This Strahlung deals automatic critical hits against individuals who have broken the terms of their social contract.

———

While that was interesting, Artorian wondered about the implications. Was this a Pag-specific LFB? He hadn't seen the size or the rest of the details yet, but having that in his back pocket could certainly be useful. "Let's check the other one."

———

Special Quality: Shelling.

Unique to the Devastating Turtle, the Shelling special quality overrides the effect of the equipped lens. Rather than any other form of expression, a blue shell of energy will be launched. This blue shell targets either the local leader of the opposition, or whoever is in the function of 'first place.' This shell does not miss.

———

Make that two LFB's to keep in the pocket! On the other hand, what caused these effects? Was it a finished Strahlung providing a set bonus, or was a component causing the majority of the effect? Because if it was a component? There would be pilfering!

K-chink!

————

Information: I don't have the variant list completed yet, but look who I found!

————

Flammenwerfer: Sturm.

Special Quality: Red-Black Rainbow.

Note: We have caught Erustrum sneaking into another pantry. He has been Mushu-fied and given appropriate punishment. Squeeze him for Ze Flammen.

————

"Red-Black? Is that some color scheme modification? It does fit the Dreadshine theme." Artorian brushed his beard while the space around him got polluted by clickety-clacks. Incursus was hard at work, so he tapped the entry. Rather than a pop-up prompt, a miniature Long popped into existence on the ground, complete with a sparkly little music cloud that he dramatically rose out from. As if announcing that he lived! Rather than an announcement, Erustrum took a breath so deep that it made Artorian think that the Long hadn't done that in a few years.

Wheezing and collapsing into a noodle-y pile, Erustrum hugged the ground like it was the single most blessed thing in all of existence. Artorian could commiserate. He'd had days like that. "Hello again, little dragon. I must know. What was so good in the pantry that it was worth…"

Artorian rolled his wrist in a circle at the dissipating mystic cloud. "All this?"

Between wheezes, Erustrum spoke only the truth. "Honey. Pie. *Freshhhhh.*"

Powerful sagely nodding followed, the sweets-loving grandfather in severe agreement of the miniaturized Long's choices. "A most worthy cause. Most worthy. A kingdom for one of Lunella's pies is well worth the price."

Artorian tapped the other entry on the miniature prompt to learn a little more about Erustrum. The dragon was listed as a weapon, and he'd heard One-Stone say the word Flammenwerfer before. He didn't like that it had been attached to Hans, but eh. "Let's see what we've got."

K-chink!

Item: Flammenwerfer.

    Type: Pocket Danger Noodle.

    Name: Sturm.

    Material: Erustrum, a Long-type Dragon.

    Rarity: Unique.

    Special Quality: Red-Black Rainbow.

    Ability: Ze Flammen.

    Maximum range: 150 meters.

    Cost: A good squeeze.

    Cooldown: 3 uses of 'Ze Flammen' per Day.

    Special Quality:

    Red-Black Rainbow is a light-beam attack mixed with the properties of fire and corrosion. This attack manifests as a gout of fire, shaped as an extremely narrow cone, that lasts for five seconds. This attack has its colors layered like a rainbow. The tags of this damage are Fire, Radiant, and Acid.

    Ability:

    When squeezed, Ze Flammen will activate, consuming one of the three daily uses. Ze Flammen deals 150 points of Fire damage, 150 points of

Acid damage, and 150 points of Radiant damage, per second, to each target caught in the cone. After Ze Flammen is used, it cannot be used again for 30 minutes.

———

"In the pocket you go!" Artorian stuffed Erustrum into the front pocket of his beach-going button-up, and thought there was no better place for the little guy to be. "That makes three out of three, and don't worry, buddy. Unlike the prior two? I won't peel you like a potato to get to your components."

Erustrum shot the Administrator a very nervous look. The dragon slowly descended deeper and deeper into the safety of the pocket until only his eyes and nose were poking out from the cloth edge. He wanted none of this smoke. He would provide Ze Flammen.

K-chink!

———

Information: Variants are ready.

———

Artorian perked up at the messenger, wanting that information so he could pick a frame and keep going. "Give them to me. Also, could you take both Tolerance and the Devastating Turtle apart? I want to know if a component is providing the effect, or the whole. If it's a component, I want to steal the effect out and transplant the effect onto an uber-sized component instead. I plan on violently cheating with Artifacting to fly through this problem and stick a cannon in Pag's face."

K-chink!

———

Information: Complying with great complaints.
    Taking both LFB apart now.
    Populating variant prompt.
    Note:
    Plus damage? More Dakka. Good.
    Plus reload speed? Shove new coolant in. Bad.
    Plus fire rate? Faster Dakka. Good.
    Plus deviation? Beam don't go where you point. Bad.
    Plus coolant capacity? More chill. Good.
    Plus coolant use? More chill used. Bad.
    Plus range? Farther Dakka. Good.
    Plus heat generation? Shots make the fingers burn faster. Bad.
    Plus fusion ignition chance? Pull trigger, get beam. Good.
    Plus minimum heat? Make more heat per beam. Bad.
    Plus beam stability? Beam stays a beam. Good.
    Plus jamming? Beam stops beaming, starts booming. Bad.
    Plus ejection speed? Removal of empty coolant container. Good.
    Plus augmentation slots? More strange Dakka. Good.

———

"There, there." Artorian rubbed empty space, pretending the turtle's tiny head was present. He eased both his hands behind his back, and patiently watched the large screens open, and fill up as the information rolled in line by line. He wondered why they looked out of place, but then it hit him that the variants were being presented alphabetically.

K-chink!

———

List: Strahlung frame variants.
    Versions listed: 20 out of 40.
    20 versions unfinished, not ready for production.
    Listing only selectable variants.

———

Alpha:
　　+15% Damage.
　　+50% Reload speed.
　　+15% Fire Rate.

———

Converted:
　　Use Wisdom instead of Dexterity in the Accuracy Formula.

———

Critical:
　　+15% Critical chance.
　　+5° Deviation.

———

Cursed:
　　-50% Damage.
　　+50% Reload speed.
　　-50% Fire Rate.
　　+50% Coolant use.

———

Elite:
　　+15% Damage.
　　-15% Fire Rate.
　　-15° Deviation.

———

Heavy:

DENNIS VANDERKERKEN & DAKOTA KROUT

Double chassis weight.
+50% Damage.

———

Hunter:
  +80% Damage.
  -80% Fire Rate.

———

Hyper Burst:
  -80% Damage.
  +80% Fire Rate.

———

Lightweight:
  Halve chassis weight.
  -50% Damage.

———

Military:
  -50% Reload speed.
  +25% Fire Rate.

———

Modular:
  Plus 1 Coolant Capacity.
  Plus 1 Augmentation slot.
  +5% Jamming.

———

New:

    +15% Range.
    +15% Minimum Heat.
    -15% Jamming.

———

Overclocked:

    +25% Minimum Heat.
    +25% Heat Generation.
    +100% Fusion Ignition Chance.
    +100% Range.

———

Prototype:

    -10% Fusion Ignition Chance.
    +10% Jamming.
    -10% Beam Stability.
    +50% Damage.

———

Reactive:

    +100% Ejection Speed.
    -100% Reload Speed.

———

Relic:

    -10% Fusion Ignition Chance.
    -50% Beam Stability.
    +50% Damage.
    +5° Deviation.

———

Scavenged:
> *Minus 1 Augmentation slot.*
> *+50% Jamming.*
> *+25% Fire Rate.*
> *-20% Range.*

———

Stable:
> *-100% Jamming.*
> *+15% Beam Stability.*

———

Standard:
> *+5% Range.*
> *+5% Ejection Speed.*
> *-5% Reload Speed.*
> *+5% Damage*

———

Ultra:
> *+50° Deviation.*
> *+50% Fire Rate.*
> *+50% Damage.*
> *+50% Coolant Use.*

———

Artorian nodded, holding his beard. He read back and forth between the notes and the effects. "I'm never going to worry about damage, or the rate at which damage is delivered. I'm choosing to stay at heavy load, and keep the LFB in my pocket until I need it. That will make me a sitting duck when firing, but I don't expect to need to do that a whole lot."

He pulled up his own prompt, and started making a handy list to cross out what wasn't going to work for him.

———

Alpha - No.
    Converted - Pointless.
    Critical - Meh, deviation bad.
    Cursed - Why? Abyss, no.

———

The old man brushed a hand over his bald head. "I think that in addition to damage and rate of fire, I can rule out anything that causes beams to go at something I didn't target, or messes with the beam in general. Back to the list."

———

Elite - Maybe? Minus deviation means accuracy bonus.
    Heavy - Ha! Funny. No.
    Hunter - No.
    Hyper Burst - No.
    Lightweight - No.
    Military - No.
    Modular - Maybe! Depends on the Augmentation side of things. More coolant is never going to be bad. Shame about the jamming.
    New - No.
    Overclocked - Why hello there. Always get a successful beam and double the range? That's enticing. Solid maybe, even with it getting hot.
    Prototype - No.
    Reactive - Instant reloads? There's a time and place for that. Solid maybe.
    Relic - Abyss no.
    Scavenged - No.

Stable - Ooooh, never jamming, with some stability? Enticing. A solid maybe.

Standard - No.

Ultra - Meh, no.

———

That rounded Artorian's list down to elite, modular, overclocked, reactive, and stable. A more sensible list of choices. He stood there and stared at the list, his beard gaining a hefty helping of fresh grooming as he muddled and grumbled over the choice. "In the end, it's between the never jam of stable, and the always beam of overclock. If it jams, I'm assuming I can't fix it and it goes boom. Though in that case? I'll just gift the ticking hot potato to someone. Therefore, overclock it is!"

K-chink!

———

Choice confirmed!

Now printing: Overclock variant Überstrahlung.

Please continue with components.

CHAPTER FORTY-TWO

Artorian liked that this was all going nice and quick! "Components are a go! If there's a size six coolant available, load up the first one you can find, unless those come in variants as well. As I see it, size six *anything* is going to be scarce, or a one-off. Go ahead and slot whatever there is only one of and don't feel the need to ask."

Incursus was glad to get to skip a few steps! He advanced straight to Go, collected two hundred Essence, and provided the Administrator with an improved Strahlung prompt.

K-chink!

———

Item: LFB.
    Size: 6 - Überstrahlung.
    Material: Treated Osmium.
    Name: Yamato.
    Variant: Overlocked.
    Coolant: Heart of a Frozen Star.
    Coolant Slotted: Yes.

Coolant Space: 1.
Coolant Rarity: Trash.
Core: None, Available: 4.
Converter: None, Available: 3.
Lens: None, Available: 2.
Chassis Weight: 2,430 lbs.
Coolant Weight: 145.8 lbs.
Expected Core Weight: 60 lbs.
Expected Converter Weight: 60 lbs.
Expected Lens Weight: 60 lbs.
Expected Total Weight: 2,755.8 lbs.

———

Grandpa made an unhappy face. "*Trash* rarity? I get one shot? *One?* Eww… Abyss no. Engage the cheatery!"

Flipping the Admin lever, Artorian watched the rainbow of Wisps pop in. The Administrator was already pointing at the relevant prompt while starting directly at the Yellow Artifacting Wisp. His will was clear and simple. "Attack."

Saluting in unison, all the Wisps sped off to go solve the problem. Whatever poor soul was currently handling that coolant was going to need an apology basket. Wait… he hadn't specified the coolant. He'd just pointed. *Oh no.* "Make that… several apology baskets."

Oh well! The thing was gonna be an Artifact one way or another! "Incursus, did you find if it was the parts or the whole that gave the special goodies?"

K-chink!

———

Information: The parts.
The lens of the Devastating Turtle provided the blue shell expression. The converter of Tolerance provided the Paradox effect. These can be applied to one of the available size six components, replacing existing effects.

We're cheating them in with brute force, so no fancy finessed stacking of effects. Whatever the components had will be gone.

———

Cores available:
Me. Pick me.
Mu. Don't, just pick me.
*Dregs - **Eruption Law**, Volcano Dungeon. Too hot-headed, still me.*
ElCazorro, a Desert Beast that has affinity with you. Too catty, pick the turtle.

———

Converters available:
Amethyst - Air typed.
Sapphire - Water typed.
Ruby - Fire typed.

———

Lenses available:
The lenses are identical, so no real choice? There happen to be two.

———

Artorian thought those all to be easy choices. "Incursus, if you're offering, I'm not going to turn you down. It just means you need a safe place I can put you if a jam happens, or that's going to get ugly. I believe you were an Earth Core? You pick the converter, buddy. Slap Tolerance in, use whatever lens you feel like, and get your Devastating Turtle back on track. I know the Strahlung is going to be big, so if you want to make some adjustments to make the thing look like a castle, or a cathedral, or both? Have at it! Express yourself."

The lack of *K-chink* was worrisome. Had that been too much? *K-chink*!

Never mind! There it was!

Item: Überstrahlung.
  Material: Treated Osmium.
  Name: Fortress Battleship Yamato.
  Rarity: Artifact.
  Variant: Overlocked:
  +25% Minimum Heat.
  +25% Heat Generation.
  +100% Fusion Ignition Chance.
  +100% Range.
  Coolant: Heart of a Frozen Star.
  Coolant Slotted: Yes.
  Coolant Space: 1.
  Coolant Uses: 85. (128 original, before Overclock effects.)
  Coolant Rarity: Artifact.
  Core: Incursus.
  Core Affinity: Earth, Water.
  Core Quality: Artifact.
  Converter: Sapphire of Tolerance.
  Converter Special Quality: Tolerance.
  Converter Quality: Artifact.
  Lens: Devastating Turtle.
  Lens Special Quality: Blue Shell.
  Lens Quality: Artifact.
  Total Weight: 2,800 lbs.

The Administrator squinted at the entry. His nose was doing that tingly thing. Incursus had clearly known and pre-planned this cheatery. Was it to quickly get classed as an item of Artifact quality? Clever! That reminded him of the ancient history that was Dale wiggling himself in as a disciple. He liked cleverness, and skipped to the next stage. "Outstanding! No reason to dally. Throw the battleship into my inventory."

His rainbow of Wisps returned, saluted, and winked out after a job well done. Returning a crisp salute before they left, Artorian studied the prompt. It hit him that the damage wasn't listed anywhere. "Say, Incursus. There's no damage formulas here?"

K-chink!

———

Commentary: Trust the process.

———

Artorian wondered if he missed when prompts had changed to include terms like information and commentary, but shrugged it off. System changes were rampant, and keeping track of them in the beta version was an act of folly. "Soni! I'm ready! Send me down."

"Down to select your chassis?" The Moth hovered over, wings folding back up after she landed with a prompt tucked under an arm like a clipboard. "You took a bit long, but better late than never to start looking at components."

Artorian pressed his fingers together in the shape of a pyramid. "*Mmmn, noooo…* I'm done-done. LFB complete and under construction with all the bits and bobs, kind-of-done. It's going right into my inventory on completion and I need to get to the rat problem."

Soni turned her head, her fronds tense. She dug visualized daggers into One-Stone, who was dancing in place around some new prompt with an Artifact-quality border. They had no

Strahlung of Artifact quality laying around. How could one have…?

She gasped hard, rounding on Sunny. "You cheated!"

"I expedited!" The old man turned his big nose the other way, sticking out his lower lip with a *humph*. "Now, are we going or not?"

Soni took the prompt from under her arm, and considered it like a stale cookie. She lifted her gaze to One-Stone, and chucked the screen at the back of his head. With a thunk, a yowl, and a big bruise forming after the screen had struck true, Soni turned and walked off. Away from the nutty professor. "He can fix his materials himself! Soni is still the Portalmancer Supreme; onto the rat problem!"

With a flick of the wrist, the Moth popped open a Scorpion Portal and stepped right through. Seeing no reason not to trust the process, as Incursus had just said, Artorian followed Soni through the breach. Thus leaving the serene plains of the Alfheim sun, and entering the dreary warzone of the crystal trenches in Pylon hold four-three-four-seven-seven.

The place was little more than a vast cavern with no end on the horizon, interconnected crystalline structures of various shapes and sizes, and a fake sky. Looking down from his current elevated position, the deep, angular cuts and busy sight told Artorian plenty. Lines of light constantly poured forth from one side of the trench, while an endless horde of rats spilled out from the other side of the Pylon fields. The rats ran face-first into those beams endlessly, and endlessly turned to particulate as the Strahlung's lasers tore into them.

A threat that stopped none of them.

From his current vantage point, Artorian thought one side was using flashlights to melon-scoop water out of a sinking boat. "How long has our side been holding like that?"

Soni was already meandering down the crystalline hill, making her way around an entrenched, building-sized Pylon that hummed and buzzed with power while lights flicked through the massive crystal. Those motes of light were processed before being sent off elsewhere, but the process was blindingly fast. "Too long. The Gnomes are field testing, and we supply them with as much coolant from Jotunheim as we can make. But this is the fourth time we've been pushed back to a deeper trench."

Artorian spotted a mixture of races in the defensive lines. Gnomes and Bashers held the line. Other Bashers, based on the ears, couriered materials back and forth. Then some Goblins. Strange Goblins. Goblins that hadn't yet learned counter-charges were not the way to go, and likely never would be?

Ah, no. They were holding scavenged-variant Strahlung, and jamming them on purpose. Goblin Grenades. G.G. for short? A few familiar-looking obelisks and totems respawned those Goblins, who rushed in for another go. "That's a tactic, I guess. That should be a book."

He'd reserve further judgment until he could talk to a field commander or something. Luckily, or unluckily, the commander had noticed their arrival. Soni's portals were good and efficient, but couldn't be hidden well and made lots of light.

The field commander turned out to be an old acquaintance!

Raile rolled up like an old memory, here to knock some doors down. Colonel Raile unfurled from his Basher form, shaping himself through Humanization into a Granite Dwarf with a grudge against all warhammers. The thick stone armor stood out, though it still took second place compared to a more prominent detail. First place went to the thick lump of wood that stuck out the side of his mouth, the end stoked with internal fire.

The armor plating covered his entire being both as a Dwarf, and a Basher. From floppy ears to toe-claws. The only reason anyone could tell where Raile's face was at a glance was thanks to the smoking stick of wood. This one was mango-flavored!

Raile insisted on calling it his 'cigar,' to the continued complaints of every single Glitterflit in his ranks. His personal guard composed of the Hops-Ecutioners slunk up behind him.

They only smirked in response, expecting a call for 'ramming speed' any second now.

Artorian didn't think he'd ever heard Raile talk before, because the voice came as a complete surprise. Dwarven? Yes! Different? *Oh yes.* What was he going to catalog this dialect as? Top Hat? Overly polite but bombastic? Churchill? "Governor Baha-Mutt! Smashing good to see you, old boy! Bring 'er here and give us a hug!"

The Administrator had only one thought, which fled through his words. "I'm going to get crushed, aren't I?"

The Hops-Ecutioners all emphatically nodded as Raile stepped in and bear-hugged Artorian like two mountains colliding together. The bone-breaking noises that accompanied the act were both free upon delivery, and entirely mandatory.

Huerk.

CHAPTER FORTY-THREE

Artorian felt like a wrenched towel, freshly squeezed dry.

Standing there like a twisted fern that had been smacked around by crushing winds, a Hops-Ecutioner bounced up. The large, wind-themed horned rabbit reared up, spread its arms, and made the Administrator squint and squirm by attempting a callous repetition. A repetition without any of Raile's politeness. "Ello gov'na! Smashin' g't see ya, ol' boy! Bring 'er 'ere an' give us a hug!"

Without the rest of him moving, Artorian replied by snapping his hand around the Basher's rude mouth. Cringing from the poor copy, he breathily mouthed the word 'no' while Raile reared back and laughed. The antics of his third never ceased to amuse. His second had more stones to him, but that was Earth Bashers for you. The muffled Wind Basher tried to complain, but couldn't pry the fingers free from his mouth and face.

Feeling worse than he looked after Raile's welcoming bear-sized Basher hug, Artorian's Aura gave him a good scrub. He wasn't dirty, but the sensation of the Cleanse made him feel better. Like the pleasure of rehydrating after being out of breath. A cup of crisp cold morning dew after a hot Socorro Desert day.

That his racial entry was responsible for keeping him well-hydrated at all times, and not his Aura, was a detail gently nudged under the carpet. The sensation was what mattered. The sensation! He could feel his equilibrium returning to normal, non-squeezed proportions as he let the Hops-Ecutioner go.

The fluffy windbag of course couldn't reciprocate, or let it go. He wasn't even ice-themed. Rubbing at his jaw, the oppressor surprised Artorian. Unlike Raile, this bun-bun didn't turn into a Dwarf. The impolite one turned into a Gnome!

One clearly not part of the Deverash faction, for the clothing was in poor taste. "Aw, c'mon bruv. We're jus' 'ryin 'o 'ave a good 'ime."

Unable to translate what the Basher, now Gnome, had said, Artorian looked to Colonel Raile as the stocky commander inspected him. Or tried to. Learning much by finding that he could learn nothing, Raile swapped out his smokestick for something a bit more refined.

Armed with a brand-new churchwarden pipe, the polite Colonel stopped the problem before it could escalate. The color of the smoke changed to a delicate brown as Raile spoke, and smelled of chestnut. "Pish-posh, Jeffrey! You trying to have a good time tends to come with being hurled from the local establishment, before I find you once more at the constable's. Much more and they'll begin allowing you to decorate that cell with the amount of time you spend there."

The Hops-Ecutioner designated as Jeffrey adopted a brash arms-crossed stance that was clearly not in line with any kind of reproachfulness. The Gnome kept his head up so high that he leaned back just to look down his nose at Raile. "I can'' 'elp 'ha' 'he guard is cu'e!"

Artorian thought he might have caught that one. The side of his own nose did the meddlesome-grandpa tingle. "You cause trouble because you can't help that the guard is *cute*?"

Suddenly bashful, the Basher blushed and lost control of his shape. One dull poof, and Jeffrey pulled his fluffy ears down over his face before looking away. *"Bruvvv."*

"What a lovely display of color!" Raile laughed, slapping Artorian far too hard on the back as the pale grandfather visually convalesced in front of them. Was Raile talking about him? Or the Hop? A mystery for the ages.

The stumble knocked Grandpa out of the twisted fern position, but worsened the expression on his face as Raile firmly clasped him by the shoulder to get a march on. "Jolly good! Don't mind the hopsies. I'm more partial to flopsies myself. I've been trying to lean into the speaking method of the hopsies, but the success has yet to be smashing. They tell me it's difficult? Pish-posh, I say! A little locution won't cost old Raile a horn and tail!"

Artorian could swear he heard one of the hops say the word 'again,' but that sound was cut when Raile rolled his other arm around Soni's neck as she attempted an escape. Soni, too, released a **huerk**. "Provisioner! Good show, my dear. A mostly lovely portal to announce oneself, I must say. Though, I do hope you've come with more coolant?"

Raile's raised eyebrow was hidden by plates of granite armor, but both Soni and Artorian could feel the expression being made with how Raile leaned toward the Moth.

Half begrudging, Soni pulled several storage rings out of her pocket and shoved them into Raile's greedy, waiting hand that was already opening and closing in 'gimme' motions. "That would be very inefficient and I don't want another One-Stone rant. Take them."

Raile squirreled the stored coolant away to his hops, which darted away and fled. Both as an excuse to skip the crushing-hugs line, and to get the frontline fresh ammo. A frontline that had not stopped firing the entire time Artorian had been here. Between the cursing from the trenches, and the squealing of attackers? Only the rats made noise. Lots of rat screeching drowned out the alternatives. Artorian did note that if the

Strahlung made sound, he couldn't pick up any. The heat, on the other hand, was very obvious. Some of those LFBs ran so hot that they looked to be ready to catch flame. The barrel of one was even cooking an egg!

"Smashing!" Soni buckled from the slap to her back after being released. Artorian would have helped, but Raile was still dragging him off with the power of Dwarven purpose. When he looked over his shoulder, Soni had two hands on her knees, one in the air to surrender, and the last waving him off to 'go ahead without her.'

Go on without her, his foot! He was being ditched. "I will remember this!"

Soni acted out a case of the vapors, pressing the back of one hand against her forehead while overly wobbly. "Alas, I am shook, I leave it to you to complete the work in thy nook. Good-byeee, important man! I believe in youuuu!"

Soni, the smug little monster Moth, fell into a brand-new portal with two hands behind her head like she was about to drop right into the pillows of a cozy bed. Artorian could hear the treacherous and soft flop before the portal closed. That was the telltale noise of a duck-feather duvet and a twenty-by-sixty-inch Basher-fluff-stuffed body pillow. With satin trim and spider silk lining.

He wanted fifty. Artorian shook his old fist in the closed portal's direction. "I'll send bunnies after you! Bashers too! That horn will mess you up!"

"What kind, old chap?" Raile's interest turned to the new direction of conversation as they kept meandering towards the front lines. They dipped down into very deep trenches that muffled the sound of rat death happening overhead. "Oppressors? Impalers?"

"Pardon?" Artorian wasn't following. "I know Bashers were one of the first, if not the first mobs Cal ever made, but these names are new to me."

"Troop composition!" Raile stopped in place to point at a half-passed-out group of miners responsible for getting more trenches in play. Three Dwarves that were dead tired, and one Gnome of boundless, bright energy. "Rock, Stone, Carl, and Bosco by honorary measure over there? They are all Earth Affinity Bashers, also called Smashers. They operate in heavy armor plating like yours truly, or handle the yardwork. Brown and blonde fur patterns."

A few steps later, Raile motioned with his pipe at a logistics train, of which Artorian recognized Jeffrey, and only Jeffrey. "I say. Although they're called Oppressors? Air Affinity bashers are quick on their feet, and better for a good guerrilla. Don't ask me why they're all some variation of green; I don't know. All Oppressors are naturally able to create sharp gusts of wind that bypass or sneak under armor. Not as useful against rats that don't use any. Can't use a needle for a job that takes a hammer."

Interested, Artorian followed in tow as the Colonel explained the groups. A quick pause at the medical tents revealed familiar sights. He knew a Sister of the Paw when he saw one, but Raile assumed that Artorian knew nothing and went over them all. "Glitterflits for Celestial, Impalers for Infernal."

Raile pointed out Nigel and Diegen. "The Impalers, the ones with the long and sharp horns? They are excellent at getting things that aren't supposed to be inside of you to be outside of you once more. Impalers are almost always albino white recently. If you're taking them into the field? Mud them up with camo."

Artorian was following. "Golden Glitterflits then make those new holes go away."

Raile leaned in to speak slowly, and with warning. "A note of worth? Obey your medic. A few of them aren't above paying close attention with a far too tight-lipped attitude while an Impaler's working on your hide."

When Raile gave them a wave, a crisp salute answered the Colonel. He took the motion in stride and carried on. There was tea and biscuits to get to. "It used to be the case that Water and Fire Bashers simply didn't exist. Time, and a healthy spot of natural evolution saw fit to plug the gaps that Great Maker Cal couldn't fill with effort."

Right at the front line, Raile motioned at rows upon rows of heavily armed Fire Affinity Bashers, who had no issues at all handling the hunks of light-blasting Osmium regardless of how hot they got. "There's two names for Fire Bashers, as evolution provided us with two separate strains. One: Flhares, the orange ones with pilot-light fire on their forehead in a rough horn shape. They liked the mix of Flare and Hare, so that's what they got. Make no mistake, that horn is all fire, it's just bright rather than hot. Two: Hot Hops, the red ones with fire on their feet. Their fire is hot rather than bright. They're responsible for turning the ground into proper paving, and smacking any rat that gets lucky and too close to the lines."

Artorian followed that logic. "A face full of fire is a blinding deterrent."

Another clap on the back from Raile sent Artorian into a stumble, but he caught himself as the polite Dwarf laughed. "Splendid show! I love a Governor that understands!"

Pointlessly brushing himself off, Artorian let the Colonel be himself without reproach. Some people were an odd mixture of brusk and gentle. He wanted to know about the water variant. "Tell me about the last one, and then explain this Governor business before I hop over this trench wall and turn myself into a brand-new rat problem."

Raile pointed out one of the soggy light blue buggers. "Bunsoons! The term used to be Haredration for a while, but they couldn't live with being a walking pun. Now the Oppressors handle all the coolant, the others lost their 'chill.'"

The Colonel took an amused puff of his pipe as Artorian added Bunsoons to his mental list of favorites. Anyone that fought the good fight against puns was a friend to remember. Raile motioned at one with his pipe. "Funny little Bashers, those Bunsoons. They're physically amorphous and can squeeze between impossible cracks, then pop out the other end whole and unscathed. Bunsoons run rations, water, and supplies for other Bashers. If you want supplies for equipment and logistics? You want the Bunsoons. They're the only Bashers without horns, and they think they're so terribly clever when they play innocent. If they didn't have purpose, they'd all be thieves. Thieves, I say! If you thought Jeffrey could give the constables a headache? Ha! One Bunsoon is a headache monsoon."

The Administrator mentally underlined their name in his tally of favorites. Ready to rumble and jump the shark, Artorian got out of the trench intersection and warmed up with his ancient stretching routine. "Thank you, Raile. Could you tell me about how you know the Baha-Mutt mention? I'll get going after. That was during... the Henry and Marie thing?"

"Quite so, old chap!" The armored Earth Basher Colonel jabbed him with the blunt bit of his fancy churchwarden pipe. The chestnut smell got much stronger as it closed the distance to Artorian's nose, but he bit the sensation away. "Bellini and Brasilia, the Heavenlies of **Rhythm** and **Celebration**, are smashingly popular in Dwarven culture. Especially the beach-loving splinter group."

The pipe made a swirly motion to point out Artorian's current pink-to-orange gradient, festive and sand-appropriate attire. Sunglasses included. "You're one of the lads in charge, so Governor it is. Dwarven social lines are my favorite, so regard-less of how else I might know you, such as from the war against Olympus? Baha-Mutt is my moniker of choice."

"I see." Finishing up his warmups, Artorian popped his wrists and shoulders, then planted himself. He watched the Flhares get restocked by the Oppressors, who came with deliv-eries of coolant-stuffed spatial rings. Could an LFB be reloaded while in inventory? That was something to try, if he even had a second frozen heart.

Raile sharply pointed his pipe up at the trench. "Tally-ho, then! Give old Paggums some Abyss when you see that maid of a lad. A solid thrashing, if you will. With Bugmageddon sorted and behind us? Once we have the rats situated, we win this bloody war and can all go on vacation! This and that Midgard storm are the last big hurdle to close out the beta, so I hear, and Old Raile still has some good floppy ears!"

Artorian laughed, then took a spare Noisy Cricket-sized LFB that Raile offered him. "An unnecessary touch, perhaps. Still, it's not safe to go alone. Take this for my peace of mind rather than your prowess in murder. I know of your stories, Governor. You breach as the spear, we will hold the line. We did it in 'Cadia. We will do it here. This time? The planet doesn't need to break before the guard does, because the guard sure won't."

Taking a deep drag from his pipe that was on its last embers, Raile tapped the chestnut shavings out and stowed it. "Just remember: no abilities in the Pylon Hold unless you want it all to go away. Your scrubby Aura is fine, but dear celestial feces, don't use anything that causes a point of damage that isn't from coming from a light source. The Pylons treat LFB interactions just like Essence shielding, and the old rules apply. No beam can harm a Pylon, and at most you'll shut it off for a while. So you're either going in unarmed, with an LFB, or not at all. Trust no other equipment. Not here, or we're all mad from mutually assured destruction."

The Colonel snapped to attention, providing Artorian a crisp, professional salute. "When not even Pag does it? Geneva knows where to draw the line. Good luck, Governor, and Godspeed."

CHAPTER FORTY-FOUR

"Enjoy planning your upcoming vacation, Colonel. I suggest you hurry." Artorian copied Raile's crisp salute, then rolled his shoulders and bounced on his toes as he verbalized his current to-do list. "End Pag. End the source of infinite rats. What a day to be an Administrator."

The Colonel grinned beneath his faceplate when he got a front row seat to something that had been detailed in many reports laden in dangerous ribbons.

Artorian, in action.

There were many opinions about Artorian and his particular doings. Some disapproved of his methods. Others argued about the order of operations, rather than the means used. Others still argued that the outcomes wouldn't match the input, playing forecaster of current and future events. Many were mad that he didn't optimize his game skills and abilities, and even threw some of them out like pocket lint. Unfortunately for those people, if they wanted to see more of a particular tool used? They were going to have to do it themselves, or find another player to do it for them.

Artorian only ever moved at one speed.

His own.

Wisps had foamed at the mouth and Gnomes had thrown chairs when Artorian looked at their creations as if a polished apple, before placing their prized goodie on a pedestal that he walked away from. Those personal gripes had been responsible for the additional difficulties he'd faced on the way. With the fall of the first Task Manager, on the other paw, the internal reviews and audits had proceeded apace and in volume. An act spurred forward by the kneecapping of Gaston.

Being 'cubed' had become the fate of many a troublesome Wisp that had pulled fey wiles too big for their britches. Being relegated to disaster cleanup was a similar fate for the slighted Gnomes. They wanted to make the disaster! To break the mold and the plaster! Instead, they had lost their prized tasks to Goblins. *Goblins*, of all people.

Yet there was golden news.

Shalom of **Discord** had finished setting up his glorious community stadium. Rooms were opening where groups of cultivators, Beasts, and Heavenlies could band together to both cheer and jeer for their favorite players. That the existence of some players had created the need for a stadium due to the number of seats required had been a happy accident. That Zelia hadn't quite told her Dreamer the whole truth about the number of people observing his vanguard adventures and front-line flag-planting speeches was another one of those nuggets that got swept under the rug.

What Shalom opened the door to was for new adventures and adventurers to take hold of a narrative and break into the spotlight. With viewers! Commentators! Narrators! In the event they were lucky? Readers! Yuki had begun a program for fresh souls to write on and about the adventures of their favorite performers. She had declared that she would read these tales once these stories existed. Of the few she preferred the most? She would reach out to the creators, and see about an inclusion into the greater whole. They needed only to have the material ready for her to peruse, and the rest was up to the eyes of the many.

There had been much fuss about where people could begin these tales, but that answer boiled down to anywhere they liked. Many of the older cultivators craved content from the days of yore. Many younger souls lived only for the Eternia game. Yet almost all the Heavenlies burned for material on what would happen when the gate opened, and the Exodus began. That glorious new pathway into whatever had become of the Old World.

Raile shared none of these views. His favorite story would always be that of Cal, and the Divine Dungeon. That did not stop him from reaching into his pocket and taking hold of a sun-sigil patch. Hand-sewn out of his own sturdy fur. There was a rarity in finding a person who both enjoyed the paperwork in the safety of the back, and now climbed up the inner rampart to stand with flag in hand at the front.

The solar sigil flag on his back bursting into being like an unfolding pair of wings was acceptable too.

"Voltekka, Trans Am." The beach-attired grandfather stepped right past the volleys of light fire to tread onto the battlefield laden and littered with Pylons in a variety of sizes. The LFBs that continued to fire behind him missed him entirely as their colored beams curved around him. Courtesy of Effortless Light Shaping, they still carved through their intended targets.

Pushing to his objective, Artorian slid into the guise of Dreadshine as the seamless suit of armor morphed over him. As an adult-sized being, his form wasn't superficially altered. The bulk and muscle beneath Voltekka's seamless folds looked sturdier and of greater volume to match the original shape instead. Swole-torian was no spring chicken, but neither was he of small stature as he advanced directly toward the endless horde.

Artorian had liked several of Raile's sayings, but had to make an alteration as his voice shifted from grandfatherly to metallic. "I like going fast. Perhaps not godspeed, but the speed of fear will do just as nicely."

Adopting the wide-armed stance as he walked into the dissolving cloud of particulated, dead rats that the trench LFBs tore into, Artorian began the show. The majority of rats had reddish fur, so using Villain thematics was out. Otherwise, he wouldn't stand out. Both Ad Astra and Trans Am were colored a very heroic white and blue. While the bright white would certainly do, it lacked the impact he currently wanted to drive home. "Incursus, I should have a new slot for effect cosmetics by now?"

K-chink!

Information: Effect Cosmetics has improved from the Beginner rank to the Student rank. Two new color scheme slots are available, with a combination of up to four colors.

Artorian thought of the yellow tulips and pink peonies that Zephyr had been growing. He knew he wanted white of some kind, which left an open fourth color. Grabbing the first rat that jumped at him by the throat, he hurled it back into the charging crowd. With a thunderclap of force that he dampened through Effortless Shaping, the nameless creature was thrown with enough force that the ball of weight turned into shrapnel as the mob traveled. Tearing itself to pieces, the dead mob cleared a path.

A path that Dreadshine kept clearing, by repeating that measure with other nearby rats as he checked in on his brooch. "Is anyone watching? I'm trying to choose a fourth color to begin the big show. I have yellow from tulips, pink from peonies, white because I'd like it, and am open on the fourth."

His brooch crackled, the already bickering voices of Zephyr

and Lucia clamoring so they could give him an answer on a question that they had apparently been debating for hours. Reminder to self: flowers were important to the fair ladyfolk. Acquire Ember some flowers. Perhaps some that spat fire and bit her enemies.

He heard Zephyr confirm that yellow tulips and pink peonies should be its own schematic mixture, then lost ground to Lucia, who spoke directly through her brooch. "Kit? Alstroemeria is a purple and white lily. The violet flower symbolizes devotion and friendship. Its leaves twist out from the stem as it grows—much like the twists, turns, and growth of friendships. The colors would be great on your armor if you apply the violets to anything that gives light, and the whites to anything static. The petals also have a very fetching stripe pattern that would look *so good* on Voltekka."

Zephyr cut in with a detail that was important to her. "That lily also has no scent, and is ideal for anyone with allergies."

Artorian was amused by the whole shebang. "Incursus? Hold the fourth slot, set the slot of the Apprentice rank to Alstroemeria. Call it something shorter and fitting. Violet glow and particle effects, static white. Embellish as you please. Let's make the ladies happy while we take out the trash and weed the garden. The Janitor must attend to pest control."

That he was buried well over his head in rats of unusual size was a cosmetic touch that would help his upcoming debut. That their bites did around six- to seven-hundred damage a gnaw, and their claws about five-hundred each, was very funny to Voltekka, who ignored up to eight-hundred damage per attack. The rats were all using slashing-typed damage, so the Iridium didn't even need to do any heavy lifting. There was the occasional addition of fire damage, but the Silverwood in his armor joined Voltekka in finding that very funny.

Thanks to the maneuver 'Is that all you've got?' The stacks of Menace that Artorian was racking up easily breached the three-digit mark, which were now skyrocketing towards a fourth. With that buff active, he swapped over from hurling rats to flicking them out of the way and putting giant holes in the pile. When Glorious Overkill combined with Flick, he boosted the effect and buffed the physics applied by a full category, thus turning each rat into another splatter-fueled projectile.

That the rats were too stupid to be afraid? That was going to cost Pag.

K-chink!

———

Skill: Effect Cosmetics.

Rank: Student.

This skill allows a user to take the system-set cosmetics of a tool and alter the assigned expression. You may alter the color of an expressed effect freely; such as to white and blue, or black and red, depending on the visual theme or style that the user is attempting to go for. This skill cannot make a tool transparent. Invisible effects are considered too potent and have been specifically added to their relevant classes. You are limited to opaque and translucent alterations.

Each rank of this skill adds an additional color scheme.

Novice color scheme: Trans Am. Celestine blue glow, snow white particles.

Beginner color scheme: Villain. Onyx black, carmine red.

Apprentice color scheme: Windu. The alstroemeria lily's purple and white.

Note: Violet particles and glow, static whites, flower-patterned designs.

Student color scheme: Unassigned.

———

With the mechanics done, his brooch chimed as Ember opened the communication lane on her end, changing their call from a peer to peer into that of a small forum. "I'm up on Jotunheim right now, honey. I heard something about color? Anything I need to stop and see? World in danger?"

With a violent swat of his arm, Dreadshine knocked a few

dozen rats free from his visor. The cleared space allowed him to look up and find the Jotunheim realm. A thought struck, and a smile followed. "With the sun at my back, I look at you, and I see my whole world."

The brooch crackled with static, Ember clearly bright red in the face as she sputtered out her rebuttal before slamming her connection closed. "Shu… shut up, you!"

The '*D'awwww*' from Zephyr and Lucia kept the sparkling grin on his face as he snickered his way through becoming a rat pile again, but he had what he needed. A secretly happy lady with a big flush on her cheeks. To the detriment of whatever Titan she was currently giving dentistry to and tearing the teeth out from. Plus, a color scheme for when he threw open the curtains and stepped on stage. Speaking of!

"Polly?" Just for show, he summoned **Pride** into his main hand when the Parrot gave him a positive vibe, signaling that the Beast-made-blade was good to go. In response, Dreadshine began to channel the energy of Determination. Hidden beneath the rat pile, a bit of tweaking altered the provided light into that of moonshine. While not yet presented to the world, a Rainbow Claymore was brightly brought to bear.

He wasn't going to use Polly in this fight due to the inherent dangers of his location, but for presentation? Blow the trumpets, beat the drums, and call for war with horns. Dreadshine had come to weed, and he wanted all the thorns.

His words were made of metal. "Effect Cosmetics: Windu."

CHAPTER FORTY-FIVE

With his colors shifted to become a lily-flame bonfire, Dreadshine knocked the rat horde off his being by raising Ex-Calibur, and shifting his Aura to that of Pressure. Having mastered that tool, he changed the direction of the push to be up rather than down, and removed the entire damage component via an act of will. Funneling determination into **Pride**'s Aura Blade special quality, he pumped up the jam and pushed Polly's **Pride** to herculean proportions.

The warning not to use skills and abilities in the hold were good and well, but Artorian had puzzled out the mystery box. So long as he did nothing that dealt damage to the pylons, that wasn't from an LFB, he was in the clear. Meaning that he could display his super-villain presentation and lay the effects on as thick as he wanted.

So long as it was all for show.

A massive moonlight-violet blade pouring forth with violet particles pierced the fake sky of the Pylon hold. A declaration that got plenty of attention. Including that of several energy globs that Artorian had long known were sources of observation. This time? He would not shoo them away.

Dreadshine breathed deep. Amplifying his call with Effort-less Sound Shaping, he roared as the rats around him went flying off into the sky, hurled away by sheer pressure and reversed gravity. *"Paaaaag!"*

The blade of violet moonshine dropped with absolute menace in the direction of the Great Rat Maiden. The direction was a rough estimation, but Nascent Being senses said Pag was that-a-way.

That-a-way it was, tacked on with a thousand and twelve stacks of Menace that made any observer currently watching Dreadshine clench their cheeks and grip something. Being menacing in general was an act of social pressure that made one opposing force feel imposing, threatening, and dangerous. Being menacing in game terms forced those feelings upon the observer, which was far less gentle and far less forgiving.

Releasing Polly, Artorian whisked the blade away to his storage bracelet and fell into a forward stride as he launched himself toward Pag's estimated location. While it took him some steps to safely pick up speed as he leaned heavily on the Hypermobility skill to not break anything, Dreadshine built up velocity just fine as all the rats coming for him took free flying lessons. This was a good movement tactic.

The lack of damage diminished his stacks of Menace, but Artorian had made his point already. To improve the show, Artorian instead flicked the lever on The Oof, forcing all the rats within thirty-three leagues of him to see him as the juicy target they needed to get to. That was going to buy the frontline some time to recoup older trenches. The Aura swap made him lose the effect of Pressure, but as effective as throwing rats out of the way was, the sight made for a poor show.

Why play toss, when you can lay down dakka? "Incursus. Is my Yamato ready?"

K-chink!

———

Warning: Equipping Yamato from storage will crash both your movement speed and you if you are not at a complete standstill when you do the thing.

Information: Überstrahlung - Ready for deployment.

Note: Fortress Battleship Yamato has two firing modes.

Mode 1: Devastating Turtle, Main Cannon.

Mode 2: Temper Temper, Area Superiority.

———

K-chink!

———

Message from: The Great Rat Maiden, Pag.

Note: The rat is upset.

You won't scare me so easily, pillow man! I know and remember you both from the glassed Socorro Desert of the Old World, and the alpha run. You're just Dawn's sidekick! Plus, I know how you really fight, so you won't find me to be easy prey. You find weaknesses that people didn't even know they had. Then after dancing around with them, you tell them about the knife you stuck into the chink between the plates, and why you won thirty minutes ago. No such thing will happen today! The rat hordes are here to play! Not even you can stop the endless vermintide, you second-rate villain!

———

Artorian figured that Pag had a direct line of sight on him right now through one of the observation globs. Time for some goading. "Big words from a fourth-rate mascot with fifth grade relevance. This sidekick is coming to put you into the ground."

K-chink!

Dreadshine gripped the sound as it finished, blocking the pop-up mid-run. "Incursus, if that's a reply, squelch it. I want no more contact from Pag until I'm in his face. We'll see what tune he sings then. It's time to see what an Artifact can really do. For comedic effect? Note down Pag's memorial on his epitaph as follows. Cause of death: offended the main character."

The confirmation chime played as the horde of rats lurched at him like ocean waves. In a few seconds, they would drown him. There was no better time to have a bigger boat just sitting in the pocket. With a jump, Dreadshine landed to plant his feet and start grinding to a halt across the ground.

K-chink!

Information: The Great Rat Maiden has engaged its Deity mode. Minions have been enhanced.

That was a problem for later. First? Thinning the waves. Then? Rat-catching duties. Dreadshine came to a halt, and moved up an arm as if expecting a heavy burden to rest on his shoulder. "Incursus? Temper Temper."

Deploying the Überstrahlung from his inventory, Artorian gained a lot of trust in the process, because the result was spectacular. While two-thousand, eight-hundred pounds was a hefty burden, that burden was visually displayed as something that could and should easily have many multiples of that weight. Rather than some house-sized stationary cannon, as Artorian had expected, his feet sank into the rocky ground as something far bigger bore down on him.

How what should be a sixty-ton warship got away with being a mere three-thousand pounds was a matter of pure Incursus magic. Clocking in at a length of eight-hundred eighty-seven feet, with a beam of a hundred and eight feet, a ship that wide was unheard of outside of Zephyr's hip standards.

Better still? This Yamato came armed to the teeth with nine individual sixty-inch Super-Strahlung lens-barrels. The secondary cannons on Incursus looked like they could obliterate mountains and keep chipping down the rest of the hilltop family until the mountain range was arable farmland.

Composed of three platforms worth three cannons each, all nine aimed every which way to begin charging. Along with a full complement of twenty units worth of thirty-inch Schwerer Gustav lens-barrels, thirty units of five-inch Ludere Launcher lens-barrels, fifty units of twenty millimeter 'The Standard' lens-barrels, and one hundred units of ten millimeter 'Kikōhō' lens-barrels. All these LFB's gleefully put on their targeting hats, finished charging, and released their joint volley at the same time. Creating a purple nova of laser emissions that turned the impeding rat waves into pixie dust.

Any Pylon hit caused the beam that struck it to divert or split, causing even more collateral damage from a big beam that turned into multiple smaller beams. Or from a big beam that suddenly went rogue as it bounced and pinballed between multiple crystals and tore through ranks of rats that weren't even remotely close yet.

Checking to see how much coolant that had cost him, Dreadshine laughed with evil cackling at seeing that this entire outburst had cost a mere, single unit of coolant. The fortress battleship hissed from accumulated heat, but that didn't stop the well over one-hundred and fifty Strahlungs from reloading their finger crossbows and pointing themselves at fresh enemies. All to the gorgeous symphony of clickety-clacks as Incursus calculated attack vectors.

K-chink!

———

Field test: Violet Calculation Engine, Evergarden

  Result: Fully functional.

  Interesting Math: 10 Super-Strahlung take up 1 charge of Über-

strahlung coolant. This can be subdivided into lesser caliber LFB, calculated per an easy category of ten. 1 unit of Super-Strahlung coolant can fuel 10 Gustavs. 1 unit of Gustav coolant can fuel 10 units of Ludere Launchers. This pattern repeats.

Note: This function is experimental. There is no stable way to use a larger coolant source for a lesser-sized LFB. This will have unforeseen consequences during testing, and the math may alter.

Request: Vessel name: Evergarden.

––––––

Artorian was grinning ear to ear, his tone hungry for more as he labored while under heavy load, and put one menacing foot in front of the other. "Request approved. Reload and fire."

The second volley broke the tide more than the first, but the heat from Evergarden clearly stacked up faster than was expected. Artorian took stock of that reality, and adjusted whatever Incursus was using for standing orders. "Use double the coolant. Your measurement might not see it, but Evergarden is already up to frying-pan-hot levels of heat, and doing a hundred-and-twelve fire damage to me per second. Voltekka is handling it for now and giving me free Menace stacks, but we can't play that way, bud. No threats to my Incursus. I will not keep this up just to end with boiled turtle soup. Double coolant, now."

K-chink!

––––––

Order confirmed: Double coolant.
    Remaining shots: 83.
    Purging a coolant charge to dump heat.
    Purge complete, heat dumped.
    Remaining shots: 82.
    Assigning double coolant order.
    Remaining shots: 41.

Continue fire?

———

Dreadshine parroted the order as he took another step, purely because he knew that Pag was watching him as the stacks of Menace built, even as the fire damage from holding the Über-strahlung took a nosedive. "Fire."

Volley three broke the wave and thinned the horde as it had done the first two times. Artorian made the quick calculation that when someone gave him information along the lines of 'infinite rats in infinite waves,' that he should believe them. There was no end to the waves coming. Not now, nor on the horizon. Forty more shots of total army-wipe field-clearing was a gorgeous metric, but he would dwindle that number to zero before Pag ran out of fresh rats.

"Incursus, Evergarden is going back into the inventory. I've made my point, and any more action makes this a downhill battle. Get me something on the Amalgams that make these rats in the first place, or get me something on Pag. I'm expecting that currently Divine nuisance to have nicked Gaston's Authority idea. If he's immune to my Inspect, I need my infor-mation another way." A confirmation chime from the Dungeon Core was enough, and Dreadshine vanished the entire fortress-themed battleship back into his storage bracelet.

He didn't need to ask Incursus what some of the special features of the Artifacting had been. The size, weight, and army-clearing cannonade was enough of a front-row-seat show-ing. No longer encumbered, Dreadshine picked up the pace and ran right for the direction that felt correct, according to the ever-reliable nose-tingle.

Shutting off The Oof, he was now confident of having provided enough of a show that there would be no fussing about his heavy use of reversed Pressure. Unlike with Cleaning Presence, investing his entire Determination bar did make it disappear, but that was worth the tradeoff.

What was the distance again? N meters in radius of pressure effect per percentage of maximum Energy bar invested, N meters in height. This meant that with the full one-hundred percent invested, any rat that came within one-hundred meters of him from any conceivable direction went flying. "Trust the nose!"

CHAPTER FORTY-SIX

Artorian learned of an important downside to Pressure now that he was using it for more than merely a touch up here and there. His Determination bar doubled as his Stamina bar. Without that bar, he was funneling a fat supply of Determination-recovery into nothing. For the first time in forever, Dreadshine became terribly tired as he had no physical energy to pull from, regardless of how fast he supposedly recovered it.

Changing his math to ninety-five percent investment solved that problem right away, but oof, what a thing to learn mid-run. If that system had just been turned on, it was likely to teach him exactly that. He was certain that he'd done this before without the massive drain to his body, but as the game was finding its footing, he was going to get away with less and less cheap bonuses. All the better for the game, he supposed.

That was the whole point of the beta run, after all. Make things better.

Except from the perspective of Pag, where all things were getting worse. His long-standing plans were collapsing like Abyss in a handbasket. He could hold against an inconceivable number of NPCs, and a staggering number of players.

One Deity? One Deity would wreck his day, and he'd known that in his endless pursuit of more power, more tricks, more cheese, and even more tricks again.

Pag had zero care on how he got certain toys or tools, so long as he got them. Whether by cheating, exploiting, pressing a bug, or causing the problem himself in the first place? Not important. Only the rush of the great victory mattered. The scene where his rats ran over all that was, and laid claim to all that could be.

In the Old World, before lazing for ages with Duke in the desert, playing endless games through the Dungeon Core of Karakum, he'd been someone! He'd been important! An Incarnate of Fire! In the most prominent, powerful capital. In the most significant province of the entire world, as part of the single most worthwhile nation that had ever stood. The glory of the Ancient Elves would never die so long as he lived. To see that glory return, even by the mere sniff of a memory, was worth the endless war that the rat brought to bear.

This was what Ancient Elves were good at, after all. The Endless War. The march to victory. The oppression of all that laid before them, as anything not part of their culture existed to be crushed underfoot. Amalgamation into the empire was an honor!

Pag realized he'd drunk too much of his own Kool Aid as, cozy on his great throne of trinkets and loot, the observation Relic showed him the insurmountable obstacle currently beelining it for him. Aside from his own stolen stash of Relics, Artifacts, and cheap cheatery? His endless army made through Amalgam Pylons was held together with spit, tape, and fringe rules that would fall apart if one looked at them for too long. His army of rats was his only real main weapon.

Artorian the side-character would get to him. Of that there

was no question. What to do when he did… What to do. Mid-thought, Pag, the most glorious of Great Rat Maidens, was punted from his throne by Dreadshine the freight train. "Found you."

Mid-flight through a shattered shield, the perturbed rat yelled at him. Unlike in the prompts, which could be narrated in a variety of voices, whether flat or snarky, Pag's actual rat voice was as squeaky and high as one imagined. "How are you here already?!"

Dreadshine's visor hummed with dark violet light as the pursuit had not paused, his voice villainous and metallic. "Clench your jaw."

"What?" Pag received a first-hand lesson in speed as the sound barrier's snap, crackle, and pop ended with him receiving a fist to the cheek that ended his upward trajectory and buried him in the rocky ground of the Pylon hold. Having crashed through the ground and gotten buried deeper after the fact, Pag the Crumpled didn't feel so good while stuck between a pocket of gneiss and granite. Which may as well have been a rock and a hard place. "*Ow.*"

Luckily, he was going to be here a bit and could recuperate. He'd get to take his time getting out while violent-shine up there waited and got swarmed by endless… *Crunch*!

Fresh rays of light were not what the Great Rat Maiden was hoping for, but the rat who had opted to dress as a maid was going to find no mercy from Mr. Magoo the Menacing over here. With pure Strength, Dreadshine had opted to rip open the crack that had formed. A crack that Pag's own descent had provided the handholds for. A spread gap which Dreadshine followed, descended through, and continued to make wide enough to pile-drive a fist directly into Pag's stomach.

An act that emptied the contents of said stomach, which didn't survive more than a few moments before becoming particulates. Dreadshine had shifted back to Cleaning Presence, and seemed to have ignored the plan to break the Amalgam

Pylons first. Grandpa had chosen to go straight for the root of the problem, and pluck it right out.

Pag was buried another hundred feet deeper from the slam-dunk, causing several of his cheated-in talismans to snap and break. Talismans there purely to keep his health fat and full. Unfortunately, he didn't have an infinite number of those. "Wait! We can talk! Diplomacy!"

Dreadshine's reply was to make the hole they were in ever deeper. Pressure showed up to play, reversed gravity, and excavated countless tons of rocks around him. This up-chuck continued until the arms-crossed and standing-in-place Dreadshine arrived at Pag's new depth level. Upon which he took a solid footing stance, and replied to the offer for diplomacy. With Diplomacy. "Evergarden, Main Cannon."

Fortress battleship Yamato appeared in Dreadshine's hands and rested on his shoulder. Presented bow-first, the one-hundred-and-twenty-inch Uber-lens charged up, in tune to the full fanfare of a musical escort. One of the bards, playing a character named 'The Witch of Mercury,' had been called for a performance by Incursus. The Witch delivered, providing the music of a duel that played loud and free though Artorian's brooch from Zephyr's and Lucia's end, amplified by Effortless Sound Shaping as the girls hollered and waved supportive glow sticks.

Pag knew he had to run.

Whatever madness the main cannon of that ridiculous fusion beamer was going to do, his cheated in protections and stolen Divinity were not going to cut the mustard. Without trying to be clever or chance speaking any words, he broke an escape stick and teleported away. Escape sticks were meant for dungeons and getting the Abyss out when things got sticky. While those dungeons weren't up and running yet, Pag had of course absconded with a box of the prototypes after having sniffed them out.

He would rat around forever! This battle was only beginning! Assured of having gotten away scot-free, Pag shook his tiny fist at nothing. "You can't catch me, pillow man!"

Having stored Evergarden in his bracelet, Dreadshine made it out of the pit as the endless rat swarm was piling into it like a bucket of sugar. He looked to be either walking on their heads, or running on the squeals they all made as they fell to their doom.

Either way, once Dreadshine stood on the rim and flicked a rat in the face to give himself some breathing space, Pag did not like the follow up. The glowing visor snapped to his direction, the villain looking not just in his direction, but exactly where he stood at the tippy top of a large floating Pylon. The glow and obscure location should have hidden him, but this accursed sidekick knew where he was? That would make fleeing troublesome.

Direct engagement was no better. Luckily, he had the height advantage and the high ground! As a bonus, his foe could not fly. Dreadshine had no recourse but to tangle and tussle with endless rat hordes, who… "Why are they all falling asleep?"

Dreadshine, having swapped to Field of Sleep, pointed directly at Pag. After which, a boring, mundane broom appeared in his armored hand. The armored foe swung the Broom of Shaka, the Boom Shaka Laka, as if to clean the floor. To Pag's extreme surprise, Dreadshine swept himself away instead.

Weighing just about nothing due to Voltekka's addition of Mithril in the set, Artorian's susceptibility to physics was far increased. The weakness was turned to a benefit in this instance as Dreadshine's arc was clearly going to land him right on top of Pag's head.

"Curses!" Pag abandoned the ship and jumped from the floating Pylon with his hands together, landing into a pile of sleeping rat bodies in order to swim to safety through their useless meat. "A thousand curses!"

Why must he have such a love for fireballs? Most of his skills and abilities couldn't be used in the Pylon holds! That accursed double-edged blade was cutting him deep right now. All those stolen goodies, and none of them wouldn't blow up the hold. Granted, it was a thing he could do in order to win the battle. Yet... he knew in his tiny little heart that if he did that, the bigshots would look at him most unfavorably, and pluck him out of his current fate by the tail.

Then, he would lose the war, and every war there ever was after that. Because Dawn would *never* let that go. If he blew up her sidekick along with the entire hold, he was the one hosed. "This isn't over, sidekick!"

"Correct." Dreadshine's armored grip snatched Pag by the tail as he was escaping between the piles of minions. Kicking the rat in the side, the sidekick pulled him free without effort before doubling down on that statement. Dreadshine's visor hummed a deep violet with each utterance. "Clench your jaw."

The thunderclap of the great face-punch displaced many— sleeping, now dead—rat bodies that were forcibly made to make way as Pag was bent to the will of physics. The bruised Great Rat Maiden either passed through them or moved them. Pag tumbled to a halt, several more talismans snapping as the danger to his health bar actually taking some hurt started to look like a very real possibility. "*Ow!* Will you stop that!"

"No." Pag felt fear when Dreadshine blocked out the unnatural ceiling lights in the way that arrows blotted out the sun. Rather than being a good distance away, Dreadshine was both there, and in striking range upon reply. A reply provided in the format of a thunderclap as Pag made the journey of the great rat-displacement again. This time with an unhealthy dent in his health bar. A feat that Dreadshine seemed most pleased by. "*There* we go."

Pag shoved himself up, tearing away dead tokens, non-functional cheated items, and broken talismans that only added weight. In dumping dead weight, Pag made an unpleasant discovery. He had broken several escape sticks. The system realized that at the same time Pag did, who teleported thirty-two times within a second around the map, before reappearing in his current location while more than a little sea-sick. "What do you want from me?!"

Dreadshine thought that to be simple. His stance gained stability, and his arms went up as if to hold a heavy item currently not present. "Run."

Pag bolted for freedom when the Witch from Mercury belted out her music through Artorian's brooch, like a white whistle being blown as a giant horn. Dreadshine merely knew his task as the Janitor, and cleaned the house. "Evergarden. Devastating Turtle."

Fortress battleship Yamato popped into being on Dreadshine's shoulder, already fully charged and ready to go. Its bow adjusted a mere touch, aimed squarely at Pag's back as the Great Rat Maiden fled through piles of rats and disappointment. "Incursus. *Fire.*"

Pag screamed at the flash of violent violet light behind him. He didn't bother looking at first, his focus only on the flee-flee until he chanced doing so when he wasn't dead right away. The act was met with imminent demise, as a massive, bright blue shell with a strong purple hue dipped and darted toward him. The shell zipped effortlessly between both dead and sleeping body piles, including the still awake and living rats chasing the other way in order to get to Dreadshine.

The unerring blue shell of the Überstrahlung struck Pag dead on. A damage calculation occurred, but what Artorian saw from his ever-growing hill was only ever going to be categorized as amusing. After he stowed Evergarden and walked up and up in order to keep line of sight, he chuckled at the way Pag died.

The blue shell hit Pag. Pag stopped in place like he was a flat poster rather than a three-dimensional creature with density, flipped upside down, then fell through the floor of the world while a little prompt made of the letters 'Dead' hovered upwards in pixelated text. A jaunty little melody played as the Great Rat Maiden died as a character.

That Divinity seemingly had done little, if anything at all, to stop the blue shell. Artorian reflected on reasons why. "Must have been something to improve his minions, rather than himself. Maybe I'll ask him later."

Clapping his hands together, Artorian considered this a job well done. Next, the infinity flood. "Incursus? I'm going to Deify myself a moment and tap into both of my Personal Holds, then toss Evergarden into the air. While you're up there? Temper Temper all the Amalgams. I'm certain you've found them by now."

K-chink!

———

Information: Affirmative!

Evergarden is prepared to set the mood.

Temper Temper is charged and ready to reduce the mountain range down to rubble.

———

Artorian eased on his stance and observed his hand a moment when the light of constellations fused with Dreadshine. The look of the armor altered to that of a see-through, cosmic galaxy. An Elden Beast. "Incursus? Fill the Student rank of Effect Cosmetics. Designation? Divine."

One confirmation chime later, and the very stern of Evergarden appeared on Fierce Deity Sunny's open hand. Perfectly balanced, as all things should be. Pointed nose-up, Artorian grunted before hurling the entire fortress battleship clear into the sky and giving the order. "Fire!"

Incursus took that order as gospel, aiming the multitudes of Strahlung cannons to their intended, pre-calculated locations.

With a flash of highly energetic victory, Evergarden's cannon nova downed all eight Amalgamation Pylons in one blow. The methods had been easy, as the type and output of the lasers matched the majority nature of the Pylons they needed to hit. Adjacents will interact. Opposites cancel. Like reflects like.

Except that like cannot reflect like when the amount of attack energy pumped in utterly overcomes the energy of the defendant. This was true in cultivation, therefore this was true for Strahlung.

Dreadshine caught Evergarden on the way down, and stopped all her momentum by directly storing the whole ship into his Silverwood Bracelet. An act that he followed by turning to all the observation globs. Spreading his arms wide as he deactivated his cosmic mode and allowed his colors to return to normal as Voltekka's armor retreated back into its core, he called the performance to a close.

"Curtain. Call." As the Amalgams continued to explode in the background as they overloaded to provide plentiful, localized multicolored fireworks? That was it, that was the show. "Next stop? New Haven! Zephyr? Come get me."

CHAPTER FORTY-SEVEN

Artorian was glad to board Zephyr after an army of Gnomes and Wisps poured from her holds to inspect and study the Amalgam remains. The remaining rats had gained some intelligence after the loss of Pag. Which they used to observe the situation, take note of the angry god in sunglasses standing on a mountain of their dead brethren, and promptly flee topside to be in the Pylon holds no more.

Rats on the surface of a realm were just fine.

Rats in the Pylon holds were a no-no.

The arrival of Raile and related troops that rolled in at ramming speed were an equally pleasant sight. He shook a quick paw with the Colonel so the big Dwarf couldn't crush him out of sheer elation. "Raile! Got your vacation all planned out?"

The Colonel was glad this was all over. "My good chap! I most certainly have. Do you need anything before you make yourself scarce? The hopsies have terrible ideas planned for you."

Artorian didn't need more reasons to leave in a hurry, so what was one more. "Could you cook up some of these dead rats and mail them to me? I'm likely going to need provisions to feed a whole bunch of starving people. Not the best option, I know, but can you do it?"

"Consider it done, Governor." Raile clapped him on the shoulder far too hard. "You best tally and ho, my friend. The hopsies are almost here. Expect bee-liveries."

Artorian took that to heart and squirreled himself onto Zephyr before anyone could pull a prank or make any funny suggestions. "Zeph, the second you're good, go. *Go fast.*"

Zephyr's neon engines roiled to life before the last decantee was free from her holds. In her playbook, 'good to go' meant going when her people needed her to. The Gnomes still in her hold could *jump*. Which they did as the yacht's nose pointed skyward and began to pump engines and burn ground.

Artorian jumped into a seat and held on as Zephyr took off like a scorned woman, fleeing deep into the night. Her bow leveled out only when they were free and clear of earshot. Only then did her door slam open for the High Elf to stomp out onto the deck. "You have another boat *aside from me*? Were you ever going to tell me?! I feel so betrayed!"

The Administrator shouldn't laugh. It was a terrible time to laugh. Yet, here he was, unable to stop laughing as he pulled up the weapon entry between unopposable giggles. Once he had it, he shoved the prompt at the High Elf before he buckled over from laughter.

Zephyr took the screen while yelling incomprehensible Elvish at him in the native High Elven dialect, then changed the target of her wrath to Incursus as she took in the knowledge. "Incursus! You freeloading balcony-squatter! The next time I see your shell, I am turning you into soup! You dare fly? Do you know how long it took me to fly?"

"I... I tossed him. *Ah, aha.* Ow, my ribs." Artorian wiped away tears. "Zephy, I tossed him. Evergarden cannot fly."

Zephyr angrily and repeatedly stabbed her perfect, manicured finger into the prompt while turning the screen to face him. "Yes. He. Can."

Not believing that, Artorian adjusted his sunglasses after a sniffle and read over the prompt. The information was dense, and even though this was supposed to be a weapon entry, the information on Evergarden was an easy twenty-thousand words big. He needed to scroll back up after accidentally moving the page, and it took him several movements to get back to Zephyr's find. Where he did confirm that Evergarden, in fact, had a flight function. Costly, but the ship had one! "Well, crunch my crackers. That's a find."

He dismissed the prompt, then leaned over to pat Zephyr's hand while she death-gripped the edge of his lounger. "You're my favorite ship, Zephy. You've taken such good care of me. I wasn't going to randomly forget that."

Zephyr turned beet red, crossing her arms over her chest as she got all flustered and looked away. "Yes. Well. Yes. I mean. Yes. No. I mean yes. I'mgoingtoplantnewflowersnowbye."

Artorian giggled as the High Elf ran away, and the ship's engines stabilized to a more sensible output. The deck stopped shaking, for one, which he considered a good sign. In addition to yellow tulips and pink peonies, fresh additions of white and purple alstroemeria lilies joined the decor. "*Oooh*, so what's what these look like? I do like this flower. Very pretty. Good call, Lucia."

The momma bun appeared at the door frame in her human guise upon being named, walking right over to him with a medical kit under her arm. She was clearly going to give him a once-over. "Thank you! Now for the bad news?"

Artorian didn't follow. "What bad news? That was a great win!"

Lucia made a swirly motion at Artorian with an accusatory finger. Oh c'mon, he wasn't cheating on the boat with another boat! "Kit, you are going to learn at least one shielding technique, spell, or ability from me before we get to Jotunheim and pick up Ember. Momma was worried sick seeing you under that pile of rats! All gnawing and frantic and… *ugh*. Momma's supportive, but you dun gave your momma a heart attack!"

The medical box slammed onto the table while Lucia kept powerful eye contact with the grandfatherly Administrator, caring none at all for his appearance. A kit was a kit! No matter the age or size. If he ever grew up to be a proper Hare, then she could stop the care. Until then, this odd little fluff was a litter runt and needed *extra* care. They always did, the fussy babies.

She clicked open the medical box, revealing a massive bowl of steaming seafood in a most sumptuous orange-colored stock. "Now you gon' eat this soup that Momma got together, and I don't wan' hear no fussin' until that bowl's empty!"

"You got it, Momma Bun!" Artorian absconded with the large bowl, quickly helping himself to dinner as he inhaled the peeled shrimp, crab, fish filet, and assorted veggies and stock. Lucia opened several healer-related prompts as he did, fussing over him while not finding anything terribly wrong. A bit of fatigue from temporarily not having a stamina bar while making stamina actions, but that was minor.

By the time Artorian's bowl was empty, Lucia had left, only to return with a several pound bag of steamed crawfish. "You ain't done! You're skin and bones, eat more!"

Swole-torian thought that might be a joke, but who said no to the divine smell of masterfully prepared, spicy crawfish? Just pinch one part and twist the other, right? A good ten or so died as casualties to the learning process, but after that Artorian had the maximum-meat strategy all figured out. The tail was where all the good stuff was! "Momma Bun, this is delicious!"

Lucia replied to him from the kitchen with a motherly yell. "*Uh-huh*! You gonna yammer or you gonna eat?"

"Eating, ma'am!" Artorian knew when to throw a fight, and this one was considered thrown. "More, please!"

A considerably happier response followed from the kitchen. "Tha's my boy! Momma gon' be right there. Next up is etouffee and chicken fried chicken."

Once fat with shellfish, Artorian kneaded his grown stomach while taking deep breaths and supping upon fresh water to help keep it all down. "*Delicious*. Is this the prep for shield theorem class? Or are you more the Dale-type instructor and throw people into the deep end like Gomei? I haven't seen that Moon Elf in a while. I should check in with Brianna."

Lucia settled herself into a nearby lounger after throwing a blanket over Artorian. "You gon' learn while you nap! Momma's been studying up on you, kit."

She tapped her sniffer and pointed at him. "Intent-based learner. You're going to think of wrapping a thin film of protection around yourself, just like that blanket. Then you're going to nap, and if you wake up because I threw something at you, we start over. The goal is for you to sleep so well you snore, while Momma shoots healing arrows at you. Now don't you fret. They'll hurt! But they won't hurt you none. It's the kind of painful love only a momma can give."

Artorian squinted his eyes at her. "That... doesn't..."

"Shushio!" Lucia swirled her hand at him as if casting some kind of spell, but it clearly didn't work, if it was even a real spell. "Momma gon' tell you about how to lead a raid, and the golden rule of cupcakes to help put you to sleep. Don't pay attention to the arrow coming your way, stay focused on intending that thin film of protection until it's actually there. This is all about the movements and shape of mana, which I heard you're supposed to be not half bad at."

Artorian gasped. "You fattened me up so I would be tired!"

"Suffer from the 'itis, son!" Lucia pushed up her sleeves without bothering to get out of the lounger, and got out her Heartstring bow. "Now! The cupcake rule."

Artorian threw up a sheet of solid light when the first harmless arrow nearly sank into his thigh. "That has nothing to do with cupcakes!"

"No cheating!" Lucia reached out with her bow to conk him on that bald head of his. "Focus on the film. Intend your protections! You've seen me throw shields up the entire adventure. You likely even licked one at some point."

Apprehensive to say the least, Artorian maintained his wall of solid light for the entire duration that Lucia tried to keep *thunking* that bow on his head. When she stopped to glare, he cautiously diminished the wall. Had he ever licked a shield? He couldn't recall, but it sounded like the kind of thing he'd do. "At this rate, mine will be salt-flavored."

Lucia slid on a pair of rectangular reading glasses, purely to look over the rim. "One bolt in the face and a back full of mace will make you not care too much, so long as your shield works. Now settle in and shell up!"

Far too wary of another arrow, Artorian pulled up his blanket as if it were a shield. Where was his Sugar Glider when he needed the boy? Actually... "Go ahead and tell me about your cupcakes, Lucia. *Blanket* will protect me."

"The cupcake rule." Missing the grandfather's inflection, Lucia cleared her throat, and told Artorian a story as if she was giving the speech to a raid group. "*He-hem.* I have made these cupcakes for y'all out of the kindness of my heart. As a show of appreciation and respect for me as your raid leader, you will eat them, and receive a buff called 'cupcakes make you happy.' As long as you have this buff, I will accept you as a member of my raid, showing that you will follow me and obey my rules and agree to the terms of loot distribution."

Artorian ducked as an arrow whistled over his head, Momma Bun snapping at him. "Focus!"

The old man threw the blanket over his head and sank between the pillows, grumbling as Lucia continued while Artorian tried to focus. "Should you refuse to eat the cupcake, you will be removed from the raid, and no further loot will be distributed to you. Should you let the buff fall off without refreshing it by eating another cupcake, you will be removed from the raid. No further loot will be distributed to you."

Another arrow shot at Artorian, but thunked off a thin film that had begun to coagulate around him. Why was it made of white fire...? Not important to Lucia. Only results! Pleased with the initial success, she continued her speech. "I made plenty of cupcakes to go around. If you act up or throw a hissy fit while you have the cupcake buff, I will give you one reminder. *One.*

For you to get yourself back in line. Cupcakes make us happy, after all, so be happy with what you get and who you're following."

Artorian peeked open an eye. "Then what?"

Lucia had a brand-new arrow pointed right at his face. "Then, if they don't get in line? I will remove them from the raid and no further loot will be distributed to them until they are willing to eat the cupcake."

The arrow plinked off the thin flaming film, and regardless of Artorian flinching, Lucia put her bow away and punched him twice in the shoulder. That likely had some cultural significance somewhere. "Great! You've got the building blocks. Now, that shield needs a name and a proper method of expression. Then it becomes a real game skill. Or ability. Personally? I support spells."

Artorian tried pressing his fingers together while the flaming film was in place, and found that he could not. He also wondered why the film wasn't burning anything it touched, but he'd take it. "Fascinating."

A different idea struck him. Looking around for a glob of observation energy, he waved at it when he found one. "Hello! Is there a Heavenly of **Shield**? Is that a thing?"

K-chink!

———

Information: The Heavenlies of Floor 117 would like to know if they have permission to visit. Guest list: **Luck. Shield. Speed. Growth. Armor. Vitality.**

———

Artorian ran his digits down his beard, noting that Lucia shrank into herself and began to look uncomfortable. "Apologies, Incursus. That is a negative. I merely wanted to know if there was one. I will be learning shielding from Momma Bun, and not the over-zealous stars wishing to butt in. Please relay my amusement at how closely they match game terminology."

Lucia's ears shot up, her eyes watery with an accompanied trembling lower lip. Her kit had read her mood and concerns just from that small moment? Throwing off her own blanket, she power-walked to the other lounger and bury-squeezed his whole face against her chest. She rocked Artorian while grinding her cheek back and forth over his bald head. "Why do the runts of the litter always end up as the best kits?"

Artorian chuckled, but hugged Lucia in turn while she went through her momma moment. She'd likely spring back to serious in no time, but for now, this was important. When she let his head go, he gave her his brightest smile. "Because the runts love their momma the most, so we're going to make sure you feel that you matter. Because you matter, Momma Bun. You matter."

A second helping of chest-smothering followed as the Basher got all emotional, but Artorian let his Aura clean up her sniffles so she didn't have to wipe her cheeks clear. "I'm going to teach you all the shields, you runt."

Artorian patted the small of her back, that beaming smile still present when Lucia released him. "I look forward to it, Lucia. Though, you're welcome to be more gentle about it. I'll never be a Heartshielder, but I sure love everything I've seen you do, you magnificent Glitterflit."

Wiping under her eyes with the back of her paws anyway, Lucia pulled up her sleeves. "Oh, hush, you. Git on up. Momma is gonna teach you some magnificent shields."

CHAPTER FORTY-EIGHT

Artorian arrived at Jotunheim having learned not one, but three shield abilities. One for himself, one for someone or something else, and one to plop down in an area. Once he'd grasped the basics of barriers, the variations had come easily enough. That first hurdle of forming the shape, density, and intent of the barrier had been the most difficult. An hour of explanation and example from Lucia had done all it needed to bump him up from a Shield Novice to a Shield Apprentice.

His learning sessions ended when Zelia and Ember boarded, both looking smug as a rug. The Spider lady smiled, unfolding a fan to cover her expression. "I told you, Kindling, he's preparing for that Soulsborne Quest."

Artorian had honestly forgotten all about that quest, given he wasn't going to get to it until... official release? He'd done an alpha run and a beta run. The next time he went through this game as a player, he wanted it to be... not complete. Playable? Yes, playable. Without half of the systems going awry.

The moment Ember and Zelia were on board, Zephyr's deck shook as she took right back off, turning her bow to face

Midgard before stepping on the neon and flaring her engines. She seemed agitated?

Artorian leaned down to touch the deck. "Zephy? Problem?"

The ship stopped flaring her engines as hard, but the High Elf was clearly annoyed when she spoke. "I'm bored."

Ah. What an incredible problem for a High Elf to have. Artorian scratched his chin, and thought of something. "What about a little race? You mentioned Evergarden can fly. Are you faster? I bet you're faster."

The lights all across Zephyr's yacht pulsed with bright light as she threw down a glove. "Of course I am faster!"

"Incursus. Be ready." Artorian stood, made his way to the balcony, and looked over his shoulder at Ember. She was waiting with her arms crossed to jump on his back and be carried around, as he seemed to have forgotten to child-ify himself to match her. Rude. "Emby? Do you still love boats?"

Ember's accosted facial expression told him that his question had been an atrocity. Before she could reply, his giant smile made her glare. "Good! Meet Evergarden. I'm guessing it's a she, so she's a Yamato-class fortress battleship."

With a swing of the arm, Artorian unloaded Evergarden from his inventory into empty space. The battleship appeared in all its multi-cannon glory, revealing brand new engines that unfolded from its aft. The tri-fold cylindrical exhausts used heat as directed propulsion. Unlike Zephyr's neon green flare of energy exhaust, Evergarden spit fire! Evergarden then also made the mistake of inching her nose ahead of Zephyr, which made the High Elf bristle like a badger.

Artorian was going to ask Dawn what she thought of Evergarden, but she ran past him and jumped ship. Aggressively boarding the Evergarden with a wild squeal, Ember became a rampant problem as she needed to know every nook and cranny of the battleship. All at the same time. A feat she couldn't accomplish, but a feat attempted regardless.

Incursus screamed when one moment her eye and cheek

were mushed against his core, only to be gone the next. If Dungeon Cores could have heart attacks? That was it. That was how.

Zephyr, being sporting in her upcoming race where she would utterly trounce this daredevil interloper, matched the length, width, and general dimensions of her fanciful yacht to that of the fortress battleship. What she would do with the extra size was a question for later. Right now, she matched bow-lengths with Evergarden and flared her engines in prideful challenge.

Artorian went ahead to go stand on said bow, as Ember had already done so on Evergarden. A massive, gleaming smile split her face. She loved boats. With one leg up, and an arm resting on her knee, she looked like a captain! Copying Ember, Artorian matched her pose to begin the countdown. While he was at it, he dipped into Effortless Light Shaping to lay down the edges of an illuminated track. Pushing the effect, he found he could go no further than a kilometer. T'was enough!

He prepared Effortless Sound Shaping and a Brilliant Behemoth, planning to turn the explosion into the starting *ka-bang*. "On wub! Three. Two. One!"

Ember dropped her arm, and boomed out the speed order at the bass drop. "All ahead flank!"

Wub!

Both ships illuminated space as their engines turned into stars, and their bows plunged forward into the dark. Both Evergarden—currently crewed by Ember and controlled by Incursus—and Zephyr—who was crewed by many, and controlled herself—shot all-speed-ahead toward Midgard. A journey that should take hours was going to be maybe... thirty minutes? Less? The ships were both booking it, which was when Artorian realized that they didn't have a set endpoint. So he took hold of his brooch, and made one! "First to breach the Midgard skies wins! Put a dent in Fuyu No Arashi!"

In terms of flat speed, Zephyr pulled ahead. Evergarden responded to this by turning all of her cannons toward her aft, and charging the output to full blast. With a bright but sound-less burst, Evergarden pulled ahead of Zephyr as the cannons unloaded. While indirectly, this provided forward propulsion, as the heat generated was rammed into the engines. She ran hot, but she was winning!

Ember laughed, Artorian laughed, Incursus laughed, and Zephyr cursed.

Artorian took hold of his brooch, needing to make sure of something. "Are we helping, or staying out of this?"

Zephyr answered for him, which Ember overheard easily enough through the connection. "Stay out of this! Everwheat is mine to beat!"

Artorian looked ahead to the other vessel, watching Ember make the 'you heard her' hand signs, before Evergarden pulled ahead too far for him to see her sign language well enough. A fact that Ember realized as well when she swapped over to using her brooch.

Mocking with encouragement, she prodded Zephyr. "Big words for a High Elf that's being left in the dust! How's that cannon exhaust look from back there?"

Artorian put a hand over his mouth so he did not laugh. Instead, he squeezed his brooch. "Incursus? Cannons are all good and well, but remember my rule. No boiled turtle soup allowed. You better cut that emission before Evergarden turns into an oven, with you trapped in there."

Sad, but understanding, Incursus cut the feed. The cannons glowed orange with heat, but the engines were eating it all up while Incursus made sure to chill what he needed to with a coolant charge. He was already riding the edge between burnout and high efficiency for Evergarden's engines, but he was ahead, and not slowing down! Wait… Not slowing down? If he kept going faster and faster, he wasn't going to be able to stop on Midgard. He'd crash through that orbit and atmosphere only to keep going.

Doing some calculations… all the time he spent speeding up was time he was going to need to spend slowing down. There was a difference between a clean re-entry, and blowing through like a fireball. Well… was that such a problem? The goal was to smack the cold storm, not stop, slow down, or drop anyone off. Abyss with it! He'd paint Evergarden red if he had to. *Whaaaagh! Da red wunz go fasta!*

Assured of his impending win, Zephyr passed him. Rather than firing her cannons, she had used the extra internal space to make more engines, and components that engines required. She'd also turned her hull green, because *Green iz da best!*

Ember laughed, Artorian laughed, Zephyr laughed, and Incursus cursed.

CHAPTER FORTY-NINE

Midgard's New Haven was in a poor state.

The sustained good weather and consistent sunny heat, both internal and external, had melted critical natural infrastructure. Left to its own devices, New Haven would have collapsed all by itself over time. The central shaft was poised to drop down, ready to serve as a staircase between the regrowing Murim Woods and Midgard's topside.

Too much of the necessary structure had been ice during The Pale, and when all that exposed hot metal was suddenly hit by another cold wave, things broke. Pipes full of water burst, heat no longer transferred well, and many segments had to be abandoned due to molten holes that could not be plugged.

What had been solid and dry permafrost was now a wet slip-and-fall hazard.

The majority populace had to hunker and bunker with the Orkharn, but the people who had come to play from Cal saw this as one giant challenge. Death for a local was very different from death for a player. Fuyu No Arashi was about to hit New Haven with its last cold wave, and every player capable of doing something about the strike before the storm was standing on the remains of the Rimward March.

Clad in Artorian's missing anti-cold set, Autarchy's Wonder, Lenore led from the front. A wave of heat rose from her O'Dachi, ready to silence another incoming horde of Thunder-horns, thunder-themed Rams who had taken pages out of the Great Book of the Moose, scaled down to proper Midgard levels.

Unfortunately for those of New Haven, much like those Moose of old, Thunderhorns spawned by the score. Handling twenty Rams per every attending person and encounter, every encounter, was no easy task. Especially when they had to do it in the scant amount of time before the cold hit and the NPCs had to bunker up. Any Thunderhorn not slain would get to chase them down as they ran while the wall of cold pinned them in, and any Ram that got into New Haven caused catastrophic damage.

Losing the city could come in many forms.

If they lost the generator, the city was gone. If they lost all the inhabitants, the city was gone. If they lost all the defenders, the city was gone. Or, if the oppressive cold and lack of food made morale die, forcing surrender? All was lost. One could not win a war of attrition against the nature of winter when it didn't let you keep the slain food. As the clock hit the beginning of the last cycle, the Voice of the World reminded everyone of the quest, and updated the text to match.

Dun-dun-dunnnn!

———

World Event: The City Must Survive.

Fuyu No Arashi, the Eternal Thundercloud, has declared Casus Belli upon the Realm of Midgard due to unacceptable weather patterns. Fuyu No Arashi demands the permanent reinstatement of The Pale, and related conditions. Until these conditions are met, Fuyu No Arashi will assault Midgard with increasing waves of ice, frost, sleet, and snow. Either until its health runs out, due to the inhabitants having weathered the storm, or by capitulation of the current most prominent city on Midgard, upon which the storm will be centered: New Haven.

Survive: Unlock 'Brave New World.'

Perish: The Pale becomes permanent on Midgard once more.

Note: Unlike the conditions of The Pale, which could dip to a constant temperature of minus fifty degrees Celsius, Fuyu No Arashi can force temperatures to dip down in waves, until a final temperature of minus one-hundred and fifty Celsius is in effect. This last temperature drop is also her last hurrah, and surviving that wave signals success.

Next wave: Minus one-hundred and fifty degrees Celsius.

Note: Boss Event! Before this last wave, Fuyu No Arashi, the Eternal Thundercloud, sends forth its final champions. Defeat them before the storm encroaches, or they will destroy New Haven, and you will fail this World Event.

Lenore and the adventuring parties of the Iron Sheep watched with clenched jaws and stern grips on their weapons while wind whipped snow all around them. This was the last hurrah for them as well. Many were tired, bordering exhaustion.

Fuyu No Arashi, the Eternal Thundercloud opened her center, and dropped in their new source of dread. One end boss, three mid-bosses, and an incalculable amount of Thunderhorns.

Lenore, the Iron, flexed her fingers around the Tsuka of her weapon. Her spare hand swept to the side, opening windows of party allotments. She had to know who she had left, and who could handle that upcoming horror show.

At a glance, the big boss was a walking Frost Turtle of some kind. Notable features were a shell covered in dark blue ice, a walking stick, and a pope hat. The three mid-bosses were Lightning Chip-Monks, and the accompanying horde was all Thunderhorns. She knew what to do about Thunderhorns, but four boss-quality monsters at once, with a time limit? That was a tall order.

———

Key: New Haven, Order of the Iron Sheep.
  Group: Team Sleep - Unavailable.
  Secret Files, Members: Artorian. Ember. Lucia.

———

Group: Nightshade - Stationed in Ur's Rest, ready to attack from behind.
  Secret Files, Members: Chandra. Rose. Brianna. Amber.

———

Group: Predator's Territory - Disbanded.
  Secret Files, Members: Raile. Snowball. Manny. Halcyon.

———

Group: Beef and Book - Stationed in the rear, ready to intercept Thunderhorns.
  Secret Files, Members: Tychus. Grimaldus. Sarcopenia.

———

Group: IcyHot - Frontlines, vanguard, exhausted but enthusiastic.
  Secret Files, Members: Tom. Yuki. Shaka. Valhalla.

———

Group: Magnitude - Defeated.
  Secret Files, Members: The Hawthorn Saplings of Discord. Chaos. Entropy.

———

Group: The Oldest Woods - Frontlines, hanging on by a thread.
 Secret Files, Members: Mahogany. Rosewood. Birch. Snowdrop.

———

Group: The Old Woods. - Defeated.
 Secret Files, Members: Olive. Baobab. Eucalyptus. Sequoia.

———

Group: The Young Woods - Stationed internally, logistics.
 Secret Files, Members: Apiculteur. Maya. Airos. Crooked.

———

Group: Nature's Secrets - Unavailable.
 Secret Files, Members: Chandra. Tatum.

———

Group: The Pirate Crew - Unavailable.
 Secret Files, Members: Zephyr. Oak. Hans. Meg.

———

Group: Four White Mages in a Trench Coat - Frontlines, out of mana.
 Secret Files, Members: Richard. Adam. Irene. Craig.

———

Group: Beasts and Beauties - Disbanded.
 Secret Files, Members: Jiivra. Astrea. Blanket. Voltekka.

———

Group: Blood and Stone - Defeated.
  Secret Files, Members: Emilia Nerys. Kellen Shadowbeard. McShane.

———

Group: InkSplash - Stationed internally, generator duty.
  Secret Files, Members: Lucky Luca. Eri. Piano. Tsuu.

———

Group: Sand and Sun - Frontlines, out of mana.
  Secret Files, Members: Ra. Set. Ma'at. Anubis.

———

Note: All 40 groups below this point are listed as Defeated.

———

Lenore's actions were decisive when she was through with her check-up. The grandmother of Iron steadied herself and spoke with pure conviction. Not a shred of surrender was to be found in her voice. "All internal groups, groups in the rear, and everyone who's out of mana, or hanging on by a thread? Generator duty. You're no good to anyone on your last legs. Prepare a last stand. All civilians, retreat to food storage, scour anything left that you can find and get it to the generator room. I don't care if it's frozen bread crust. If we don't hold here, we don't hold at all and this is over. Get them every last calorie you can get paws on."

That accounted for Sand and Sun, InkSplash, Four White Mages, The Young Woods, The Oldest Woods, Beef and Book, and... No, that was it. This left Lenore only herself, IcyHot, and Nightshade. Quick math said that with eight groups of four members each, that was thirty-two instances of a Thunderhorn score to deal with.

Six-hundred and forty horns? That was a lot, plus her personal twenty tacked on for a total of six-hundred and sixty Thunderhorns. Three mid-bosses. One big boss. She squeezed the brooch that came with the item set, the communication clip included when she'd received the package. "Nightshade? What information can you get me on those bosses? IcyHot? On me."

The information from Nightshade was quick and on point, as always. Pure professionals, those women. Lenore wanted a whole city of them, and was vocal about that opinion.

Ding!

———

You have encountered: Oogway, Turtle Pope.
    World: Eternia.
    Realm: Midgard.
    Region: Ur's Rest.
    Terrain: Snowy, the corpses of the fallen.
    Circumstance: Event Boss Encounter.
    Local Event: Fuyu No Arashi Storm.
    Unique Properties: Resurrected.
    Racial Template: Undead.
    Species: Elderly Rime Tortoise.
    Detected Trait: Martial Master.
    Detected Ability: Compress.
    Detected Ability: Lifesense.
    Detected Ability: Nothing Personal, Kid.
    Detected Skill: Martial Arts: Way of Excommunicado.
    Detected Skill: Snow Mastery.
    Detected Skill: Cloud Surfing.
    Detected Skill: There are no accidents.
    Protection: Undead Traits.
    Protection: Immune to Cold and Ice-typed Damage.
    Vulnerability: Greater Weakness to Fire, Holy, and Melee.
    Main Attack 1: Martial Maneuvers.
    Main Attack 2: Shelling Palm.

Special Attack: Excommunicado.
Special Attack: No, You Didn't.

———

Note: Filtered results.
You have encountered: Alvin, Theodore, and Simon, The Chip-Monk Cardinals.
Species: Lightning Chip-Monks.
Detected Trait: Martial Disciple.
Detected Skill: Martial Arts: Way of Excommunicado.
Detected Skill: Snow Mastery.
Protection: Resistance to Cold and Ice-typed Damage.
Vulnerability: Weakness to Fire and Melee.
Main Attack 1: Martial Maneuvers.
Special Attack: Excommunicado.

———

You have encountered: 780 Thunderhorns.
Species: Thunderhorn.
Detected Trait: Ramming Speed.
Detected Skill: Give 'em the Horns.
Detected Skill: Snow Mastery.
Protection: Resistance to Cold and Ice-typed Damage.
Vulnerability: Weakness to Fire and Melee.
Main Attack 1: Thundering Headbutt.

———

Lenore squinted at that last prompt. "Seven hundred and eighty Thunderhorns? Where are those extra one-twenty Thunderhorns coming from? We have six mystery people engaged in this fight? *Where?*"

Shaka and Yuki stood behind Lenore with Tom and Valhalla. Team IcyHot was well prepared, all members clad in matching furs and covered with strong cold-protection spells. Tom and Shaka were both even on fire, acting as localized bonfires that roasted everything except their own teammates.

Adopting formation, Tom tried to steady their assigned leader with a smile full of honor and staunch confidence. "It matters not, great lady. We are here. We are the wall that stops the horde. The shield that breaks their advance. We will not quit. We will not give up. We will stand, defiant!"

Valhalla gripped Lenore's other shoulder, copying Tom's bright confidence, mixed with her own fervent steel. "We will stand. To the last. Regardless of mountain-sized martial foes, and colossal undead turtles."

Lenore's hidden trembling had perhaps not been so hidden. Her shuddered breath exhaled thick and visible in the cold. She nodded, inhaled sharp and fresh, then gripped her brooch. "Nightshade? Do something about that Turtle, then get to the generator before the window closes. Our equipment and spells can't hold against the cold that's coming. Do what you can and get out of there. IcyHot and myself will... somehow... handle the horns and the monks. It looks like Fuyu is about to thunder-clap? Engage on the clap. That's getting very bright up there. Much brighter than usual."

Lenore's ear twitched, a distraction and odd noise crackling forth from her brooch. Was that... music? A feeling, and nothing more, made her free hand slip into her pocket and grip her hand-sewn cloth patch. Warm to the touch, she fished it free. Her chest swelled when she felt the warmth grow between her cold fingers. It was there to give hope. Her Child of Light had seen her through until now. Today, however, she needed a bit more than hope, and a passive health regeneration boon that kept her standing. "I wish you were here."

Opening her palm slowly to reveal the sigil, the music from her brooch increased in strength. In front of her eyes, her cloth patch, like every other cloth patch within New Haven, lit up along with a burning star that fell from the sky.

CHAPTER FIFTY

"Shoot me from the main cannon." Artorian knew something was wrong before they got to Midgard. A pesky, growing, awful feeling that twisted the stomach kept growing as his Nascent Sense tapped its foot nervously on the ground. Zephyr had a front-facing cannon like Evergarden, but her Staravar Macro-battery was not a kinetic projectile type deal.

This did not deter Artorian one bit. He had his brooch in hand and Voltekka already morphing over him as he prepared to walk off the front of Zephyr's bow. "Emby? We're going to get there too late. I don't know how I know, but I know. I'm going to have Zeph launch her Staravar, and I'm going to shape the resulting light beam into a platform. One that I can stand on and ride to be ahead of the curve."

Zephyr and Incursus both grumbled at this, but they had both overdone it with their all-ahead flank. That speed was not meant to be sustained, and after twenty-five minutes of sustained burn, they were both feeling that burn. They'd both been forced to slow down, but still tried to keep their nose just barely in front of the other. Neither knew how engines could cramp, but *oooooh*, they could cramp. They were both going to break atmo and be forced to keep going, but that was a rub they would recover from.

The crews would have to orbital drop while they both got maybe one volley off at whatever threat might be present before momentum carried them out of the battle theater. No matter how much they wanted to, neither of the ships were going to be able to slow down enough to be part of the tussle. Still, one volley from Temper Temper and one volley of High Elven Pride was going to ruin *something's* day.

Ember hopped the fence from Evergarden to Zephyr and linked up with Zelia and Lucia. There was no need to orbital drop; they had their own way to get to Midgard. As Zephyr charged her Staravar with Artorian steadying himself at the opening of the cannon's cylinder, Zelia stopped Kindling before she could tell him not to. "Let him do it."

When Ember gave her an odd look, Zelia provided intelligence. "Deverash wanted to test Effortless Shaping. There won't be a better chance. As for us? That thundercloud is cheating. Fuyu has cheekily spawned a boss underneath New Haven, in the Murim Woods. My Dreamer will be of sufficient help topside, but New Haven has nothing to defend against the hidden threat coming in from behind and below."

Zelia laid her gaze on Kindling, expecting decisive action, while informing her with a facial expression that she herself would not be helping beyond offering transport. "Do you want to do something about this?"

Ember grit her jaw and caught fire. She reached for her brooch, and upped her age. If her boy couldn't match her child-like antics right now, then she was going to step up onto the platform of the great adult. With all childishness gone, Dawn spoke to her dearest with her delicious voice. "Sugar? Go get 'em. We're going to handle another problem that has cropped up in the Murim Woods. One that believes that it's being clever."

Artorian's unmodulated grandfather voice returned through

the connection, secretly smiling at the change in her speech. "Affirmative! See you at the generator?"

Dawn leaned into the persona of Astarte, her abilities ticking into activity one after the other. "See you at the generator, boo. Let me send you off?"

Artorian wasn't going to say no to that. "You got it!"

That was enough for Astarte, who released her brooch and snapped her fiery eyes to Lucia. "Momma Bun? Shield me up. I have a boss to solo, and until we know what it is? I want you running circles around it and me to slap down any unexpected grunts that may accompany the big one. There's always unexpected adds."

"One Momma Bun special, comin' up!" Lucia instantly paw-bapped the grown team lead with the most expensive shield modifier she had. "High Lenity!"

The shield thumped into being around Dawn as she was coated in a shimmer of fading color, who was happy about the extra health-point shield. One could never be over-prepared, and she was trying to hide that she was looking forward to this bout. The majority of her best abilities created indiscriminate area of effect damage, so tackling a boss alone was a treat.

She then thought to get her boy a treat when they met back up in New Haven. What was something he didn't know yet? Oh, easy! "Momma Bun, what does the 'High' modifier do?"

"High Prosperity." Lucia followed with the shield enhancement, but instantly looked tired. "The prefix? 'High' is a magnitude alteration. Ten times cost for ten times output, but it also costs you that amount in Stamina, and has a cooldown that ticks per individual ability or spell you apply it to. So, while I can throw them out, if I am not in a bunker or otherwise not expecting to be in any more combat for a while, that prefix makes me a sitting duck. Using that modifier exhausts me, and if I need to use any more spells shortly after? I sploot on the spot and bury my face in my paws."

She shuddered with a nasty look on her face as she tacked on a normal Sanctity, Integrity, and Tenacity. Her features rapidly lost humanization after that, her sploot imminent. "I tried casting Greater High Lenity once. *Once.* I was out cold for a week."

Wiggling her nose as she returned to Glitterflit format, Lucia groaned from a Stamina headache and buried her face in her paws as advertised. Grumbly and displeased, she also warned Astarte about an additional downside. "That prefix also adds a timed modifier to the shield. Use it or lose it, because you've got an hour before it's gone all by itself. My forte and specialty is all about shielding and protecting large groups of people, whole raids, or small armies. I did not specialize in single target protections, which was a boon way back when, but my bane now. I'm ready to go, but I won't be mobile right away."

Zephyr broke up their conversation with action. "Staravar, ready!"

Astarte, having filled the shoes of her character, tugged up her brooch. She was going to be supportive of this madness, and believe in her Artorian. "Sugar? Fire when ready. We're all set on this end. Send off."

Artorian wasn't going to admit that he was nervous, and that those nerves were climbing as a Capital-class weapon charged at his feet. He'd be fine with Loved by Mana ready to eat the effect and the damage, but he needed his trait *not* to eat the damage. He needed that beam as velocity. He nodded to his dearest while fully clad in seamless armor, and forgot entirely that she couldn't see him. Instead, he took a deep breath, and set his gaze on Midgard. "Zephyr? You heard Dawny. *Send me.*"

The neon green blast of Zephyr's Staravar Beam Cannon punched Dreadshine into the black of space at a speed that broke a few system metrics and overloaded at least one calculation Pylon. Dreadshine himself focused on Effortless Light Shaping. The diminishing Staravar under his feet was quickly used and altered into a solid pane of light that sustained his footing. That was problem one sorted! Nascent Sense was no longer as nervous. He was going to get to the bout on time now, even if the Staravar ran out.

Problem two! What to do when he got there?

"Trans Am." With his voice fully mechanical now that he eased into Dreadshine, Artorian enacted a color change, and shared an idea. Ephira's cooldown on El Kabum hadn't clicked over yet, so the Nagamaki was out. Sorrow and Compassion both had side effects he couldn't risk at the moment, so they were out. Time for **Pride**! "Polly? How much maximum *oomph* can you store through Aura Blade, and do you have anything in the Tsukiyomi Series that can be used during orbital drop? Because even with Pressure in reverse and affecting myself, that's going to be *hot*. I know for sure! I've done it before."

A *splat* prevented Polly from replying as Artorian shoulder-checked through something unknown, murdered it dead, and kept going without any change to his velocity. "The Abyss? Incursus! What did I hit?"

K-chink!

————

You have encountered: Clown.

Origin: Space Station 13.

Additional Data: Redacted.

You have killed the Clown before it could infect a realm with the disease Honk Honk. Cleansing Presence has prevented the disease Honk Honk. The area of effect of Cleansing Presence has destroyed all remaining particles of the disease Honk Honk.

Eternia rejoices.

Ask no questions. The Clown is a Memetic Being. Knowing of the Clown allows the Clown to revive. All knowledge of the Clown will be scrubbed from my memories. Right now.

Warning: Destroying this prompt.

Inquiry: Would you like to erase all memories of the entity Clown?

————

Artorian smashed the yes function, and never wanted to think about this again. Blissfully, he did not. The entire affair was scrubbed and forgotten, to the permanent end of the Clown. Who could never have made the joke that out of the entire emptiness of space, it would get smashed into by a janitor. That was like walking head-first into the only palm tree in a desert.

No longer aware of a pause in stride, Polly picked up the thread on what the Tsukiyomi Series could do for the current problem. Having some difficulties with communication, Polly worked through Incursus.

K-chink!

———

Message from: Polly.

Lakelight Legend, into Fallen Pride, will transfer physics damage into flat damage. This will cause a split in the landscape if Aura Blade is of significant size. Aura Blade's maximum capacity is unknown. Pour it in!

———

Dreadshine started early, pouring his energy regeneration value into the Aura Blade. Beginning with the blade aimed low, he swung in the upwards arc of a crescent moon. As he did, lambent Determination sang and hummed from the color-shifted Rainbow Greatsword to fuel the movement.

"Tsukiyomi Series. Excalibur Style. Lakelight Legend." The visual speed of the upwards swing appeared too slow. Each few inches of the blade's path, a silvery-white with an imprinted blue afterglow artfully showcased where Ex-Calibur had been. This arc continued until the image of a waning crescent remained imprinted in front of Dreadshine. With the blade held high above his head, Artorian completed the image, then focused on pouring in the fuel.

Ex-Calibur's blade grew enormous as the power pooled. The proportions were so bonkers that the system required

Cadastral Maps to puzzle out how much damage that guillotine cut was going to accomplish. Breaching the exosphere, he shoved his Aura into Pressure while focusing on the effect. Wanting to push down in the hopes that it would slow his descent. He'd done this too soon, but given that he was holding a sword-to-face pose with a technique effect active and being sustained, too early was just fine.

The thermosphere changed nothing, the mesosphere made him feel awfully close to Midgard, the stratosphere allowed him to lock onto his target from above, and the troposphere was where all the action was about to happen. Fuyu No Arashi was in no way expecting an attack from above to happen twice.

"Trans Am isn't what I want here. Incursus? I won't be loading up Fierce Deity this time, but give me Effect Cosmetics: Divine!" Dreadshine aimed for an opening as his colors began to shift from white and blue to a swirling, cosmic mass of black and gold. Unfortunately, aim was a strong word for an uncontrolled fall that one hoped nudged him into the right spot. Then again, with a cosmic sword this big? He could miss his impact zone by a country and still cut something valuable.

That still required him to fall in a neighboring country. Eyeballing it? He was way off. New plan! "Archimedes! We're chain stepping. It's time!"

Flash-Stepping to the goal ever faster without making any stepping motions was surprisingly difficult. He had to hold the sword technique! Eschewing the damage and stun components, he blipped. Then he blipped faster, faster, and faster still, until his Determination bar flashed back at him. Each jump still cost him five percent of his bar, and he was not regenerating anything right now. That forced him to stop teleporting, and stop pouring energy into Aura Blade.

He could not get mixed in with that bar empty.

Current problem? He still wasn't remotely close enough, and breaking into the troposphere introduced the heat, turbulence, and drag problem. His armor was holding up, and the Silverwood in Tekka's composition was eating up the Fire damage, but that number was climbing fast. "Abyss! Polly! Change of plans. I'm improvising to get us close now that I've got some air to surf on, and I'm doing the whole Tsukiyomi movement over again when closer. We're going to use your block value as a heat shield. Big blade means big sword to surf on, and you're made of light! I'm giving you wings. Let's goooo!"

Abandoning Lakelight Legend and breaking the technique, he swung down and twisted the blade to lay flat, before moving himself on top as if Ex-Calibur was his average flying sword. Wait... Polly *was* a flying sword. What was he doing? Abyss with it, too late now! "Polly! Remember that *you can fly*. Adjust us!"

Polly, having forgotten they could fly as well, did as told and carefully adjusted their descent angle. Wide sheets of light slid out from the sides of the Rainbow Greatsword designed in spirals of black and gold constellations. With the extra control, the point of the sword fixed their descent and shot them straight toward the storm cloud's center. "Tekka, Polly, get ready!"

Hoping this was enough, Artorian both retracted the wings and moved himself back to the hilt before redoing the entire Lakelight Legend maneuver. He was coming up on the pissy storm cloud far too quickly, but he was only going to make it more angry than it currently was anyway.

"Tsukiyomi Series. Lakelight Legend." Finishing the movement barely in time, he followed up with the kicker and enacted the swing of destiny. "Ex-Calibur Style. Fallen **Pride**."

CHAPTER FIFTY-ONE

Dividing the sky into two neat widdle halves, Dreadshine descended through the dreary thundercloud with stellar force. From Lenore's perspective, Fuyu no Arashi was cleaved in twain by a sky-splitting, burning line. Without the rumbling dark ceiling that spanned from one horizon to the other, the scenery altered. No longer a dim and dull scene of wintery oppression.

Revealing the blinding sun and its bright rays, people missed the angry messenger it had yeeted their way. Which was sensical, as the messenger was hard to spot compared to the country-sized guillotine coming right for the undead Tortoise.

When the scenery changed as the bisection of clouds made onlookers shield their eyes against the unannounced brightness, Pope Oogway paused in his advance on New Haven to lean on an oversized walking stick. The papal ferula. Light was bothersome to an undead, but less so for one who had no eyes. Craning his head to look right at Dreadshine instead of the burning line, the turtle pope gently broke into a grim smile. As if observing a funny monkey, the pope spoke to him.

Artorian couldn't hear the spoken words, but a prompt came up to relay the message regardless. Artorian did not like the message. For it was smug, haughty, and he would have done it too. Complete with the scheming grandpa giggle.

Ding!

———

Nothing personal, kid.

———

With a blink and you miss it moment, Dreadshine and the Tortoise Pope switched places. With their locations swapped, Fallen **Pride** cut both Alvin and Ur's Rest in half. This prevented a song and dance number that died along with its central member, when the burning red line and bass dropped after a skipped beat.

Artorian hit the Midgard realm hard and fast. He did not stop as the ground cracked open underneath him like a grand canyon fault line being split.

With Oogway playing a sneaky reversal card, he no longer had the time to do any kind of fancy adjusting. With the ground suffering the same fate as the cloud, the only way to go was down. As Polly reverted to being a broken claymore, wings of light plumed from his back. He was going to fall, but he could keep away any and all sharp edges as the ravine continued to crack open and widen under him.

This allowed him the moment for a quick tally. He'd felled one of the mid-bosses instead of the main target. While this was cause for grumbles, a win was a win. He'd accomplished this directly along with the murder of several hundred Thunder-horns when Polly's empowered strike hewed through them. As cherry on top of the honey pie, another few hundred Thunder-horns had blindly added themselves to the death toll by changing vectors and trying to attack him, causing an unexpected third win. Or impending win. Death by gravity may not be death by orbital cut, but less enemies was less enemies!

One look up, and Artorian could see the Thunderhorn mobs tumble down above him. Many struck the sharp edges of the ravine as they all fell straight through the freshly cleft wound into the Murim Woods.

Dreadshine scowled. Of that view, it was not the Thunderhorns giving him grief. It was, instead, the same sight that Lenore didn't know how to feel about. Artorian knew exactly how to feel about a creepy undead end-boss with a big smile on its face while it tried to sky-swim toward him. Oogway only went as fast as gravity, but something about the very attempt was unsettling.

For Lenore, this was a mixed bag. The orbital slice left her with considerably less enemies to contend with, but the resulting quake was going to cause lingering problems elsewhere. Ignoring the collateral for now, since that was out of her hands, she took stock.

A scant two-hundred and three Thunderhorns to face? Manageable. Two remaining Chip-Monks? Far healthier numbers to contend with, considering their remaining forces. One end-boss who cheerily fell down into the new worldwound while holding onto its pope hat without a care in the world? Problematic, but not for her.

The Tortoise, after looking back and forth between her and the hole in the world, appeared cryptic. Lenore was certain that rather than observe New Haven, that Tortoise had looked right at her, and made an unconventional choice. Before the pope vanished from view, Lenore received an odd prompt. One she dismissed out of hand.

Ding!

One often meets his destiny on the road he takes to avoid it.

Lenore didn't need to put down gold in the gambling bin to know where her money landed on the identity of the mystery helper. If it hadn't been for Oogway's tongue-in-cheek castling maneuver, Sunny would be working on adding cubed Chip-Monk to the field kitchen soup in a half-shell.

He'd be alone against an end-boss, but those were good victory chances. The match up was in their favor, unless Oogway had some truly devious tricks up his shell.

That calculation left them with dark odds, but it was not a calculation that remained constant. Breaking into the battlefield from above and bringing their own hurricanes, Evergarden and Zephyr bore fresh holes in Fuyu No Arashi's wedged-apart thunderclouds. Still trying to one-up each other, they entered the field by firing their cannons! Figuring out whose nose made it to Midgard first was a bust, but whoever killed more things was something they could compare with prompts!

Aiming for what they could see beneath the travel vector of the other, the light shows unleashed from both ships crisscrossed each other in the sky. They were only going to get one volley, so rather than focus on adjusting speed, they poured all their power into ever more projectiles! Struck by both a Staravar and Temper Temper, the landscape gained an overhaul as it was scored by copious lasers in a variety of sizes. While this dropped the number of remaining Thunderhorns down to nearly none, the two remaining Chip-Monks were on their toes after losing Alvin, and reacted with trained chipmunk speed.

Rather than allowing both vessels to enter the theater and slip back out again, both of the oversized chipmunks leapt straight into the air, moving in tandem while holding a martial pose. Avoiding the majority of the joint barrage, they swirled into a martial spin and grabbed the noses of both ships. Mid-twist and on their way back down, they suplexed the battleships down onto frozen Midgard soil.

While this tilled a great chunk of freshly scored landscape and killed the remaining Thunderhorns like a hot iron flattening the wrinkles out of cloth, it also spelled the end for both ships. Their tumbling momentum brought both mid-bosses straight to New Haven's front door, and being used as landscaping tools hadn't been good for their flashing red health bars and bent sails. Getting ground-slapped with great velocity was good for nobody, but extra poor for those who needed their shapes to remain rigid. Neither Zephyr nor Evergarden were going to be combat capable for a while after that forced crash.

Triumphant, both Chip-Monks stood on their smoking remains, snapping into a dabbed pose before punching the air in front of them a few times, as if both of these hamster-rejects were going through the motions of a martial form.

Before Lenore could shout orders, she learned important secrets that changed them. The Way of Excommunicado did not do what she assumed. With both of the Chip-Monks activating the skill at the same time as they reached the correct movement, her eyes got plenty of worrisome information.

A red circle with that word present under the outer edge blipped into being above the monks. Filling with the symbolism of a red skull adorned with a crown, the floral innards of the circle completed as the chipmunks paw-struck the downed ships in unison. Zephyr and Evergarden both turned bright red before being booted out of Eternia with a single red blink.

The missive she got from Nightshade confirmed her worries.

Ding!

———

Message from: Brianna of Nightshade.

Excommunicado does not deal reputation damage per hit. That particular martial arts move does something much worse. Excommunicado tosses you out Eternia entirely! My Moon Elves say that both ships just showed up in Cal. Evergarden is in pieces, and there's a turtle stuck on his back between all the wreckage. Zephyr is back in an Elf form, but she looks rough and is being rushed to the bunnies.

————

Lenore's hand snapped to her brooch. "Change of plans! Don't get hit by that move above all else. IcyHot, take Theodore. Nightshade, fell Simon. The mobs are—"

The Lady of Iron turned pale as twenty new Thunderhorns spawned in and burst out of the snow less than a hundred feet from her, but those were not the cause of her distress. Twenty Thunderhorns merely signaled the addition of a new combatant. One that had coiled out of the red blip of Simon's victim as Zephyr got booted from the game.

Not amused by having his leisurely walk interrupted, Señor Louis unspooled from the person-tight confines that he had adopted for convenience. Mantis blades first, he made his presence known by sticking them into and through a nearby spine.

The wet, living, fleshy, sharp blades pierced Simon with cringeworthy damage. Damage that was joined by an eel-like form which entrapped and coiled around the mid-boss. Unfortunately for the Chip-Monk, those blades cut ever deeper and wider gashes as the horrifying tri-skull monstrosity continued to grow without end, at a frighteningly fast pace.

The fate of Simon, who was soon stabbed by far worse than mantis blades, was sealed.

Unceremonious, and certainly annoyed, Señor Louis bit the chipmunk's head off. Tearing the rest of the body up from within with sheer force, the eldritch horror roared out a high-pitched, tinnitus-inspiring screech. One that made stack after stack of failed Will-save prompts appear and compound for every local player. While it was ongoing, that single screech forced everyone to cover their ears as a sudden flurry of waking nightmares and mental debuffs hit them.

"No más!" Still annoyed, but having gotten both a treat and vengeance against the rude chipmunk, Señor Louis absconded back into space with what was clearly his afternoon snack.

Lenore had failed to let go of her brooch, but was the first to be free of negative mind-affecting statuses. The feeling had been terrible and terrifying, but she was Lenore the Iron, and she would stand and lead when everyone else feared to.

Steadying herself and trying not to let the recent sights get to her, she croaked out a change of plans as Señor Louis disappeared into the depths of space. "I am so glad that thing was on our side. I am going to pretend it was. Nightshade? Focus on Theodore along with IcyHot. I will hold the line against the Thunderhorns."

Releasing her brooch as she didn't have time for a reply, she found her strength when both of her hands squeezed the Tsuka of her O'Dachi. The new Thunderhorns were already charging her. One bleated at her with great cacophony, sending a paralytic cry her way so she would stand there and take the bonk head on. Lenore bit through the effect, leaned forward, and counter charged as her blade flared with might. She spoke flawless Sheep; how dare they think that an insult to her mother was going to root her to the spot?

Ten Thunderhorns experienced instant regret as her weapon sailed and sliced through their flock, leaving a Nike wave of lingering death behind.

When she came to a standstill on packed snow, she shifted her grip to follow up on the remaining ten. Lenore felt the sun hit her back like hands to support her shoulders, and accepted only victory as she leaned into a brand-new combat style, her soul aflame with determination. "Sunshine Style, Morning Dew."

CHAPTER FIFTY-TWO

Artorian was a fool, but not a fool that would fool around when something actually clever was hot on his tail. The Tortoise had no eyes, but Artorian wasn't going to pretend that the glint of cleverness and malice wasn't there, bright and shiny for all to see.

This old Tortoise was not the kind of dumb, shambling undead you could tell stories of to a group of giggling children. This Oogway was the kind of undead that had originated from something with wit, and was now bent to the will of something far more evil-aligned. In another life? Oogway would have been a fast friend. In current circumstances? Artorian wasn't going to be able to play around, nor take this bout anything except seriously. His nose was shaking him by the lapels, but Artorian was ahead of his nose.

"Ad Astra." Copying the colors of Trans Am, since the system knew what he meant, Dreadshine turned white and blue. Along with that change, Artorian received an unwelcome notice. What was Quackbang doing here?

Uack!

Message from: Quackbang.

Your calculation engine and associated chosen Dungeon Core are incapacitated, or no longer in Eternia. Their services have been suspended; you will be assigned a new Dungeon Core at random to continue experiencing quality gameplay.

Uack!

Assigned Core: Boreas, Dungeon Core of stormwind and winter.
Warning: This Dungeon is Fowl.

Artorian blinked, not liking that he hadn't gotten a choice. Since he was freefalling to the Murim Woods, perhaps it was not the best time to be snarky about hotfixed help? Not leaning on Voltekka's voice modulation, Grandpa tried conversation. "A cold core against a cold foe? What a chilling choice. Hello Boreas, are you a talker?"

Buh-gawk!

Artorian reminded himself to stay calm. They had assigned him a Rooster? A *Chicken*. What kind of Karma was this? "Never mind, Boreas. Nice to have you, and a pleasant cluck to you as well. Can you run my numbers?"

―――――

Buh-gawk!

―――――

If there was a difference between those chicken calls, Artorian couldn't tell. "Grandpa's gonna take that as a yes and move the cluck on. Quackbang? Alternatives?"

Uack!

―――――

Information: Alternate Dungeon Cores Available.
  Currently Assigned: Storm Core, Boreas.
  Dungeon Thematic: Pale Reminder.
  Populating other Beast-Typed Dungeons.

―――――

Origin - Beast:
  Wasp Core - Vajra.
  Dungeon Thematic: Caves of Ambrosia.
  Bee Core - Honey.
  Dungeon Thematic: Flower Glades.
  Goose Core - Untitled.
  Dungeon Thematic: Quack.
  T-Rex Core - Munchies.
  Dungeon Thematic: Park.
  Tiger Core - ElCazorro.
  Dungeon Thematic: Desert Tavern.
  Lizard Core - Ogden.
  Dungeon Thematic: Oasis Tavern.
  Raccoon Core - Rack.
  Dungeon Thematic: Smuggling Operation.
  Skunk Core - Smellums.

Dungeon Thematic: Parfumerie.
Squirrel Core - Cheeks.
Dungeon Thematic: Mount Nut.
C'towl Core - Madame Mew.
Dungeon Thematic: The Original Crème de la Crème à la Edgar.
Basher Core - Schnell.
Dungeon Thematic: Race Track.
Cat Core - Poussin Boots.
Dungeon Thematic: Cuddle Corner - The Scratching Post.

Uack!
Available Beast Origin List Complete.
Populating Special Entry.

Origin - People:
Goblin Core - P'Dunk.
Dungeon Thematic: Shiny Loot Cave.

"Goblins got classed as people? Nice!" That made his day. That must have been one firetrap of a debate. "What was the rule again? Anything with a core or crystal is a Beast, anything without just a normal animal? I do recall something about Bob using a cultivation technique."

Artorian wondered if Dale ever had a core. If he did, would that have made him a Beast? He shook the thought from his head, for it went to a terrible place. "The first time Dale ever says 'rawr,' Minya's arm would be down his throat and getting that core out of him. Her only response would be, 'Minya, kill.' *Mhm*, I can see it now."

Uack!

———

Would you like to know more?

———

Artorian could pick from this list, he supposed. Anything beat out the chicken. He did not want to hear a *buh-gawk* every time he got a message. That would drive him bonkers. Quackbang was saving his sanity right now. He should oblige. "Keep it going until something stands out, or the fat lady sings. This fall could use some elevator music."

Quackbang confirmed that with the expected noise.

Uack!

"Thank you, Jodocus." Knowing he wasn't going to fall forever, it oddly felt like he'd barely gone down at all with how the light from the ceiling gap didn't change. The only consistent factor in his drop was Oogway's flawless chase, and an ever-diminishing number of falling Thunderhorns that got snagged on something sharp.

Something sharp tended to be the walls, which were closing in. Oogway, who had matched his own centered-as-possible position, was unfortunately going to be fine.

Uack!

———

Inquiry: You remembered my name? How unexpectedly kind.
Populating information.

———

Origin - Natural Dungeon:
Volcano Dungeon - Dregs.
Dungeon Thematic: Volcano Innards, Active.
Bag Dungeon - Mu.

Dungeon Thematic: Dire Turkeys.

Origin - Silverwood Dungeon:
  Harris Hawk - Caladrius.
  Dungeon Thematic: The Hall of Scrolls Art Museum.
  Cloud Giant - Roberts the Ruminating.
  Dungeon Thematic: Cyclopean Tomb.

"Stop!" Artorian snatched the prompt from the air to pull the screen against his helmet. "Did I hear that narration right? Roberts the Ruminating. From Skyspear's olden times? The same source that Lucia and others have been getting gameplay lessons from? Please tell me they're one and the same."

Uack!

Information: Affirmative.
  Would you like to replace Boreas with this choice?

Artorian used his face to accept the prompt. "Gib!"

B-doop!

The notification sound was akin to a drop of water falling into a larger puddle, with all the discord that ensued. The sniff of waking up from thinking followed, as if from a person already awake, but not fully present until that moment. The voice of Roberts was gritty, cultured, low, and like every realization was a revelation. "Your tongue knows how everything you look at will feel."

The Core then realized he was supposed to be using prompts instead of talking to a player directly, and fixed that.

B-doop!

———

Hello. I am Roberts, the ultimate source of shower thoughts.

CHAPTER FIFTY-THREE

Grandpa-torian kept zero metallic alterations from Voltekka in his words as he got all giddy. He beamed like a love bug named Herbie. "What a pleasant surprise! Hello! Your statues were all over Skyspear, though I never thought you were a Cloud Giant. How quaint! I admit, I have a thousand and one questions, and some of them are from about half a billion years ago, give or take a stone's throw with a timeline or two."

B-doop!

———

This puddle is exuberant, and cannot wait to ruminate upon the ripples of your pond water. To be a Cloud Giant is a choice, not a fate I was saddled with. In the wise words of Mew the Second, 'The circumstances of one's birth are irrelevant. It is what you do with the gift of life that determines who you are.'

I cannot wait to exsanguinate the topic of Dungeon Core body options. All the new discoveries and advances have me salivating for the next update nearly as much as I do when encountering pistachio-flavored ice cream.

Mmmmmm. Pistachio.

Before that? As I push my reading glasses up the nonexistent nose of my Core and catch up on recent events, I must inform you that an impending recent event will impact your situation. A scheduled meeting with… the itinerary says 'the floor'? Is going to put a damper on our conversation. This puddle currently can't help you yet, but I can run your numbers. Are you able to muddle along until I can?

———

Taking a page right out of Raile's playbook, Artorian shifted his attention to the problems at hand. "I keep calm, carry on, and muddle along! *B-doop* me!"

Roberts the Ruminating confirmed that with a cheery *b-doop*!

"This is so much better than a buh-gawk!" Needing to actually pay attention, he confirmed that impact with the ground was imminent. A realization knocked on his door, handed him a paper, and Artorian felt silly after review. Opening and closing his wings of light, he sighed. "Y'know, I have been making wings of light since the earliest of days. Why did I stop doing that? They were so effective. Polly? How are you holding up?"

The deflated *plfblrblblrt* of a raspberry being blown was enough of an indicator that Polly was out of the fight. The limit to the size of Aura Blade might have been hefty, but Polly was pooped after letting all of that energy go in one big blast. Stowing Ex-Calibur back into his bracelet, he continued the rounds. "Tekka? Holding on?"

Tekka also giving him the deflated *plfblrblblr* was unexpected, but Artorian would have to roll with the punches. His dinosaur sent him feelings and imagery of being really hot during the fall, and then suddenly really cold in Midgard. The duality had put cracks in his seamless plate, and he wasn't doing so hot as a result. Tekka could handle either the hot, or the cold, but not both. "We made it, and that's what matters. You did well, Tekka, take a break."

With a happy roar, the seamless plate swirled off his being, unmorphing and being recouped by the Core in his chest. This was not looking great for a one versus one against an end-boss, but what was he gonna do? He valued his connections and adored people more than the benefits they happened to give him. It was a matter of priorities, and making sure they felt considered. "Since that changes the plan, I may as well alter the narrative. Rejuvenescence."

In a flash of light, Grandpa-torian was Young-torian. His beach attire had been swapped out for his Faith Foundry pajamas, but those weren't going to cut it here. Shame that he had no other gear.

Piiii!

While Blanket could not read his thoughts, the Sugar Glider would most definitely not agree with that statement. Shooting past the end-boss at Mach speeds to slam into Young-torian's chest—to the unhappy sounds of his health bar—Blanket chirped in victory. He'd made it in time! Artorian had called for him earlier, and the Glider had scrambled to get going.

Waiting for neither confirmation nor initiative, Blanket chirped and hugged Artorian before shifting into his itemized Eternia form! A clothing set that was some odd cross between a tracksuit, a hoodie with glider wings, and a martial arts Gi.

Granted, those items came in stacking layers, and the hoodie had the most adorable little ears.

Young-torian implicitly felt what Blanket was able to do, and traded his light wings for glider wings. Once he cleared the ceiling of the Murim Woods, he transitioned from a fall into a clean glide. "Blanket, you beauty of a Beast! That's where your group got the name from, didn't they?"

Artorian forgot his voice had changed, momentarily taken aback by it. "I will get used to that one day. Until there comes a day where I no longer have to. On with the show! Glad you're here, Blankie. I see you went for clothes instead of armor? You'll definitely get hurt less that way. I'll check your full stats later. We gotta make some advantages over that Tortoise first!"

"Ufufufufufu." Pope Oogway, considerably smaller in size, found that terribly amusing. Nearly matching Artorian's current child-like height by a difference of maybe an inch, the undead elderly rime Tortoise floated next to them on a literal cloud. One that appeared pasty and thick, like it was plucked from the brush strokes of a painting.

Artorian hadn't expected an undead boss mob to be able to chat.

Oogway's smug, overtly amused, and slightly condescending words came accompanied with a repeated staff-bop to the top of Young-torian's head. As if the Tortoise was giving him head-pats. With a big smile, the Tortoise sounded all wiser-than-thou with a surprisingly smooth and fun-seeking tone that Artorian didn't expect an undead could have. "Oogway knew it was right to abandon destiny and follow you. This will prove far more amusing. Yes-yes."

Artorian, arms-wide to use the glider feature of his hoodie, decided on combining in light-wings anyway in order to both take a sharp turn and nose-dive toward the Murim Woods.

Oogway thought that too, was terribly funny, and he poked a single spot on Young-torian's back. "No, you don't."

This poke completely cramped up the youngster, preventing him from taking that action as his body locked up for a moment and sent him tumbling into a freefall. "*Yeowch*! Why did that poke hurt?! Pokes aren't supposed to hurt!"

"Ufufufufufu!" Pope Oogway clapped, on a leisurely descent after Artorian with his fancy schmancy comfort cloud. Artorian wanted a comfort cloud! "Come now, show me, show me. I may no longer feel after becoming an undead, but my tail tingle never betrays me. You're different, and fun! I would like some fun. Amuse Pope Oogway! I will keep my malice packed away in my shell if you do. What you say? *Hmmm*?"

Hypermobility hard-carried him. Artorian was too busy bouncing across the Murim canopy that was slowly recovering and showing the first signs of fresh bioluminescent greenery as new plants grew on the deadwood. The new plants loved all that delicious nitrogen. Nom nom!

When he hopped down and could slow down to a mere run on the ground, Oogway was already overhead, blocking out exactly his shape with the cloud's shadow as light poured in through the new ceiling crack above.

Young-torian grabbed the trunk of a dead tree to help with a sharp turn, but Hypermobility couldn't help him with that one. The deadwood crumbled under his fingers and forced him into a hard roll that sent him crashing through several more trees. A painful experience that was followed up with an energy-shaped palm-strike from above that flattened him and all the space around him.

B-doop!

————

Trait: 'Loved by Mana' considered the Martial Arts Move: 'Shelling Palm' to be irritating, as it uses Chi, rather than Mana. Loved by Mana warns that none of the tricks of the entity: 'Pope Oogway' can be interacted with. Shield up!

————

Artorian had beaten Loved by Mana to the punch, currently moderately safe in—amusingly enough—a turtle-shell shield-projection. The irony. "I'm gonna get Momma Lucia the *best* Timothy hay."

Pushing himself up, he cycled into his Field of Sleep Aura. Oogway landed, leaned on his frozen walking papal ferula stick, and smacked his lips. "*Ufufufuuu!* Tasty! That would have done me in had I been a living being. Undead don't appear affected. Still, Oogway like! Another!"

Artorian swapped to Pressure, which buckled the rime Tortoise down a few inches while flattening all the surrounding landscape and deadwood that Shelling Palm had missed! Aha! Progress! Plus, a bonus arena. All the better for a good bout.

Smacking his lips again, Oogway pushed up against the effect and performed a curious wiggle. "How fun! I seem to be too strong to handle this potion you are serving me. Let us try a different drink."

Both astounded and feeling downright grumbly, Youngtorian didn't bother with unloading 'The Oof.' Anything he could attract by annoying everything in his environment wasn't going to hold a candle to this opponent. Oogway would knock them all out of the way.

Shifting back into his tried-and-true Cleaning Presence, the rime Tortoise curiously inspected himself as a pasty vapor bled out of him. "Oh my, I appear to be smoking and taking damage? Yes, yes, that is the minimum requirement. It would be boring if I smacked you down one-sidedly."

Artorian momentarily felt really bad about what he did to Pag. Mostly because the Tortoise had a point. He did like that his Aura cleaned him up from his fresh and splintery tumble as he got up enough to hop on his toes and brush himself off. "Why me?"

"There are no accidents." Oogway looked at him with those empty eye sockets of his, then momentarily couldn't suppress the obvious, oozing malice that poured free like a sickening miasma. The rime Tortoise wiggled the bottom of his walking stick at Artorian's chest. "I have no heart. You have two. I thought, maybe you have one spare?"

This clued Artorian in that Oogway could see in one of the many non-traditional senses of the word. What did he have? Developer view of outlines? Future-sight? See-through-ness? "Apologies, oogie-boogie, I need both. Can I maybe interest you in a stabbing?"

Moving his arms wide, Sowwo and Compassion both unsealed themselves from his inventory and floated in a half-circle around him. He took hold of them with Telekinesis rather than with his hands, but that did leave them free!

He had to squint for a moment as he did. Had the uchi-gatana just pulled a prank on him? He could have sworn he thought of Sorrow with Ws instead of Rs. The katana was already heavily leaning on him with wide-eyes and eye-brow thumping mental imagery to use the villain mode color themat-ics, while Compassion replied with a nose-scrunched look of disgust. Clearly Trans Am was the way to stay. Oogway had too much purple in that miasma effect for Artorian to consider Windu; he didn't feel like the villain here, and Divinity was too much.

Oogway, stowing his malice back into his shell, stole Artori-an's move of the pensive beard rub. Even if the Tortoise lacked any such beard. "*Mmm…* Oogway does not find this interesting."

Artorian felt insulted. "You know what? I'm gonna pull something out of my pocket, just for you."

This intrigued Oogway, who lit up and papped his front paws together. Hands? What was the correct name for turtle appendages? Let's go with those being called hands for now. An explosion in the distance distracted them both. An accompa-nying heat wave that set nearby deadwood on fire was easy enough to ignore, but the sight of a black and white Panda getting utterly trashed black and blue by Astarte was a pleasant sight.

Artorian forgot all about being insulted, his expression dreamy and voice bubbly. "Ah, there's my sweetheart!"

Oogway had far more to be interested in all of a sudden. His face made several back and forth squinting and scrunching movements, as if internal calculations were being reshuffled. Oogway clearly believed that he was going to mop the floor with Artorian, but the associations with someone who was going to be a very different matchup changed that deliberation.

"Anyway!" Artorian pulled himself back to task, and slid into a martial stance of his own as he changed out where his energy was being directed. Dropping the stationary shell, the image of a tree flickered over his body before dimming out of sight. A personal shield was better than a stationary one if you planned to move around! "You know Fancy-Fu. I know Fancy-Fu. Let us learn more Fu, together."

"Ufufufufufu!" Oogway laughed with his head and neck bobbing, loving this. "You are a foolish youngster. Oogway likes you."

CHAPTER FIFTY-FOUR

The rime Tortoise lolled himself back and forth. "Unfortunately, Oogway is no fool. Oogway would like to fight you, but has a proposition for you."

The master leaned on his stick, and adjusted his pope hat. "I would like to fight you *properly*. In the right venue. Not some burning backwood where if I fall, I fall forgotten. That is dull. Not to mention the extra weight that currently lies on your shoulders. I am no fan of being pressed for time, youngster, no matter how much of it I have. That final cold wave from Fuyu weighs on your mind, and our fun together."

Stealing another move from Artorian, the Tortoise tapped the side of his flat nose with his papal stick. "You know that if you keep hashing it out with me down here, there's a very good chance you won't get back up there in time to do things that matter to you. Your sweetheart may, but *you* won't, and it's written all over your Aura that you want to be there."

Artorian despised that the Tortoise was right, his face a pure scowl. "I'm listening."

Oogway tried so hard not to let his undead miasma and malice break free, but the wrinkled face couldn't stop itself from betraying his true feelings. The decidedly evil undead wanted to play with his food. "I let you go! I make something nice down here. You come back after. Fuyu is about to hit New Haven up there with its last wave in a few minutes. You'll need that time just to make it up there, even if the lady of pure heat currently rapidly approaching us flies you up."

The Tortoise looked up, finding this all so very interesting. "We're in the lower layers of the woods, not the top layers that are conveniently close to the bottom of that central shaft. What a strange thing to see from all the way down here. It's like that generator and associated structure is alive."

Without changing the rest of his stance, only his face craned creepily towards Artorian. "That sword of yours cut deep. Do bring it? I don't know why it's not in your hands, and that disappoints me. Something must be wrong. You're fighting me with an arm tied behind your back. I don't like it. If I'm not the one responsible for making you squirm on the ground, then I'm not happy. Showing up to a bout with a handicap... *Bleh*."

True to his word, Astarte burned into view while on a beeline vector towards them, the ripped-off head of a Panda still roasting in her offhand. Oogway didn't have to look, he nodded and knew it was true. "Good proposition, no? You go do what's important to you, now. You come back at the beginning of your next... What do we call it? Volume? Book? Yes, come back at the beginning of your next book, and make *me* the first big adventure before you venture off. I want lots of your time, more than you currently have. I want a proper boss battle. Not some rushed bout. I wish to learn more about Fu with you. I'll even let the lady coach you from the sidelines."

The Tortoise clicked his tongue. "I wish I had an audience, or more contestants."

Astarte arrived ready to roll and prepared to throw down, only to find her boy and an elderly turtle chatting away and making some backroom deal. The heat in the local area spiked, but as her feet touched the ground, she controlled that output to observe the goings on. Her Elven ears had easily picked up the majority conversation on her way over, and she too was pressed to get to New Haven herself. That cold wave really was coming.

"*Mmm...*" Young-torian recalled his weapons, who both pouted at the lack of battle. "Roberts. Thoughts?"

B-doop!

———

Min your Maxes. Max your Mins.

The race here is not against the enemy's health, but against your own mistakes per minute. I will tell you of my favorite lesson that I love to teach: When there is doubt, there is no doubt. Trust your instincts and trust your doubts, for to doubt is to question.

A pool reflects best when it is still. Trust your questions, and begin with certainty, with stillness. Reflect, then act with that certainty. Action disturbs stillness, disturbance changes perspective, and perspective leads to new questions. When you lose perspective, return to stillness, then, act with certainty.

From what I gather, your main fighting style is: 'No, you don't.' You can stop an action in motion. You play a counter. Oogway seems to have your predecessor. His style is: 'No, you didn't.' He can stop a thing from happening in the first place. He plays with action negation.

Your matchup isn't good, even if you can create his damage vulnerability types, and Cleaning Presence is slowly scrubbing away his health. I don't know why that works yet.

If you want puddle advice? Take the deal.

B-doop, out.

———

Artorian extended his hand. "Deal."

"Ufufufufufu." Oogway reached out with his walking stick and tapped Artorian's open palm, his wicked smile spreading from ear to ear. A most unsettling sight when combined with those vacant and dark eye sockets. "Then by my fancy pope hat, I will see you when you slink back like a heathen cat."

Turning on his stick, the rime Tortoise merrily waddled off

while talking to himself. "I'm thinking… an arena? Yes. Something large, and official. Something where all squares make a circle. Maybe in some kind of confined cell? I could call it the cell games? *Oooh*… Why stop there? A Tournament of Power! *Mmm*, we can make that better. Something fancy. Budokai? Yes, The Tenkaichi Budōkai. The Number One Under Heaven Martial Arts Gathering! I like it! That's what I'll do with the Murim Woods. Make it all about Martial Arts! Oogway, out!"

Artorian watched the rime Tortoise go as an evil fit of giggles erupted from Oogway's direction. "I may have just made a horrible mistake, but he was right about every last celestial feces slathered little thing. Sugar, can you fly us to New Haven?"

The skull in her hand had become dark and flaky. Staining her skin. The remains in her hand turned to what was probably coal before she threw it away. Cleaning Presence cleaned the stains right up regardless.

Not interested in what was left of an unworthy opponent, Dawn instead leaned over and played with the adorable little ears on his hoodie. She was taller now, given she had aged up, and Artorian had aged down. "*Mhm*! Don't fuss about the deal, sugar. We do what we gotta do. Is that Blanket? This is adorable! You look so precious in your soft, sporty little fluff-bundle. Now you hold on tight. We have a good way to go, and don't mind the forest fire. The place needed to burn."

Not about to argue, Artorian wondered how to do that. Then he sighed, and moved his arms up so Dawn could pick him up. Something she'd clearly been waiting for as she scooped him from his feet with a humongous smile. Artorian snuck her some side-eye. So she got fussy if she was young, and he was old. But all was right as rain if she was old, and he was young? *Uhu.* Sure. No double standard to be found here or anything. He sighed again, dropped it, and squeezed his arms around her neck as she carried him with one-handed ease.

Dawn nodded. She seemed to be able to read his mind just

fine, and kissed the top of his head. "Don't fuss. I'm happy. Vongola Burst."

"I'm not fussing!" Artorian fussed as he lied, like a liar.

Dawn smirked, giggled, and held him close as she took off like a fire-propelled Gnomish rocket.

He grumbled about several things not having gone according to plan. How was Oogway even trusting him to come back at all? *Oh,* who was he kidding? He was going back and throwing the gauntlet down. There would be a satisfying fight! He wanted it! It was exciting!

Young-torian huffed all indignant, still fussy. "Fine. New Haven, then a rest, then an Oogway. I want one more big fight before we book it out of Eternia. I want to walk around the rest of Avalon with you. See all the segments. I don't know... do some paperwork. I'm starting to miss paperwork."

Dawn giggled louder. Her face was starting to hurt from smiling too hard as his antics tickled her in all the best ways. "You make me happy, sugar. We'll be there soon. I'm going straight to the generator. I can push heat into the system and keep the structure warm, but all that warm is going to bleed out."

Artorian's mind instantly flipped over to solutions, but he kicked himself from the pun. Cal had far too great an influence on him. "I may have to wait for my time with the turtle, but I have one shell of a shield to help with that!"

He squirmed in mock pain and groaned instantly after. "Nope. Still hurts. Can't do it."

Dawn couldn't stop laughing the entire way back to New Haven.

CHAPTER FIFTY-FIVE

Dun-dun-dunnnn!

———

World Event: The City Must Survive.
  Final phase!
  A cold wave of minus one-hundred and fifty Celsius is in effect.
  Survive!

———

Lenore marched into the central-most chamber of New Haven to a lot of sniffling and shivering. The generator wasn't able to keep up, and most everyone who had mana to spare had already been pouring their supply onto the pile. Anything to keep the pilot light lit and the heat going. No matter how much their environment creaked, cracked, or fell apart around them.

The sudden addition of biting cold in between breaks of heat played havoc with New Haven's structure, and the main shaft itself was already leaning. A slight tilt to a big structure made a big difference when the floor was no longer flat, and the continued popping shelves of remaining ice made a terrifying noise when they moved the tiniest bit.

Worst of all, they had been out of food for a while, and had lost an entire wing of supplies when those chambers had simply... fallen off the rest of the ice structure. One moment they had stores of behemoth meat, the other they had exposed hallways billowing with frostbite.

Everyone who survived was huddled together, but no food and severely reduced energy regeneration of any kind was causing pain. The players with heftier statistics were holding out longer, but even the veterans and advanced parties had come home tapped. Multiple days and waves of Thunderhorns, with some of them getting in and wrecking pipelines, had been a bad time. The cold fronts had been manageable, but New Haven's populace and adventuring parties had been forced to retreat closer and closer to the generator every time.

While it was warmest there, the air by this point was toxic. A feature that the Mechanicus Steamlord apologized for, but could do nothing about if they wanted heat. They could either breathe the fresh, crispy air of frostbite, or the cough-inducing pollutant of all that carbon dioxide it spewed out. A funny Gnomish name for the pollutants that got trapped in after the roof had collapsed. With the generator floor already being a quasi-basin after all the buckling, it didn't matter that carbon dioxide was heavier than air. The people had to go somewhere, and staying still on a slanted surface while low on stamina was a bad time.

The slip and slide problem was real, and when someone slid right into an invisible cloud of carbon dioxide and couldn't clamber their way back out fast enough? That was game. All in all? This was a celestial feces show, and Abyssed all around.

Lenore stabbed her O'Dachi into the metal ground next to the generator and left it there, using the handle as leverage to pull herself up those few extra inches so her hand could grasp onto one of the exposed mana pipes. Those rods that had been peeled free from the generator so people could feed the device in great numbers. Back when they had great numbers. "Status report."

Everyone in the vicinity groaned; those farther away didn't even give her that. Shaka gave her a miserable look, but at least he reacted. They'd lost Tom and Valhalla to the Chip-Monk before Team Nightshade could show up to end the problem. He was in a poor mood, and far from his jovial self. Having tapped out of mana a while ago, he was watching his mana regeneration occasionally dip into the negatives.

The area was tapped, that was all there was to it.

Too many people with too much draw all added to the growing problem that everyone was out of mana, and nobody could replenish while they were all packed in like sardines on an ever-increasing height level. They couldn't get rid of the carbon dioxide by dumping it to deeper levels anymore. That had been an early solution. Now, those pathways had the frozen variant of the stuff clogging them all up. Not something they'd wanted to see. Turned out that carbon dioxide was a gas at room temperature, but freezes solid at a much lower point than water: minus one-hundred-nine degrees Fahrenheit, or minus seventy-eight Celsius. A threshold that the biting chill outside laughed at any time the frost waves came in, which was of course, when they needed to dump the pollutant the most.

Adding in her last few hundred points before she got sick and her meter tapped out, Lenore released a defeated bleat and let go of the pipe. Shaking her hand while feeling unwell, she looked out over her people and failed to contend with the reality.

All that work, and still, eradication was pending.

A loud explosion rocked the structure, tilting the shaft even more on its axis as New Haven groaned. That was a bad sign.

Until Dawn kicked the door in with Artorian in her arms, who was shooting everyone a big smile and double-V symbols as his Cleaning Presence began scrubbing that carbon dioxide pool away like that one bathroom stain you needed to spend an hour on. It was going to die. It was. Complete with the squeaky noises and curse-filled shouting.

"Guess who's baaaaack!" Dawn, with her fire-flight, pushed through the new hole she'd made and head-smashed some extra room in order to make it through without a hitch. The howling cold followed her, but she clearly did not care. As far as Dawn was concerned, this problem was solved. Especially with some of the things that her boy had told her about on the way. "With great news!"

Everyone was hungry for good news. Great news was even better, but that wouldn't fill an empty stomach. Which, Artorian and Dawn knew, was the bit that made it great. Putting Youngtorian down as he raised both his arms, Dawn made her way directly to the generator. She sat on the machine, slapped a rear panel, and winked at the confused Mechanicus Steamlord before pouring a frankly ridiculous amount of heat into the process. "Hey, hot stuff."

Artorian laughed and watched her flirt with an innocent Golem, who sputtered now that the energy was being provided to the generator. With that first matter well in hand, he took care of both that pesky air-quality problem and another minor nuisance. "I brought food!"

This declaration, while initially positive, was followed up by a sight and sound that made hopeful faces turn to screaming mouths.

A swarm of *Bees*!

The screaming went on for so long that people didn't notice an important detail. Each Serenity Bee smuggled in a carefully bundled package of sliced, diced, and roasted meat. The meat was unrecognizable, and after a few seconds on an exposed heat pipe, smelled divine to the weary and hungry alike. The few that figured out the origin of the meat tactically kept their mouths shut. Preferably around a second helping.

"Why is the world slanted? Let's fix that." Annoyed by the

central shaft's tilt within the minute, Artorian light-shifted solid panels into place with some small aeration holes. Purely so people could stop awkwardly hanging onto the slanted flooring. That bowl also annoyed him, so it was included in the floorplan.

This solved the food and air issue in about five minutes flat as the Serenity Bees barreled in and out of the area with all the brusk shoulder-bashing efficiency of Dwarven marines. The Alliance of Cold could suck their pollen, Serenity Bees braved the very depths of the black! Against a wee little bit of cold? People would be fed, and they'd be coming back. With a bonus brown coat added to each and every delivery.

Did people need more than one brown coat? Probably not. Were they getting multiple? A-buzzling-lutely. Artorian topped this off by slapping down his area of effect stationary shell shield. Thanks to lessons from Lucia, he traded out its durability and thickness for size without too much trouble.

With the entire room encased in a warmth-retaining cocoon, and his Aura keeping all the air tip-top? Along with giving everyone a good scrub, the dreary mood was turned upside down in fifteen at the most.

The shield stopped more food deliveries, but by the time the turtle-shell shield was up and running, those had been expended. All in all, Artorian laid on the flattened light-panel floor, exhaled deep from being on time, and shot everyone a thumbs up as if he was on his last remaining digit of HP. The endeavor had not been damaging, but it had definitely been draining on the psyche.

New Haven would make it.

The city would survive.

So long as nothing creaked.

Artorian squinted at the ceiling. He'd just jinxed himself, hadn't he? "Lenore!"

The Iron Lady, now steady in her footing, clicked her heels over to the new floor-layer when called. Her steps left minor illumination behind. She was tired, but food had put pep in her step. "My Divine?"

A devious plan was already midway to forming, the gears spinning to life behind his eyes. "What all actually *counts* as New Haven? Is it the structure? Or is it the *people?*"

Not certain she understood the intent of the question, Lenore related what she knew without pause. She didn't know where her Divine was going with this, but when the person in progress of solving all your problems was on a roll? You didn't stop that ball. "The generator is a person, and considered part of the New Haven people. We lose if all the inhabitants perish. We lose if all the adventurers perish. So I suppose... none of the structure matters, and it's all about the people."

New Haven creaking again with threatening pops that buckled part of the ceiling, which Artorian could see directly above him, made the decision process particularly snappy. "Thank you, Paladin Lenore."

He sprung up and clapped his hands together. "New plan! Dawny! Rip the generator from her housing. We're going mobile! Where's Lucia? I need her!"

Dawn threw her head back, cackled, and pulled out a bag before getting up. The Mechanicus operating the generator could be heard going '*nonononono*' in the background. Upturning that bag, Lucia tumbled right out. She enlarged moment by moment until she reached full size in her Glitterflit form, and posed magnanimously on arrival. "Momma Bun is here!"

She stretched, popped all over, and bristled with pleasant chittering in the Cleaning Presence field as the Aura gave her a good once-over. "That is never going to get old."

Once she was stretched and settled, she pressed her hands to her hips as she shifted into her human form and her ears flopped out. "What do y'all need?"

Artorian grinning wide betrayed that she was in for one of those fabled wild rides. "I need you to take over shielding duties, because I am going to need all my Determination to make a sliding ramp out of hard-light for the downwards borehole that

Astarte is going to melt for us. All we need to finish the quest is for the people to survive until the storm is over. Nothing in that quest says we have to do that here. In this collapsing, buckling, and falling apart remnant."

Young-torian put his fingers to his mouth and whistled sharp. "Everyone find a buckle on your new brown trench coat and strap in! Dawny? Let 'er rip!"

Lucia cursed a thousand curses as, without any more warning, Artorian let his shell-shield go. "Boy!"

After pulling out the Mechanicus Steamlord and setting her down in the middle of a very concerned group of people, Astarte rubbed her knuckles against her chest and walked to what she deemed to be the front. They wanted to voice their complaints, but were stuck between the rock of that maybe not being a good idea, and the hard place that they couldn't really stop the Divines if they tried.

Lucia got her own shield up as Dawn used that shell as brand-new footing. Pressing her hands together, she began rhyming out words that sounded something akin to turtle-wave. Ka-Me... something. Lucia only caught the roaring '*ha*,' before the floor turned into vacant space. As her entire protective shell began the slip and slide into freefall, that vacant space was filled with hard light railings. The protective barrier shaped into a half-tube anywhere there was open space rather than icy flooring. Similar railings were added to the inside of the shell as well. Complete with bucket seats and something to hold for dear life.

Shaka sat in a bucket seat and strapped in, starting the warcry. "Alululululululu!"

Down the entire populace of New Haven went, the whole city going right down the tubes in a wild adventure where everyone could do nought but find a seat, hold on, and pray. Admittedly, Artorian received a lot of new D.E. point pop-ups. He hadn't seen Divine Energy in a while! "That can wait! Dawny! I'm running out of open track too fast. Escalate!"

Going faster was not what the populace of New Haven was

hoping for, but when the adventuring groups gave in, joined Shaka, and shot their hands up to have one scream of a good time? The local inhabitants knew this was a one-way trip, regardless of the outcome. New Haven as a structure proved that when it crumbled above them. The big hole in the ground carved out by Astarte's sustained incineration blast, combined with Artorian's earlier addition of a new canyon, killed all the necessary critical support infrastructure to keep any of it where it was.

A race against time, this was not. The populace had enacted their evacuation via a mad plan far too early for the collapse to have been a problem. Astarte was doing well on her heat supply, Artorian was having—at worst—limited difficulty with the floors and rail, and Lucia empowered herself and kept her shield steady via an unyielding and unending holy verse filled with nothing but curses. Which Artorian got D.E. points for as well, as they were mostly about him.

This mad journey lasted until they'd breached the first, second, and third layers of the Murim Woods. Their trajectory flattened out in the fourth, bottom-most layer. The sight that greeted them amused Artorian to no end. Oogway had completed his first arena! He was upset at it. One of the corner pieces was wrong.

Channeling Effortless Sound Shaping, his voice boomed ahead of him. "Hey, Oogway! I heard you were starting a martial arts tournament. Do you need some contestants and people for the stands? I brought some!"

Oogway looked up, didn't believe what he saw, and threw down his walking stick. "You are my new favorite person."

Artorian laughed, Oogway laughed, Dawn laughed, and the arena laughed. Dawn blew up the arena, and Oogway faltered from a laugh to shriek. His precious mimic!

The entire populace of New Haven smoothly and gently slid to a halt, allowing them to get off the ride. Something all of them did with so much enthusiasm that the act was what broke the last hit point out of Lucia's shield, her own shell falling apart as people hugged the dirt and kissed the ground. That made so much more sense now.

Once more standing on solid ground in the Murim Woods and refusing to acknowledge how hectic of a sudden trip that had been, Artorian inhaled deep, and exhaled slowly. "I think… that's a win!"

CHAPTER FIFTY-SIX

Dun-dun-dunnnn!

———

World Event: The City Must Survive.
    U win!
    An event has started: Brave New World.
    Midgard will now reset, but retain its current shape.
    All players, please return to Cal.

———

The toot of royal horns followed that announcement and cut the confetti before all the party favor cannons could properly launch. A little bit fell, but the Wisps responsible all stopped upturning more buckets as something more important happened.

———

Pa-pwaaaap!

An announcement will now play.

Thunk-thunk-thunk.

"Is this thing on?" The word of Cal rang through all spatial worlds and every Dungeon Core. "Looks like it; the Farnsworth device smells successful. Good news, everyone! Remember that thing about leaving my Soul Space, and going back to the Old World? Well, this timing is a bit funny, but I'll take it. We got the door working! It doesn't work... *well*. But it works! Exodus is a go! If all my round table people could step into the portals that Zelia, Grace, Amber, and Soni are about to throw open? Please come up. You can go back to what you were doing after, I need you all in Eternia. Thanks!"

Lenore blinked, her head slowly turning to Artorian. Rather than appear elated, her Divine looked utterly exhausted and like he was about to fall over and cry.

"My vacation." Young-torian held his sniffly face as Zelia's gate opened, his Spider secretary walking out calm as a fiddle. "I was about to start my vacation."

"Very good, my Dreamer." Zelia stepped out of the way of her gorgeous door-themed celestial gate, and moved her hands toward the pillowy light. "Tell me again when you're two days from retirement."

"*What* retirement?" Artorian threw his hands in the air, lamented out loud, and stomped over to give Lucia a massive hug. "Thank you for the help, Momma Bun. Dawny and I will be back. We have to go find out what new workload we are being saddled with. If we see you in Cal first? Also good."

He checked himself when he let go after Lucia ground her chin into the top of his head, realizing he was still in the quasi-embarrassing Blanket attire that Momma Bun was taking full advantage of. Her litany of curses had mysteriously stopped… She was grinning wide while playing with those adorable ears on his pulled-up hoodie. Ah, it was because she had blackmail, now. Of course. "Potentia."

With a flash of light, Young-torian was Grandpa-torian. Ready and set with his beach attire to begin that vacation. If Cal was going to saddle him with new work, he was going to make the dungeon feel bad about it!

His huff and puff plan got as far as Dawn sliding an arm in along with his, and tugging him along to lead the way. "Be back soon, Momma Bun. *Oh*, don't trust the Tortoise. Not your pope."

With that sole cryptic warning, Dawn and Artorian left through the gate. Zelia gave everyone a cutesy wave, then followed in after them before the portal-door closed. Leaving everyone bewildered, confused, and a good part lost until the confetti finally popped and everyone's reward prompts began rolling in by the dozens.

Their disappearance was quickly forgotten in favor of *loot*.

Everyone loved loot, especially when some of it was more food!

––––––

Dawn and Artorian walked into a scene from history. The round table of Niflheim had been a long time ago, but he remembered his spot! Except he didn't remember which table. There had only been one table last time, but there were five this time around.

Luckily, Dawn knew the correct table, and walked him over as others began arriving. He knew many of these faces, and even more that he did not. Perhaps they were teams in charge of other things? Too much went on in Cal for just him to handle, and he doubted that he was the only Administrator.

As Cal popped in with the Wisps Dani and Grace, he

strolled right to the center in the borrowed body of Scholar D. Kota. Some in attendance stood, most sat, but either way he had everyone's attention without needing to ask. "Dearly beloved, we have gathered here today—"

A swat to the back of his head from Dani made him break into a giggle fit, while Grace shot her father side-eye. "Mom, I told you he wasn't going to be able to help himself."

Dani hovered ominously close with a third, much smaller Wisp cradled against her. "Oh, I know, baby. I know."

"Alright, alright, I'll get to it." Clearing his throat, throwing out a beaming smile, and clapping his hands together, Cal started over. "Hello everybody! This meeting is for special people in charge only. I wanted all the brightest minds in one place for the next problem we need to tackle, because I want my involvement to be minimal. I've done as promised in getting everyone here, but I've done enough, yes? Once you're decanted, and people's deals and oaths culminate? I don't want people back unless it's for the game, and even that is happening only in Eternium."

Cal shot Tim finger crossbows. The portly Dungeon who sat next to Yuki waved at everyone. "To be clear? I will be a most gracious host for the rest of the ride, but I want everyone out when everyone can safely *be* out. I will not be accused of murder where I didn't get all the Essence from it. If you're not dying in my Dungeon, then I don't care."

That was an odd segue, but he was giving a table of people who were likely other Dungeons his own version of severe side-eye. Dungeon politics? Dungeon politics.

Clapping his hands again, he threw them up at the sky to clear the cloud layer. Springtime pleasantry was in effect on this Niflheim recreation, but what was really important was the sight visible in the sky.

Señor Louis, high up in the depths of space, had twisted himself into an Ouroboros. The space that was so very vacant outside of that circle was very much not vacant inside that circle. Noticing that he had the attention of the only people that remained in Eternia as everyone else was leaving in a hurry, he waved an appendage so large that they could see it from where the groups sat. Size was a funny thing, one quickly forgotten as Señor Louis was given the floor by Cal, and spoke.

The voice, with some Cal cheatery, carried as if Louis was speaking from the center of every round table. Where an image of the being copied itself into place.

"Hola, amigos!" Señor Louis gave them all his best smile, which caused a handful of Heavenlies to faint. "It is Louis's great pleasure as the gatekeeper to announce the beginning of the new dawn, and a much-missed daybreak. Louis gives you the Old World!"

The portal flared to life within the Ouroboros, showing a scene and blowing through air with a smell that was pure, Essence-devoid nostalgia. The sight of a sunrise happening in real time, in the real world, with real air coming through the opened gate assailed everyone. Tears were swiftly repressed as they all couldn't look away from the real sun coming up over a natural horizon, proving that the way out was no myth.

Dawn squeezed Artorian's hand, but possibly because he'd squeezed hers first.

Señor Louis gladly moved his many arms to make welcoming motions, drawing them towards the open portal. "Welcome, one and all, to Amanecida!"

ABOUT DENNIS VANDERKERKEN

Hello all! I'm Dennis, but feel free to call me Floof. Credit of the name now being accumulated by the vast and powerfully cultivated viking beard, that grows ever more in potency. I'm now counting my writing experience in years, so let me say it is my great pleasure that you are reading this, and welcome back to the goodness!

I have been the designer, plotter, and writer of Artorian's Archives since its inception, and look forward to gracing your eyes with ever more volumes of the story. Indulging my dear readers in secrets otherwise forever obscure.

If you have any questions, or would like to chat, I live on the Eternium discord server. Feel free to come say hi anytime! I will keep you entertained for years to come!

Connect with Dennis:
Discord.gg/mdp
Patreon.com/FloofWorks

ABOUT DAKOTA KROUT

Associated Press best-selling author, Dakota has been a top 5 bestseller on Amazon, a top 6 bestseller on Audible, and his first book, Dungeon Born, was chosen as one of Audible's top 5 fantasy picks in 2017.

He draws on his experience in the military to create vast terrains and intricate systems, and his history in programming and information technology helps him bring a logical aspect to both his writing and his company while giving him a unique perspective for future challenges.

"Publishing my stories has been an incredible blessing thus far, and I hope to keep you entertained for years to come!" -Dakota

Connect with Dakota:
MountaindalePress.com
Patreon.com/DakotaKrout
Facebook.com/DakotaKrout
Twitter.com/DakotaKrout
Discord.gg/mdp

ABOUT MOUNTAINDALE PRESS

Dakota and Danielle Krout, a husband and wife team, strive to create as well as publish excellent fantasy and science fiction novels. Self-publishing *The Divine Dungeon: Dungeon Born* in 2016 transformed their careers from Dakota's military and programming background and Danielle's Ph.D. in pharmacology to President and CEO, respectively, of a small press. Their goal is to share their success with other authors and provide captivating fiction to readers with the purpose of solidifying Mountaindale Press as the place 'Where Fantasy Transforms Reality.'

Connect with Mountaindale Press:
MountaindalePress.com
Facebook.com/MountaindalePress
Twitter.com/_Mountaindale
Instagram.com/MountaindalePress

Wolfman Warlock by James Hunter and Dakota Krout

Axe Druid,
Mephisto's Magic Online, and
High Table Hijinks by Christopher Johns

Skeleton in Space by Andries Louws

Dragon Core Chronicles by Lars Machmüller

Chronicles of Ethan by John L. Monk

Pixel Dust and
Necrotic Apocalypse by David Petrie

Viceroy's Pride by Cale Plamann

Henchman by Carl Stubblefield

Artorian's Archives by Dennis Vanderkerken and Dakota Krout

Vaudevillain by Alex Wolf

Made in the USA
Coppell, TX
28 October 2023

23532811R00281